BATTLE OF JERICHO

BATTLE OF JERICHO

KENDRA NORMAN-BELLAMY

www.urbanchristianonline.net

Urban Books
1199 Straight Path
West Babylon, NY 11704

ISBN-13: 978-1-60162-959-3
ISBN-10: 1-60162-959-1

First Printing April 2008
Printed in the United States of America

10 9 8 7 6 5 4 3 2 1

Submit Wholesale Orders to:
Kensington Publishing Corp.
C/O Penguin Group (USA) Inc.
Attention: Order Processing
405 Murray Hill Parkway
East Rutherford, NJ 07073-2316
Phone: 1-800-526-0275
Fax: 1-800-227-9604

Dedication

He delivered me from my strong enemy,
and from them which hated me:
for they were too strong for me.
(Psalm 18:17)

On some level, I desire for this book to serve as a tribute to my father, my brother, my godfather, and every other man and woman who now serves or has ever served in the United States military. On a daily basis, you unselfishly put your lives on the line for our peace, safety and freedom. In troubled times like these, who you are and what you do is especially essential. I pray for your lives. I honor your heroism. And on behalf of all of us who benefit from your valor, I say, "Thank you."

Also, in memory of fellow author and friend, Katherine D. Jones (1965-2007): Because military spouses are brave too. And because you are sorely missed.

Acknowledgements

In everything give thanks for this is the will of God concerning you.
(I Thessalonians 5:18)

To my **Heavenly Father**: You sent your Son to pay a price He didn't owe, all because I owed a price I couldn't pay. There is no greater love. Thank you!

To my husband, **Jonathan**: Thanks for allowing me the space and quiet time that I desperately needed in order to get this book complete. I know your personality; therefore, I realize how much of a sacrifice that was for you. I love you.

To my firstborn, **Brittney**: You're a "Mama's girl" to the core and the more I see your desire to be like me, the more I strive to be a better person. As you continue to grow into womanhood, there are many who wish to see you stumble and fall. But with Christ, I am persuaded that nothing or no one will separate you from the love of God. I can't wait to see just how high God is going to elevate you as a person and a writer.

To my baby, **Crystal**: The "C" stands for confident, colorful, creative, comical and yes, quite a character. God has gifted you on so many levels—some of which we have not yet seen. I don't know how or when, but somewhere down the road, through a divinely powerful reveal, the world is going to know your name.

To my parents, **Bishop H.H. and Mrs. Francine Norman**: You have always been living examples of righteous parents; and to know that you're proud of me means the world. The older I get, the more I love and appreciate you both.

To **Crystal, Harold, Cynthia and Kimberly**: If I could close my eyes and wish into existence the perfect siblings, when I opened my eyes, the people standing before me would still be the four of you. Smoochez!

To **Jimmy** (1968-1995): You said I'd never forget you and you were right. I thank you for so many things; but most of all, I thank you for Brittney and Crystal.

To **Terrance**: We were born cousins, but we are so much more. You have served in so many pivotal capacities in my life. I'm thankful to have you in my corner. I honestly don't know what I'd do without you.

To my godparents, **Aunt Joyce and Uncle Irvin**: Whether it was a prayer, a pillow, or a piece of advice, I've always been able to count on you. Much love!

To my attorney/agent, **Carlton**: From the moment we met, you believed in me. Because of that, I can't think of anyone else that I'd rather have serve in your capacity.

To **Rhonda**: It's not always easy to find a publicist who has the full respect of the literary community. I found that in you and I'm grateful.

To **Heather**: You said it best when you called our friendship "a miracle." Most people find it hard to believe that I define a girl I've only met twice in life as my "bestest best friend" . . . but you are. For nearly thirty years, you and I have shared hearts and souls—first through letters, then through phone calls, then through emails, then finally, face to face. If ever there was a friendship made in heaven, ours is it.

To **Gloria and Deborah**: We developed solid ties during our elementary and high school days, respectively; and though our lives have settled us in different parts of the country since those formative years, the camaraderie remains as strong as ever. You ladies exemplify what true friendship is all about.

To **Lisa**: You really have no idea what you mean to me. Through your company (Papered Wonders) you have blessed me with more than just wonderful promotional and marketing material. When I hold your products, I feel your prayers. Thank you, most of all, for your prayers.

To **Dama**: Who knew that one request for an appearance at your ministry's function would turn into such a meaningful association? God knew . . . and I thank Him.

To **Vivi, Tia, Michelle, Norma, Shewanda and Vanessa**: The Anointed Authors on Tour group has become like a sisterhood to me. This ministry is ordained by God and I am humbled to be named among you.

To **Victoria, Jacquelin, Stephanie and Patricia**: I will always value you for the part you played as my mentors and motivators, especially in the early days of my career.

To **Timmothy, Travis, Hank and Keith**: Y'all are some gifted brothas of the pen! The world needs more strong men, good fathers and great writers like you.

To **Eric** (The E-fect!), **Fredrick** (Hey, classmate!), and **Alexander** (Way to go!): A special thanks goes out to each of you for the inspiration, ideas and insight that helped to make *Battle of Jericho* possible.

To **Keven**: You deserve this shout-out, soldier. You are a true hero. I continue to pray for your complete recovery and I thank you for your bravery. Hang in there.

To my **Urban Christian** family: Thanks for the challenges and the growth opportunities that have been afforded to me. I embrace them with appreciation.

To the clients of **KNB Publications**: Each of you represent a piece of my destiny. And because of that, the success of your careers will always be in my prayers.

To **The Writer's Hut** members: You are definitely what I had in mind when I founded this support group in 2005. Thank you for being a diversified, yet respectful, professional and enjoyable online writers' family.

To **Revival Churches, Inc.**: My spiritual roots will always remain among you. Your prayers and support have been a blessing to my life, my family and my career.

To **Bishop Johnathan and Pastor Toni Alvarado and the Total Grace Christian Center family**: There is no place like Total Grace! Thank you for providing me with a spiritual home away from home.

To **Pastor Timothy Fryar (Christ Centered Church)**: God definitely orchestrated our online introduction. Your prayers and spiritual counsel were on point and on time. Thank you!

To **book clubs and other readers**: I don't take a single one of you for granted. Your support is appreciated to the highest level.

To **Shunda, Jamill and Booking Matters, Inc.**: A season . . . a reason . . . a lifetime. Although I thought ours was a bond that was meant to last a lifetime, I am abundantly grateful for the season.

Finally, to **Brian, Fred, India, Deitrick, The Williams Brothers and Five Men on a Stool**: God said faith without works is dead. For me, the same goes for writing without music. So, thank you for the lyrics, melody and harmony that helped bring life to this project.

BATTLE OF JERICHO

Prologue

Dear Daddy,

Thank you for the earrings! You're the best daddy in the whole world. Mama said they're pretty, but she thinks they are too expensive. I told her that y'all got stuff for cheap over there. Grandma doesn't like them. She said that no thirteen-year-old girl has any business with "earbobs" and she called out some scripture that she said meant that it was a sin to wear them. Grandma says a whole lot of stuff that doesn't make sense to me, but she's old, so I try not to laugh. I know you would, though.

I miss you so much, Daddy, and I'm glad that you'll be coming back to the States in a few weeks. You've been gone a long time. Mama misses you too. She didn't say that, but I know she does. Last week, when I was putting away laundry, I found a calendar in her bedroom where she's been marking off days. She has April 14th circled. I know it's high-

lighted because it's the day you're supposed to be back. I can't wait!

School is fun and I'm still making good grades. I'll send you a copy of the certificates I got on Honor's Day. My favorite subjects are English Composition and World History. The weather has warmed up here now, so I've been wearing the new spring clothes to school that Mama let me buy with the money you sent for Christmas. My friends say I'm rotten, but I tell them that I'm just a Daddy's girl, and proud of it (ha-ha). Only two more months and the school year will be over. Can you believe I'll be in high school next year? You're getting old, Daddy! I laughed when I read your last letter when you asked me if my friend, Malik Greene, was my boyfriend. No, he's not my boyfriend, Daddy, and no, you don't have to bring a gun when you come to Atlanta. He's just a good friend. Did I tell you that he taught me how to ride a horse last summer? I'm a real pro now. I feel like a cowgirl when I'm at Greene Pastures (smile).

I have to go now. I have to get to the bus stop. One question, though. When you get out of the Marines, can we move to Atlanta? I like it here. Think about it, okay? Write back soon. I love you, Daddy.

Kyla

"Kyla, are you ready? I'll drop you off at school on my way to work if you're ready to leave. That way you don't have to stand out in the rain at the bus stop."

"I'm ready, Mama," Kyla called back.

She wasn't fooled. Kyla knew that the real reason Jan wanted to transport her to the stop that was only two streets over was because her mom was no longer comfortable with her walking there. Especially during a downpour. Not since that rainy day two weeks ago when she nearly got hit by a car that sped through the neighborhood. The driver of the fancy car almost seemed to purposefully sway toward Kyla as he raced on the wet pavement, disregarding the twenty-five miles per hour residential speed limit.

Kyla didn't feel that her mother had reason to worry, but she was glad for the opportunity to pack away her umbrella. It only took her a few seconds to kiss the signature line of her letter to her father as she always did, and fold it so that it would fit into the envelope that she'd already addressed and stamped. Then Kyla took a moment to double-check her belongings, making sure that she had packed the proper uniform. An active eighth grader, she kept a mental calendar in her head of what she had to do on which days. Her after-school cheerleading practices ended when her middle school basketball team failed to make the finals, but her track and field obligations would keep her past dismissal today.

Jan's voice called out again. "Come on, sweetie. I really have to leave. I'm running late."

"Coming, Mama."

There just didn't seem to be enough minutes in the morning to get everything done without hurrying. No matter what hour Kyla set her alarm to sound, it seemed that she was always racing against time. The thirteen-year-old hated being rushed, but for her, the time passing quickly meant that the weeks that stood between now and her father's return would disappear fast. The letter that she was sending today could possibly be the last one that she would write. Well, maybe one more. After that, she'd be able to talk to her dad face to face. Knowing that was the one thing that made the rushing bearable.

"Kyla . . ."

"Coming." Grabbing her book bag and her letter, Kyla sighed, took one last look into the mirror and then rushed out of her room, just in time to join her mother as she headed for the front door.

Chapter 1

It all happened so fast that no one could have seen it coming. One moment, the military truck packed with tired and hungry soldiers was cruising down the dusty road in the middle of the night; the next, the driver had lost control. The tires of the vehicle were secured by what the military called Run Flat, a hard rubber that kept tires from deflating due to a blowout. But amidst loud bursts of gunfire, something happened, possibly an exploding mine, to make the sturdy vehicle roll over more than once. Cursing filled the truck as the five soldiers inside clutched on to whatever they could in hopes of preventing themselves from being tossed onto foreign soil and crushed under the weight of the heavy Humvee. But they soon found out that being thrown to their instant deaths would have been their choice if they had it to do all over again.

As the soldiers caught in the mix tried to drag their battered bodies to an impossible escape, the words being yelled by the armed men that surrounded them sounded like gibberish. But it didn't take genius or even bilingualism to know that the only way they could possibly save themselves was to surrender. Even then, their fate was in question.

Master Sergeant Peter Kyle Jericho's mouth was filled with the dust from the ground as he felt the heel of one of his captors press against the back of his neck. But the dirt was the least of his worries. All he could think about was his still-broken home and the wife and child that had lived apart from him for more than a year. Peter had promised Kyla that he'd return safely and make things right between him and her mother. He made it a point never to lie to his little girl, but this one was out of his control.

Peter had survived two previous orders and spent a total of more than four years fighting this seemingly unending war. With the twenty-year service mark just weeks away, Peter had decided that this would be his last deployment; he had just completed eleven of the twelve months he'd been assigned to on the battlefield. Twenty-eight more days and he'd be home. That was the plan. But now . . .

"Ugh!" Peter grunted in pain as his already sore arms were mercilessly yanked behind his back.

"You stand!"

Those were the first two words of English that had been spoken by the enemy. As he struggled to get to his feet, Peter could feel the barrel of a gun pressed firmly into the back of his gear. Through the darkness, he saw the other four men from his unit who had been riding in the covered back of the truck; but Peter didn't see the driver. Ramsey must have somehow managed to escape. While the gunmen forced the five of them into their vehicle, Peter found a glimmer of hope in the possibility that Ramsey would be able to seek help.

As the truck began moving, Peter tried to catch the eyes of his comrades, but none of them would look in his direction. They belonged to the few, the proud, the

Marines, and they were trained to be prepared for the worst of the worst. But Peter could hear his heart pounding in his own ears, and he could feel the fright and panic that had set in on his normally brave counterparts. Realistically speaking, no matter how much training they'd gone through in preparation for the "what ifs" of war, none of them expected it to happen to them. And realistically, none of them were prepared.

Peter made an attempt to swallow, but there was no moisture there. What the dust hadn't absorbed, fear had. The armed man standing near him must have noticed the dry discomfort of the men because he reached down to the floor of the truck and picked up a metal bucket with a ladle inside. Maybe there was some humanity in them after all. But despite the refreshing look of the liquid that was now being held right beneath Peter's lips, the look in the eyes of the man holding it was anything but friendly. Peter turned his head as an act of refusal and quickly felt the butt of a neighboring gunman's rifle ram into his stomach. It hurt badly, but Peter was given no time to recuperate.

"Drink."

The command made it clear that accepting the water wasn't an option. Peter took in a few swallows and almost choked. It wasn't as revitalizing as he thought it would be. Now, instead of his mouth feeling dry and dusty, it felt muddy and pasty. He needed more; but more wasn't offered. Peter watched as the enemy took the bucket to his comrades. Unlike Peter, they didn't refuse. They'd already seen the consequences of rejecting the goodwill gesture.

The fear that multiplied on the inside of Peter was getting out of control. So much so that he began to feel numb from his waist down and the organs inside his body seemed to tremble. He knew he had to get a grip so that he could think clearly and maybe devise some plan of escape. None of the training he'd received could help him now. Peter was in for the battle of his life and he knew it. There was only one hope of getting out of this alive and being reunited with the family he hadn't seen in months. Closing his eyes, Peter did the only thing that he knew to do. He prayed.

Chapter 2

"I think we got married too young." Wearing a plain white T-shirt and a pair of denim shorts, Jan sighed and rested her back against the living room couch. "We were just kids who didn't even know ourselves yet. We had no business getting married at that age."

As she talked, Jan stared at the ottoman that she used as a prop for her tired feet. It was a beautiful piece of furniture, but no one would ever know with the ugly plastic that covered it as well as all of the other matching pieces of the living room set. The covering reminded Jan of the bubble packing material that Peter used as cushioning in the box he'd used to send Kyla's latest gift. For as long as Jan could remember, her mother had kept her home furnishings covered in thick plastic, except on rare occasions when she was expecting "important company." The last time the true beauty of the rose-colored living room set was seen was right after Christmas, when the pastor of New Hope Church had stopped in to have prayer with Jan's mother following surgery to have cataracts removed. Only Leona Grimes could make such a minor surgery need the attention of blessed oil and the laying on of hands from one of the city's most prominent pastors.

"You got married young . . . so you *really* think that's all it is?" The thoughtful challenge came from Rachel Ross, Jan's cousin; and it was laced with sarcasm.

"Don't start," Jan warned. She knew what Rachel was hinting, and on most days, Jan could kid about the fourteen-year-old running joke. But not today. Today, in spite of everything that had transpired over the past fifteen months, she missed her husband more than usual; and a sense of humor escaped her.

"You know it's the truth," Rachel said with a giggle, clueless of Jan's level of annoyance. "He was supposed to be mine. You stole my man, girl, and that's why the two of you have had to endure all of the 'Peter and Jan Brady' jokes over the years and that's why y'all are having this problem."

"Rachel . . ."

"No, it's true and you know it. I was supposed to be Mrs. Peter Jericho and Kyla was supposed to be *my* daughter. You stole Pete right from under my nose. So, now I'm thirty-six, single and childless, and you're living my life."

The way that Jan and Peter met was no secret to anyone in the family. Their relationship had lasted so long that Kyla often told people that her parents met in high school, when in fact, they were both young adults at the time. What was supposed to be a match-making connection between Peter and Rachel back in the day turned out to be anything but. Rachel's older brother, Carl, was the mastermind behind the set-up, but he failed to tell his sister that he'd be bringing his college roommate by her apartment that evening. When the reunited former high school football teammates arrived, it was Jan who greeted them at the door, wearing a peach sundress that accentuated her slender curves, and four-inch-heeled sandals that lengthened her legs and masked her true petite five-feet-one-inch height.

At the time, she and Rachel shared a living space, a small two-bedroom apartment near Florida A&M University, where both girls, at age twenty-one, were weeks away from graduating from the School of Nursing. Jan invited her cousin and his friend inside to wait, but it would be another hour before Rachel would arrive from her impromptu Saturday afternoon shopping spree at Tallahassee Mall. By most people's definition—men, especially—Rachel was the more beautiful one. She was taller, had longer legs, and a more curvy body that she showed off in one form or another with every outfit she wore. Even her conservative garments accentuated her power points. But despite that, Rachel's failure to be in place provided more than enough time for Jan and Peter to form an unspoken bond. The mutual attraction between the two had been instant, but while Peter made no effort to hide his, Jan succeeded in pretending one didn't exist.

At the time, twenty-four-year-old Peter was a corporal, well on his way to earning his sergeant insignia. Upon graduation from high school, Peter infuriated his mother when he shelved an athletic scholarship to Florida State University, and instead chose to follow his lifelong dream of becoming a U.S. Marine. Carl accepted his scholarship, and when the two parted ways, their childhood camaraderie waned, but never totally dissolved. The weekend trip that Peter had made to Tallahassee from Beaufort, North Carolina, where he was stationed at the time, turned into much more than the Marine had expected.

Jan was fascinated with the handsome and witty soldier, who towered over her true height by eleven full inches. His wide, warm smile captured her, making it hard for her to look away whenever he flashed it. Carl saw the attraction between the two and made a valiant effort to redirect his friend's focus once his sister got home. He even volunteered to treat Jan to a movie that evening so that Peter and Rachel could share an intimate dinner at Anthony's, a local restaurant located not far from the campus of Florida State University. But for Peter, it was too late. He was already smitten, and Rachel wasn't the object of his affections.

For a while, the fact that he had chosen Jan put a strain in the close cousins' relationship. Jan's loyalty to Rachel made her feel obligated to ignore Peter's advances and refuse his telephone calls. But in the end, love won; and over time, Rachel accepted defeat and moved on, indulging in many satisfying relationships along the way, but securing none. Despite that, she was the happiest, most fulfilled single woman Jan had ever known. As Jan saw it, a relationship between Rachel and Peter never would have worked out anyway. Her husband didn't much approve of her always attractive, but often boisterous best friend.

Rachel's last comment drew another sigh from Jan. "Well, lately it hasn't been the best life. If things don't change, a divorce is a realistic possibility, so I guess if you really want him, he'll be single soon and you can throw your hat in the ring."

A brief silence was followed by a loud laugh from Rachel that filled the room. Jan never told Rachel how much Peter hated her unrestrained laughter that always included at least one disgusting snort. "Girl, please! I don't want your sloppy seconds," Rachel said after gaining some level of control. "Besides, you and Pete ain't getting no divorce and you know it. You love that man, girl."

"Well, I'm here and he's there, so that proves that love doesn't necessarily save a marriage."

Rachel rested Indian-style on the carpeted floor, opting not to sit on the plastic that was already sticking to the skin of Jan's exposed thighs. "Y'all have been apart for over a year now, Jan. Pete will be back from Iraq in less than a month. Maybe this tour of duty was God's way of giving y'all some space. Who knows?"

For a girl who rarely went to church and was never one to even come close to claiming salvation, Rachel was famous for tossing around God's name like an ace in a deck of cards.

"I don't know, Rachel. The separation can't truthfully be blamed on the tour of duty. Kyla and I left California to come here weeks before Pete got his orders." Jan squirmed in her seat, not sure if it was the plastic covering of the couch, or the mental revisit to the last time she saw her husband that was causing her heightened discomfort. "Pete and I had never argued like that before, and especially not in front of Kyla. I mean, we've been married for thirteen years, so of course we've had disagreements before. But we always managed to keep our disagreements out of Kyla's listening range."

"Kyla's a mature girl," Rachel reasoned, smacking her lips and flipping her wrist in a carefree manner. "She got over that mess a long time ago."

"Yeah, but she's never gotten over being apart from her dad. When it comes to looks, she's half Pete and half me. But make no mistake about it; she's a one hundred percent Daddy's girl."

Jan couldn't help but to laugh at the harsh reality of her statement. When she and Peter separated, he'd been so upset with her that he didn't even want to chance calling his mother-in-law's house and have either Jan or her mom answer the phone. Less than two weeks into the separation, Peter shipped Kyla her own cell phone, already powered up and ready for use. The two spoke to each other almost every day until Peter was sent to war. Even then, he was sure to call his daughter on a weekly basis.

"He called me two weeks ago. Did I tell you?"

Rachel's eyes widened. "No, you didn't tell me. How could you not tell me something that important, Jan? What did he say?"

"I didn't speak to him directly. He left a message on my cell, claiming that he'd made a mistake and dialed my cell number instead of Kyla's." Jan couldn't help but smile as she spoke. She knew that Peter's so-called blunder was just an excuse to talk to her. Or maybe that was just wishful thinking on her part. But her reasoning made good sense. If it were really an error, why didn't Peter just hang up and call the number he claimed he meant to call? Jan knew her husband well. She was almost certain that his call was a ploy to open the lines of communication between them.

"Did you call him back?" Rachel asked.

Jan bit her bottom lip and nodded. "I waited three days, though," she said. "I didn't want him to think I was anxious or anything. I got his voicemail and I kept my message just as vague as he kept his."

"What did you say?" Rachel pried.

"I just told him that I'd gotten his message, asked him how things were going in Iraq and then thanked him for staying in contact with Kyla. His contact with Kyla has been real good for her, so I wanted him to know that I appreciated it."

"Has he called you back?"

Jan shook her head slowly and tried not to look as disappointed as she felt. "No."

Today was Saturday and Jan had allowed Kyla to spend the afternoon with her school friends, who were riding horses in Greene Pastures, the horse breeding farm owned by the parents of one of Kyla's friends. Unless Peter had called his daughter on her cell today, a full week had now passed since Kyla last heard from her father, and the span of silence was odd. Jan could partially understand why he may have decided not to return her call, but, *Why hasn't he called Kyla?*

Jan's fleeting thought was interrupted by Rachel's voice. "I've asked you this before, Jan, and you've never given me a straight answer; but you know you might as well tell me 'cause I'm not gonna quit asking until you do. Where did the trouble begin? You guys used to be such the perfect couple and then all of a sudden everything seemed to fall apart."

"I wish I knew, Rachel. All I know is that I came here to help Mama adjust after Daddy up and walked out on her, and when I got back to Cali, Pete was acting the fool."

"There has to be more to it, Jan."

Finally tired of wiping perspiration from her skin, Jan stood from the sofa and joined her cousin on the floor. "When I came to visit that September, I was only supposed to be staying for seven days. Well, you popped into town and said you were moving here and needed help, so I wanted to stay a little longer to assist you."

"So, you're saying I'm the cause of all of this?"

"Of course not. See, that's why I didn't want to tell you. I knew you'd say that. I was the one who made the decision to extend my stay, so it had nothing to do with you," Jan said, then continued her story. "Besides, the extension was only supposed to be for a couple of days, but then you strained your back while we were putting your furniture in storage and . . ."

"Okay. Once again, this is sounding like it's all my fault," Rachel protested.

"Are you gonna let me tell the whole story or not?" When Rachel sat in silence, Jan spoke again. "If you remember, it was my fault that you hurt your back. I didn't lift my side of the couch at the same time you lifted yours and that's what caused the injury. So, you know I couldn't walk away until you were better. Then Mama had a few issues . . ." Jan's voice trailed and then returned. "It just became a much longer visit than I had planned. Pete was calling me and ranting and raging about the fact that I missed his birthday party, then I missed seeing Kyla play lead in a production that the church's youth ministry put on, and when I missed the Soldiers' Masquerade Ball that the Marines threw on base and he had to go stag . . ."

"Daaaang, girl," Rachel sang. "No wonder the man was mad. I didn't know you were only supposed to be here for a week. How long did you stay? A month?"

"Yeah, but it wasn't intentional. Honestly. But Pete made it seem like I left California with the premeditated intent to be here that long. He all but accused me of it, but nothing could have been further from the truth. But I do think that my being here was a good thing on many levels. How would you have gotten anything done while you were flat on your back for all that time? And Mama . . . well, she's getting up in age, and since Daddy abandoned her, she needs me more than she used to."

"You ain't the only daughter your mama's got. Besides, Aunt Leona don't need nobody but Jesus, and she'll tell you that herself. You act like she's old and decrepit or something. She's only sixty-two, and you know what they say about age being nothing but a number. When Oprah turned fifty years old, she changed everything about the aging process. Fifty became the new forty and sixty became the new fifty. Aunt Leona, by today's standards, is only fifty-two."

"She's still my mother and she still needed me whether she admits it or not," Jan insisted. "That was a rough time for her, and Pete should have understood that."

Both women sat quietly for a long while. Jan replayed her own words in her head and wondered how hypocritical she was being. In all of her explaining, was she trying to convince herself as much as she was trying to convince Rachel? Looking at the situation in brutal honesty, Jan couldn't help but admit that she'd do things differently if she had the chance. She'd missed some very important dates and appointments with Peter and Kyla that had been penciled on their family calendar for months in advance. She knew how important it was to Peter for her to be at his birthday bash. She knew how excited Kyla was about both her parents seeing her in her first stage production. And she definitely knew how keyed up Peter was about the masquerade ball.

Jan had every intention of getting back home in time for all of those things, but somehow, she just couldn't seem to get away once she'd flown to Atlanta for the visit. One unexpected event after another happened, and all of it served as a form of bonding glue that kept her adhered to her mother's house even though she knew her absence was causing major problems back home.

"Maybe you should have stayed somewhere else when you were here visiting back then," Rachel said, breaking the lengthy silence and Jan's deep thoughts.

"What?"

"Maybe you should have stayed at a hotel or something. You know what they say about Shelton Heights." Rachel's voice had dropped to a whisper, as though she thought the deceased namesake, whose family still owned the upscale subdivision, would awaken from his eternal sleep if she spoke too loudly.

Jan laughed. "I know you aren't superstitious, Rachel."

"Laugh if you want, girl, but that's why I only stayed with Aunt Leona for a few days when I moved here. As soon as I was able, I had to get up outta here. Old Man

Shelton Heights was a warlock and everybody knows it. And people call it superstition, but can't nobody deny that crazy stuff happens to folks who live out here."

"Child, please." Jan rolled her eyes and smacked her lips.

"It does, Jan. Look at what happened to that preacher down the street. That crazy fool kidnapped him and kept him tied up in his basement with a dog for two months before anybody ever found him."

"That had nothing to do with the fact that the Reverend Tides lives in Shelton Heights. You said it yourself. The man who abducted him was crazy. Crazy people do crazy things."

"And what about the little boy, in December, who mysteriously shot himself in the eye? Imagine that! Losing an eye from a misguided pellet from your own gun."

"Rachel, that was no mystery and the pellet wasn't misguided. The boy was looking into the barrel, trying to see if he could watch the pellet as it discharged. That wasn't a mystery; that was an ignorant kid who didn't know enough to realize that he'd shoot himself in the eye if he did something so stupid. I fault the parents for that. If their kid was that naïve about guns, they never should have bought him one for Christmas."

As if Rachel didn't hear a word of Jan's reasoning, she continued. "And what about that other lady? You know, that woman whose house is located in the cul-de-sac; the one who was sitting on her porch one day and was dead the next. Not a thing wrong with her on Monday and then on Tuesday, she was as dead as a doorknob. Just up and died in her sleep."

"Just up and died? She was *ninety-eight*, Rachel," Jan said emphatically. "That woman probably had so much stuff wrong with her that it ain't even funny. It was just time for her to go."

"And for forty-five years, Aunt Leona and Uncle Ted were married," Rachel persisted, "and as soon as they moved in Shelton Heights, he all of a sudden couldn't keep his britches up."

"Rachel . . ." Jan's voice was warning, but Rachel ignored it.

"*Forty-five* years, Jan. Was it just *time* for them to break up? No. I'm telling you, this stuff only happens in Shelton Heights. Uncle Ted is what? Sixty-six?"

"Sixty-seven," Jan corrected. "But Daddy isn't the first sixty-seven-year-old man to decide to go astray after years of being married, and he won't be the last. People go through midlife crises all the time."

Rachel's roaring laughter returned, and in that moment, Jan understood why Peter couldn't stand the signature emotional outburst that nearly always revealed the slight overbite Rachel had had since her childhood thumb-sucking days. Jan found herself resisting the urge to put her fist through the large gape in Rachel's mouth in an attempt to cork the annoying sound.

"Midlife crisis? Girl, Uncle Ted is way closer to the end of his life than the middle. And he worked in the school system for years. Seems to me that if he was gonna start chasing young girls, he would have done it then, when he had all his hair and a stronger back. How you gonna get old and then decide you like girls your daughters' ages? Ah-uh," Rachel refuted, shaking her head for emphasis. "This ain't about him getting old and straying; this is about him getting old and moving to this godforsaken neighborhood."

"I refuse to believe that, Rachel."

"Well, you'd better start believing it before something even worse happens. Didn't you say that Kyla almost got hit by a car a couple of weeks ago?"

"That was just a—"

"Coincidence?" Rachel finished. "Well, if you know like I know, you'll get out before more *coincidences* happen. Dealing with the abandonment of your husband has you jacked up enough. If you mess around and lose Kyla too . . ."

"Stop it, Rachel. You are making way more out of this than it is."

"Am I?" Rachel's face was set and her eyes were serious, yet filled with concern. "I honestly don't think so. Trust me, Jan. The legend of Shelton Heights has gotten y'all, girl, and that old dead warlock's spirit has torn up both your mama's family and yours!"

Chapter 3

Peter didn't know if it was day or night. All he knew was that it was dark. Not just dark, but dark and hot; so hot that sweat ran down his face and into his eyes. He squinted in an attempt to see anything at all, but couldn't. He strained to hear sounds around him, but didn't. Peter thought hard—trying to remember what had happened between the time he was put on the back of the truck and now; trying to remember how much time had passed, but everything in his mind was as black and empty as the room he now lay in.

Not only was the space uncomfortably hot, but it also carried the strong stench of urine. It wasn't long before Peter became conscious of the fact that the unpleasant odor was coming from his own body. Trying to bring himself into a seated position, he realized that his hands were bound behind his back and his legs were restrained by some type of material that had been used to bind together his ankles. His body was dreadfully sore; no doubt from the combination of the accident and from lying against the hard surface under him. The skin beneath his pants legs itched and suddenly, he could barely breathe.

Have I been buried alive?

The walls were closing in on him in the darkness and the initial fear that he felt when he and the other troops were captured had returned with a vengeance. To make matters worse, his bladder was full again and he needed to relieve himself. Apparently, whenever it had happened before—however many times it had happened before—he was unconscious and had no control over it, but now, being awake, he couldn't do it intentionally. It would be degrading even with no one around to see it. Besides, not knowing where he was or what would happen to him overrode the urgent need for a toilet. Peter tried again to sit up, but the toes of his boots hit something, causing it to fall to the floor. The sound of it brought a new sense of terror. In Peter's mind, he wondered if he'd just knocked a grenade to the floor beneath him and sealed his doom.

God, help me. If his tongue wasn't so dry, the words would have been vocal.

"Who's there?"

Peter froze as he heard the harrowing whisper that seemed to come from a place not ten feet from him. Not knowing who it was, he wondered if he should answer. The voice spoke in a clear American accent and that should have offered some comfort, but it didn't. Peter said nothing. Instead, he chose to lie still to see what would happen next. Two, maybe three minutes passed with no sounds. *Could I have imagined it?* Then suddenly, the silence was broken again.

"First Sergeant Fletcher Owens of the United States Marines here. Anybody there?"

Peter's eyes widened. "Owens? Flex? Is that you?"

"Yeah, yeah, it's me. Who are you? State your name, sir." The last sentence was added after a brief, thoughtful silence. First Sergeant Owens had probably done so as a precautionary measure; in case the person he was addressing was one of his superiors.

"It's Peter."

"Jericho?"

"Yeah."

The whispers of both men came to a sudden silence as if both of them were trying to get a grasp on reality. Just knowing that Fletcher Owens was in the room with him decreased Peter's fears. At least he now knew that he couldn't be in a casket-sized box. He was still in danger and Peter was well aware of that, but something about knowing that he wasn't alone gave him hope.

"You okay, Flex?"

"Yeah. You?"

"I think so. Are we alone?"

"I don't know."

The room returned to its quiet state. Peter knew that if any of the other members of his fire team were in the room and able, they would have spoken up by now. That meant one of two things: either others were in the room but had been killed, or if there was anyone else there, they were wearing the uniform of the enemy. Peter knew that Fletcher was thinking the same, which was the reason for his silence as well. At least, he hoped that was all it was.

"Flex?"

"Yeah?"

"Just checkin' to be sure you were still there."

Fletcher let out a chuckle. "Where could I have gone, man?"

"I don't know, man. I was just checkin'. Are you tied up like me?"

"Hands behind the back and ankles together?"

"Yeah."

"Yeah."

Quiet reigned once more as Peter thought hard about what they could possibly do to save themselves. *Lord, please help us.* Now that he knew Fletcher was there, Peter couldn't be selfish; he had to pray for both of them. As soon as the prayerful thought ran through his mind, Peter wondered if it was God who was putting him through this to begin with. Maybe this was his punishment for not apologizing to his wife and for allowing her and Kyla to pack their belongings and leave. He had been too upset to care at the time, but that initial anger had subsided a long time ago. Fifteen months had passed since then. Although Peter had desperately wanted to, it was pride that wouldn't allow him to call and beg Jan to come back home. In his mind, she was the one who owed him an apology for knowingly screwing up all of their family plans. He understood the devastation that his mother-in-law must have felt when her longstanding marriage fell apart so suddenly. But to be brutally honest, Peter always wondered how his father-in-law stayed as long as he did. Leona wasn't the easiest woman to live with. She was argumentative, melodramatic, and downright irksome. On more than one occasion, Peter had described her as "a sanctimonious pain-in-the-butt."

Why Jan couldn't have just spent that one week with her mother, Peter didn't know. But what baffled him even more was how that decision on her part led to a separation that had lasted for more than a year. Up until now, being in Iraq had made Peter feel better about the situation. Being here, he could make believe that it was only his duty to his country that was keeping Jan and him apart. He knew it wasn't the whole truth, but blaming it on the war felt a whole lot better than reality. Having to face the truth went far beyond having to come to grips with the fact that his marriage had fallen apart. Having to face the truth also meant coming to grips with the fact that given recent developments, there was a good chance that he'd never have the opportunity to make it right. Peter had no idea how he would get out of the dark hole that he'd been placed in. He didn't even know how he'd gotten *in* it.

"Flex?" he whispered. It had been some time since either of them had spoken.

"Yeah?"

"How did we get here; do you know? I don't even remember them throwing us down in this hole."

"Are we in a hole?"

"I don't know. It's so dark in here that I'm just guessing we're underground. I keep trying to remember what happened, but I can't. Can you?"

"It was the water," Flex said in a confident tone. "There had to be something potent in that water they gave us. I couldn't taste it, but you were the first to drink and a minute later, you dropped to the floor of the truck like a dishrag. Then Silas went down and I must have been next. Don't remember anything after that until I woke up a little while ago. I wonder what they did with Silas, Chuck and Louis."

Peter thought for a moment. "Guess they didn't think it was a good idea to put us all in the same place."

"Yeah." The room came to another momentary hush and then Fletcher spoke again. "They're gonna kill us, aren't they?"

Peter didn't want to answer that question. He didn't even want to think of answering it. He loved being a soldier, but dying in this manner wasn't what he desired for himself. If he died now, Kyla's last sight of him would be one of a heartless father, helping her mother take their suitcases to the car. And he couldn't let Jan live the rest of her life remembering that the last words that he spoke to her face to face were, "I'll help you move, doggone it. You want to live with your mammy? Fine. See if I care. Goodbye and good riddance." Peter cringed at the thought of it all.

From the moment Jan pulled out of the driveway, he'd ached for her return. In his mind, he'd convinced himself that she would just drive around the desert for a while and return once she'd let the dry heat evaporate her emotions. He had no idea that she'd take the more than two thousand mile road trip all the way back to Atlanta, Georgia and never return.

Peter determined that even if this was the end for him, he couldn't think like that. As dismal as it seemed, he had to find his faith. *Lord, please help us.*

When Peter didn't readily answer, Fletcher continued. "As much as I've always known about the dangers of this battle, I never thought I'd be a casualty." Normally a jokester who found humor in everything, Fletcher now sounded grave. "I never planned to go out like this."

"We're not going to die here, Flex." Peter sounded far more confident than he felt. "I refuse to entertain the thought. I got a wife and kid and they need me."

"Me too."

"You have a kid too?" Peter didn't know much about Fletcher's personal life. Before now, the brotherhood of the Marines was the only bond that held them together. But being in this place and in this predicament, Fletcher suddenly felt like the only friend Peter had in the world.

"Yeah," Fletcher answered. "I got a son and a wife back in Ocilla, Georgia. She's staying near her parents while I'm away."

"Ocilla? Never heard of it. Is that somewhere near Atlanta?" It felt good to be talking about something other than the anticipation of their doom.

"Not really. There are about two hundred miles between the two. Why? You got people in Atlanta?"

"My wife and daughter," Peter said, momentarily drifting again as his thoughts became absorbed with snapshots of Jan and Kyla.

"Really?" Fletcher said. "Is that where you're from?"

Reality was harsh, but Peter saw no need to hide the truth. "No. Actually, I'm originally from Seattle, but I've lived as far south as Florida. Me and the wife . . . well, we've been separated for a few months. She's from Atlanta and her mom still lives in the area."

"Sorry to hear that, man. Not that your mother-in-law is still living," Fletcher added with a laugh. "I mean, I'm sorry to hear about your wife."

"Yeah." In the midst of all of his other thoughts, Peter missed the humor. He couldn't help but wonder what time it was and how long they'd been tied up in the dark place that held them mentally captive just as much as the ropes had kept them physically bound. He wasn't even sure about what day it was, but he was almost certain that whatever substance had been added to the water they drank had kept them unconscious for several hours.

"Man, I gotta pee," Fletcher said. "And judging from my pants and the smell in this space, this ain't the first time I've had to go."

Peter had all but forgotten about his own urge until Fletcher's words reminded him. The conversation had kept him occupied with other matters. Now his bladder felt as though it had little feet tap dancing on it, and the uncomfortable itch of his legs increased. Peter desperately needed to get his mind off of his discomforts.

"I know our ticket out of here, Flex."

"Shhh!" Fletcher warned. "If you got some secrets, I don't recommend you voice them. We still don't know if we are the only ones in here." His voice took a sudden increase in volume. "For all we know, one of Osama's stupid goons might be standing in the darkness aiming to blow our heads off. The big, dumb, psychotic idiots don't know nothing to do but serve their murderous master. Well, they'd betta kill me now, 'cause if they let me live, I'm not only gonna kill them, but I'ma kill all their ugly, big-behind mamas and all their snaggletooth babies, too!"

Fletcher's tone made Peter hold his breath for a moment. If there was someone in the room with them, their fate was sealed for sure. He had heard reports from some who'd been wounded in other violent incidents that being shot didn't hurt. They said it was a very warm feeling, but not a painful one. As Peter squeezed his eyes shut and waited for the ratting sounds of gunfire, he prayed that the rumor was true.

"Okay, go 'head and talk," Fletcher said with a short laugh. "If they didn't kill me just then, I don't think anybody's in here. What were you saying about getting out of here?"

In spite of the potentially deadly consequences of the situation, Peter chuckled too, more out of relief than humor. But it was a laugh that he needed. "Mike Ramsey," Peter said. "Ramsey didn't get captured during the incursion. Did you notice that he wasn't with us in the truck? I think he hid out until we left and then he went for help."

Silence.

"You heard me, Flex?"

"Ramsey's dead, Pete." Fletcher's words were somber and when he spoke them, they hit Peter in the pit of his stomach much like the butt of the rifle had done when the enemy had hit him with it hours, maybe days earlier.

"Dead? How . . . How do you know?"

"His body was next to me when we were all on the ground following the ambush. I guess he got thrown from the truck, but I think he was dead even before then. At first I thought he was lying there like the rest of us, but as we were being forced to our feet, I got a good look at him. He had a bullet hole in his head. They must have shot him, which would explain why he totally lost control of the truck. Ramsey's dead."

"Jesus, help us." This time Peter whispered the prayer aloud. For the first time, he felt the threat of oncoming tears. Clenching his jaw to fight them, Peter swallowed hard. He was trying to find a glimmer of optimism to hold on to, but at this point he didn't feel that things could get much worse.

"Do you believe in—?"

Fletcher's words were cut short by a sudden loud commotion. Both men flinched, and from somewhere in the distance came a gleam of light. Someone had just opened a door that led to where they were held captive, and in the shadows, Peter could see men approaching with raised guns. He had been wrong. It *could* get worse—and it just had.

Chapter 4

"*Baby . . . tomorrow I'ma have to fight . . . leaving at first light . . . but all I can think of is you. . . .*"

Jan made a conscious effort to erase from her mind the tune that had been seared there ever since she'd picked up the release by Brian McKnight yesterday during her afternoon of shopping with Rachel. It was a love song, but also a tribute to the soldiers fighting in Iraq. Jan had played the melody so many times that she'd learned the lyrics. Every time she thought of Peter, the anthem resurfaced. When she first heard it, she had to lock her bedroom door to be sure that her mother didn't walk in and see her crying. Kyla would have knocked before entering, but Jan knew her meddlesome mother wouldn't. And it would have been a situation she would have had to spend the rest of the day trying to explain away.

Now, as she sat in church sandwiched between Leona and Kyla, Jan fought the persistent threat of new tears as the song lingered in her head, not allowing her to fully enjoy the choir that was singing from the stand in front of the church.

Ever since Reverend Tides had come by their house and prayed with Jan's mother following her minor eye surgery, Leona had been visiting the church on a regular basis—at least two Sundays of each month. It was almost as if she now had dual church membership. Her official connection was with a much smaller church that was closer to where they lived, but Leona didn't mind driving a few extra miles to hear the preacher who took the time to tend to her over-dramatized discomfort when her own pastor didn't see the need.

Jan knew her mother would never admit it, but Leona was falling in love with New Hope's ministry just like thousands of others already had. Jan felt the same way and actually found herself looking forward to first and third Sundays. The services at New Hope reminded her of what she had become accustomed to at the church she and Peter attended in California.

Baby . . . tomorrow I'ma have to fight . . . leaving at first light . . . but all I can think of is you. . . .

There it was again.

As Reverend Tides finally took the stand, Jan tried to focus her eyes and thoughts on the words in her Bible. Reverend Tides was such a captivating speaker. In the time she'd been visiting the church with her mom, Jan had come to love his style of preaching. His ministry was so diverse that she never knew what to expect. His messages were sometimes humorous, sometimes fervent, sometimes prophetic, and always far-reaching.

Kyla liked the church, too, and that meant a lot to Jan. Her daughter had been through quite a bit over the past fifteen months or so. Being away from her father had required a lengthy adjustment period. Even now, the girl struggled with Peter's absence. They both did.

"Amen," Jan spoke in response to something the preacher had said. She hadn't heard him, but hearing the one-word affirmation echo around her with an especially loud one coming from her mother, Reverend Tides must have said something profound. It only seemed right to join in.

Glancing over at the boy who sat next to Kyla, Jan smiled. Malik Greene was a major part of the reason that Kyla had been able to adjust to Atlanta and to New Hope. He was a year or so younger, but he was one of the first friends Kyla made when she began attending her new school.

Although the children were friends, Jan had done little more than speak in passing to Malik's parents. Hunter and Jade Greene had only been married for a few months, and although Jade wasn't Malik's biological mother, an outsider would never know. Jade, who also happened to be Reverend Tides' daughter, nurtured the boy as though she'd gone through ten hours of labor to bring him into the world. And the love that Hunter and Jade had for one another was certainly no secret. They didn't mind publicly displaying their affections. Whenever Jan saw them together, she struggled with the onset of depression and maybe even a bit of jealousy. They reminded her of a happier time in her life. A time not too far in the past. A time when she and Peter . . .

Baby . . . tomorrow I'm a have to fight . . .

"Be not afraid nor dismayed by reason of this great multitude; for the battle is not yours, but God's." When Reverend Tides read the last portion of II Corinthians 20:15, the words rescued Jan from being completely sucked back into the tune of the soldier song.

"When many of us think of battles, we immediately

imagine natural struggles with fleshly enemies," he continued. "But often times we are crusading for our souls. Every battle isn't natural, saints of God. Some are spiritual. The Bible tells us that we wrestle not against flesh and blood, but against rulers of darkness and against spiritual wickedness."

"Amen, amen, amen! I know what you're taking about, Reverend." Leona yelled it with such vigor that those around her could only guess that her soul was on the warpath for sure.

If the preacher's words hadn't hit a tender spot with Jan, she probably would have found her mother's dramatic outburst comical. Leona blamed the devil for everything in life that didn't go the way she planned. When the aging car she hadn't had serviced in three years finally broke down back in March, Leona said it was a "trick of the enemy" trying to stop them from getting to church for Sunday morning worship. When the doctor told her that she had cataracts, Leona's reply to him was, "The devil is a liar!" and then she accused the doctor of being a messenger of Satan, passing along bad news to the saints. Most recently, when the cable guy came and disconnected her service in the middle of her favorite soap opera for nonpayment, Leona stood on her front porch holding a bedroom slipper, shaking it over the hedges that grew nearby, saying, "Mark 6:11 says I can shake the dust from underneath my feet and leave it as a testimony against you, you evil-doer! God said it's going to be more tolerable for Sodom and Gomorrah than it will be for you."

Between the time she was a child and now, Leona had read the Bible from cover to cover on more occasions than she could count; and she could recall scriptures better than she could her own grandchildren's names. But rarely did she use any referenced biblical citation in the context that it was intended. So, whereas Jan's mother's interpretation of the scripture that Reverend Tides read may have been misguided, Jan knew exactly what it felt like to be in spiritual combat. Her soul had been at war with her flesh ever since she left California. At the time, leaving seemed like not only the best choice, but the only one. The discussion that started out as merely heated had turned into a fiery shouting match that sank to the level of childish name-calling, something that never happened before in their marriage.

When Jan denied the calculated intent to extend her stay in Atlanta, Peter called her a selfish liar. As an act of verbal retaliation, Jan accused Peter of being an overgrown, jealous juvenile, claiming that he was just resentful because his family was not as close-knit as hers. The emotional disconnection of Peter's family members had always been a sore spot for him and Jan knew it.

As it replayed in her mind, Jan sighed, trying to unburden the heaviness in her chest. Both Jan and Peter had accepted Christ as their personal Savior less than a year after they exchanged wedding vows. An unplanned pregnancy had been the determining factor in the two of them making a mad dash to the altar after only a few months of dating. But their decision to make Christ the head of their lives was what had made good of what otherwise may have been a disastrous union.

But nothing had changed. God was still the Lord of our lives when the marriage fell apart. What happened?

"Fear not!" Jan heard Reverend Tides proclaim as he strode across the pulpit sounding as if he was talking directly to her. "Sometimes you have to suffer awhile, but if God said the battle ain't yours, then it's not yours! Stop trying to figure it out, my brother. Stop trying to reckon within yourself of why, how and when, my sister. God already has the answer and in His own time, He will grant you the victory."

"Amen!" Leona jumped to her feet, waving her arms in the air as though she was stranded on a deserted island and had suddenly seen a rescue aircraft hovering overhead.

"Amen," Jan whispered, whisking away a single tear.

Chapter 5

In Iraq, weeks could pass with barely a cloud in the sky. Rain didn't make a frequent appearance, and most times, even when it decided to fall, the spill would be brief. But a momentary downpour was all that was required to take Iraq from being a miserable place to being a miserable and messy place. A fifteen-minute shower was enough to turn the dirt roads to mush, and apparently at some point, while Peter and Fletcher were unconscious and tied up in the dark room, the skies had opened up outside.

The men were dry and warm now as they sat quietly in a twelve by twelve concrete structure, staring at each other from across the room. But not long ago, they'd been anything but warm or dry.

More than twenty-four hours had passed since they were ordered to complete silence, blindfolded and forced to hold on to a rope while they followed their captors to another unidentified place of imprisonment. It felt as though they'd walked for miles, and with every step, Peter could feel his combat boots sinking into the wet soil beneath him. He didn't say a word, nor did he hear one from

Fletcher during what had to be an hour-long trek. There were many times that Peter wanted to yell out for his comrade, but he could still feel the tenderness in his ribcage from his last act of rebellion, not to mention the soreness that lingered from the ambush. He could only hope and pray that Fletcher was all right and was somewhere in the caravan leading him to wherever.

Still blindfolded when they finally arrived at what would be his new temporary home, Peter was overcome with fear when he was suddenly hit by a strong dash of water that nearly knocked him to his knees. He guessed that the men got tired of smelling the stench of urine that his uniform held. The water kept coming, bucket after bucket; and while they tortured him with the cold bath, Peter took the opportunity to empty his bladder, which had at last reached its capacity. Once the water stopped, the men, speaking mostly Kurdish, stripped Peter of his soaked military garments, dried him with what felt like a towel made of alligator skin, and covered his naked body with civilian clothes. Peter clenched his jaw throughout the shameful ordeal, having a desire to protest, but a stronger yearning to live.

After he was manhandled into the building and made to sit down in a corner, the blindfold was snatched from his face. Peter looked directly into the eyes of an Iraqi soldier. Their threatening gazes locked for a long while, each looking at the other as though his greatest desire was to see the other slaughtered. Peter was the first to look away. In a fair fight, he knew he could rip the skinny man's arms from their sockets and use his dismembered limbs to beat him into oblivion; but with other men holding loaded guns surrounding them, Peter knew he couldn't win.

The skinny one suddenly grabbed Peter's legs and placed them together. Peter didn't flinch. He watched as the man took a rope and bound him at the ankles. Then the man did the same with Peter's hands. As bad as it was, having his hands tied in front of him was far more comfortable than having them behind his back as they had been earlier.

Shortly after the man double-checked to be sure the knots were secure, he and all but one of the armed soldiers left the room. It was then that Peter released a sigh of relief. He was almost certain that he saw Fletcher do the same as his body relaxed against the wall behind him. Peter knew that Fletcher was just as thankful as he was to see the friendly face sitting across the room.

Neither had repositioned himself since being placed in their assigned locations. Peter had dozed and taken several short naps since being seated there, but every sleeping moment was spent in the same position as the wakeful ones. And in the hours since they'd been brought to the room that was void of any furniture, there had always been an armed guard watching over them. Until now.

Peter turned his head to face the door when he heard it open and saw a soldier walk in. The men exchanged a few words that neither of the Americans could understand, and then they both walked out together after giving their prisoners a quick once-over. When the door closed behind them, Peter immediately returned his eyes to Fletcher.

"You okay?" Peter kept his voice to a whisper. He knew that although they were alone, the enemy wasn't far away. He imagined that they were standing right outside the door.

"Man, I want me some fried pork chops so bad right now."

Unprepared for the amusing remark, Peter found himself fighting an outburst of laughter. His whole body shook as he laughed inwardly at the scowl on Fletcher's face.

Peter couldn't think of anyone else he'd rather be going through this hellish ordeal with. None of the other guys would have been able to keep him smiling despite the fact that the sands in the hourglass of his life were slowly draining. The mention of food made Peter realize just how hungry he was. They hadn't eaten since their capture, and he felt the draining effects of being malnourished.

"You still gotta go?" Peter asked, changing the subject.

"Are you kidding? Man, I went while we were walking from that other place to this one. I couldn't hold it any longer. You?"

"I went while they were giving us our showers."

"And what was up with that?" Fletcher asked. "I wanted to say, 'Look-a-here, fool, this ain't the sixties. Brothas don't take getting hosed no more.'"

"Yeah? Well, why didn't you?"

"Pshhhh. Man, that would have made *me* the fool," Fletcher said. "I'll tell you what, though; that pitiful bath made me gain a new appreciation for the showers that we had to use back at camp."

"Yeah," Peter said, thinking back to the many days he complained of having to walk across the street to use the showers that were in place for the soldiers living in Camp Taji.

A movement just outside the door hushed both men and they sat quietly for several moments before Peter felt comfortable enough to speak again.

"Flex, we gotta get out of here."

"I know, but how? You got any ideas? You were sleeping so soundly over there one time that I thought you'd decided to jump sides and change your citizenship."

"Not hardly," Peter said, shaking his head. "All that time that my eyes were closed, I wasn't 'sleep. Some of that time, I was praying, man."

"You do a lot of that, huh?"

"What? Sleeping or praying?"

"Both," Fletcher said. "But I was talking about praying."

Peter took a moment to think and then gave an honest reply. "I used to. Lately, I haven't done it as much as I should. I've been doing more praying since we got ambushed than I'd done in a while."

"I don't know, dude," Fletcher said. "Look around. I don't think it's working."

"We're still alive, aren't we?" Peter challenged.

Fletcher's immediate reply was a quiet concurrence, a slow, thoughtful nod of his head. Afterward, he said, "I wonder if everyone else is still alive."

It was a thought that had been rotating through Peter's mind ever since the soldiers cleared out of the room and he saw only Fletcher. During the long walk to get from one nowhere to another, Peter concluded that either they were being taken to their deaths or they were being brought to the place where the other prisoners were being kept. But as the hours ticked by, it seemed that neither was the case.

"I'm sure they're alive," Peter said, despite his own doubts.

They'd been divided along racial lines, it seemed. Peter and Fletcher, the two African Americans, were together, and the others, all Caucasian men, were somewhere else; status unknown. All of the men had their own personalities and some of the characteristics of the missing men concerned Peter. Lance Corporal Silas Bigalow was young and short-tempered, often struggling with respecting authority. If he didn't control his emotions and his tongue, he could find himself in a world of trouble. Staff Sergeant Louis Malloy was fairly level-headed and full of loyalty to his country. If the absent part of their fire squad were all in the same place, Louis would probably be the voice of reason among the three of them. And Peter shook his head when he thought of Private First Class Charles Klauser, who they'd all come to know as Chuck. He was just a kid, barely out of basic training. At just nineteen years old, he was too young to die. He hadn't even started living yet.

Peter rid his mind of the mounting negative thoughts. "Chuck, Silas and Louis are probably all being kept in the same place, and I'll bet they are sitting around having this same conversation, wondering about our status."

"You think Colonel Goodman knows we're missing yet?" Fletcher asked, referring to the leader of their platoon.

"Are you kidding?" Peter replied. "If my estimation is right, we haven't returned to camp in at least two days. He knows we're missing."

"You think our families know?" Fletcher asked. "If Chantel and Flex, Jr. have been told about this, I'd hate to think of what they're going through right now. They're not ready to lose me, Pete; and I'm not ready to lose them. You know what I mean?"

Peter's eyes watered as he thought again of Jan and Kyla. With their relocation to Atlanta, the word of his capture would be delayed in getting to them. They most likely wouldn't find out until the media did, and Jan and Kyla deserved better than to find out along with the rest of the world. In spite of everything, those were his two favorite girls and he loved them. Peter wished for a chance to make right his wrongs, but the longer he remained in captivity, the more he felt like the opportunity would never come.

I'm sorry, Jan. If I could turn back the hands of time, I'd do so many things differently. So many things . . .

A tear fell from his eye as the thought lingered. Peter

didn't bother to try to hide his emotions. There was only one person there to see him; and if anybody could understand his growing feeling of hopelessness, it was Fletcher.

"Yeah," Peter whispered as he used his bound hands to wipe away the tear. "I know what you mean."

Chapter 6

Listen,

There's no real sense in beating around the bush, okay? I've been trying to think of a way to be tactful about this whole thing, but I can't keep up the charade. We're both reasonably smart, reasonably attractive adults and technically speaking, we both still have more years ahead of us than behind us. I think the best thing for us to do is call it quits now and move on. I got your message the other day, but sometimes it's just best to cut things off cold turkey. I was wrong to ever call you because it is apparent now that my call was misleading. I will always care about you, but I don't love you. And no, it didn't take me all this time to figure that out. It just took this long for me to get the courage to tell you.

The fight we had turned out to be for the best because it opened the door for me to say what I should have said some time ago. I'll always owe a certain level of debt to you. If it wasn't for you, I would never have been able to hold in my arms the most precious gift God could have ever given me and look into her eyes with love. For that reason, I can't see our connection as a complete waste of our time and efforts. I'm sorry we couldn't work it out, but some things just aren't meant to be. For the sake of our irreversible family ties, I hope we can somehow still be friends.

Best regards,
Pete

"What?!" It was a literal scream. Jan couldn't believe what she'd just read, and her eyes burned as she continued to stare at the paper she pulled from the envelope that was wet and smeared from the outside rainfall. A hundred—no, a thousand curses danced on the edge of her tongue, threatening to escape in the midst of her near-uncontrollable anger. Her tears were hot and they clouded her vision as she read the one-page letter for the second time. The paper trembled in her unsteady hands, and Jan was more grateful than ever that she'd worked the day shift today at Northlake Medical Center instead of her regular evening schedule. There was no way she would have been able to go to work and give the patients the attention they deserved after reading the letter she'd just received from Peter.

All this while, Jan had been worried about why Kyla hadn't heard from him in so long, and now she knew. Peter was laying low, waiting to see how she would react once she received his latest letter. He'd probably mailed it several days ago. The mail that Kyla got from him usually took a week or so to arrive, and since Kyla had also received a letter in today's mail, Jan could only assume that both letters were mailed on the same date.

"So you hope we can still be friends, do you? Did you take private lessons or were you born that stupid, Peter

Kyle Jericho?" In the face of her tears, Jan laughed aloud at the gall it must have taken for him to even suggest such a thing. "And what did you say in this letter to Kyla, huh? Did you tell her that you'd decided you didn't want to be her father anymore but you hope that y'all could still be friends too? Is that what you said, you no good—"

Jan struggled to keep her words righteous just as much as she struggled with the decision of whether to open her daughter's letter. Yes, it would be an invasion of Kyla's privacy, but it would be for her own protection. She would hate for Kyla to find out from a piece of paper that her parents wouldn't be getting back together after all. She didn't think that Peter would be so cruel as to explain something like that in a letter to his daughter, but since he did it to her, Jan no longer knew what Peter was capable of.

"The least you could have done was wait until you got back to the States and came to me like a man," she said through clenched teeth. "But I guess you'd have to *be* a man in order to do what a man would do." Jan couldn't recall the last time she'd been so angry.

Using the skin of her arms, she wiped her tears. Her first instinct was to ignore the ringing telephone on the nightstand beside her. Usually, Leona would answer, but she must have been resting in her bedroom down the hall and didn't want to be disturbed. That was the only possible explanation, since Jan's emotional outbursts hadn't sent Leona running to her room to find the source.

Three more rings and it would go to voicemail. Kyla had stayed after school for track and field practice, and while it seemed too early for her to be ready for pickup, if she were calling for a ride home, Jan needed to know. So, she took a deep breath, cleared her throat and answered.

"Hello."

"Hey, cuz." It was Rachel. "I just called your job and they told me you worked a different shift today. You wanna hang out with me this afternoon? I have to go and buy a new outfit."

Jan tried to sound interested. "Oh yeah?"

"Yep. I have a date," Rachel sang.

"You say that like you haven't had a date in years," Jan said, wiping away residual moisture from her cheeks. "You have a date every other weekend."

"I know, but this one is with one of the staff cardiologists' interns. And he's cute to death!" Rachel exclaimed. "Be still my heart. Get it? My heart? He's a cardiologist, so the heart is his specialty. That's why I said be still my—"

"I got it the first time, Rachel."

Rachel released a single swear word and then added, "What's wrong with you?"

"I'm sorry," Jan said through a heavy sigh as she fought back a flood of new tears. "I'm just not in a good mood right now."

"Why? Is Aunt Leona getting on your nerves again?"

"No, it's not Mama. It's just . . ."

"Just what, Jan? Now you got me concerned. You don't sound like yourself. What's the matter?"

Jan sighed again. She really didn't want to get into this now. The words of the letter were just too fresh in her memory and too painful for her to talk about rationally. "Nothing."

"Girl, I know you not lying to me. This is Rachel Marie Ross that you're talking to, not some stranger who doesn't know you. You'd better talk to me. Do you need me to come over there?"

Jan's intent was to give a verbal reply, but her only response was a burst of tears that she could no longer keep in custody. She found herself weeping so heavily that she couldn't respond to any one of the many questions that Rachel asked following the sound of her cousin's outburst. Jan still sat, holding the telephone to her ear even after hearing Rachel say, just before hanging up, that she was on her way.

"Jan? What's wrong with you, girl?"

Looking toward her bedroom door, Jan realized that the situation had only gotten worse. The last thing she wanted to do was involve her mother, but it was too late now. Leona stood in the open doorway wearing a full-length duster and rollers that represented every color in the rainbow in her hair. Jan gasped to try to control her sobs, but failed.

"What's wrong with you, I said?" Leona rushed to Jan's side, took the handset from her daughter and placed the receiver to her ear. "Hello? Hello?" she repeated, trying to find out who was on the other end and what they'd said to upset her child. "I know you're there 'cause I hear you breathing, you cross-eyed, gap-mouthed, pigeon-toed devil," Leona said. "I command you to get behind me, Satan, in the name of Jesus! In Matthew 18:6, the Lord said it would be better for a millstone to be hung 'round your neck and for you to be drowned in the bottom of the ocean than for you to hurt any one of His children. So who-sun-ever this is, the Lord is gonna—"

"There's nobody there, Mama." Jan was finally able to speak.

"Oh," Leona said, taking a moment to gather herself before pressing the OFF button and returning the phone to the nightstand. "Well, something must have happened to make you cry. What's going on, Jan?"

In silence, Jan slowly extended her arm toward her mother so that she could see the still-damp letter for herself. There was no use in trying to hide the truth. Soon enough, everyone would know that Peter had so callously ended their nearly fourteen-year relationship. She couldn't believe she'd spent the last thirteen years of her life married to a man who could treat her so badly with no sign of remorse. Their fight had been bad, yes; but Jan thought they would be able to work it out. She'd been praying on a daily basis that they would, and after she got the voice message from Peter—the one he called a mistake—she'd gained a new reason to hold on to her hope.

Jan watched as the expression on her mother's face turned from confusion to repulsion. Leona sank on to the mattress beside her daughter and seemed to read the letter three more times before speaking.

"I told you from day one that that boy wasn't the one for you. Didn't I tell you that?"

"Mama, please," Jan begged to no avail.

"I told you from the beginning, Jan. I told you that ain't no man worth marrying if he out serving in the military. But you had to go and get yourself pregnant by this boy so you could marry him anyway."

It was a conversation Jan had had with her mother a countless number of times. Leona was never fond of Peter and it was a fact that she never tried to hide. The ill feeling between the two was mutual, but Jan was convinced that things would have been better if it weren't for her mother's overbearing and oftentimes disrespectful approach. In fact, for many of the same reasons, none of Leona's three sons-in-law cared to spend much time around her.

"I didn't have to get pregnant to marry Pete, Mama," Jan reminded her. "I got pregnant because I made a stupid decision. I was a grown woman when I got pregnant and we got married, so I didn't need your permission."

"Don't you get smart with me, lil' girl," Leona warned. "This boy done wrote you a letter that is just as foul as if he had-a spit in your face. You sitting in here boo-hooing over something that never would have happened to begin with if you had-a listened to me. That boy was in sin when you met him and—"

"I was in sin when I met him too, Mama."

"Yeah, but you got saved."

"And so did Pete."

"That boy wasn't never saved. If he was, he would have left the Marines. The military is a sin, and you can't be saved and in sin at the same time."

"Mama . . ."

"The Bible ain't never lied, Jan. Exodus 21:12 says any man that kill another man is 'sposed to be put to death. So that means that killing is a sin and that boy that you brought into this family gets paid to kill folks. He ain't no better than them Guatemalan folks in the Mafia who be killing for money. He over there right now killing folks and that proves he ain't no true Christian."

Jan shook her head. By Leona's definition, every person who wasn't American was from Guatemala. "Mama, that's not what that scripture means."

"Girl, I been reading the Word of God for more years than you been alive. You can't teach me nothing 'bout what the Lord meant when He said what-sun-ever He said. I can't even believe you would even shape your lips to try and defend that rascal after what he just did to you."

"I'm not defending him, Mama. Nothing about this letter is right, and Pete was dead wrong for writing it. But he wrote it and I have to deal with it. I can't waste my time hating him or even talking about him for that matter. I have to think of Kyla and how I'm going to break the news to her." Jan's eyes momentarily fell back to the envelope on her nightstand that bore her daughter's name. She quickly refocused them on her mother and added, "This is going to be devastating to her, and I have to try and make it as bearable as possible."

Leona stood. "I don't know what it is that gets into these men folks. At least your fool of a daddy waited 'til all y'all was grown and out of the house. This scamp ain't had enough dignity to do that. He probably been messing 'round with some military woman and decided that he wants to be with her full time."

Jan closed her eyes and turned away. As angry as she was with Peter for sending the heartless letter, she wasn't prepared to consider the possibility that he was being unfaithful. An image began to form in Jan's mind of Peter entangled in a passionate embrace with a woman in uniform, and it was too much to deal with on top of everything else.

The ringing of their doorbell interrupted Jan's response to her mother. Without even looking out of her bedroom window, Jan knew that it was Rachel. She watched as her mother disappeared into the hallway on her way to answer the door. Just the thought of having to relive this ordeal all over again brought new tears streaming down Jan's cheeks.

"Oh, God, help me to get through this," she whispered. "Please help me get through this."

Chapter 7

"Oh, it is *on* now!" Rachel declared as she slammed the palm of her hand against the open-faced letter on the dining room table where she, Jan and Leona had been sitting and talking for the past two hours. "He didn't even give you the courtesy of putting your name at the top of the letter. What decent man starts a letter off like this? Especially when writing to his wife. Girl, he might as well had called you a—"

"Watch your devilish tongue," Leona quickly jumped in, knowing how loose her niece's language could get.

"The B word," Rachel said, barely missing a beat. "He might as well have just straight up called you the B word. I'll bet you a thousand dollars that's what he was thinking when he wrote it."

Jan's tears had ceased a long time ago. She'd stopped talking a long time ago, too. For the past forty-five minutes, she'd been sitting in silence, staring at the untouched glass of iced tea that had been placed in front of her. She mindlessly watched the ice as it melted, forming a layer of clear liquid on top of the brown liquid. *I wonder how the water stays separated from the tea like that.* Her body felt numb and void of emotion; like a dead woman who somehow still had the capability to see and hear, but no longer had the wherewithal to comprehend or care.

Rachel continued the rant she'd started ten minutes earlier. "And I'm not even believing that he wrote you and Kyla on the same day and makes his letter to her sound like he's all sweet and caring and then makes his letter to you sound so hateful. You know what he's trying to do, don't you?"

When no one answered, Rachel answered her own question. "He's trying to set you up, girl. He wants to come out looking like the good parent while you look like the bad one. When Kyla looks back on all the letters and gifts that he has sent her since all this got started, when this mess hits the fan, she'll think that you had to do something to cause it all. You know why? Because Pete made himself look like a king leading up to it. Kyla's not going to believe that the same man who bought her those gifts, sent her those letters, and gave her a cell phone would be capable of breaking her heart like that. He's setting you up real good, Jan. Can't you see that?"

Any other time, the revelation that Peter was trying, in some underhanded way, to turn their daughter against her would have brought Jan to tears. But she was all cried out, and after reading the tone of Peter's letter, she was no longer shocked at what he was capable of doing. Jan had heard Rachel's question and even without looking directly at her, she could see Rachel staring at her and awaiting an answer. But Jan said nothing.

"When the time is right, he's gonna have to answer to God for this," Leona said, ending the brief silence.

"Well, I wish God would put him to the head of the line," Rachel mumbled. "The best thing God could do is let him get gunned down before he has a chance to change the beneficiary on his life insurance policy."

"Girl, hush," Leona said with a slight chuckle. "The Lord don't deal with people the same way we would, but you best believe that when He gets through, they know they been dealt with."

"Brothers can be so stupid," Rachel said in a raised voice. "They don't know how to appreciate a good black woman. All they know to do is mess us over and then break our hearts. Did I tell y'all that the cardiologist intern that I'm going out with this weekend is white? That's right; pure snow white—blonde hair, blue eyes, the whole nine. He's so white that his mama's name is probably Lily. But I don't care. I'm broadening my horizons. I'm tired of all these no-good brothers. It's too many of us and not enough of them. They know we outnumber them and they know our choices are limited if we want to keep our affections in our own community. Well, bump that. I'm getting ready to add some flavor to my coffee."

Leona nodded in agreement with her niece. "Might as well. And our black men don't know this, but God requires more of them than He does from other races."

"What?" Rachel said, giving Leona her full attention.

"Oh yeah," Leona emphasized. "God ain't never liked no ugly black man."

Even in her disoriented state, Jan's eyes locked on her mother. But it was Rachel who spoke.

"Auntie, what are you talking about?"

"Girl, you need to read your Bible sometimes and stop running the streets. If you spent some Saturday nights wrapped up in God's arms instead of hugged up with some no-good man, you might know sumthin'."

"You're telling me that the Bible says God doesn't like ugly black men?" Rachel could barely contain her laughter as she asked the question.

"In Song of Solomon, the first chapter and the fifth verse, the man of God introduced himself by saying, I am black, but *comely*," Leona said in a matter-of-fact tone. "Just in case them folks at the college didn't teach you what *comely* means, it means attractive. That don't mean you have to be attractive on the outside, but what it does mean is if you're born black, you gonna at least have to have a good spirit about you. You can't be both black *and* ugly. If you're going to have a bad attitude, you need to be white. That's why God allowed slavery and segregation for all them years. Them folks was white and He let them get away with it until He was ready to send Dr. King and all them other black folks to get things straight."

Rachel's head leaned against the wall behind her to support the deafening fit of uncontrollable laughter that she released. Jan would have laughed too, but that would have called for some type of sensation, and at the moment, she had none.

"You ain't hurting my feelings none," Leona said. "Go right on and laugh. When Jesus preached the Word, folks laughed at Him, too. So, who am I to think it will be any different for me? You gonna laugh your way right into hell."

"Who told you that that's what that scripture means, Aunt Leona?" Rachel asked, wiping water from her eyes with her napkin.

"I'm a praying woman. Ain't nobody had to tell me nothing. The good Lord revealed that one to me a long time ago." Leona slid forward in her chair and leaned across the table so that her face was closer to Rachel's than before. "Let me tell you something, child. Man is limited in his knowledge, but God knows all things. You know what that means?"

"What?" Rachel played along.

"It means that there are some things that you'll never learn in a classroom no matter how many years you go to college. But God is the master professor. He can teach you stuff that man can't. So, no matter how many degrees you got through going to college, you won't never be as educated as I is."

Finishing her sentence with such substandard English only made Rachel's newest roll with laughter louder and her signature snort more annoying than the ones before it. Jan was just about ready to leave the table and close herself in her bedroom for some much-needed alone time when her mother spoke again.

"Jan, baby, are you okay?" She placed her hand on top of Jan's and searched her face.

Jan's only response was a nod.

"No you're not," Rachel injected, "and you have every right not to be. Girl, you need to say whatever it is that's on your mind and stop holding it in. The only reason I'm not saying everything I want to say is because I'm in Aunt Leona's house. If we were at my place, I would tell you how I *really* feel."

"Well, you just make sure you keep all that foul language at your house," Leona cautioned. "Pete ain't worth me going to hell for. God is gonna take care of him, and whatever words God speaks against him will do a lot more damage than anything I can say."

"Yeah well, God can be my backup, 'cause if He don't get Peter Jericho before that tired piece of crap gets back to California, I'm gonna make a special trip and get things started. Then God can bring His slow self in and finish the job."

"Shut your mouth, girl; that's blasphemy."

"Whatever, Aunt Leona. What are you gonna do? Just sit around and wait for lightning to strike Pete from the sky? Well, that's you. But I can't just sit back and do nothing after what he did to my cousin. And what about what this is going to do to Kyla?"

"I need both of you to promise me that you won't mention any of this to Kyla." Jan had finally broken her silence.

Rachel and Leona immediately quieted their chatter and exchanged glances. Rachel's eyes dropped to the table and Leona began to slowly shake her head from side to side.

"The child has a right to know, Jan," Leona said.

"I know, Mama. I'm just saying that I need to be the one to tell her. I don't want her hearing it from anywhere else."

"Are you going to tell her today? She shouldn't be kept in the dark about this," Rachel advised.

"What's the rush?" Jan asked. "We peeled the letter open while it was still wet and we know that Peter didn't tell her. My baby has been through enough. I'm not going to spring this on her and destroy all of the progress she's made over the past year. I will break it to her gently when the time is right."

"I don't think there's ever going to be a right time," Rachel said.

Leona agreed. "Of course there won't be."

"Maybe not, but there will be some times that are better than others. Today is not a good time, and I need for both of you to promise me that you will respect my wishes on this."

Rachel nodded her head and took that moment to swallow the remaining liquid in her glass. Looking back at Jan with concern, she asked, "Are you going to be okay?"

"I really don't have much of a choice, Rachel." Jan got up from the table, leaving her tea untouched. "I *have* to be okay. I've just learned that I no longer have a husband. I mean, in all of this time that Pete and I have been apart, I had been seeing it as just a temporary separation that at least had the potential of being mended. Now, I know differently." Jan took a moment to control the trembling of her chin and then she continued. "I have to be okay for my daughter's sake. It's going to take a lot of prayer and trusting in God, but we'll be fine."

"And you know you always have me," Rachel said, reaching up and stroking Jan's arm.

"I know."

"And the one thing you ain't got to worry about is a place to live. I've always told you and your big sisters the same thing," Leona said, standing and walking to the other side of the table to be beside her daughter. "You can always come home if you need to. I can tell you firsthand that men come and men go, but y'all always got your mama, who will be here for you whenever you need her."

"I know, Mama." Jan's voice cracked as she accepted the hug that Leona offered. As her mother released her, Jan added, "Maybe I should call him and make him talk to me directly and say the same things he said in the letter."

"Absolutely not!" Rachel said, sounding like a scolding mother. "What good is that going to do? He'll just lie or say something even more hurtful. Then I'll have to kill him for real, Jan. You know that hearing him say he no longer loves you will crush you even more. Don't let him hurt you any more than he already has."

"I agree with Rachel," Leona said. "Don't give the devil no more room in your life, baby."

Jan stood in silence, knowing that Rachel's words were true. If she heard the words from Peter's lips, it would be devastating. She couldn't believe she'd even considered the idea of calling him. She never wanted to talk to Peter again for as long as she lived. *How could he?*

"Jan, why don't you go lie down for a while," Rachel suggested. "The rest will do you good."

Jan used her finger to wipe away the onset of a tear as she stepped away from the table and turned her back to the other women. "I can't. Kyla will be calling at any minute for me to come and get her from practice. I'm just going to go and take a shower to refresh myself. By the time I get out, I'm sure she'll be ready. Can I use your bathroom, Mama?" Jan added, taking a quick look over her shoulder. "I want to use the massage setting that your showerhead has."

"Stop calling it my shower. It's yours too. You live here now, baby. Sure, you can use it."

"Thanks, Mama," Jan said just before she started the short walk to her bedroom to retrieve a fresh set of clothing. She appreciated her mother's generosity, but more and more, Jan wondered if there was more truth to Rachel's earlier words than she'd first given credit.

Maybe Shelton Heights really is a community of misfortune. Could the simple act of my being here really have cost me my marriage? For the life of me, I can't find a justifiable reason for my life falling apart like this. And when did Pete turn into such a cold-hearted man? How could he just lay something on me like that?

By the time Jan reached the bathroom and turned on the shower, her thoughts were beginning to jumble. She could barely complete one before another would bombard her brain. The pulsating hot water that beat against her body did little to bring the relaxation that she needed.

He used to be so romantic and considerate; what happened? It wasn't that long ago that we were making long term plans to renew our wedding vows on our fifteenth anniversary. How did we go from planning a wedding to planning a divorce? How could he say that his heart didn't belong to me, and then in Kyla's letter tell her to tell me hello? Is he really trying to set the stage to ultimately turn Kyla against me? This is crazy!

Pretty soon, tear ducts that had at one time run dry were once again overflowing. The irrigation from Jan's eyes meshed with the downpour from the shower, creating a heavy salty waterfall. It was at that moment that Jan made up her mind that one of the first things she had to do was find a new home outside of Shelton Heights. She couldn't risk the chance of anything worse happening to her or her daughter. Enough was enough.

Chapter 8

The room was so dark that Peter couldn't even see his hands as he stretched his locked wrists in front of his face. The windows were covered with black curtains that wouldn't allow even the smallest glimmer of light inside. It was the perfect setting for the agonizing imprisonment.

By Peter's calculation, more than eleven minutes had passed since the last armed guard had left the room. There was no clock on the wall, and the watch Peter had been wearing at the time he was captured had long ago been stripped from his arm. But the dark quietness left little else for him to do than to count the seconds the way his elementary school teacher had taught him as a child.

One thousand fifty-seven, one thousand fifty-eight, one thousand fifty-nine, twelve minutes. One thousand one, one thousand two . . .

"Pete? You 'sleep?" From across the room, Fletcher's whisper seemed to echo in the barren room.

"No. You?"

"Man, what kind of crazy question is that? Didn't I just

ask you if you were asleep? If I were 'sleep, could I ask you that?"

Peter turned his body over on the hard concrete floor and stared directly into the space where the ceiling hid in the darkness. "You could if you talked in your sleep."

Fletcher grunted and then said, "Okay, that was a pretty good answer."

Peter smiled. He thought so too.

"What was that that we ate?" Fletcher asked.

As quickly as Peter's smile appeared, it vanished. He had no idea what it was that they'd been fed, and he wasn't sure that he wanted to know, either. Their meals had been delivered in tin pans that reminded Peter of the disposable foil dishes that Jan used when she made homemade sweet potato pies. He missed those pies and he missed Jan even more.

As famished as Peter was, he still would have turned down the foreign-looking meal if he thought he could have done so without being physically reprimanded. The men who brought them the food spoke no words. All they did was set the pans in front of their hostages and then stand over them, guns in hand, as if daring them not to eat it. While Peter was eating, he was thinking the food had been laced with something that would knock them out like the water they'd been force-fed before. But this time, nothing happened.

"I don't know, Flex," Peter admitted. "But it didn't taste too bad and it satisfied my hunger, so I just pretended it was Creole, prayed over it, and ate."

Fletcher chuckled. "Creole? You must like spicy foods."

"Yeah, man. I love to go to New Orleans—even considered moving there once my twenty years were up. They have the best Cajun food, you know."

"So I hear."

"I guess you were superimposing slices of fried pork chops over whatever we were actually eating, huh?"

"You guessed right. But not city-fried. I was picturing it fried, just like we did it in the country. You don't know nothing about that."

"If you say so," Peter replied. As far as he was concerned, fried pork chops were fried pork chops.

"But maybe I should have prayed over mine too because my stomach doesn't feel all that great right now."

Peter raised himself up on one of his elbows as if being in that position allowed him to get a better view of his friend. "You mean you ate that mess without praying first? Are you crazy?"

The space grew quiet, and for a moment, Peter thought he'd missed seeing a soldier enter the room. He and Fletcher were always quiet when they weren't alone.

"Flex?"

"I'm here. I was just thinking, that's all," Fletcher said.

When he offered nothing more, Peter said, "Thinking about what? And don't say anything about dying because I don't want to talk about that right now."

"That's not what I was thinking about, but thanks for planting it in my head. You're such the motivational speaker. You ever thought about giving Les Brown a run for his money?"

The laugh, though it was a quiet one, did Peter good. "Sorry. What were you thinking about?"

"Prayer."

Peter struggled into a seated position and rested his back against the wall. "What about it?"

"We used to pray a lot when I was a kid growing up in the country. I remember praying at home and going to church and praying there too. My mama used to say the Twenty-Third Psalm like it was a prayer. Anytime bills needed to be paid but we were short on money, or anytime one of us got sick, she'd recite that Psalm. So, I grew up around prayer, but when I graduated high school and started my own life, I didn't really pray much. I mean, I went to church, but not that often; and I can't remember the last time I really prayed about anything."

"Why?" Peter couldn't fathom a life without prayer. He'd slacked from the fervent prayers he used to say early in his Christian walk, but cutting it totally out of his life had never been a consideration.

"I don't know. I guess it was no real big part of my life to begin with. I did it when I was a kid because the people around me were doing it. I don't know that my relationship with God has ever been personal. It was just . . . I don't know, practiced, I guess. I just did it when I was told."

"So your family—you, your wife, your son—you all don't pray or worship together?"

"I always close my eyes and bow my head at church whenever somebody is up praying, but I can't really say that *I'm* praying at that time, you know what I mean? Mostly, I'm just going through the motions. Man, that sounds horrible even to my ears, so I can only imagine how it sounds to you."

"Sounds like you're just being honest," Peter said.

There was a brief break in the conversation and then Fletcher asked, "What's your wife's and kid's names?"

"My wife's name is Janet, but everybody calls her Jan; and my daughter's name is Kyla. My middle name is Kyle. Jan took it and feminized it for our daughter."

"Do you all pray together?"

"Yeah."

"But you said you and your wife are separated, right?"

"Yeah." Peter braced himself for what he knew was coming next.

"So, what good did it do? I mean, I admit that my family

doesn't do much praying, but we're still together and your family is split up. What does that tell you? I mean, don't get me wrong, Pete. I don't have anything against praying and I'm not trying to make a joke out of the fact that you and your wife are separated. I'm just saying . . ."

"I know what you're saying, Flex, and you make a good point," Peter said. "But my family didn't fall apart because God came up short on His end. What happened to us is what happens to anybody that does a lot of talking to God but not enough listening to Him. You know what I mean?"

"Honestly? No."

"Well, prayer mostly consists of talking to God; thanking Him for stuff and asking Him for stuff," Peter explained. "But I think if a lot of Christians are truthful about it, we'll admit that we do a lot of talking but not enough listening. We tell God all the things we want Him to hear and then we say 'amen' without ever being quiet and giving Him a chance to tell us what He wants us to hear."

Fletcher released a thoughtful grunt and then whispered the words, "So is that what you've been doing? Talking and not listening?"

"Up until a few days ago when we got jacked, yes. But since the capture, I've been listening like crazy."

"So, God's been talking to you?"

"Yeah."

"What's He been saying?"

Peter could hear the sound of Fletcher's boots scraping against the concrete floor and imagined that he was bringing himself to a seated position too. It wasn't easy to do with bound ankles and hands that were restricted from giving the needed amount of support.

"He's been telling me how stupid I've been and how much I've taken for granted. He's been reminding me of all of the secrets I've never confessed and the lies that have followed me since I was a kid. He's been forcing me to look at myself, showing me all my shortcomings."

"He sounds tough," Fletcher said. "Maybe that's why folks just talk to Him and not listen. I mean, it seems like He'd be a bit more considerate, seeing the mess you're already having to put up with from these crazy Iraqis."

"It's all in love. Sometimes love, like truth, hurts. I guess God had to strip me down to this to get me to shut up long enough to hear Him."

"What about the rest of us? Are we guilty by reason of association?"

"I guess," Peter said, smiling at Fletcher's choice of words.

"Has He told you whether or not we're going to get out of this alive?"

Peter shook his head from side to side as if Fletcher could see him. "No. But He's reminded me that those who die in Christ end up in a much better place."

The silence that followed was so thick that it could almost be felt. Peter's mind filled with thoughts of being brutally killed by inhumane soldiers, and he was sure that the same unwelcome thought had bombarded Fletcher as well. Peter needed to change the conversation that now felt as though it was smothering him.

"Where'd you get a name like Jericho?" Fletcher must have felt it too.

"What kind of question is that?" Peter asked. "Where does every person get their last name?"

"You're the only black man I've ever met that has that last name. As a matter of fact, you're the only man I've ever met period who had that last name. It sounds like something off television or out of a book. Like an Indian name."

"It is."

"So, you're Indian? You don't look like an Indian."

It was a story that most people in Peter's life didn't know in detail. His family life was one that he rarely talked about, but Peter hoped that telling it tonight would create new images in his head. Not that his family history was bestseller material, but almost any mental pictures would be more welcome than the current ones of him being murdered.

"My stepfather was two-thirds Indian and one-third African American. He was the only real father I ever knew since my biological father jumped ship before my mother even gave birth to me. I was very young when my dad and mom got married, so my dad adopted me and gave me his last name."

"Did they have any kids together?"

"No."

"So, you're an only child?"

"No. My dad—my stepdad, that is—had a daughter. My biological father had other kids too, all daughters; but I never got to know any of them. My family was never really close. Me and my mom have always been cool, but that's about it for me as far as family is concerned. Jan's family is real close and they do a lot of things together. I never had that. Her daddy left her mom after about a hundred years of marriage, and although it shook up things, Jan and her sisters still have a relationship with him. Both the men who once carried the title of my father ended up leaving my mom and me alone. I barely know one and hardly ever speak to the other." Peter paused and with a short laugh, added, "Funny thing is that I have an Indian name, but Indian cuisine is probably my least favorite food. That doesn't have anything to do with the fact that my stepdad didn't stick around, though. I never liked Indian food."

For a moment, the lapse of quiet that followed made Peter think that his rambling had managed to put Fletcher to sleep, but his cellmate's eventual reply broke the lingering silence.

"My family is like your wife's, I guess. I have cousins that are as close to me as brothers. A lot of us were close in age, so we went to school together and everything. I was always the jokester of the family." Fletcher chuckled and then continued. "When I was a senior in high school, I was voted wittiest boy in my graduating class."

"In other words, you were the class clown," Peter said.

"Yeah, I was a fool. Believe me, the title was well deserved."

"You don't have to convince me, man. I believe you."

"That's why everybody was so shocked when they heard that I'd decided to enlist," Fletcher said. "Even my parents were taken aback. Basic training and joking around didn't mix. The military is so structured that it just seemed so unlike my character to want to be a soldier. But I did and so here I am. When I got married five and a half years ago, I promised Chantel that I wouldn't get killed in battle. She told me that the only way she would marry me is if I'd make her that promise. So I did and the moment we said 'I do,' I had everything I wanted. I had my son, a wife who loved both me and the child that wasn't biologically hers, and I was a soldier. Now here I am; captured in a strange land that is threatening to make me go back on the word I promised Chantel. I can't even tell her and Flex, Jr. that I love them. I'd give anything to talk to them right now, Pete. Anything."

"Me too," Peter agreed, with mounting regret for his own recent actions.

"Even if it's just to say goodbye," Fletcher concluded.

Peter was certain that the pronounced quiver he heard in Fletcher's voice was a failed attempt to hide tears. A pool was forming in the bottom of Peter's eyelids too, but this time, he was able to control them. He filled his lungs with air, held it for a moment, and then released it as slowly as he could. When Peter was sure that he could talk without breaking, he did.

"Flex?" Fletcher didn't respond, but Peter knew he'd heard him. "I know you said you haven't prayed in a while, but I want to pray now, and I want you to pray with me. Are you cool with that?"

"Yeah, I'm cool with it," he replied after a sniffle. "But I'm not like you, man. Me and God . . . well, I wouldn't know what to say, Pete."

"You don't have to say anything. Remember what I said about listening to God and how we don't do enough of it? Well, I'll pray, and if you want to talk to Him, you can do it in your heart. You don't have to do it out loud. Then when I'm done, we'll both be quiet and just meditate and listen. The only way we're going to get through this—if there is any chance at all of us getting through this—is by trusting in God and being prayerful. We have to do it for our families, man. Okay?"

Peter couldn't see him, but he heard the heavy breaths that gave away the fact that Fletcher's tears were falling heavier now. In the midst of the gasps for air, Peter heard Fletcher whisper his single-word answer.

"Yeah."

Chapter 9

It was past midnight when Peter and Fletcher finally drifted to sleep, and as Peter's eyes opened only a few hours later, his body could feel the results of the abbreviated rest. Peter groaned, closed his eyes and tried with no success to grab back the first good dream that he'd had since being arrested.

Trying to move quietly so that he wouldn't wake Fletcher, Peter repositioned himself so that he was flat on his back and stared straight up at the ceiling. He could feel the need for another bathroom break, but decided to hold it as long as he could. He and Fletcher were no longer forced to relieve themselves in their clothing, but what their captors had given them for a restroom was barely any better. And they could never go to the dark hall alone. There was always an armed guard standing over them whenever they did whatever they did.

Even if you are left-handed, remember to use your right hand when patting a friendly Iraqi on the shoulder or when touching him in any way. Never even make an attempt to shake the left hand of an Iraqi. Using your left hand to touch them in any way, or allowing them to touch you with their left hand is considered disgraceful. For the most part, none of them have tissue. So, in their culture, the left hand is the hand they use to wipe themselves after using the bathroom.

Peter shook his head to rid his mind of the disgusting thought that had been drilled into his regiment of soldiers on his first mission to Iraq. Closing his eyes, Peter figured that if he could go back to sleep, he could not only shut out the fact that with or without tissue, his body needed to flush itself of whatever it was that they'd eaten yesterday, but he could also get back to his dream. It was one that made him ache for the company of his wife more than ever. Peter longed for Jan's touch and to hear the sound of her sensuous whimper as she lay across the bed and allowed him to massage her body. He had never had any formal training in massage technique, but Jan raved about his skilled hands and she would request their services often. Those relaxing moments were just as enjoyable for Peter as they were for his wife. He savored the feel of her skin as the massage oils seeped into her pores, giving her brown flesh an enticing glow. Those sessions almost always turned into more—much more. But Jan was more than just attractive in her outward appearance. She had poise and class that seemed to escape the bulk of her family members; especially the females.

After a few attempts at trying to appease his college friend by fostering a relationship with his sister, Rachel, Peter made an impromptu visit to Tallahassee and stopped by the cousins' apartment at a time when he knew that Rachel wouldn't be at home. The night before, Rachel had left a message on his answering machine, telling him that she would be out of town. Although Jan had been successful in avoiding Peter, he wasn't convinced that she didn't share his affections. He'd seen it in her eyes the first day he met her, and hoped that it wasn't just wishful thinking that she still harbored an unspoken attraction.

Peter's perfectly timed visit was the start of a whirlwind romance that quickly escalated. Severing the nonexistent emotional ties he had with Rachel wasn't that complicated for Peter. A part of him felt badly that because of him, there was a temporary strain between the two cousins, but Rachel's avoidance of Jan meant that Peter didn't have to deal with her either. The selfish side of him hoped that they'd never make amends; but eventually, they did, and to his disappointment, the after-bond that Rachel and Jan shared seemed stronger than ever before.

Relocating to the West Coast was the move that saved Peter and Jan's marriage. The first three years, living within a day's drive of Jan's family, were trying ones. Peter's disparagement for his in-laws was very much mutual; neither side tried to mask their dislike for one another. Even after Peter accepted Christ, tolerating his wife's "holier than thou" mother, her overprotective father, and her irritating cousin remained a chore. In Leona's eyes, nothing he ever did was good enough, or as she put it, "Christian enough." He was constantly told by his mother-in-law that he needed to go back to the altar and allow the Lord to "complete the work that He started" in him. According to Leona's definition, Peter hadn't allowed God to "fully" save him.

"Whenever you get *fully* saved," she stressed at every opportunity, "you'll take off them stripes that the Marines gave you and take on the stripes that Christ endured when He was nailed to the cross for your sins. When you get close to God like me, He'll tell you exactly where you need to be, and the Marines ain't it; I can tell you that."

All that talking she claims God does to her, but He didn't tell her that Marines don't get stripes? How 'bout you stop worrying about my prayer life and start worrying about yours, Mrs. Grimes? Oops . . . I mean Leona Ellis. I hear that some other woman is about to be Mrs. Grimes now since she took your husband. Peter felt a moment of renewed anger and then an override of guilt for reveling in his mother-in-law's misfortune. But sometimes, he felt that she had it coming.

Nine years ago, when Peter first got the orders to uproot his family from North Carolina and move them to California, the thought of living in the desert of Twenty-nine Palms didn't set well with him. Peter was born and raised in Seattle and had always enjoyed living in one progressive city or another. But Uncle Sam's orders had put him in a place far away from his intrusive in-laws, and in the Jerichos' new surroundings, their marriage found a new level of peace. In California, they were free to make human mistakes when raising their daughter without each one of them being pointed out and magnified by Leona and Ted. Perhaps best of all, Peter didn't have to endure Rachel's frequent unwelcome visits or her determination to stick her nose in all of his and Jan's personal affairs.

Life in California had been progressing just fine until Jan's visit to Atlanta; the one where she only packed one suitcase to make him think the trip was going to be short when all the while, she'd planned to be there much longer than she voiced.

Why did she have to lie?

"Wake up!" The door to the room that was once near empty and quiet suddenly flew open, letting in sunlight and at least a dozen armed men. "Stand on your feet! Get up now, both of you!"

Only the educated citizens of Iraq spoke fluent English, so it was safe to assume that the one man speaking, who was now standing over Peter brandishing a large knife, was one of the fortunate ones. It was the familiar skinny man, who seemed to be the leader of the pack.

Peter used much exertion to obey his captor's demands. The simple act of sitting up wasn't so simple when hands and legs were not at liberty to move as needed. His heart skipped a beat when the knife-toting man lowered himself to his level and held the knife directly in front of his chest. Then in one swift, sweeping motion, the man cut the rope that held Peter's wrists together. The blade came so close to Peter's flesh that he winced. Then the man did the same with the ropes that tied his legs. Without a word, he left Peter and was replaced by two gunmen, who directed their rifles at Peter's face, daring him to make a move while their leader freed Fletcher.

"Stand to your feet and come with us, now!" the man yelled from across the room as though Peter and Fletcher were a hundred feet away, or hard of hearing.

Unlike Peter, Fletcher hadn't been awake prior to the men's entrance. As Peter massaged his raw wrists, he watched Fletcher rub his eyes and then fumble for the glasses he'd removed from his face the night before. Both men followed the group's assigned leader and found themselves outside of the building for the first time since they'd been placed in confinement. Two trucks, very much like the one they had been forced to ride in on the first day they'd been taken into custody, awaited them.

When the men separated and Peter was directed to get into a different truck than Fletcher, Peter's heart plummeted. All this while, he and Fletcher had had one another as a source of comfort. But now the twosome had been divided. Just before getting into their separate vehicles, the two men exchanged glances, their eyes filled with a mixture of questions and fear. In a quick, but subtle movement, Peter placed his palms together and brought his hands to his face in a prayerful pose. It was a silent gesture, reminding Fletcher of what it would take for them to survive.

Their time with God last night had been a life-changing one. After the prayer that Peter initiated, he felt humbled when Fletcher asked him for direction on how to accept Christ on a personal level. The two men prayed together, wept together and then prayed some more. As he directed Fletcher toward the path of righteousness, sharing memorized scripture references and other encouragements, Peter felt a spiritual growth of his own.

The last words Peter heard Fletcher whisper to him, just before they drifted to sleep were, "I want to get out of here alive, but at least now I know that if I don't, I'll go to heaven when I die."

Peter had the sinking feeling that once the enemy closed the doors of the trucks, both he and Fletcher would be one step closer to the reality of what it meant to die in Christ.

Chapter 10

"Hi, Jan. Please come in. It's a pleasure to actually get a chance to sit down and speak with you. I feel that this is way overdue, and I do accept my part of the blame for it taking a setting like this to get us together."

Jan reached and accepted the outstretched hand that belonged to Dr. Jade Tides-Greene. Jade's smile was warm and her office, with its neutral colors, had a calming feel; but it was Jan's first time ever walking into the office of a licensed therapist, and she could feel her heart pounding in her chest.

"It's really mostly my fault," she replied, trying to sound far more tranquil than she felt. "Kyla really enjoys being around your stepson . . . I mean your son . . . I mean Malik . . . and you and your husband have invited me over for dinner and to enjoy your horses many times. I've just been too busy . . . I've just . . . well, I, I, I guess I just don't adjust to people that I don't know well as easily as my daughter does. Kyla is more like my husband . . . I mean her dad . . . I mean Pete, when it comes to stuff like that." Jan's nerves were getting the best of her.

"Children are very resilient," Jade said as she walked to her water cooler and filled a paper cup before bringing it to Jan and inviting her to sit on the couch that she'd been standing beside.

"I'll stand if you don't mind," Jan said. *You're not getting me to lie on this thing and suck all the information out of my brain, sister.*

"I don't mind at all."

Jan watched as Jade took the short walk that brought her behind her desk. She was such a pretty lady, with unflawed skin that looked luminous even in the low lighting in her office. Jan knew that Jade was not much younger than she, but with her naturally wavy hair pulled into a fresh ponytail, Jade had the youthful appearance of a woman in her early twenties. Having never been inside of a psychologist's office, Jan came into Jade's place of business planning to expect nothing, but also not to be surprised by anything. Yet, she was unprepared for Jade's next words.

"Because I feel that I know you, I'm going to ask you if you are okay with the notion of us talking in a way that is a little different than I do with my regular clients."

"What do you mean? What do you mean by 'talking in a way that is a little different'?" Jan felt the need to guard herself, although she wasn't quite sure what she was defending herself against.

"Well, I know that you regularly attend New Hope. I don't know whether you know it or not, but I was recently led by the Lord to establish a mental health ministry there specifically geared toward the needs of the women in the body of Christ."

Mental health? Jan was offended. "Are you trying to say that I have a mental problem?"

"Not at all," Jade said, shaking her head and still sporting the same kind smile and level voice that she had upon Jan's arrival. "When you contacted me, I made an attempt to tell you about the weekly meetings at the church, but you interrupted and told me that by no means did you want to meet in a group setting. While that is certainly understandable, I just wanted to ask your permission that I not be so formal and technical with you. Many of the women who come to me in this setting, I've never met or have no connection with outside of this office. Quite honestly, the overwhelming majority of the women who come here have little or no personal knowledge of God. You do. Therefore, if you agree, I would like to speak to you more from the heart than from the textbook."

Jan sipped from her cup and walked toward one of the office windows. She wanted to look out and pretend that something on the outside had captured her attention, but the closed blinds wouldn't allow her to use that method as a way to keep her inner agony from revealing itself. Still, she stared in the direction of the window as if the covering didn't exist. At least this way, Jade wouldn't be able to see the hurt that her eyes would be sure to give away. Jan's choice not to respond didn't go unnoticed by Jade.

"Don't feel pressured in any way, Jan. The decision is totally up to you. I can function effectively in a clinical capacity as much as I can in a spiritual one. We'll stick with whatever makes you most comfortable."

"If I did what made me most comfortable, I wouldn't be here at all," Jan said, not turning away from her idle stare.

"What would make you most comfortable?"

"Being at home in my bed," Jan answered.

"You can always relax on the couch if you like. That's what it's there for."

Only loony people lie on the couch, sister-girl. I ain't

crazy. I don't need to lie on your couch. "I said I'd be most comfortable in *my* bed, not on your couch."

"Then why aren't you there?"

"Where?"

"At home in your bed."

Jan turned away from the window and faced Jade. "Are you asking me to leave?"

"No. I'm asking you to tell me why you decided to come to me. What lured you out of your comfort zone and brought you here to a place where you are obviously not at ease?"

Jan shrugged and walked back in the direction of the brown leather couch, but walked around it and came to a stop with her back against the neighboring wall. As long as she avoided the couch, she would be able to leave still owning a shred of dignity. "I don't know, really. Everything within me told me not to call you, so I don't know why I ended up picking up the phone and doing it anyway. I think I was just desperate, to be honest. If I could have thought of someone else . . . anyone else I could have gone to, I would have."

"That sounds rather personal. Is there something about me personally that had you not wanting to call?"

"It's not that I have anything against you, if that's what you're thinking," Jan said, shifting her feet. "It's just that, well, everybody knows that you and your husband have a great relationship. I figured that the person I chose to talk to should be someone who could relate to being brutally mistreated and hung out to dry."

"Jan, I don't apologize for having a good marriage. By most definitions, Hunter and I are still newlyweds, so it would stand to reason that we wouldn't be having any major problems right now."

"See, you can't relate. Look at you; over there grinning like a school girl. That's why I didn't want to come here."

"Jan, the only me you know is the one you see sitting in front of you. But I've not always grinned like a school girl. Hunter wasn't my first love. Just because I'm experiencing a great relationship now doesn't mean I always have. I know what it's like to have a broken heart and to have the man I loved treat me with disgrace. Don't let my today be the yardstick by which you measure my yesterdays. I've experienced being terribly misused by a man. I even know what it's like to be fully dressed in a wedding gown waiting for the music to start so that I can march down the aisle, only to be delivered the message—while I'm in the bridal chamber, mind you—that my groom is a no-show."

Jan looked at Jade in shock. She could only imagine the embarrassment that a situation like that would cause. "You were left at the altar?"

"My wedding was called off twenty minutes *after* it was scheduled to start."

"I'm sorry."

"I used to be sorry too, but I'm not anymore," Jade revealed as she stood from her seat and walked around to the front of her desk. "You know why? Because had that marriage taken place, my marriage to Hunter wouldn't have. God does everything in divine order. My parents had tried to tell me that George wasn't the right man for me, but I was grown; I thought I knew more than they did. But they were right all along and if I had listened to them, I never would have been made to look like a fool in front of a church full of my family and friends. Yet, by the same token, because I was left at the altar, I was ultimately made a stronger woman and a more dedicated Christian."

Jan's eyes dropped to the floor as she thought of years past. "My parents told me not to marry Pete, but I did it anyway. Is this God's divine order for my life too? Is all of this to make me a stronger woman and a better Christian?"

"I've not yet heard your full story, Jan. I'd never make a statement to that end with the little information that I have on your marriage. I was only sharing my testimony to let you know that everything God's children go through in life is for His purpose and for His plan. How long have you and Pete been married?"

"Our thirteenth anniversary was last month." Jan didn't want to get into how miserable it had been to spend it apart from her husband. She'd spent most of the day crying, wanting to cry or trying not to cry.

"That's a long time, Jan; especially to have married as young as the two of you apparently were at the time. The fact that you survived all these years speaks volumes to your dedication to one another. Have things always been a challenge where your union is concerned?"

Jan's mind took a quick journey, reviewing her marriage. Almost all of her memories were fond ones. She and Peter had been spontaneous and adventurous in their relationship. Lovemaking was a frequent sport in their home. He would break away from his job on base during the lunch hour and show up at home, saying that he had a taste for a "different kind of cuisine." Jan always knew what that meant and she served her husband well. Even on days when they weren't on the best of terms, each of them knew that no matter what room the argument started in, it would eventually end in the bedroom.

"No," Jan said, feeling an urgent need to redirect her thoughts. "We had the normal problems, but we had a very good marriage until a year or so ago."

"And both of you are saved, correct?"

"Yes."

"If you and Pete were married for twelve years before you began having major issues, and Christ was the head of your household, I have to question your parents' opinion that you should not have married him."

"Apparently they were right."

"It's not apparent to me," Jade said, leaning against the side of her desk and crossing her legs at the ankles. "Why don't you tell me what happened to lead to your breakup."

Jan struggled at the start of her reveal, but the more she shared with Jade, the better she felt. Not better in a jubilant way, but her heart felt lighter, as if telling Jade somehow was a means of sharing the load she'd been carrying alone for all these months. While Jan spoke, Jade stood quietly and listened to all that had transpired from the early years of their marriage to the final days that resulted in Jan's relocation to Atlanta. At times, Jan's eyes overflowed with tears and she used the sheets of Kleenex that Jade handed her to absorb the resulting streams.

"Like I said, we'd had little problems here and there before," Jan said as she neared the conclusion of her story, "but I never thought we would end up like this. I never thought Pete could be so cruel as to tell me that he didn't love me. Not only did he tell me he didn't love me, but he basically told me that he hadn't loved me in a while and just hadn't mustered up enough courage to admit it."

"Jan, you've talked about the years that Pete has spent in the service. War has been known to affect soldiers in various ways. Have you given consideration to the fact that Pete was not himself when he wrote the letter to you? I mean, it makes little or no sense that he would write such a wonderful letter to Kyla and with the same pen and on the same day, write you one like the one you've described."

Jan walked to the sofa and grabbed her purse. She briefly fished through it, pulling out the letter in question and extending the folded paper toward Jade. "Here. Read it for yourself. I've read it so many times that I've memorized it. Pete fought in the Persian Gulf War in 1991, so this isn't his first time in active combat. And before you say it, I know that this war has gone on much longer and has been much more deadly. But I don't think for one minute that the pressures of war had anything to do with him writing that letter. Even before he wrote the letter, before we separated, and before he was sent on this most recent mission to Iraq, Pete accused me of being a liar, saying he could no longer even trust me to tell the truth. Now he tells me that he doesn't love me anymore? It's just cruel and I didn't deserve that."

In the time that it took for Jan to rant her feelings, Jade read the brief letter and folded it back in the way that it was handed to her. "The tone of this letter hardly fits the person that you described Pete to be prior to your breakup."

"Well, that just goes to show you that people can really change. He definitely wrote it and he definitely mailed it to me. My mom and Rachel believe that he's having an affair and that maybe *she* gave him an ultimatum and he chose her over me." The words left a bitter taste on Jan's tongue.

"Who's Rachel?"

"My cousin."

"She sounds like my best friend, Ingrid, back in Virginia. She's a tell-it-like-she-sees-it kind of girl. She doesn't hold back very much. If Ingrid thinks it, she says it."

"They could be sisters," Jan said. "Rachel's my best friend, too, and she's the one person that I can trust to be brutally honest with me whether I want her to be or not."

"They could be twins," Jade said with a laugh. "But I think everybody needs somebody like that in their lives."

"I agree."

Jade quickly sobered and then asked, "Do you want this marriage to be over? An even better question would be, has God told you that it's over?"

Jan frowned at the query and the way it was posed. "God? You read the letter, Dr. Greene. It doesn't matter what I want or what God has told me. Pete wants out and he's made that clear. I'm not going to run after him or try to get him to reconsider. He's not going to disrespect me like that and have me sitting over here hoping that he changes his mind. I'm not going to be an afterthought; the woman he decides he'll go ahead and stay with after he's rolled in the hay with what's-her-face. As far as I'm concerned, *he's* the idiot. I'm a darn good catch if I must say so myself. If Pete can't see that . . . if he lets some other woman, who probably just wants him for what she *thinks* he has, make him leave me, then so long, soldier. Get gone. Hit the road, Jack. Adios, amigo. To the left, to the left."

Jade was silent for the duration of Jan's words and accompanying hand gestures. Once the room was quiet, she took the short stroll across the room and stood beside her client, whose hour-long session was nearing its end. Placing her hands on top of Jan's shoulders, Jade's voice was full of compassion when she asked, "If you really mean that, Jan, why are you here?"

When Jan opened her mouth, her intention was to yell at Jade for questioning the validity of the words she'd just spoken so adamantly. But instead, all that escaped was a burst of uncontainable tears. Jan didn't want to break down, but she did. It seemed that all she'd done in the past few days was shed unwanted but insuppressible tears. She was tired of crying, tired of questioning, tired of caring, tired of hurting. Just plain tired.

Chapter 11

I'm free! I'm free!

The words screamed from within, but Peter managed to contain them. He couldn't believe what had transpired over the past several hours, but he dared not ask any questions. He dared not speak at all for fear that he'd find out that it was all a dream and would wake up only to find himself still confined by makeshift shackles. Peter watched Chuck Klauser, Silas Bigalow and Louis Malloy exchange conversation and celebrate with gulps of bubbling champagne, complements of Uncle Sam; but he chose to just sit. Every few minutes, he would look at his raw wrists, touching the places where the ropes used to be, and would pray a silent prayer of thanksgiving. None of what had occurred in the last several hours made sense to Peter, but he gathered that he'd somehow lived the last scripture he'd read the morning before being captured.

God has chosen the foolish things of the world to confound the wise. Peter repeated the words of I Corinthians 1:27 in his head as they were brought back to his remembrance. The last day, maybe two, had definitely been crazy, foolish, whatever the definition, but none of that mattered now. He was going home. Finally.

"Are you sure you're all right, Jericho?"

"Yes, sir," Peter whispered, almost cringing as he shifted his body to prevent Colonel Alfred Goodman from touching his shoulder.

The commanding officer was tall and broad-shouldered to the point of intimidation. He had the physique of a professional bodybuilder and at age forty, could outrun and out-bench-press most soldiers that were half his age. With his extremely fair skin and grey eyes, Alfred could embrace his mother's heritage and easily "pass," but he chose not to. He could be hard-nosed and downright rigid at times, but Alfred had a tender side that few of the soldiers in his care had ever seen. When the five battered men who had been missing for days were returned as quickly as they'd been snatched away, Colonel Goodman tearfully embraced each one of them. Now, as he personally escorted them home, he cared for them as though they were his sons.

Despite Peter's declaration that all was well, Alfred brought him a cup of water and then sat on the floor of the helicopter beside him. Peter said nothing. He kept his eyes fixed on Fletcher, who occupied the space directly across from him, just as he had for days as the two of them shared the same place of imprisonment. Fletcher stared back, appearing to be just as dazed as Peter.

Peter wanted to yell, "See? Our prayers worked!" but he didn't. Fletcher didn't need to be reminded of the power of prayer. He'd experienced the same fears and dangers as Peter had, and they had both lived to tell the story. It was nothing short of a miracle.

"We couldn't find your wife, Jericho," Alfred said. "We sent word to your home several times to alert her that you were headed back, but she was never there. Do you happen to know where she is?"

"Yes, sir."

"Is there somewhere in particular that we need to transport you once we land? We should be arriving in California soon."

For the first time, Peter looked directly at Colonel Goodman. "She's not in California; she's in Georgia. I need to get to Atlanta."

"Then we'll get you there."

"Thank you, sir."

"No, Jericho; thank *you*."

When Colonel Goodman raised his hand to pat Peter on the knee, Peter drew back his leg. He knew that Alfred was wondering what was going on with him, but Peter hoped the colonel didn't ask. If he did, there would be no real explanation. It was as though his body had a mind of its own, and right now, it didn't want to be touched. To Peter's relief, Colonel Goodman said nothing. Instead, he gathered himself, left Peter to his own thoughts, and went to tend to the other soldiers.

At some point, Peter dozed. He was awakened by the helicopter's landing. The level of commotion escalated when the doors opened and the men began descending the stairs. The thick darkness was lit only by the outside lights of Los Angeles International Airport, but from where Peter sat, he could hear the screams and cheers that came from family members and fellow soldiers alike. Just before Fletcher made his exit, the eyes of the two men connected again.

"Thanks, man, for everything," Fletcher said.

Peter smile and nodded in silence, hoping his friend would leave before threatening tears broke. They'd gone through so much together that he felt closer to Fletcher than he did any of his natural family.

"I'm praying for you," Fletcher added. "Go get your family back, man. And let's get together soon, okay?"

"No doubt, Flex. No doubt."

Almost as if Fletcher knew that touching wasn't allowed, he gave Peter the thumbs up sign and then put his hands together in a prayerful pose, much like the one that Peter had given him just before they were forced into the trucks two days earlier. Then Fletcher took his turn to exit the helicopter just as the others had.

From the place onboard where he continued to sit, Peter watched Fletcher shake the hands of several men in uniform and endure the blinding flashes of cameras before the shadows of two people who had to be Chantel and Flex, Jr. rushed toward him. The sight of them embracing was the last image Peter saw before the doors closed.

"You're not getting off, sir?" he asked when Colonel Goodman returned to the space beside him and sat.

"Soldier, I don't go home until you get home," Alfred said. "I've spoken to my wife. She knows where I am and she understands my need to see you to safety first. We should be in Atlanta by five in the morning, Eastern Standard Time. We have clearance to land at Hartsfield-Jackson Airport, but you won't get the kind of fanfare that the boys got here. Nobody was expecting us to fly into Atlanta. I hope you don't feel any less appreciated."

"I don't want the fanfare, sir. I just need to see my family."

"I understand, Jericho. If I'd been through what you've been through, I'd feel the same."

As the helicopter returned to full flight, conversation was nonexistent between the two men for the first two hours that followed. Alfred busied himself by making military contacts, calling numerous people and giving them play-by-play updates on what was going on. Much of his time was spent in the cockpit, talking to the pilot, making sure that they were making good time and that everything at the airport in Atlanta was in order.

"You have to be hungry, Jericho," Alfred said. "We still have plenty of food onboard. Can I get you something?"

"There won't be anyone there waiting for me, sir." It had nothing to do with the question, but that was Peter's reply.

"What?"

"At the airport. There won't be anyone waiting for me."

"We can get word to your wife."

"No," Peter said, shaking his head. "She . . . I . . . we split up a few months before I went to Iraq. We haven't talked in a while."

"You don't think she'll meet you?"

"No, sir."

Alfred sat back on the floor and released a heavy sigh. Peter knew that he was trying to decide whether or not he should push the issue and dig for more information. He waited for Alfred to say something, but when he didn't, Peter spoke again.

"Can I get a ride from the airport to Stone Mountain?"

"Jericho . . ."

"Please, sir," Peter said. "I need to see my family. I have to make things right."

Alfred continued to sit for a few moments, seeming to contemplate his next move. Without a verbal reply to Peter's request, the colonel picked up his telephone. Peter listened to the one-sided conversation while Alfred spoke to someone and made arrangements for a car to be ready for their arrival. When the conversation was complete, he disconnected the call and attached the phone to the waist of his pants.

"I'll get you there," Alfred said, looking straight ahead.

"Thank you, sir."

Peter didn't know how Jan was going to react to his unannounced return, especially after everything that had happened between them. She'd be asleep when he got there, but he knew that his mother-in-law would be awake. For as long as Peter could remember, Leona made it a practice to get up at precisely four o'clock in the morning and have a quiet devotional time with God. Knowing that he'd have to get through her to get to Jan wasn't the most encouraging feeling.

Days of sparse sleep got the best of Peter once more, and he failed in his fight to remain alert for the duration of the flight to Atlanta. Just like in California, he awakened as the aircraft made its landing. From that point, everything seemed to move at warp speed. Peter scrambled to get off of the helicopter, and an unnecessary police escort delivered him and Alfred to a waiting limousine. A driver was already in place, and Peter was surprised to find himself not climbing into the backseat alone.

"You're going all the way to the house with me?"

"I don't go home until you get home," Alfred reminded him while pulling the seatbelt across his expansive chest.

The half-hour drive to Shelton Heights was mostly quiet, and during it, Peter's thoughts rested heavily on Jan and Kyla. But he couldn't help wondering if his reunion with them would be even a fraction as exuberant as the other guys' had been. Peter had no doubt that Kyla would be happy to see him, but his first concern was Jan. She hadn't bounced back from all of the turmoil like his daughter had. Peter had said some things and done some things that affected Jan far more deeply than Kyla.

"Do you need me to walk to the door with you?" Alfred asked. He was already reaching for the buckle of his seatbelt.

Peter envisioned the likely scene that Leona would create upon seeing him at the door. If Alfred were standing there with him, hearing every word that was exchanged, the ordeal would be all the more embarrassing.

"No, sir; it's not necessary."

"Are you sure?"

"Yes, sir. I'm very sure. I appreciate it, though. I really do."

"All right, then," Alfred conceded. "We'll wait for you to get inside and I'll be in touch with you again in a couple of days. I can stall for that long, to give you a little quiet time to spend with your family. But after that, we'll have to give the world what they want. You know the press is going to want to talk to you. I'm going to set up something on the base in Twentynine Palms so that you and the other four can do a joint press conference and just get it out of the way. Are you okay with that?"

"Yes, sir. Thanks again, Colonel Goodman. I didn't mean to be so much trouble—having you bring me all the way to Atlanta."

"It was an honor, Jericho. You deserve it."

With that, Peter rendered a faint smile, closed the door of the car and traveled the short walkway that would lead to his mother-in-law's door. *God help me*, he prayed within himself before ringing the doorbell. The prayer had worked in Iraq, so it seemed like a good idea to use it here too. Only seconds passed before the front porch light came on and Peter could hear the locks on the door being disengaged. All the while, he could hear Leona mumbling on the other side.

"Lord a mercy. What in the world is he doing here? I'm sho' glad I got up and read my Word before having to deal with this. Satan, I bind you in the name of Jesus . . ."

As the door crept open, Peter swallowed. "Good morning, Ms. Leona. May I come in?"

"Wha'chu doing here, boy? Ain't you caused enough turmoil in this family?"

"Please, Ms. Leona," Peter begged in low tones. He knew that if he didn't talk his way into the house soon, he would arouse the suspicions of his commanding officer. "I just need to see my wife and daughter."

"You mean the daughter you ain't bothered to come and see in over a year and the wife you said you didn't want no more?"

No longer in the mood for a word war, Peter edged past his mother-in-law's slow reflexes, and once inside, closed the door behind him. Leona reached to grab his arm, but once again, Peter was too quick.

"Boy, don't you come mustering your way up in my house like no common criminal. I didn't invite you in. You know what that makes you? A thief—that's what it makes you. And God says that thieves ain't nothing but murderers. In John 10:10 the Word of God says—"

"Ms. Leona, please," Peter said, raising one hand and struggling not to do the same with his voice. "I promise that I'll let you preach to me all day tomorrow and I won't interrupt a word you have to say. You can pray, prophesy, speak in tongues, lay hands, cast out demons, quote scriptures . . . whatever. And you have my word that I'll listen with both ears. But for now, can I please just see Jan? *Please*?"

After a long moment of thought, perhaps to see if the scales tilted in her favor, Leona said, "She's 'sleep, I'm sure. She's in the first room on the left." As Peter turned to walk in that direction, Leona stepped sideways in front of him. "Take note that the only reason I'm letting you in is so Jan can throw you out. You got five minutes, and don't think that I ain't timing you. And don't let me hear her holler, scream or nothing that even resembles a cry. If you upset or hurt my daughter, I'm gon' kill you dead. You hear me, Pete? The Bible ain't the only weapon that I keep in this house."

"Yes, ma'am. You have my permission to kill me. I won't try to stop you and I won't try to press charges, seeing that I'll be dead and all."

"Don't get smart with me, boy."

"Just let me see her, Ms. Leona."

Giving him one last glare, Leona stepped aside and allowed Peter to pass into the hallway. Standing at Jan's door, he turned and gave his mother-in-law one last look, and was surprised to see that she wasn't following close behind. Peter's heart pounded like that of the thief he'd been accused of being, as he slowly opened his wife's bedroom door. When he closed the door behind him, he quietly locked it for added insurance. The five minutes he'd been given wouldn't be enough, and Peter knew that when his allotted time was up, Leona would surely attempt to make good on her promise.

Using painstaking motions, Peter slipped out of the clothing he'd been wearing since leaving Baghdad. The last bath he'd taken was the one all of the former captives had enjoyed just hours before they were ushered to the helicopter that would bring them back to American soil. That was more than twenty-four hours ago, but as Peter did a quick smell-check of his armpits, he deemed his hygiene to be acceptable. He'd take a bath in the morning.

Walking around the full-size bed, he carefully pulled back the covers just enough so that he could slip under them without waking Jan. She was lying peacefully on the left side of the mattress, just as she'd done for the extent of their marriage. To Peter, it felt like she'd left the right side available, just for the day of his return. He lay still for several moments, taking slow, deep breaths. The smell of her familiar fragrance was in the air and in the fabric of the bed linen. It excited him.

Inching closer so that his skin touched hers, the hairs on Peter's arms came to full attention. Jan moaned softly, causing Peter to tremble with mounting anticipation. In a fleeting second, he forgot all of the bad things that had led up to this moment. The fight that caused their separation, the orders that sent him to battle, the capture that nearly cost him his life, the letter—memories of it all, against the warmth of Jan's body, dissolved like melting snow. Bringing his lips to his wife's neck, Peter kissed her. With his face still lowered, he spoke her nickname in her ear.

"Bay," he whispered. "Bay, I'm home."

"Hmm?" She stirred and then turned her body so that she faced him, but her eyes remained closed and soon, her sleep was sound again.

Propping himself on one elbow, Peter smiled and took a moment to search Jan's face in the dim light provided by the moon outside the window. She was beautiful. *God, how could I have ever let her leave? I'm such a fool. I have to make it right.* Peter kissed Jan's lips lightly, refusing to part from them until she opened her eyes.

In momentary fear of the face that rested so close to hers, Jan slid away quickly and sat up with widened eyes, pulling the bed covers close around her chest. She opened her mouth to scream, but Peter's hand covered it just in time.

"It's okay, Jan; it's me." His whispered words were quick, knowing that if she even screamed a little, Leona would shoot the lock right off of the bedroom door.

"Pete?"

The word was muffled behind his hand, but Peter heard

it. He slowly removed his hand from her mouth and used it to caress her cheek. "Yeah, Bay. It's me. I'm sorry, I didn't mean to frighten you. I-I-I . . ."

"Who . . . Why . . . What are you doing here?"

"It's a long story, but I don't want to talk about it just yet. There're so many more important things that I need to say to you; things I want to do to . . . with you. I'm sorry for everything. I'm so sorry. I'm so, *so* sorry. I'll do anything to get my family back, Bay. Please say you feel the same."

"But you said—"

"I know what I said," Peter cooed, stroking the side of her face with his fingertips. "I was stupid. I was selfish. I was wrong, and I won't even try to make any excuses for it. Please don't hold me to it, Jan. I've been through so much over the past few days that I don't even know what day of the week it is. I've been praying every day, though. I've been praying like a sinner who had a taste of hell and knows that prayer is the only thing that will keep him from spending eternity there. God put me in a place where prayer was all I had, and I asked for His forgiveness, Jan. God has granted it to me. I need you to forgive me too."

The darkness in the room hid her facial expression, but Peter felt a moist tear come to rest against his finger. He hoped it was a good sign, but he couldn't be sure.

"I love you, Bay," he whispered. "Please say you still love me."

"I do," she whimpered. "I do still love you."

It was only at that moment that Peter felt a sense of relief. He leaned in to deliver another gentle kiss to her lips, and when he did, in a passionate motion, Jan threw her arms around him, pulling him close to her.

* * *

Peter opened his eyes and sat up straight just before the truck he was in began coming to a slow stop. The wheels had barely stopped turning before Peter received his first order.

"Get up! Let's go!"

Peter looked into the face of the English-speaking captor and realized that his precious freedom was as brief as a dream. The lack of sleep the night before had apparently hit hard. He had fallen asleep in the truck he was placed in for transport just a short while ago.

"Let's go!" the man repeated when his initial command wasn't obeyed quickly enough. For emphasis, he pointed his gun directly at his detainee.

Peter stood, longing to return to the dream that had been snatched away from him for the second time. In the midst of it all, he found reason to be thankful. At least this time, he'd been able to apologize. And at least this time, he'd been able to kiss her. In the previous dream, Peter never made it to his destination. Colonel Goodman broke the unconscious journey when he patted Peter on the knee shortly after securing the freedom of his soldiers. His firm touch had awakened Peter before he had the chance to get to Atlanta and make a plea for his wife's forgiveness. Like the one before it, this dream ended too soon, but at least this time, he'd said he was sorry.

Climbing from the truck with his captors, Peter immediately knew that he was in Baghdad. Early morning darkness hid most of the scenery around him, but the offensive smell of Iraq's capital gave it away every time. *What are we doing here?* He knew better than to ask the question that swirled in his mind, but Peter didn't have a good feeling about whatever plans the Iraqis had for them here. A few feet ahead, he spotted a shadow of Fletcher being aggressively manhandled by the other men and forced through the doorway of a building about twice the size of the one where they'd spent the last few days caged. Following the lead of the enemy, Peter headed in the same direction, having no clue what would be found on the other side of their new prison's doors.

Chapter 12

"Girl, I cannot believe that you're going to a shrink," Rachel said for the fourth time as she and Jan walked up the steps that would bring them to the double glass doors of New Hope Church.

It was a humid evening and the smell of rain was in the air, making the curls fall from Jan's hair. The thirty minutes that it took to style it in preparation for her first meeting with the specialized women's ministry now seemed a waste. Jan reached for the metal door handle and pulled, allowing Rachel to enter before her, and then waiting until the door had closed completely before she responded.

"Jade said—" The acoustics inside the church made Jan's voice echo, bringing her reply to a temporary halt. After a moment, she began again, this time with her voice just above a whisper. "Jade said that she thought it would do me some good to hear the testimonies of some Christian women who'd lost faith due to failed or troubled relationships, but found courage through this ministry."

"May I help you?" asked a woman sitting so low in her chair that neither Jan nor Rachel had noticed her.

Jan approached the information desk with caution. “Oh, um, I’m here for a meeting.”

The middle-aged woman pushed her glasses up on her nose and then looked over at the cousins and smiled. “Which meeting, honey? We have several engagements going on tonight.”

Jan shifted, suddenly feeling demoralized by her own ignorance. “I’m not even sure what the meeting is called. I just know it starts at seven o’clock and I was told to try to get here around six-thirty.” She glanced at her watch as she spoke. It was 6:45, so she was already fifteen minutes late.

Rachel tapped her fingers on the countertop. “Can you just call somebody and tell them that she’s here?”

The woman never took her eyes off of Jan. Ignoring Rachel’s question, she asked, “What’s your name, sweetie? Do you have an appointment with Reverend Tides?”

“No, ma’am,” Jan said. “My name is Janet Jericho. I’m here for a group meeting with Reverend Tides’ daughter.”

“Dr. Tides-Greene?”

“Does he have more than one?” Rachel blurted, sounding like an exasperated paying client who’d been waiting for hours.

Jan gave her impatient cousin a look of warning, but it was no match for the one Rachel received from the woman behind the counter.

“And you are?” the lady demanded.

“With her.” Rachel’s disrespectful tone was to Jan’s chagrin.

The lady was neither intimidated nor amused by Rachel’s blatant sarcasm. She stood—all five feet of her—from her desk and removed her glasses. “Excuse me?”

“I’m sorry,” Jan quickly said. She knew that she needed to step in or she’d never get to the meeting in time. In fact, if she allowed Rachel to continue talking, they’d never make it to the meeting at all. "I guess if I'd just given you all of the details to begin with we wouldn't be having this confusion. It's my fault," Jan added, hoping desperately to pull the woman's attention back to her. "Yes, ma'am. I'm here to see Dr. Tides-Greene. There is a women's group that meets each Friday night and that's the group that I'm— that we are supposed to be a part of tonight. Dr. Tides-Greene said that I could walk down the main hall, make a right, and the room would be the third classroom on the left. Does that sound about right?"

It worked. The woman returned to her seat and replaced her glasses on her nose. "Yes, honey, that's right. They don't start until seven, so you should be right on time. I just need you both to sign here and you can go straight back."

They did as they were told, and Jan breathed a sigh of relief when they passed the information desk and rounded the corner without further incident. Only then did she speak.

"I can't believe you did that, Rachel. That was just rude. You could have gotten us thrown out of here."

"Good," Rachel said. "You don't need to be here anyway. I keep telling you that."

"I'll be the judge of that, Rachel. You just behave yourself. Just because you hate stuff like this is no reason to be uncouth."

"I'm not being uncouth and I don't have anything against stuff like this. I just never thought it would be something you'd be interested in."

Jan stopped when they were within a foot of the closed door. "Neither did I, Rachel; I also never thought I'd be in this situation, either. You think I made prior plans for myself just in case this happened? I wasn't ready for any of this, and it has affected me more than I was willing to admit. I'm just trying to find the best way to cope, and who better to go to than God?"

"I'm all for going to God, Jan. But why here at this big church with the mean little old lady at the counter?"

"Because this is where Dr. Greene holds her group sessions."

"I'll bet you anything that 'gossip sessions' is a better term for it."

"Rachel . . ."

"It's a bunch of women, Jan; and you know what that adds up to. All I'm saying is don't be telling them all your business and don't be up in here crying and stuff. That's what those doctors want you to do. They're just like preachers at funerals—they don't think they've done their jobs until somebody's falling all out on the floor crying." A profane word escaped Rachel's lips and when she saw the look of horror on Jan's face, she immediately covered her mouth with her hand and took a quick look around. When Rachel was sure that her transgression hadn't been overheard by any of the staff, she continued as though no harm had been done. "You ain't got nothing to cry about, Jan, so don't let these folks make you fall apart. If you'd just listen to me and realize that Pete ain't worth your tears, you'd be fine.

"How did you let that doctor talk you into this group thing? When Aunt Leona was hung out to dry by Uncle Ted, she didn't need to see a psychologist. And do you know how many breakups I've had in my life? If I had a hundred dollars for each one of them, I could retire. But I've never been to a therapy session. I know how to deal with these situations all by myself. I pray, yes. But, girl, God designed a woman so that she is naturally equipped to deal with stupid brothers. Men are like Pringle's potato chips. Way more than one comes in a container, and if you pull out one that's burnt on the edges or that's got a chip on his shoulder, you can throw him away and pick up another that's just like him, only without the issues.

"I'm sorry, Jan, but in my opinion, reducing yourself to therapy is sending that dog a message that you don't know how to find your own bones. The best revenge is letting that no-good man see you looking good, walking with your head held high and moving on without him. Attack him where it hurts the most. That's the best revenge and it's the best therapy."

"I'm not trying to get revenge, Rachel. Didn't Mama just quote you the scripture where God said that vengeance was His and that He would be the one to pay?"

"Well, here's my theory. If you let God do whatever it is that He's going to do and then you do whatever it is that you want to do, then his . . . *behind* will get twice the whipping that it deserves."

"Rachel . . ."

"Jan, you're an Ellis woman and we got it going on, girl. You think you can't find another man? Sure you can. Show Pete where he can go and what he can do for you while he's there. Let Kyla start getting attached to another man who plays a visible role in her life. That's how you get back at a fool like Peter Jericho. Do you think he's sitting in a shrink's office right now? Heck, no. He might be lying on a couch, but I guarantee you there's some woman underneath him."

"Rachel!"

"I'm just saying."

Both women quieted when the door to the room opened. Jan's elevated voice had penetrated the walls that separated them from the assembly of women.

"Jan," Jade said, flashing a brief smile in her direction. Then her eyes glossed over with concern as she looked from one woman to the other. "Is everything okay?"

"Yes," Jan mumbled.

"We're sorry for the disruption," Rachel said, extending her hand in Jade's direction. "I'm Rachel Ross, Jan's cousin. You must be Dr. Tides-Greene."

"I am. You may call me Jade, though. I encourage that in the meetings here at the church. Here, we don't have to be so formal. I've heard some wonderful things about you, Rachel. Will you be joining us in today's session?"

Rachel's grin gave away her pleasure in hearing the compliment. "I came to support Jan. I hope you don't mind."

"Not at all. Please come in and grab a seat. We will be starting momentarily."

Following Rachel's lead, Jan sat in a vacant chair that was nearest the door. She kept her eyes on the sheets of paper that Jade handed her, staring at the words but not truly reading them. Feeling a sudden strange sense of embarrassment at being in a place such as this, Jan didn't want to look directly in anyone's face.

What if someone here knows me? New Hope is a big church. It wouldn't be farfetched for some of my coworkers to be members here and possibly be a part of the group. Outside of Mama and Rachel, nobody knows the extent of my marital discord. How will I explain my presence here? I'll be the topic of Monday morning's gossip. Rachel was right. This was a bad decision. Jan was just about to turn to Rachel and suggest they leave when Jade's voice interrupted her actions.

"Good evening, ladies. As you take your seats, I want to thank you for coming. Every week that you make the decision to attend our Women of Hope ministry meetings, you are a step closer to the total victory that you are in search of. I see a few new faces among us tonight and I just want to welcome each of you to our family. I've given our newcomers a packet that I'd like for you to take home and read over. It tells you all about Women of Hope and our purpose in the Kingdom of God.

"This is not a male bashing session and I always stress that at the beginning of each gathering; particularly when we have guests or new members. You are not here to slander the men in your lives, whether they are currently a part of your existences or a part of your pasts. That's not our purpose at all. What you are here to do is to share your experiences and your testimonies, gain strength and encouragement and to open your hearts to hear what the Lord will share with you through me. Are we ready to begin?"

Jan winced in her chair, unprepared for the thunderous applause and accompanying cheers that the group gave, apparently as a means of telling Jade that they were all set and eager to get started.

"Good. Please stand, join hands with the sister beside you, and let's usher in the Holy Spirit through prayer before we go any further," Jade instructed.

Since Jan had opted to take the seat on the end of the front row's semi-circle, Rachel was on her left, but there was no one standing to her right. Her hands felt clammy, and she hoped that Jade would remain at the podium and not join in the human chain. When she saw Jade walking toward her, Jan discreetly wiped her palm against the denim fabric of her skirt before placing her vacant hand in Jade's.

"Dear Heavenly Father," Jade began, "we thank you for being a keeper for each sister who has gathered here this afternoon. Many women who have gone through what some of them have endured did not choose to turn to you. Instead, they took their own lives, unable to bear the pain that comes with a broken heart. But you allowed each of the sisters in this ministry to be living testimonies of your delivering power and examples of survival. We claim this for them as if it were already done. We thank you because we know that you will continue to use this ministry to be a source of hope and healing. For those who are still married, we pray for their husbands, whether they are with them or estranged. All souls are precious in your sight, Lord, and we pray that you bring those that don't know you into the knowledge of your will for their lives. Forgive sins and give total deliverance. Mend those marriages that you ordained, and make their latter stronger than their former. Let your will be done and give us the wisdom to accept whatever your plan is for our lives and our relationships. We ask these blessings in your Son, Jesus' name. Amen."

Echoes of "Amen" filled the small room, and each woman returned to her seat, some already in tears.

"See?" Rachel leaned and whispered. "Bring on the Kleenex."

Ignoring her, Jan turned in the direction of the door as it opened. When she saw a police officer dressed in full uniform walk in, for a moment, Jan thought that trouble was on the horizon. But Jade and the man exchanged a quick embrace and then she proceeded to introduce him to the class.

"I mentioned last week that we would have a special guest at tonight's gathering, and here he is."

He's about the prettiest shade of ebony I've ever seen, Jan thought. She heard Rachel release a less-than-appropriate moaning sound and knew that she wasn't the only one who'd taken note of the attractive visitor. One of the women sitting on the opposite side of the room caught the officer's eye and even went so far as to wave at him. He smiled and waved back like the attention was something he was used to.

"Some of you are familiar with Officer Lyons, and others of you are not," Jade continued. "He serves as the head of security here at New Hope. I know that all of you are not here because of domestic violence issues, but a great deal of you are. So, I asked him to come by and share a few words with you all."

The officer removed his hat and his eyeglasses, giving the audience a clearer view of jet-black eyebrows, a matching mustache and a cleanly shaven head. "Good evening, ladies. I just want to start out by saying in spite of everything, God is still good. You with me?"

"Amen," the women responded. A few even clapped and waved their hands, as they would if they were in a church service.

"I'm Lieutenant Stuart Lyons, and aside from my position at New Hope, I am also a part of the Dekalb County Police Department. Like Dr. Greene said, thankfully, not everybody here has experienced a violent domestic situation, but an unbelievable 5.3 million women are victims of domestic violence annually; so, the likelihood is great that everybody here knows or has heard of someone who is now, or at one time, was victimized. You can never be too careful, and it's imperative that while we know that God is a protector, you also know that He has given you the wherewithal to protect yourselves. You with me?"

A chorus of women agreed in the form of, "Amen," "Yes," or "That's right."

As the officer went on to talk about the dangers of not reporting domestic violence, Jan couldn't help but notice his teeth as they played peek-a-boo, hiding and then reappearing from behind his lips. Lieutenant Lyons had the whitest teeth she'd ever seen. Jan couldn't determine if they were really as pearly as they appeared to be, or if his onyx skin just made them seem that way. Hurling back to earth and tuning in to what was being said, Jan became painfully aware of how similar physical abuse and emotional trauma were. She couldn't imagine that being hit by the man you loved was any more agonizing or humiliating than being dumped by him.

Jan scanned the faces of her classmates for the first time. She knew none of them, but felt as though she knew all of them. Every woman looked normal, just like her; not anything like women who needed professional counseling. In the first few minutes, while Lieutenant Lyons took questions, some from women who clearly just wanted to hold a conversation with the handsome uniformed officer, Jan began to feel more at ease. But as soon as the man with the "you with me?" crutch bade everyone farewell and Jade began the meeting, asking each woman to share of herself, once again, Jan wanted to grab her cousin's hand and run.

One after the other, every woman spoke, sharing a different, yet similar story. Some of their experiences were sordid and horrific. But despite their misfortunes, many still had a sense of humor.

"This Sunday will mark my fifth week as a member of New Hope, and this is my third week as a part of Women of Hope," the well-dressed, curvaceous woman who had waved at the cop and introduced herself as Kenyatta King, said from across the room. Her smile was beautiful and her makeup looked like it had been applied by a professional. "I have to admit that I'm starting to feel better and I don't live in as much fear as I used to. I'm currently staying with family, so that helps. I'm pretty sure my ex won't follow me here, but I still keep my pistol close by just in case. Y'all keep praying for a sista, okay? Like Stuart just said, I believe in God's protection, but my mama didn't raise no fool. His rod and His staff surely do comfort me, but so does my lead."

Chuckles ran around the room at Kenyatta's confession, but somehow Jan doubted that any of what she said was a joke. She imagined that there was a loaded gun in Kenyatta's purse that could back up every word. When Kenyatta sat, other women followed with their introductions. All of them looked to be perfectly content with sharing their personal stories with a room full of strangers, but the closer it came to be her turn, Jan's stomach tied into knots.

"Well, I'm Rachel Ross," Rachel said, seeming all too happy to have a chance to have all eyes on her. "It's easy to remember my name. Just think of the hit series, *Friends*, and think of Rachel and Ross, the couple who really made the show. I was here before the show came out, so they didn't make me a star, I made them."

That drew a laugh from the onlookers, but Jan shook her head when Rachel's own cackle ended with a snort. She had gotten everyone's attention and she should have stopped there, but Rachel wasn't quite ready to relinquish the spotlight.

"I'm not married now, nor have I ever been; and after listening to everybody else, I'm starting to think I'm the luckiest person in the room."

Rachel's laughter rang out alone following that statement, and Jan sighed in embarrassment. *Please don't mention that we're related.*

"I'm just here with my cousin, Jan. I'll let her tell you about what her man had the nerve to do to her, but I just want to say to Kenyatta, before you get complete deliverance, we might need to call you 'cause Jan's husband needs to be shot."

Jan's head drooped lower. *Jesus . . .*

"Nobody's going to be doing any shooting," Jade said from the front of the room in a tone that clearly called for Rachel to bring her ill-timed humor to a close. "Thank you for being here, Rachel. I hope you'll be a positive support system for Jan. In the healing process, it is important that these sisters surround themselves with spiritual influences that can help them stay strong even in their most vulnerable hours. Jan, you're next."

As soon as Rachel returned to her seat, Jan stood, cleared her throat and then smoothed out non-existent wrinkles from her skirt. As much as Jan dreaded her turn to speak, once she opened her mouth, the words poured out. "I'm Janet Jericho, soon to be returning to Janet Grimes. I feel like my story is a little different from everybody else's because there were no warning signs; at least none that I saw. My husband wasn't verbally, mentally, nor physically abusive, and my home life wasn't unstable. I had a solid marriage for twelve years, but a year and three months ago, it unraveled for no apparent reason, and I'm here because dealing with this breakup and the manner in which it happened has proven to be a lot more difficult than I thought it would be. But as hard as this has been—and still is for me—I believe that with a little time and a lot of prayer, I will be fine. The most challenging part of all of this is the knowledge that at some point, I have to tell my daughter that her father's not coming back home."

Jan's voice broke and she knew she'd just disappointed Rachel with her display of emotions, but it was too late to try to regroup. The tears flowed as Jan continued speaking. "For twenty years, my husband has served as a United States Marine, and all of our married life, I worried that the day might come when I'd have to tell our daughter that her father was killed in a military accident or had become the latest casualty of a war somewhere overseas. I would squirm at the thought of having to do that. But I think that as hard as a situation like that would be, it would still be much easier to tell her that than to tell her this. At least if Pete had been killed in active duty, his not coming home wouldn't have been by choice. For the life of me, I don't understand any of this."

By now Jade had vacated her spot at the podium and stood by the distraught woman, offering fresh tissues and a comforting hand around her waist. Other women in the room cried with her as if the story was their own. Jan's words were barely intelligible as she continued.

"I don't know what happened that was so terrible that it caused my marriage to collapse; I don't understand what I did to make my husband's love for me suddenly evaporate; and I have absolutely no idea how I'm going to look in my little girl's face and tell her that her daddy, the man she adores more than any man in the world, no longer wants to be a part of our family."

Chapter 13

It was Peter's worst nightmare come true. In fact, what he knew was about to take place was worse than anything he'd ever dreamed or imagined. He knew death was a real possibility for him and his troop members, but this wasn't the way he anticipated it would all go down. As poorly as he and Fletcher had been treated in the recent past, Peter now looked back on those days with a newfound appreciation, even wishing he could return to them. Those times of urinating on himself, being doused with cold water and stripped naked, being fed once a day with food that didn't look fit for human consumption; all of it seemed like five-star treatment compared to what they now faced.

When Peter and Fletcher were brought to their new home, they were temporarily relieved to see other familiar faces. Their comrades were alive. Silas, Chuck and Louis sat together in a corner of the brightly lit room, not bound like Peter and Fletcher had been for several days, but with armed guards standing behind them. The relief that Peter felt came to a screeching halt as the scene before him began to look oddly familiar. The men standing behind Silas, Chuck and Louis were not only armed, but wore masks to cover their faces.

"You sit here." The commanding words thrown directly at Fletcher were heavily accented, but spoken in English by the skinny, hard-faced man who had cut the ropes from their wrists and ankles just before they left their former cell. When Fletcher complied, occupying the space beside Louis, the man then turned to Peter. "Now you; you sit here."

Peter squeezed into the less than adequate space that was left between Fletcher and the wall. None of the men shifted to make more room for him, probably out of fear. Peter couldn't blame them. They were surrounded by more guards and more lighting than at any other time of the ordeal; yet, for Peter, this moment was more eerie than any of the nights of lying on the hard concrete floors, unable to see or hear anything through the darkness. Flashes from broadcasts seen on CNN resurfaced in Peter's mind and he knew what was transpiring. By the terrified looks on his fellow soldiers' faces, they knew too.

The bright lights that had been illuminating the space from the time they entered it came from video cameras set up in front of the five men. There was no dress rehearsal and no makeup artist to powder away the shine on the prisoners' faces.

"You speak, you die. Understand?" The skinny one tossed out the threat while pacing in front of the men. "You love your country so much that you allowed it to send you over here to kill us. But you failed. Now let's see if your country loves you enough to save your pathetic lives."

With that, the man released a haunting laugh and then stepped out from in front of the prisoners, allowing the lights from the cameras to shine directly on them, scanning each one of their faces, one at a time. No words were spoken, and when the camera reached Peter's face, he stared directly into it, hoping that someone was watching who could get word to his family. He knew Jan wouldn't be watching. Every time any story broke on the news concerning the war, she would change the channel. But Peter was certain that whenever the feature was aired, somebody would be tuned in who could get word to Jan. *Please, God; let someone be watching.*

As soon as Peter prayed the prayer in his heart, the lights of the cameras dimmed and he was among four who were ordered to move to a neighboring wall. Only Silas remained.

"Read this," said the man in charge, forcing a slip of paper in front of Silas' face.

Peter watched closely and could see the trembling of his comrade's hands as he held the paper as told. Glancing to his left, Peter saw Fletcher, sitting with his head bowed and his eyes closed. He wasn't sure whether Fletcher was in prayer or just making an attempt to shut out the image of what was going on in front of them. Whichever was the case, he remained that way, not even opening his eyes as the camera lights brightened and Silas began speaking.

The words he read were calculated ones, almost the exact words that many before him had been forced to read in months and years past. In the message to the United States government, the letter demanded that the president grant the release of war criminals connected to Iraq's government, who were being held in American prisons. The U.S. had twenty-four hours to comply or Silas would be slaughtered. The letter assured the United States that one by one, the captured soldiers would be brutally murdered until either Iraq's demands were met, or until every soldier was dead.

Peter had always been under the impressions that Iraqis, since ninety-five percent of them are Muslim, don't drink alcohol; but when the captors were finished with their mission, they shut off the camera, removed their masks, shackled the Americans with ropes once more, and celebrated their day's work by sharing glasses of something that looked like whisky. While the video equipment was dismantled and removed from the room, the five men, whose days had been officially numbered, looked on helplessly. No doubt, the footage would be blasted on every American television network before the end of the day, and despite Silas' pleas, the United States would never bow to the enemy's threats.

Speaking a language that none of the Americans could comprehend, the enemy soldiers who remained in the room laughed as they downed one glass after another of the liquid substance. For them, it all appeared to serve as some type of amusement. To them, life—even their own—meant nothing. They couldn't care less that children would be left fatherless and families would be devastated if they carried out their vile mission.

For quite some time, Iraq's finest sat around drinking and making merry, but gradually, the crowd thinned. By the time the sun was fully up, only the lanky, English-speaking man remained. Ordering the men to spread out so that they were no longer sitting within touching range, he gave them all one last hate-filled glare before walking out and closing the door behind him.

The Americans were alone, but for a long while, they remained silent. When the quiet was finally disturbed, it was broken by the utterance of a loud spew of profanity that brought all eyes to Silas.

"Shhh!" Fletcher said, eyeing the closed door.

That reaction resulted in another angry and frustrated

blasphemous outburst. "Don't tell me to be quiet," Silas added. "I got less than twenty-four hours. I ain't got nothing to lose."

"You conceding already?" Louis asked. "You're a Marine, Silas. You can't give up. We live in the best country in the world and if there is a way to save us, the United States armed forces will do it. People have been rescued in the eleventh hour before and it can happen again. Remember Ronald, Shoshana and the rest of those soldiers? Remember Jessica Lynch? We're not going to let you give up, Silas. It's not the American way."

"We have to think, fellas," Chuck injected. "We have to think fast. Do any of you have any ideas?"

"Have you guys been here, in this room, all the while?" Peter asked, trying to buy time while he tried to think of ideas for escape.

"No," Louis said. "They brought us here just a little while before you guys arrived. We were driven here from some other shed that they had us locked in."

"Were all of you kept together?"

"Yeah. What about you two?" Louis asked. "Where have you been all this time? We thought you might have been killed."

"We thought the same about you," Fletcher admitted.

Peter nodded in agreement. "We hoped you were alive, but we just didn't know. This is the third stop for me and Flex. I can't tell you where we've been because we couldn't see where they were transporting us from or to, but this is the third place they've brought us. I wish I knew where we were in comparison to where Camp Taji is."

"We're in Baghdad," Fletcher said.

"I know," Peter replied. " I could smell—"

"What does it matter where we are?" Silas snapped through clenched teeth. "You all are worried about the wrong thing. Instead of trying to figure out where we are, how about we put our heads together and figure out a way to get out of here?"

"Quiet down, man; we're thinking," Chuck said.

More swear words filled the room and then Silas said, "Didn't I just tell Owens not to tell me to be quiet? That goes for you too. Don't forget who outranks who, *Private*."

Chuck's posture sank. "I'm sorry, sir."

"Come on, Bigalow," Peter said. "The kid was just trying to help. Besides, rankings don't mean nothing here. We're all in the same predicament, and the only way we even have a chance of survival is if we keep a level head."

"It's easy for any one of you to tell me to be calm or keep quiet. At worst, you have twenty-four more hours to breathe than I do. I'm the one who's about to be shot, stabbed or . . . burned alive. So, if I want to talk, I'm gonna talk, and I'll keep on talking until I'm good and ready to stop."

The door to the building opened suddenly and it was all that was needed to end Silas' rant. The man in the doorway aimed the gun in the direction of the prisoners and all but pulled the trigger. Peter closed his eyes. If he was going to die, he didn't want to watch.

"Shut up!"

The door slammed, and Peter opened his eyes to see that the man who had issued the demand disappeared just as quickly as he'd arrived, leaving them to themselves once more. Minutes passed before any of them gathered enough nerve to speak again. Even then, the exchanges were in whispers.

"I had a dream, Pete."

Peter turned to his left and looked at Fletcher. "Yeah? When?"

"In the truck on the ride over here." Fletcher shifted his body so that he faced Peter. It was obvious that he didn't want the others to overhear. "All of us didn't make it out alive, Pete; and I was one of them. It was like I was dreaming the dream and seeing you and one or two others going home, but I had been killed. I think I'm gonna die in here, man."

Peter shook his head, refusing to accept it. "No, Flex. You're not."

"I think so, Pete. The dream was so real."

"Well, I had a dream that felt real too," Peter revealed. "And in my dream, all five of us were released alive."

"That's not going to happen, and you know it."

"No, Flex. I don't know that. All I know is that we've come too far to look back now."

Fletcher dropped his head and shook it from side to side. Peter could see his waning faith and knew he had to do or say something to bring him back. He needed Fletcher to stay strong because although Peter didn't admit it, he felt just as doubtful as Fletcher sounded.

"Think of Chantel and Flex, Jr., man. Remember last night after we prayed and you accepted Christ? What did you say? You said that you had to make it back home to share the new you with your family. You said that as the head of household, you wanted to be the one to introduce your wife and son to Jesus. Didn't you say that?"

"Yeah."

"Well, you can't do it if you're not still around."

"What are you guys whispering about over there?" Louis asked. "Got any ideas you want to share with the rest of us?"

Peter and Fletcher exchanged knowing gazes.

"Yeah," Fletcher said as he repositioned himself so that he could look at each of the men. "Let's pray."

"What?" Silas, Chuck and Louis sounded like an out-of-tune male chorus.

"We need some help, y'all," Fletcher said. "Let's face it.

If we're going to get out of here, we're going to need more than us."

"He's right," Peter chimed in. "This battle that we're in has gotten way too big for the five of us. God is the only one who can help us now."

Chapter 14

It had been a full Saturday afternoon and Jade moaned as she lay stretched across the sofa, while her husband sat on one end of it, massaging her tired feet. Malik's twelfth birthday party had been a big hit with his friends and a big responsibility for his parents. Friends from church and school had begun arriving as early as ten o'clock for the noonday celebration. Jade had expected nineteen guests, but ended up with nearly sixty. Good thing she'd taken her mother's advice.

"Our folks will show up every time, knowing full well they didn't RSVP like they were supposed to," Mildred had told her. "Make sure you have enough food for at least twice the number of people that you think are coming—maybe more. And my name ain't Mildred Tides if some grown folks don't be among those that will come without giving you notice. And they will eat more than the children who the party is for. It's better to have too much than not enough."

"But I didn't invite any adults, Mother," Jade replied.

"This is a party for Malik and *his* friends; not for his friends' parents."

Mildred's only reply was an experienced grunt followed by a knowing chuckle—and she was right. More guests came than invitations were printed. A half hour into the festivities, Jade had to enlist the help of her older brother, Jerome; by two o'clock, Hunter was forced to make a phone call to his best friend, Kwame. The men answered the call of duty and willingly helped to keep the forty-three children and twelve adults entertained and occupied. Malik and his friends had more food and fun than they could stand, and for Jade, that was all that mattered. Except for the wall-mounted flat screen television that played at a low volume from across the room, the house was quiet now and most of the children had gone home. Malik and his closest friends were with Kwame and Jerome, riding in the pasture.

"Feel good?" Hunter asked when Jade released a gratified whimper under the pressure of his fingers.

"Very good," she replied. "Thank you, baby."

"Don't thank me yet, sweetheart." Hunter winked, kissing the ball of her foot. "This pampering session just got started. This is only phase one."

Jade grinned. "Oh yeah?"

"Oh yeah. I promised the legendary Reverend B.T. Tides that if he gave me his blessings to marry his baby girl, I'd take good care of her. And I'm a man of my word."

"Yes you are," Jade said. "You take very good care of me."

Reaching for her hands, Hunter pulled Jade to a seated position and then in a single heave, drew her close to him, so that her legs straddled his hips and her face was within inches of his.

"How good?" he whispered

Something about the look in his eyes made Jade want to lock all of the doors to ensure that they would not be disturbed. “Sometimes so good that it’s frightening.”

Hunter removed the elastic band that held her thick tresses in a ponytail and ran his fingers through her hair as it fell to her shoulders. Ripples of chills ran down Jade’s back when he lowered his head to her ear and kissed the lobe. She slipped her hands around his waist and tried to pull him closer, wanting more. But Hunter just allowed his lips to rest there.

“Thank you,” he whispered in her ear.

Jade gasped lightly at the feel of his warm breath on her neck. “For what?”

“Everything,” Hunter said as he pulled away, placing some space between them. “But right now, I’m specifically talking about this party. Malik has never really had a birthday party before. Not like this one anyway. He had a lot of fun, Jade. Having his friends share in this day meant a lot to him, and it means a lot to me that you would do this for him. Putting this together was a lot of work, sweetheart, but I never heard you complain; not even when folks we didn’t even know started showing up today. You did what you had to do and didn’t miss a beat. Thank you for doing this for my son.”

Jade felt her cheeks flush. “You don’t have to thank me for doing this, Hunter. I wanted to do it. Besides, he’s my son too.”

Jade noted the brief expression that crossed Hunter’s face. For a fleeting moment, he looked like he wanted to burst into tears, but he masked it well.

“I know.” He brushed his fingers across her cheek. “And you know what? Motherhood looks beautiful on you, baby. You’re a natural.”

Unprepared for Hunter’s compliment and unable to manage her emotions as well as her husband had, Jade’s eyes filled with water that pooled around the roots of her eyelashes. Hunter brought his lips to hers, and when she closed her eyes to savor the moment, the waiting tears escaped, flowing down her cheeks. Hunter wiped the moisture away with his thumbs while deepening the kiss and heightening the flames that licked their bodies. Using his hands as exploration devices, Hunter showed no signs of restraint; but as much as Jade was enjoying his touch, she was very aware that there were children on their property who could reenter the house at any moment. It took every ounce of strength that she owned, but Jade managed to grab his hands and pull them away.

"Hunter, we can't. Not here, not now. The children . . ."

"I know. I told you this was a session," he said, continuing to plant small kisses on her face. "You ain't seen nothing yet, baby. This is only phase two."

"There's more?"

"Uh-huh."

"How much more?" Jade's breaths were coming in short, quick pants.

"If I told you, it would scare you."

Jade's intention was to respond, but his lips were covering hers again. The kiss was deep and profound, sending a message to Jade that Hunter never verbally uttered. When he finally released her, it felt to Jade as though he'd literally inhaled and taken her breath away in the process. When she opened her eyes, he was sitting quietly, looking into her face.

Wrapping his strong arms around her, Hunter pulled her into his chest and allowed her to rest there. Jade could hear the rhythmic, upbeat drumming coming from the inside of his chest. As she relaxed in her husband's arms, Jade's mind floated to the women in her ministry class, and she couldn't help but face reality. At some point in their relationships, those women had probably had days just like this. No doubt, their husbands or significant others had made them feel like royalty—much like Hunter did her. Only a few months into their marriage, Jade and Hunter had not yet had their first major disagreement. Their appetites for one another ran high, neither of them seeming able to get enough. Aside from the day Jade accepted Christ as her personal Savior, accepting Hunter as her husband was the best experience of her life. Still . . .

"Hunter?"

"Hmm?"

"Promise me that you'll always love me just like this."

"I promise."

His reply came too quickly for Jade. "I'm serious, Hunter," she said. "I need to know that five, ten, even twenty years from now, you'll still love me like this. *Just* like this."

Breaking away from their embrace, Hunter cupped her face in his hands and looked at her with intense eyes. "Where is this coming from? Why do you sound concerned?"

"Because I am."

"Why? Have I given you a reason to doubt me?"

"Of course not."

"What then?"

Jade sighed. "I'm a psychotherapist, Hunter. And every day that I'm at the office or at the weekly meetings at the church, I counsel women who were once just like me—so much in love that they could barely see straight. But somehow something went wrong and their marriages fell apart."

"And you think that's going to happen to us?"

Careful not to break the confidence that the sisters at the church placed in her, Jade said, "There was a woman at last night's Women of Hope meeting who was married for several years and thought she had a good, solid marriage. Then all of a sudden, totally without warning, things fell apart. Her husband left her and he didn't even have the decency to tell her of his decision in person. He basically wrote her a Dear Jane letter, telling her that he no longer loved her and no longer wanted to be with her."

"And you felt her pain, didn't you?"

Jade looked into her husband's eyes and knew that he already understood why she felt so much sympathy for Jan. "I really did, Hunter. I know what it's like to think you're with the perfect man and then have him break off the relationship for no valid reason. This sister is in almost the exact same position I was in. She is in so much pain right now, and I feel the need to really take her under my wings and encourage her on a more personal level than the other women in the class."

"Then maybe you should."

"I will." Jade nodded. "But I still need to know that it won't happen to us."

Hunter kissed her forehead and then locked his eyes onto hers once more. "Baby, all I can do is promise you that it won't. It's up to you to trust me and know that I'd never hurt you like that. This right here," he said as he pointed at himself, then at Jade, then back at himself again, "is forever. Believe that. I'm going to be loving you for a lifetime."

Words were fleeting and Jade wasn't ignorant to that fact. But she believed Hunter. As he spoke, the doubt that had somehow intruded her thoughts was shooed away. Jade reached up and wrapped her arms around her husband's neck, holding him as tightly as she could.

"I love you," she said.

"I love you too, baby."

"Man, back up off my sister!"

Neither Jade nor Hunter had heard the front door open, and both were caught off-guard by Jerome's commanding voice. Their startled movement served as a source of hilarity for Jerome, who stood in the doorway doubled over with laughter at their expense.

"Man, you jumped back like you the hired handyman and I just walked in the house from work and caught you wrapped up with my wife. You look like R. Kelly in that video; you know, the one where Mr. Biggs walks in and catches him with his woman."

"You stupid, boy," Hunter said with a laugh.

"You're contagious, touch me baby . . ." Showing off his gifted voice, Jerome sang the lyrics to the song that the video accompanied.

"Whatever, man," Hunter said, cutting into the tune. "How 'bout you need to update your video collection. That's old and played out now."

Jerome nodded. "Yeah, but Chante Moore . . ."

Hunter laughed and raised his hand to accept the high five that Jerome was already in the process of delivering. "Oh yeah," he said in agreement to the unfinished sentence.

"Oh yeah, what?" Jade demanded, slapping Hunter on the shoulder and giving him a look that challenged him to say the wrong thing.

"Huh? Oh. Oh, no. I just meant, oh yeah, she's the one who played the part of the woman in the video. That was what I was talking about. She played the part good, so I was just like . . . oh yeah, that was her . . . she was the one in the video. I don't know what Jerome was talking about. What were you talking about, Jerome?"

Hunter's innocent face was so endearing that Jade couldn't help but laugh as he struggled to wiggle his way out of the tight spot he'd wedged into.

Jerome shook his head. "Dang, man. She got you on lockdown like that already? See, that's why I'm not getting married anytime soon. Me and Kwame, we got to hold it down for the brothers, 'cause once you say 'I do,' you're really saying, 'I don't, as in, I don't look at no other woman, I don't talk about no other woman, I don't smile at no other woman . . ."

"Don't you have children to watch, Jerome?" Jade interrupted.

"Shut up before I send you a babysitting bill for all these rugrats y'all had me entertaining," Jerome teased. "You and Hunter need to take a break anyhow. You're always in each other's faces or down each other's throats. Take a cold shower or something, dang. Besides, the kids were getting prepared to come inside. K.P. and the Lowman boys just left; so the only ones still here are Tyler, Malik, and his lil' girlfriend."

"Malik doesn't have a girlfriend," Jade interrupted. She hated when the family spoke of Malik and Kyla as though they were a couple. In her opinion, the children were just too young for such labels.

"Believe that if you wanna," Jerome said, unfazed by his sister's tone. "Anyway, they're all coming in to play marbles."

"Out of all the gifts he got for his birthday, he's choosing to play with the marbles?" Hunter remarked.

"Well, actually, it's me and Kwame that wants to play with them, but since they belong to Malik, we figured we should let him play too."

As soon as Jerome finished his statement, the door opened and the children poured in with Kwame following close behind. As was standard procedure, they all removed their shoes at the door so that the dirt picked up from the pasture wouldn't be trekked into the house.

"We had fun, Daddy!" Malik exclaimed as he walked over to the sofa where his parents sat.

"That's good, sport. I hear you're getting ready to shoot a few rounds."

"Yeah," Malik said with a laugh. "Uncle Kwame and

Uncle Jerome think they can beat us, but me and Tyler are gonna to show them how it's really done."

"Mighty big words for somebody who's barely twelve years old," Kwame said as he sat on the floor and tied his dreadlocks into a ponytail in preparation for the pending showdown. "Let's do this thing, gentlemen."

Jade looked at Kyla and noticed she was checking her cell phone. She knew that the child was wondering why her father hadn't called. After the dismissal of last night's meeting, Jade had pleaded with Jan, telling her that it was imperative that she tell Kyla the truth about what was going on. Jade had spent enough time around Kyla to believe that the girl was mature enough to handle her parents' permanent split. It would hurt for a while, but Jade was certain that Kyla would adjust as long as she knew both parents would still be a part of her life. It was apparent that Peter wasn't going to call her and tell her, so Jade suggested to Jan that she be the honest mother that Kyla needed her to be.

"You don't want to play with the guys, Kyla?" Jade asked, hoping to take the child's mind away from her silent phone.

"No, ma'am," Kyla said, smiling. "I'll just watch. My grandma called a little while ago, so she'll be here to pick me up in a minute."

"I told Kyla that we could take her home," Malik said from the floor. "We could take her home, couldn't we, Daddy?'

"If her mother gives permission; sure we could," Hunter said.

"Thank you, Mr. Greene," Kyla said. "Grandma is already on her way, though. She doesn't mind."

"Well, at least I'll finally get the chance to formally meet her," Hunter said. "I don't think I've ever met your grandmother."

"Is your mother coming too?" Jade asked the question

in hopes that she would get another chance to talk to Jan and perhaps convince her to tell Kyla today. Maybe with the support of the other adults, Jan would feel more comfortable doing so.

"She had to work," Kyla answered. "She'll be getting off in a couple of hours, but I'll be home by then."

"Aw, man!" Tyler called from the floor.

"Yeah, baby!" Kwame exclaimed from the floor as he and Jerome gave one another high fives. "Who da man?"

"That's a shame," Jade said. "Y'all act like you're doing something big. You're beating babies, for goodness' sake."

"Babies with a lot of lip," Jerome said. "They don't want none of this. What you got, Malik, huh? What you got?"

The doorbell rang and Hunter stood to answer it, stepping over the competitors in the process. "I think this is your grandmother, Kyla," he said after looking through the peephole.

"Good afternoon," Leona said when Hunter opened the door. "I'm Mother Leona Grimes and I'm here to pick up my granddaughter."

"Hey, Grandma," Kyla said as she slipped on her shoes and tied the laces.

Jade had never formally met Leona, although she'd heard the story from her parents of how the woman carried on so theatrically after her minor eye surgery months ago. Jade noticed right away that Jan bore very little physical likeness to her mother. She must have looked more like her father.

"Come on in, Ms. Grimes," Hunter said while stepping aside.

"*Mother* Grimes," Leona corrected. "I got my church Mother's license and everything, so I'm genuine, praise the Lord."

Jade stepped forward and reached out her arm. "We've really enjoyed having Kyla with us today; we always enjoy having her here. She's such a sweet, well-mannered girl. By the way, I'm—"

"Oh, I know who y'all are," Leona said. "You the pastor's daughter and that's your husband. That Reverend Tides is a true man of God, yes he is. I enjoy hearing him preach 'cause he is anointed. He ain't no jack-leg preacher like some of these here other men that be standing behind the pulpit. Yes, ma'am, Ms. Greene. Your daddy is a sho' 'nuff man of God."

"That's *Doctor* Greene," Hunter said.

"Say what?" Leona looked bewildered.

"Yes, ma'am," Hunter said despite Jade's elbow to his rib. "She has her doctor's license and everything, so she's genuine . . . praise the Lord."

"Oh," Leona said, clearly taken aback.

"Bye, Malik," Kyla called.

"Bye," Malik replied, standing from the floor where he'd been playing with the others.

"So this here is Malik," Leona said, stepping around her granddaughter and walking farther into the living room for a better view. "We done heard an awful lot about you, son. I've seen you in church sitting next to Kyla, but I don't believe I've ever heard you talk before." Leona walked closer and with raised eyebrows asked, "What y'all doing over there?"

"We're playing a game of marbles," Malik answered.

"Marbles?" Leona's word was spiked with disapproval. "Y'all letting that boy of y'all's play marbles? And who are these other folks y'all got sprawled all over y'all floor, bringing corruption in your house?"

Kwame and Jerome turned from their game for the first time to face their accuser, and Hunter and Jade exchanged glances.

"There is no money involved," Jade said, assuming that Leona thought they were gambling.

"Money or no money, the Lord said in His Word that playing marbles is a sin," Leona stressed. "Your daddy is a man of God; I know he done told you this at some point in your life."

Jade shook her head slowly. "Actually, no, he hasn't."

"Where in the Bible does it say we're not supposed to play marbles?" Kwame challenged in a voice two octaves higher than normal.

"I don't think it says that," Jerome said.

"Are you doubting the Word of God? Are you calling God a liar?" Leona charged, clearly offended by the two men who dared to question her knowledge of the Bible. "I'll have you know that I read my Word every day; that's right, *every single day*, and I know the Word of God like I know the back of my hand. In John 3:7, Jesus says not to play with marbles. He said, and I quote, 'Marble not, I say unto you. You must be born again.'"

A hush rested in the living room, which had minutes ago been filled with chatter. Jade held firmly to Hunter's arm, and she could feel his body trembling as he fought to hold back a fit of laughter. If Jade could somehow get Kyla and her grandmother to leave now, she wouldn't have to be embarrassed by the outburst of laughter that was forming in her husband's stomach, and no doubt, in the stomachs of Jerome and Kwame too. Jade was just about to usher the visitors out the door, but she didn't make her move soon enough. First it was Jerome, then Kwame, and then Hunter. All three men laughed heartily at Leona's expense, and her pursed lips were evidence of her displeasure.

"Y'all think it's funny to disobey the Lord?" Leona looked at each of the men as though they weren't fit to live. "I'll tell you what—"

"Daddy!"

All eyes turned to Kyla and then followed her pointing

finger to the flat screen television. It was at that moment that all laughter ceased.

"That's my daddy! That's Daddy, Grandma!"

Jade gasped, immediately knowing what was taking place on the screen in front of her.

"Oh no," Hunter whispered in a tone filled with despair. He knew too.

Malik grabbed the remote control and turned up the volume so that they all could hear. For a little while longer, the camera lingered on Peter's face and through it, he appeared to stare straight into the Greenes' home—right into the eyes of his perplexed daughter.

"What's going on?" Kyla asked as the camera cut away from her father's face and then focused on only one of the soldiers, who stared at a sheet of paper he held in his hand. "Why didn't he say anything? Who are those people wearing the masks? What are they doing? Where did my daddy go?"

Jade left Hunter's side and edged closer to Kyla, placing her arm around the little girl's shoulder, but saying nothing. The child hadn't yet grasped what was happening, but as the Channel 2 news anchor began speaking, she soon would have all of her questions answered. And Jade knew that once reality set in, Kyla was going to need all the emotional support she could get.

Chapter 15

"This must be what it feels like to be on death row," Peter whispered to the only man to whom he cared to talk.

Once again, brief heavy rains had fallen on the outside, and in his mind, Peter could envision the sands on the ground that had barely had the chance to dry out from the last fifteen-minute downpour, turning into a muddy mess. Rains like this were uncommon this time of year in Iraq, but they were a perfect match for the dismal hearts that waited impatiently on the inside of the concrete structure. The men were now sleeping—all but Fletcher and Peter.

Fletcher nodded his head in agreement. "I used to say that men on death row were fortunate. At least they knew the date and time of their deaths, whereas most of us would have to find out whenever we came face to face with it. At least they had time to prepare. But even sitting here and knowing that our marked time is just a few hours away, I don't know how to prepare myself. Now, I think not knowing is better."

"Yeah." It was all that Peter could think to say. He didn't know exactly what time it was or how many hours had passed since the cameras had been removed from the room, but Peter knew that the end of the first twenty-four hours wasn't far away. He'd dozed off in five- and ten-minute increments, but had never slept soundly. Neither had Fletcher. Looking at Silas with his head resting against the corner wall, Peter supposed that even when life hung in the balance, the body couldn't win in a fight against the need for sleep.

"You scared?"

Peter looked in his friend's direction and wanted to give a courageous answer, but opted for the truth. "Yeah."

"Really?"

"You seem surprised. I guess that means you're not, huh?"

In response, Fletcher stretched out his arms in front of him. Even with his wrists bound together and in restricted lighting, Peter could see the trembling of Fletcher's hands. "I've never been this scared in my whole life, man." He returned his arms to his lap. "I just didn't think you were."

"Why?"

"You just look so calm, like you got a plan that you ain't let the rest of us in on yet."

Peter tried to laugh, but his numb body would only produce a half smile. "I wish I did. All I can do is keep praying. That's all I know to do, man. If God don't perform some kind of miracle for us, we're not going to be rescued, so there's nothing left to do but pray."

"I know." Fletcher paused and then asked, "You don't think He's going to give us that miracle, do you?"

"Truth?"

"Yeah."

Peter turned his eyes to the floor and shook his head. "No. I mean, I want to believe it. I don't doubt Him—I know He's *able* to send a miracle. I just somehow feel that He won't, and a part of me thinks that I'm the blame."

Fletcher looked at Peter in bewilderment. "What are you talking about? How are you the blame?"

"You ever read the biblical story of Jonah?"

"The one who got swallowed by the whale?"

"Yeah. That's the one."

Fletcher nodded. "Yeah, but what does that have to do with you?"

"Remember when he was on the boat and the waters started getting so choppy that the folks on board thought they would all drown?"

"Uh-huh."

"Well, Jonah had disobeyed God when he was told to go to Nineveh and preach, and because he had done something that was displeasing to the Lord, a whole boatload of people were about to die. So they threw Jonah overboard to get rid of the cause of the pending tragedy. Once Jonah was gone, they were saved."

"Is this about Jan and Kyla?" Fletcher asked, his voice level rising in the process. "You think we're all going through this because of your split from your family? I can't believe you're even contemplating something as crazy as thinking this mess is all your fault. So, what are you saying—you want us to throw you overboard? Tell these animals that you want to be killed first in hopes that doing that will save the rest of us?"

Before Peter could answer, Silas spoke from across the room. "What are you all talking about over there? This is whose fault?"

"Nobody's," Fletcher said. "Go back to sleep."

Silas sat up straight, not at all convinced. "No, no, no. Don't say 'nobody's' 'cause I heard you say that Jericho said it's his fault. How is this your fault, Jericho? Are you telling me that we're all in this mess because of something you did? What are you, some kind of spy for the enemy? You set us up? You're a traitor?"

As a result of Silas' loud accusations, the other men had now fully awakened. Peter looked across the room and watched Silas wiggle himself into a frenzy, trying unsuccessfully to stand in spite of the shackles that held his feet together. He was fuming and wanted to come to blows with Peter, but there was no way the men could get in a physical altercation with the restraints that had been placed on them.

"What are y'all doing?" Chuck asked, looking from one soldier to the other.

"Oh, I ain't done nothing yet," Silas stated, still squirming. "But I'm about to whip Jericho's—"

"You're not doing anything to anybody," Fletcher said. "Stop it before you pull a muscle or bust a vein or something."

"And when I'm done with him, you're next," Silas warned Fletcher.

"Ooooh, I'm shaking," Fletcher said

"Man, sit still over there," Louis called to Silas, cursing in the process. "What you gonna do? You're tied up just like the rest of us." Then he turned to Peter and scowled. "You're a traitor, Jericho?"

"No, I'm not a traitor," Peter said, looking beyond Louis, directly at Silas. "That's not what we were talking about, and if you weren't trying to hear a private conversa—"

"Hey, I know what I heard. I heard Owens say that you thought you were to blame!" Silas spouted, trying to catch his breath after finally giving up on his quest to stand. "I'm not crazy, and I ain't about to go down because of something you did. Now tell us what you did to get all of us in this mess."

"Man, shut up!" Fletcher yelled.

"Who are you talking to, punk? Why don't you shut up and go'n over in the corner somewhere and pray? See if it does you any more good today than it did you yesterday."

Before long, all five of the men were arguing, and the more they talked, the more tempers flared. The heat, misery and fatigue were taking a toll on all of them. Angry words were tossed around like a leafy salad, and the men, who just hours ago were longing for one another's company, wondering if their comrades were dead or alive, were now at each other's throats like enemy forces. All five men immediately recoiled when a single shot was fired from the doorway.

Peter felt his heart pounding in his throat as he lay flat on the floor, trying to shield himself from harm's way. He fully anticipated more gunfire, but there was none. The one shot that was fired continued to ring in his ear.

"Sit up!" The command was given from the doorway, and none of the men hesitated to obey.

When Peter looked at the front of the room, there were five guards standing there. Four of them carried small plates of food and cups of water, and the other, the English-speaking one, held the gun that had fired the shot. The aroma from the food was delicious, but Peter didn't know if the food was actually appetizing or if his near-famished state just made it seem so. One by one, the meals consisting of some type of meat, a bed of rice, and fruit that looked like dates, were placed in front of the prisoners. None was given to Silas.

Instead, when the men backed away from the plates that had been placed on the floor, two of them firmly grasped Silas by his underarms and began carrying him away.

"No! Wait!" he shrieked to no avail. "Take him! Take Jericho! He wants to die first. He said he wants to die first! No! No! Let me go! No! Please! Oh, my God . . . No! Ahhhhhhh!"

The blood-curdling scream that faded behind the closed door was heartrending. Only one Iraqi soldier remained. Through vision clouded with tears, Peter saw Chuck bury his face between his arms and Louis use his restrained hands to draw out an imaginary cross, as was a part of prayer in his Catholic faith. Peter didn't look directly at Fletcher, but from his side vision, he saw Fletcher's hands clasped together as his body rocked back and forth. The agony could be felt from each of them.

Peter hadn't cared much for Silas' attitude over the past twenty-four hours, but that was still his brother who had been snatched from among them. It wasn't fair. Silas had done nothing wrong. *None of them* had done anything wrong. Suddenly, the meal that once smelled delectable was now foul to Peter's nostrils. In a mixture of frustration and fury, he picked up the plate and hurled it across the room, smashing it against the wall.

The armed guard immediately reacted, taking quick, decisive steps toward Peter, all the while pointing his gun directly at his target's face. Peter clenched his jaws and set his face. There would be no reenactment of Silas's screams or pleas. He wouldn't dare give the enemy the satisfaction. Peter wouldn't breathe his last breath without dignity. If he was going to die, he would die like a man—like a Marine. When the man came to a stop, he stood so close that Peter could see into the barrel of the gun. He heard Fletcher holler, "No!" and after that, Peter's world instantly went black.

Chapter 16

Word spread like fueled wildfire. Jan had never known so many cars to be parked at her mother's house; and as she looked at Leona lying across the sofa with a cool towel draped across her forehead, Jan knew that her mother was going to milk the situation for as much as she could get.

Most of the people who had crowded into the home in Shelton Heights weren't familiar to Jan. Others were recognizable, but she couldn't put names with the faces. Some were from New Hope and others were from Glory Temple. Leona's faithful dual church attendance had paid off in a major way. She had more attention than she knew what to do with. Reverend Silverman had come by earlier, but left after an hour-long failed attempt to console Leona. Shortly after the first family of Glory Temple left, the Tides family arrived and had been there ever since, offering prayer and encouragement. The telephone had been ringing constantly. Jan hadn't talked to her older sisters so frequently in ages.

A combination of supporters and just plain nosey folks

swarmed the living room and gathered around the television as though it were movie night at the Grimes' house. To try to gain a smidgen of much-needed alone time, Jan retreated to her bedroom for a moment to breathe. The simple act of inhaling and exhaling had become difficult from the moment she saw Peter's face plastered on the television screen as she did her last rounds at the hospital yesterday.

The image of her estranged husband, combined with the words spoken by the television newscaster, caused Jan to collapse, spilling the medicine she was supposed to be administering to the woman in the bed in front of her. Jan's body felt weak, as though all of the blood had been flushed from it. She reached for the side rails of the patient's bed, but could not grab them before stumbling backward and losing her balance. She didn't lose consciousness, but for a while, Jan was unable to move. The frightened bedridden woman pressed the emergency button to call for assistance. In the thirteen months that Jan had been employed at Northlake Medical Center, it was the first time she'd known a patient to have to call for emergency medical help for her attending nurse.

"Jan, if you don't calm down, I'm going to have to admit you," Loretta Summerland, her shift supervisor warned. "Your blood pressure is anything but stable, and I can't let you leave as long as you're teetering on having a stroke. I know this was a shock to you, but no matter how much you want to go home, I can't allow it as long as you're producing numbers like this."

No matter how hard Jan tried, she couldn't gain control over her emotions. She wasn't visibly falling apart, causing a scene, or even crying, for that matter. On the outside, she appeared to be taking the news better than most, but on the inside, Jan felt as though she were dying. The result was a one-night stay in the same facility where she was employed to give care to others. When her vital signs returned to normal, Jan was released into the care of her trusted cousin, Rachel Ross.

"There you are," Rachel said as she walked into Jan's bedroom uninvited. "Are you okay?"

Jan nodded while staring down at her bare feet. The pale pink polish she'd applied to her toenails three days ago still looked fresh; nothing at all like the matching coat on her fingernails that had been all but eaten away as Jan nibbled at them uncontrollably. The mattress beside her sank a bit when Rachel joined her.

"This is me, Jan. If you're not okay, tell me you're not okay. I don't need to be around here worrying about you."

Jan looked at Rachel and forced a smile. As much as Rachel got on her nerves at times, it was days like this one that made Jan appreciative of the solid blood ties that kept them friends in spite of it all.

"I don't know." Jan spoke as honestly as she could. "I don't know if I'm okay or not, Rachel. I'm not even sure what I'm feeling right now."

"What do you mean?"

Sighing heavily, Jan put her thumbnail between her teeth, only to have Rachel forcefully pull it away. Then Jan returned her eyes to the fibers of the carpet that peeked through the spaces between her toes. She spoke in low tones. "Just what I said. I'm not sure what I'm feeling. I have so many different emotions that I can't distinguish one from the other. It's the most confusing thing that I've ever felt, and I don't even know what to do to change it. I'm angry, I'm confused, I'm shocked, I'm hurting—"

"Hurting?" Rachel cut her off. "I can understand all of the other emotions, Jan, but I can't say that I understand why you're hurting."

Looking back toward Rachel, Jan said, "He's still my husband, Rachel."

"The husband that sent you a cut-throat letter, telling you that he was leaving you for another woman."

"He never said there was another woman."

"Not in so many words," Rachel agreed. "But he did tell you that he didn't love you and that he no longer wanted to be with you. Isn't that enough? You may not know what to do to curb those other emotions that you're feeling, but any time you start to feel hurt, you can just re-read that letter Pete sent you."

"It's not that simple," Jan said. "I wish it were, but it's not. Yes, he said some cruel things to me, but I don't know . . . I guess love is just one of those things that takes some time to get over."

"Aunt Leona said that God was gonna get him, and if she's never been right about nothing else, she nailed this one. You can't be upset about something that God is doing, Jan. Pete got just what was coming to him."

Jan shook her head slowly. "As angry as I've been with Pete over the past months, I never wished anything like this on him. Those people are threatening to kill them one at a time, and we know they don't mind doing it. How many soldiers and civilian workers have been murdered over there?"

"I hear you, Jan. But I guess you're just better than me, because if a man had treated me the way Pete has treated you, I wouldn't care what happened to him over there. They could put him in a big pot over an open flame and let him cook alive like a lobster as far as I'm concerned."

Jan turned her head away from Rachel. It was a silent but clear gesture that she didn't want to hear any more. Secretly, she was angry with herself for caring so deeply about the anguish that she was certain Peter was being forced to endure. She'd heard the stories of U.S. soldiers being tortured, shot execution style, and even beheaded for the sake of their country. None of those images rested well in her mind, and they constantly kept her from a peaceful sleep.

A loud burst of laughter resonated from the living room that was still packed with visitors. Jan couldn't help but wonder what they found so amusing at a time like this.

"I want all of these people to just go home," she mumbled.

"They're here to support you, Jan."

"Are they?"

"Sure they are," Rachel said. "Would you feel better if you heard a bunch of wailing? Would that seem more supportive to you?"

Jan hung her head, but lifted it again at the sound of a tapping at her bedroom door. She had fled the living room in hopes of finding quiet solace. Now, the crowd she'd abandoned was finding her. When Jan didn't move to answer, Rachel stood and walked to the door and eased it open just enough for her to peek out and see who was on the other side.

"Hi, Rachel. Is Jan in here?"

Jan sat up straight. She would know Jade Tides' voice anywhere, and it was one of the few voices that were a welcome sound. "It's okay, Rachel. She can come in."

Jade brushed past Rachel and took careful steps toward Jan. "Are you okay, sweetie?"

"Don't answer that until you know she's not going to charge you for it," Rachel said while closing the door and locking it for additional security.

Jan knew that it was an attempt to lighten the mood, but she found no reason to smile, let alone laugh. "Yeah, Jade. I'm okay. What are you doing here?"

Jade claimed the spot on the bed that Rachel had vacated, leaving her to stand by the doorway. "I came by to check on both you and Kyla. Dad . . . Reverend Tides said a special prayer for your family during the church services today."

"I know," Jan said, nodding. "He told me when I was speaking with him earlier."

"Your mother seems to be taking it rather hard."

Rachel huffed and then said, "Child, please. Aunt Leona is just a drama queen, that's all. She doesn't even like Pete."

"Stop saying that, Rachel," Jan scolded.

"Why? It's true and you know it."

"Still," Jan offered in a quiet voice, "she could very well be authentic in her actions."

Jade agreed. "That's true, Rachel. Even when it comes to people who aren't on our list of favorites, we generally don't wish this kind of devastation on them. The human side of us won't allow us to celebrate in these types of tragedies. To do so would be equivalent to wishing one's soul into hell. Anyone who would want another person to be sent to an eternal damnation is quite possibly on their way there themselves."

Rachel chuckled lightly and reached for the doorknob. "On that note, I'm going to get a glass of water and just hold on to it for a while. You know, just in case I drop dead anytime soon; 'cause I would surely need something to cool myself off if I bust hell wide open for what I think about this whole thing." The noise level increased when Rachel opened the door, and became muffled again when it closed behind her.

"She's quite a character, isn't she?" Jade observed.

"I told you she was. She thinks this is God's punishment to Pete for breaking up our marriage the way he did. What do you think?"

"I think there are some thoughts that should be kept to

one's self. That's one that I think Rachel should have never voiced."

Jan stared back at the carpet again. She, too, wished Rachel had never voiced it. Jade broke the lingering silence.

"Well, I didn't mean to run her away, but I am thankful for a moment to speak with you alone. How are you *really* doing, Jan?"

Perhaps it was the nature of therapists, but for whatever reason, Jan found Jade easy to talk to. She was so non-threatening and not at all judgmental. "I'm holding my own," Jan said, not wanting to go back through the whole story of her frenzied emotions. "It's Kyla that I'm most worried about. She's taking the news of her father's capture very hard."

"I know. She was inconsolable for a while on Saturday. I'm sure your mother told you."

Jan nodded. "She's okay now because there are so many people—children her age—around. But I don't know how she's going to react once the crowd clears."

"She likes the horses, and maybe they can serve as a means of taking her mind off of things, even if only temporarily. She's welcome to come to our house anytime, Jan. I know that having Malik around her will help. He's a sensitive kid and likes Kyla very much. He'll help her through it."

"Thank you," Jan said, fighting the onset of a gathering pool in her lower lids.

"I hear you had to be hospitalized yesterday after you heard the news."

Jan had no doubt that her mother had been the one to give away the information, and probably had done so unsolicited. "I was just shocked, I guess. The whole day was going along as normal and then, bam! All of a sudden, there was Pete's face on the screen in the room. I wasn't expecting it. It was the first time I'd seen him since . . . well, since we separated. He looked . . . thinner, like maybe they're not feeding him." Jan hoped that Jade didn't hear the vibration in her voice.

Jade stood and walked around the standard-sized bedroom, admiring the photos that were displayed. Her tour gave Jan just enough time to wipe away tears that had gathered at the corners of her eyes. As she used her fingers to dab away the moisture, Jan wondered if Jade's move was calculated—if perhaps she had purposefully allowed her the brief regrouping time she needed. No words were exchanged during Jade's admiration, and after a short while, she returned.

"What are you thinking about, Jan?" she asked, sounding like the therapist that she was.

After a momentary thoughtful hush, Jan said, "Just yesterday, I was thinking about how unprepared I was to be a divorced single mother. Now, I'd give anything to be that. It's crazy, Jade . . . just crazy. Like Rachel said, you'd think I wouldn't care one way or the other. Look at the way Pete disrespected me and ended our marriage. You would think I wouldn't even care what happened to him. As a matter of fact, I *should* think that he has it coming for being so dirty. But as stupid as this may sound, I'd rather be a divorced mother than a widow. I don't know what Kyla will do when—if they kill him, Jade. Her daddy is her hero. If they kill Pete, my baby will never be the same again."

Chapter 17

". . . but I ask for your favor and grace. Don't make me go through this alone. I'm not ready. I need my brother, God. Please don't let my brother die. Please don't let him die."

At first, Peter thought he was dreaming—or maybe even dead; he wasn't sure. He struggled to lift his heavy eyelids, and when he did, all he could see was blackness. *Is this what heaven is like?* He opened his mouth to try to call for somebody to help him, but no sound came out. He hadn't been a great Christian over the past year. *Maybe it's hell.*

"I don't deserve anything good, Lord, but I ask for grace in spite of the many years that I questioned your reality and all of the time I spent astray, not even bothering to acknowledge your holy presence. But God, if you never hear another prayer I pray, I ask you to hear this one. Don't let my brother die."

Who's dying? The thought stumbled through Peter's head. *And who's praying? Am I having another dream?* Peter tried to move his hands. If he could move them, he could pinch himself and be able to distinguish truth from fiction. Like all the times before, if he was dreaming, a sudden touch would wake him. If he could somehow touch himself, pinch his skin, he would know how to handle this new quandary that he was in. But none of his muscles would obey the commands from his brain. The whispering beside him continued.

"I know I'm being selfish, God, and I'm sorry. I could pretend my feelings for all of my comrades were on the same level, but you know all things and you know that I would be lying. I do love all of my brothers, Lord, and I pray for each of them. We're all scared and we don't know where to turn or what to do. Bless Chuck and Louis. Give them courage and bring them to the knowledge of you so that if we all have to die like Silas, we'll do it knowing you."

Silas is dead? Attempting again to determine if he was asleep, Peter squeezed his eyelids shut, and when he did, a massive pain unlike any he'd ever felt shot through his head and seemed to permeate every fiber of his being. "Ughhhhh!"

"Pete?"

"Oh, God!" Peter moaned. The pain in his head was almost unbearable. Tears trickled out of the corners of his eyes.

"Hey . . . Malloy, Klauser . . . Jericho's awake, guys! Jericho's awake!" The exuberance was obvious in Fletcher's voice.

"Jericho, you okay?"

Peter could hear Chuck's question, but he was in too much pain to answer. His breaths came in short pants, and he lay with his eyes closed, trying to wish away the hurt. "Jesus, Jesus, Jesus," Peter whispered repeatedly.

"That's right, man," Fletcher encouraged. "It's going to be okay. I know you're hurting, man, but Jesus is here. He's gonna make it okay."

Peter wanted to believe it, but right now, he felt as though his head were being smashed between two cement walls. "Jesus, Jesus, Jesus." He could feel the closeness of the others as they inched their way over to the area where he lay, writhing with pain.

"He got you good, Jericho," he heard Louis say. "You got a nasty gash near the back of your head, and a knot the size of Texas, too. That's why you're in so much agony."

Moving was still not a viable option. Peter tried once more to bring his hands to his head, but once again, he failed. If he could somehow find a way to apply pressure, he felt as though he could ease the anguish. *Am I paralyzed?*

"Don't try to move, Pete," Fletcher said when Peter released another distressing groan. "They just about got you wrapped up like a mummy, man. If you feel like your whole body is in restraints, it's because it is."

Just knowing that the blow hadn't made him a paraplegic seemed to give some sense of relief. Peter's breaths still came quickly, but the longer he lay still, the more the pain seemed to diminish. He opened his eyes for the first time since the aching became magnified. It was still dark, but less than it was before. He could see shadows of his troopmates as they hovered over him.

"Did I get shot?" he whispered.

"No," all three answered at once.

"I thought he was gonna shoot you," Fletcher said, "but at the last moment, he turned the gun around and walloped you one good time. You're lucky to be alive, man. Blessed," he said, quickly correcting himself. "You're blessed to be alive."

Peter lay quiet, feeling the rhythmic throbbing in his head and wondering if—had he had a say-so—he would have chosen death over the torment of being in severe pain and bound by the tight fabric wrapping that kept his arms pinned to his sides and his legs glued together from his thighs to his ankles.

"You thirsty?" Fletcher asked.

Peter's throat felt parched. "How'd you know? Is lint flying out of my mouth?"

"I got you, man." Wiggling a short distance away, Fletcher returned with a cup grasped between hands that were bound together at the wrist. "It's not cold and I've drunk out of it, but beggars can't be choosers," he said, holding the cup over Peter's face. "Open up."

Just the act of parting his lips was painful, but Peter grunted and tolerated it, feeling the room temperature liquid fall against the back of his throat. It was refreshing to his dry mouth. It felt like days since he'd last hydrated his body. Peter wondered just how long he'd been unconscious.

"Thanks, Flex."

"I saved a piece of veal, too. I figured you'd regret throwing yours across the room when you woke up," he said with a short laugh. "I wrapped it in a cloth napkin. Don't know how clean it is, but if you want it, it's yours."

"Is it still any good?" Peter's question was rhetorical. He was going to eat it regardless.

"It's only been a few hours," Fletcher said as he accepted the folded cloth that Chuck handed him and carefully unveiled the meat.

It took only a short time for Peter to devour the leftovers and drink the remaining water. And although he was grateful, his body wanted more. The room was quiet now, and Peter needed to talk to take his mind away from his hunger and lingering pain. "What time is it?"

"Probably around six," Louis said.

"In the morning?"

"Yeah."

Peter thought hard. He had been struck about twelve hours ago. No wonder his bladder was full and his stomach was empty. "Flex, did I hear you right? Is Bigalow—?"

"Yeah."

"How do you know?"

Peter tried to look around to see why his question wasn't being answered, but his head was still hurting too much for any extensive movement. No one had entered the room, but the three men suddenly shut down like a city that had just suffered an unexpected power outage.

"Flex?" Peter repeated.

"Let's just say that there was a minute there when I was jealous that you were the one knocked out and not me."

"What? What happened? Did they kill him in front of you guys?"

"No." Fletcher's voice sounded labored.

"Those cruel, ruthless animals brought his head in here and showed it to us," Chuck whispered.

The little food that Peter had just eaten begged to be released. He wanted to tighten his jaws, squeeze his eyes shut, anything to try to rid himself of the images that replayed themselves on the big screen in his head. But knowing the pain that any sudden facial or head movement would bring was enough to persuade Peter to control his emotions. "Oh dear God," he whispered.

"Wonder who's next?" Louis thought out loud.

"Don't talk like that, Malloy," Fletcher said. "We've got to believe that God's gonna save us."

"Like He saved Bigalow?" Louis shot back. "Come on, Owens, you've been locked up with Jericho for too long. Reality bites, but it's still reality. We're not getting out of here alive unless the good old United States armed forces rescue us. That's what you need to be trusting in right now."

"What? God can't use the armed forces?"

"Look, dude. I believe in God as much as the next person, but this is war, and we're not only outside the wire and out of the range of the protective eyes of our own, but we've been captured by the enemy. *Captured*, dude. That means we belong to them and they can do whatever they want to do with us. And you know what they want to do? They want to kill us. What do you expect God to do? You think He's gonna send Colonel Goodman up in here with the Calvary to save us? It just ain't gonna happen.

"We're either going to be saved by our country's finest, or we're gonna die, Owens, and that's just the way it is. We took an oath and said that we were willing to die for our country, and now we've got to put our money where our mouths are. See, that's why Bigalow lost it when they came in and got him, because he didn't ready himself for the worst. If we accept that we might just be killed by these assassins, then we'll be mentally prepared when they come and get us. I've accepted the reality, and if I'm that person, then so be it."

After Louis' rant ended, the room seemed quieter than ever before. Peter continued to lie on the floor, listening to his own heartbeat. Were it not for Kyla and Jan, he, too, might be able to concede to death. But Peter had made his daughter a promise, and he couldn't keep it if he didn't live through this. He was in too much pain to even try to argue the point with Louis, but Peter wasn't ready to give in just yet. Until he took his last breath, he'd keep believing that where that breath came from, another one awaited. The sun was beginning to rise now, and as Peter looked up into Fletcher's face, he knew that he didn't stand alone in his faith.

"They're coming," Chuck whispered, bringing all of the men to attention. "I hear them coming."

Within seconds of his declaration, the front door flew open and once again, the armed men entered with as much noise as they could muster, shouting orders for the prisoners to relocate to another area of the room. As the men moved away, their presence was replaced by the skinny soldier who seemed to take pleasure in pointing his gun in Peter's face. The man hovered over Peter, looking down at him with laughter in his eyes.

"Throw any food lately?" he taunted.

Saying nothing, Peter returned his long, intimidating stare. There was a ruckus going on on the other side of the room, but Peter had no idea what it was until the room suddenly brightened. The cameras were back.

The skinny guard said something in gibberish over his shoulder, and immediately two of the others came to his side and then knelt to the floor to cut away Peter's body restraints, replacing them with the normal rope around his wrists and ankles. All the while that they worked, Peter made a conscious effort to keep from moving his aching head.

"Get up."

Peter looked up at the man, for the first time, with pleading eyes. There was no way he'd be able to sit up without horrendous pain.

"Get up!" His voice was louder and sterner this time.

Peter closed his eyes and made a valiant effort, but the pain was too great. "I can't," he said through clenched teeth. "My head—"

His explanation was interrupted by four strong hands pulling him mercilessly into a seated position. Peter tried to swallow the squeal that rose in his throat, but the best he could do was control the octave so that he didn't sound like a school girl as his heartrending yell echoed off the walls. The tears that ran down his cheeks were embarrassing enough. He didn't need any further humiliation. When he was in a seated position, the men began wrapping a makeshift bandage around the circumference of his head. Their handling of him was not tender and the pain was harrowing, but oddly enough, when they were finished, the throbbing slowly decreased. The pressure of the tight bandage was offering a strange level of relief.

As the two men grabbed Peter by his armpits to take him where the others sat waiting, Peter saw the small pool of blood that had gathered on the floor beneath his head. They dropped Peter in the space beside Louis, and he used his arm to wipe away the wetness from his face. He couldn't let Jan see him in tears. His eyes needed to be clear so that she could read the message he was trying to convey to her.

Just like they had done before, the lights from the camera traveled from one face to the next while the rifle-toting soldiers stood behind them in daunting poses. *I'm sorry for everything. If I don't make it out of here, please remember that I love you.* Those were the words Peter said in his mind as he stared into the light. He hoped that Jan and Kyla would understand that message when they looked at the airing. The room suddenly darkened.

"You, you, and you—move over there," the skinny soldier instructed.

The orders were directed at Louis, Fletcher and Peter. The three men hesitated as they watched an expression of frightened anticipation overshadow Chuck's face. In the pit of Peter's stomach, he felt a pulsating knot; the knowledge that there was nothing he could do challenged his faith, despite his attempt to hold strong. As quickly as the dismal look had engulfed Chuck's face, he held his head high and tried to substitute it with an expression of bravery. Peter's eyes watered at the sight of it.

"Move!" the man yelled.

Fletcher and Louis scooted away as quickly as their restraints would allow them and Peter followed, clenching his jaws to better manage the pain that pulsated in his head.

Chuck kept his composure as he read the note that had been forced into his hands by the enemy soldiers; a note that they already knew wouldn't result in any adherence from the United States government. Peter rested his head against the stone wall behind him and looked at the ceiling, searching for the hope that was draining from his heart at the same rate as the blood that had drained from his wounded head.

Chapter 18

The sounds of snoring filled the space where the captured prisoners slept. Peter wasn't sure who the second culprit was, but for certain, the loudest was Fletcher. During the nights that Peter and Fletcher had spent together in confined quarters, Fletcher's chainsaw-sounding snore had become a familiar one. He didn't do it every night, but tonight, it seemed worse than at any other time. Peter remembered, in one of their conversations, Fletcher telling him that the more tired he was, the louder he snored. Tonight, he must have been exhausted to no end.

Peter wasn't certain why sleep escaped him. Maybe the lengthy unconsciousness that had resulted from his blow to the head was the reason that his body wasn't tired and his eyelids weren't heavy. Whatever the reason, Peter remained seated in the same position he'd been in since he and his Marine brothers had returned from relieving themselves ten hours ago. That was five hours after they'd been forced to make another recording that had probably already been blasted on televisions across the United States.

I wonder what Jan is thinking. Is she worried? Afraid? Sad? Does she even care? "Why should you?" Peter whispered into the air, his soft words overshadowed by the heavy breathing around him.

With death so close that he could taste it, he reviewed his life, taking inventory of both the good and the bad. Coming from a broken home, Peter's childhood wasn't easy, but he'd survived it and made his mother proud. When he looked back over his life, he realized that it wasn't until he met Jan that he found complete happiness. Before her, he had spent countless hours feeling as though much of his life had been wasted on people who used him—taking what they could get from him and then leaving him feeling empty and bruised. Jan had changed all of that. There was no way they should have ended up apart, living in two separate states and leading two separate lives.

Why did she have to lie to me? Why didn't she just tell me the truth? These were questions surrounding the mystery that had bombarded Peter ever since the breakup. Their marriage had been founded on truth and trust—*Well, most of the time*, Peter thought. He had to admit that he didn't always volunteer the truth, but he'd never stood in Jan's face and told a boldfaced lie like the one she had told. Peter didn't understand her reasoning. If she wanted to spend extra time with Leona, why didn't she just say so? He didn't particularly care for the cantankerous woman, but she was still Jan's mother. He would have agreed to Jan's spending time with her mom, just not *that* time. They had too many plans as a family—just the three of them. Leona could have been worked into the calendar, but at that particular time, there were approaching dates that were important to their family unit. Why she decided to fabricate all of the disasters in Atlanta that supposedly kept her there was beyond Peter's understanding.

He had never known Jan to lie to him before, but knowing she was so blatantly doing it this time around made Peter question everything she'd ever said to him. During their argument, he had the proof in black and white, folded up in his pocket, and in hindsight, he wished he'd just retrieved it and tossed it at her. It wouldn't have changed the fact that Jan had been lying to him, but at least it would have stopped the snowball effect and brought things to a head before they could get out of control.

"Even after I tried to confront you, you lied," Peter whispered in remembrance.

Jan had been so infuriated by his accusation that she'd closed herself in the guest bedroom and spent the night there. The following morning, he had every intention of showing her the proof he found to validate his charge, but when he woke up, she'd already packed her bags and said she was going back to Atlanta to stay with her mother until he was ready to apologize. *Apologize? What did I have to apologize for?* Even all these months later, Peter was insulted that she would go to such lengths to try to cover her lie. That's why he helped her carry the suitcases to the car amidst his daughter's tears. He didn't really want his family to separate and he never thought Jan would actually take the long drive back to North Georgia, but she did.

All Peter wanted was for her to admit the truth. He was happy with their marriage and he thought Jan was too, but apparently, his wife had been suffering silently for quite some time. They could have gone to their pastor for counseling and gotten the help that they needed, but Jan never even gave the marriage a chance. Even at the moment that she pulled out of their driveway, she held strong to her story that her extended visit to Leona's wasn't planned. All the while, Peter knew differently.

Dear Rachel,

I need to get out of here and get some air. The resentment is too thick and I can hardly breathe. I feel like the life is being smothered right out of me. If I had known that getting with Pete would be like this, I would have tried harder to keep him out of my heart. I love him, yes. But I'm starting to wonder if love is worth the sacrifices and heartache. I've been trying to think of some crazy reason to give as to why I need to go and stay with Mama for a while, but I'm sick and tired of trying to drum up a convincing lie. I've never been a good liar. I'm leaving because I need some time away. I'll be gone for a few weeks, maybe a month. However long it takes to give me the peace of mind that I need.

Yes, like you and Daddy always say, Mama gets crazy sometimes. But whatever her faults, staying with her will be a whole lot better than the situation I'm living in now. It's time I start thinking about myself for a change and doing what is right for Jan. If that makes me lose important family ties, then maybe that's a chance I should be willing to take. I have to do what I have to do, and I'll let God be the judge. All I ask is that you don't tell Pete about this. I'm not ready for him to know how much damage his presence in my life has caused, and when he hears about it, he needs to hear it from me. I'll think of a reason to tell him as to why I need to get away.

As for you, Rachel, I love you dearly and I always will. If you want to get together and talk, you know where to find me.

Love,
Jan

It was less than one page long, but the magnitude of the words it immortalized was strong enough to shake up Peter's marriage with the strength of an earthquake, uprooting and ripping apart everything he'd worked so hard to establish. All his married life, he'd prided himself on being a good father and husband. Peter loved his family and protected it with the same fervor that he protected his country. Admittedly, he had a savior complex and his greatest fear was ever getting to the place where he couldn't care and provide for his wife and daughter.

"Oh God, how could this have happened to me? How could it have happened to *us*?" Peter said while looking up into the dark ceiling as though expecting a verbal answer.

"Who are you talking to, Jericho?"

The voice startled Peter, sending his heart into overdrive.

"Sarge, are you talking to yourself?"

Peter's eyes darted toward the darkness across the room to the area where he knew Chuck had been sitting before nightfall. "Klauser? Is that you?"

"Yeah."

"I thought you were asleep."

"Not hardly. Who can sleep knowing that they are about to be put to death?"

Peter didn't know how to respond, so he remained quiet.

"You know why I joined the Marines, Sergeant Jericho?"

Peter had his opinions, but he thought it was best that he didn't play the guessing game. "No. Why?"

"To prove to my daddy that I was a man."

"What do you mean?"

"My whole life, I've been labeled a punk," Chuck explained. "I never won when it came to video games, contact sports, fights, girls . . . nothing. My father always told me that I made him ashamed. Anytime I came home with bruises after getting beat up by some bully at school, I had to get another beating from my dad."

Peter's heart was heavy. He shook his head from side to side, thinking of how Chuck's father must feel now, after seeing his son's face on television.

"I forced myself not to show too much emotion when they had me read that statement this morning. For the first time in my life, my dad was proud of me when I entered the Marines. He hugged me when I graduated from basic training, already being promoted to Private First Class. Before that day, I couldn't remember the last time he hugged me. I couldn't let Dad see me scared on camera. If they kill me—*when* they kill me and if my body ever gets sent back to Missouri, I need my dad to be able to stand over my casket and say he was proud of me. If he can say that, then I believe it'll be worth it."

A tear rolled down Peter's face as he listened to the teenager talk, but he was careful to conceal his sniffles. Fletcher's loud snores helped. Peter could not imagine going to such lengths to gain his father's affections. He was never there for him as a child, and Peter couldn't care less what he thought of him now. But Chuck's words were heartfelt. By most definitions, he'd been an abused child and didn't even realize it. Or maybe he knew and just loved his father in spite of it.

Peter thought again of Jan and the letter. It had hurt him to know she'd lied. Had he never found the letter tucked in the back of Jan's Bible that was left on the backseat of his car, he never would have known of her scheme. But none of that really meant anything now. He had to totally forgive her, even if it was just for his own sake. His feelings for Jan and his commitment to his family were strong enough to love her past her error in judgment.

Peter wished he'd come to that knowledge before being sent again to active war. He would have brought his family back together and been sure that Jan and Kyla were proud of him as they stood over his flag-draped coffin. Now, he wasn't sure what they would feel; but still, he had to forgive.

"Did I tell you I have a daughter?"

A pain shot through Peter's head when he frowned. "You? You have a kid? You're just a kid yourself."

"I know." Chuck's voice gave away his smile. "Me and my girl have been together for nearly five years, though. I didn't find out she was pregnant 'til a month after I got here. The baby is five months old now. Her name is Charlene."

"Named after you?"

"Yeah. All I've ever seen are pictures of her. Pretty, just like her mama. Even though I haven't seen her in person, she's always been my heart. But now that I know I ain't ever gonna see her. . . ." Chuck's voice trembled as it drifted. "You got a daughter too, right?"

Peter paused to manage his own emotions before saying, "Yeah."

In a short while, the nineteen-year-old had unknowingly shared two messages with Peter; one of forgiveness and the other of gratitude. Life was too short to not have either. Now it was Peter's turn to share a message of his own.

"Chuck?"

"Yes, sir?"

"Have you ever been introduced to Jesus?" Peter couldn't save the soldier's life, but he had to try to save his soul. When Chuck didn't reply, Peter spoke again. "When Owens and I were confined at one of the other locations, I told him about Christ, and he accepted Him as his personal Savior. He was concerned that he would die and not go to heaven. Does that concern you too?"

"I really hadn't thought about it."

"Do you believe in heaven?

"I guess. I don't know, really."

"Chuck, there's a very good possibility that all of us are going to die here, and like you, in the event that I do, I want my family to be proud of me too. But sometimes we have no control over how family feels. The most important thing is that God is pleased with us. And although our deaths may be brutal and painful, the eternal life that we get to live with Him after this mortal life is over is beautiful and painless."

"You really believe that, Sarge?" Chuck's voice trembled.

"I really do."

"What if you're wrong?"

"What if I am?" Peter challenged. "For the sake of argument, let's just say I'm wrong. What would you have lost by giving it a try? It's too big a risk not to give it a try. Everybody's gonna know, sooner or later, that He's real. But if we die before we come to realize it, it'll be too late to turn our lives over to Him. I'm not wrong, Chuck."

The space that the men shared was quiet for several moments. Peter wanted to say more, but he didn't want to pressure Chuck and have the young man shut him out, thus never establishing a relationship with God. Peter leaned his back against the wall again. He hadn't noticed until now, but fatigue was beginning to set in, and although morning was just a few short hours away, he foresaw sleep in his future for the first time tonight. Peter closed his eyes and relaxed his body.

"Sergeant Jericho?"

Peter's eyelids flew up. "Yes?"

"Please don't go to sleep. I know I'm asking a lot, but I don't want to spend my last night all by myself, and although you guys are over there, I'll feel alone if you go to sleep."

The wretchedness in Chuck's voice tore into Peter's heart. He inhaled and exhaled slowly. "I won't go to sleep."

"Keep talking to me, okay?" Chuck pleaded.

"Okay." Peter sat up straight and tried to think of any conversation piece that would make the situation less stressful. "What do you want to talk about?"

"Heaven. Tell me more about heaven."

Chapter 19

Jan lay motionless on the living room sofa, listening to the quiet that the room provided for the first time in days. It was now nine in the morning, but at nine last night, her mother's house was the most crowded it had ever been. More church members stopped by, along with coworkers from the hospital, families of Kyla's school friends, sisters from the Women of Hope support group; even military personnel came by to offer whatever level of comfort they could. People were bringing home-cooked covered dishes and leaving sympathy cards as if Peter were already dead. Carl, Rachel's brother, had flown in from Florida, and before he finally retired to his sister's house for some much needed rest, he sat for hours, reminiscing on "the good old days" that he spent in school with Peter, playing sports.

Reverend Tides had come by again, too, and he intently watched the activities that went on around him. Mrs. Tides helped play hostess with both her daughters-in-law as they offered refreshments to the house guests who came and never seemed to leave. Jan spent most of her time in her room, just like before, talking to Rachel and trying to make some sense of the turmoil that had all but wholly swallowed her family.

"You need to get out of this neighborhood, Jan," Rachel said. "You and Kyla can come and stay with me for a while until you can find your own place. It's not as big as your mom's house, but if you don't mind sharing a room with your daughter, you are welcome to bunk at my apartment. Whatever it takes, I just want you out of Shelton Heights. It's too late to save your marriage and it's too late to save Pete's life, but if you get out now, you can prevent anything worse from happening."

"Worse?" Jan scowled. "What could be worse, Rachel? It can't get much worse than this."

"Yes, it can. Have your forgotten Kyla's near accident? Not to mention you could get hurt or sick . . . or die, Jan. What if something happens to you and you end up dead?"

Jan sat in silence for a moment, shaking her head from side to side. "If it weren't for Kyla, I wouldn't even care. I feel like I'm dying anyway."

"Don't ever let me hear you say anything like that again, Jan!" Rachel's tone was filled with admonishment. "How many times do I have to remind you of what Pete did to you? He already broke your heart. You gonna let him break your spirit too? Why would you wanna die because of something that's happening to a man who gave you his butt to kiss after you gave him your heart *and* your body? I don't understand why you're not as angry as . . . as all get-out. Ain't that much love in this whole world, Jan. Pete dumped you. Don't you get it? He wooed you, he wined and dined you, he slept with you, he made you think that the two of you would be together forever and then he dumped you like gutter trash. And you want to die off of something like that? If that Dr. Greene woman ain't giving you no better therapy than that, then you need to get your money back."

Jan couldn't even rebut the statements because much of what Rachel said made good sense. She understood her cousin's frustration with her. Jan often got frustrated with herself. Still, she couldn't shake the feeling of total desolation at knowing that Pete's life was dangling by a thread.

It had neared midnight by the time everyone left last night. The Tides family had been the last to go. After sitting quietly for hours, Reverend Tides had Jan's family and his family join hands, and he sent up a prayer that propelled chills up Jan's spine. The power of God seemed to run through the house, touching everyone who stood in the circle. Something about that man's prayers, whether at church or not, moved Jan every single time.

Before leaving, Hunter and Jade hugged her and told her not to give up. Malik looked as if he hated to leave Kyla's side with her crying the way she was following Reverend Tides' prayer. Jan hadn't returned to work since the story of the soldiers' capture made headline news. Kyla hadn't returned to school either. Nothing about life seemed normal anymore. Even the plastic covers that protected Leona's furniture as a general rule, hadn't been put back on since they were removed on Saturday evening.

The fan attached to the ceiling turned and Jan watched it, almost feeling as if the motion was hypnotizing her, taking her to a place in time when life wasn't in such disarray. She recalled all of the good times she and Peter had shared. There were years' worth of them stored in Jan's memory bank. The laughter, the "date nights," the Sunday drives after church, the vacations, the lovemaking sessions . . . *Oh, how that man knew how to love me!*

The first time they'd been intimate was before they got

married, and as repentant as she was for the ill timing of it, Jan still recalled the night with fondness. Peter had been so gentle with her, all the while promising her that they'd be together forever. He loved her with all that he had within him, and she returned his affections, not once giving consideration to the repercussions of their immoral actions.

But God had been gracious despite their sins. Jan remembered being petrified when she found out that she was pregnant. The first time they were together was the only time they'd done so without protecting themselves, but apparently once was enough. Jan's first fear was that her parents would be deeply disappointed in her, and rightfully so. She had been taught better, but had somehow let her emotions and physical desires get the best of her. She and Peter had never discussed having a family, or even getting married, for that matter. They had only been dating a few weeks. Jan had no idea how she would break the news to him or how he would react. She'd known women to give themselves to men they thought loved them, only to be abandoned when they became pregnant. If Peter did the same, Jan didn't know what she was going to do.

"I told you that boy wasn't no good!" That was the first thing out of Leona's mouth when she got the news of her baby daughter's plight. "He ain't never cared nothing about you. All he wanted to do was get under your dress, and now that he's done that, you won't ever hear from him again 'less you call them military folks and have him run down so he'll at least have to pay child support. Girl, I can't believe that you done went and let the devil use your body for his playhouse.

"We brought you up to know the way of the Lord, Jan. Do you know what happens to girls whose parents are true saints of God when they go off and get themselves pregnant out of wedlock? They die, Jan. You gonna die in childbirth, girl." Leona's voice quivered as she spoke. "You won't never even live long enough to make that scoundrel pay child support. Was laying up with that boy worth your life?"

Knowing her mother's heart was crushed made the pain of what Jan had done even worse for her. "Mama, I know what we did was wrong and I'm sorry; but you don't have to think I'm going to die because of this. I'm not going to die in childbirth, Mama."

"Of course you're not, baby," Jan's father said.

"Shut up and stop lying to the girl, Ted. Both of you are blaspheming God's Word! If God said it, He's going to do just what He said. The Bible says, in James 1:15, that when lust is conceived it brings about sin, and when sin is finished, it brings death. Now, you can say what you want, Jan, but when you allowed your lust to make you give your body to that boy, you conceived this baby. And when the pregnancy is finished, when that baby is born, you're gonna die. That's what God said."

"Now, Leona, that's not what the Lord meant."

"Ted, you don't know nothing 'bout the Lord. If you could stay awake in church sometimes, you would know what the Word of God says."

"Mama, I'm not proud of what I did, but it's done now and I'm going to live with whatever the consequences are. But I don't believe God's going to kill me because of this. Do you know how many girls get pregnant out of wedlock whose parents brought them up in Christian homes? They don't all die in childbirth."

"That's because their parents weren't *true* saints of God," Leona stressed. "Your parents are. Well, at least your mama is anyway. And you need to stop trying to explain away God's Word and get your soul right so that you can enter into the kingdom of heaven after you die on that delivery table."

"Leona, you sound like you want the girl to die."

"Of course I don't want her to die, Ted; stop saying stupid stuff. I love Jan. I love all my children. But I can't compromise God's Word, not even for them. I have to tell them the truth. Otherwise, God is going to hold me responsible. Now, them other girls' parents wasn't real Christians, or else they wouldn't have been around to raise them babies."

As Jan now lay on her mother's sofa, thinking about the fourteen-year-old conversation, she almost laughed in spite of her heavy heart. Not one time since she left the hospital with both her daughter and her husband, the man her mother swore wouldn't stand by her, had Leona mentioned a word about the exchange they'd had. To do so would force her to consider that she might not be a *true* saint, and Jan knew that her mother would rather die than to regard herself as such.

From where she lay, Jan turned onto her side and stared into the blackness of the floor model television set. Last night, the newscaster announced the beheading of the first soldier, noting that there were online sites where the taping of his beheading could be seen. *Who in their right mind would want to see that?* Then they showed the remaining four captives. Jan had to gather reserved inner strength from somewhere just to be able to console Kyla when she saw her father with his face slightly swollen and a bandage wrapped around his head, stained with blood.

"What did they do to Daddy?" she wailed, looking at Jan for answers she couldn't give.

Already, Jan had been torn over whether to even allow her daughter to see the footage, but Leona insisted that it was best.

"If you don't let her see what's going on, she will think things are even worse than they are," she'd said.

Worse? There was that word again. How could it get worse? They were killing the American soldiers as though life had no value. Jan decided that she had to draw the line somewhere, especially after Kyla spent the whole night having bad dreams. As her mother, Jan felt the need and the responsibility to shelter her child from as much pain as she could. She ultimately had to go in Kyla's room, climb into the bed with her, and spend the night there. Neither one of them slept soundly, but they did better together than either had done apart.

"She still 'sleep?"

Jan turned her head slightly and saw her mother entering the living room still wearing her nightgown. Leona had been up with them for most of the night too. She knew what a hard time Kyla had falling asleep.

"She was still 'sleep a half hour ago." Jan sat up, yawned as she answered, and then used her hands to smooth down her hair. "I'm going to take her to spend some time with Malik at the pasture this afternoon. I think it will do her good to get out of the house today."

"It'll probably do you some good too," Leona said from the kitchen over the noise of clanking skillets.

Jan agreed. "Yeah, I know. Jade said that she could fit me in at five, so I'll go by her office after I drop off Kyla."

"Fit you in what?"

"Counseling. I'll be her last client for the day."

When the kitchen suddenly became quiet, Jan knew she'd said something her mother didn't agree with. Leona slowly appeared from behind the partition that separated the living room from the kitchen. The look on her face showed her displeasure and disbelief.

"You mean to tell me that you're going to see her as a patient?"

"Yes, Mama." Jan must have sighed too heavily because Leona walked closer with her hands perched on her hips.

"Don't be breathing hard with me, Jan. You wrong and you know you wrong."

"Wrong about what, Mama? Does the Bible say something against me going to see a therapist?"

"As a matter of fact, it does, Miss Flip Mouth," Leona said, clearly not amused by her daughter's sarcasm. "In the book of Amos, the sixth chapter and the first verse, the Word says, 'Woe to them that are at ease in Zion.' Then 'round about the third and fourth verses, it goes on to say that in the evil day, they will lie on beds of ivory and stretch themselves upon couches."

Jan waited for her mother to say more, and when she didn't, Jan said, "And that means that it's a sin to go and see a therapist?"

"Who else you know that have people stretched out on couches?"

"Mama, I was stretched out on a couch right before you walked in this room. Was I in sin?"

"Watch your mouth, girl," Leona said. "Now, I can't believe you going to see no shrink. Jesus is the wonderful counselor, mighty God, Prince of peace and everlasting Father. He is the only counselor that you need, Jan. Them folks just be out to get money. They'll have you telling them your whole life story and they make you break it down in parts so they can keep you coming and paying. And on top of that, they put you on medication that you end up having to be on for the rest of your life and you still don't get no better. You know why? Because Jesus said we are healed by His stripes, not by laying up on no devilish couch, spilling our guts to no educated fool."

"Mama, Jade is not a fool. She is a Spirit-filled woman of God."

"Not when she in that office, she ain't. She got to do

stuff just like them textbooks told her to. She probably be up in there hypnotizing folks and everything. They there to twist your mind and try to make you believe stuff happening to you for one reason, when God got a whole 'nutha reason for doing what He do. It ain't Godly, I tell you. Get on your knees and talk to the Lord, Jan. Not to no shrink."

Jan opened her mouth to reply, but as soon as she did, the doorbell rang, stopping what would have been a pointless argument. Jan waited for a moment, thinking that her mother would hide in the kitchen so that whoever was at the door wouldn't see her in the ugly, thick orange nightgown and non-matching yellow slippers. When she didn't move, Jan proceeded to the door and was shocked by who was on the other side.

Jan heard her mother huff from somewhere behind her. "Oh, the devil *is* a liar!"

Chapter 20

"Daddy!" Jan fell into his arms and wept, not even certain where the flood of tears had been hiding themselves.

"It's all right, baby," Ted said in a comforting voice, stroking Jan's back as she soaked his shirt. "Everything is going to be all right."

"What you doing here, Theodore Grimes? And I know you better not have your little harlot with you."

Ignoring Leona, Ted held Jan tighter and then led her to the living room sofa, where they both sat.

"You heard about Pete?" Jan asked through gasps of breath.

"Yes, I did. Why didn't you call me and tell me what was going on, Jan? Why did I have to learn about this from your oldest sister? I rushed to turn on the television for the six o'clock news, and when I looked at the television screen, I almost jumped out of my skin when I saw my son-in-law up there. Why didn't you call me, baby?"

Before Jan could answer, Leona said, "If you hadn't have run off with that Guatemalan gal who's young enough to be your daughter, then you would have known what was going on in your real daughter's life."

"Leona, now ain't the time or the place for this. I didn't come here to see you; I came to see my baby."

"Oh yeah? Well, your baby's been staying with me for near 'bout a year and a half, and she ain't seen your face not one time 'til right now, so you can't be all that concerned."

"Mama, please," Jan begged. "You're going to wake up Kyla."

"How's my grandbaby doing?" Ted asked.

"Your granddaughter has been here for over a year too, but you ain't—"

"Shut up, Leona. I'm not talking to you right now."

"He who commits adultery destroys his own soul," Leona barked. "That's what Solomon said."

"She who is sanctimonious and got her nose so far in the sky that she can smell Jesus' breath, destroys her own household," her ex-husband contested. "That's what Ted said."

"Blasphemer!" Leona gasped in horror.

"Battle axe!"

"God is going to judge the selfish sinner, Ted."

"He's also going to judge the self-righteous, Leona."

"Daddy, Mama, stop it!" Jan shrieked, bursting into tears once more. "Can't the two of you stop arguing long enough to see that I need both of you right now? My life is in shambles and my world is falling completely apart! My home has been destroyed, my daughter is hurting, her father is about to be butchered and all the two of you can do is point fingers and call each other names?"

"I'm sorry, baby," Ted said, kissing Jan's forehead. "I didn't come here to argue; I came to see if there was anything I could do. I was hoping you'd be here alone or that there would be so many other folks here that I could avoid a confrontation. I lost out on both ends, but I still had to come and see you."

Jan rested against her father's chest. "I'm glad you came, Daddy. I don't think there is anything that you can do, but I'm glad you came."

"I'm sorry too, Jan, but I'm not like you when it comes to how we handle the men who mistreat us. You grieving over Pete like he ain't done you no wrong, and while I believe in forgiving, I don't believe the Lord wants me to allow the devil back into my life or my home. Now, I need your daddy to get out of my house. Y'all can sit out on the front porch and talk, but I can't allow him to sit on my sofa where the invited guests sit."

Jan looked at her mother in disbelief, but could see the sincerity in Leona's eyes right before she turned away and headed back to the kitchen to finish the task she'd started before Ted entered.

"Have you eaten?"

Jan turned and looked at her father. "No."

"Why don't we go and get a bite to eat? We can talk over breakfast."

Jan shook her head slowly. "I can't. Kyla is sleeping now, but she barely slept at all last night. I don't want to wake her, but I can't leave her either. I need to be here in case the nightmares come back."

"Oh. I didn't know," Ted said, nodding as though he understood. "Let's go sit out on the porch, then. Your mama's got good reasons for not wanting me in her house, I suppose."

He reached out his hand and Jan held on tight. Her family had gone through some major changes in recent years and all of it was unexpected. Still, she loved her father and she knew he felt the same for her. Together, they sat on the wooden bench that Jan and Rachel had made a project of painting as soon as the weather began warming up a few weeks ago. The warm breeze and early morning sunshine was refreshing. It was Jan's first time outside in days.

"I'm sorry I haven't been here to see you before now, Jan. I just couldn't . . . well, I didn't feel like being bothered with . . . I'm sorry."

"I know, Daddy." Jan looked out into the community and saw the houses around them. Everybody was either at work, at school, or indoors. The only signs of life on the outside were the green grass, tall trees, colorful flowerbeds, and the occasional squirrel that scampered from one yard to the next. It was a beautiful sight, not at all resembling the stigma that was attached. "You think this neighborhood is cursed, Daddy?"

"Say again?"

"Shelton Heights. You know the rumor. Do you believe it?"

Ted chuckled and patted Jan's knee as he settled back on the bench. "I ain't never been one for believing much superstition, baby. I don't think there's no truth to that. Who's been putting that craziness in your head? Leona?"

"No. You know Mama doesn't believe in folklore, and until recently, I never really gave it any thought either. But I look at all those years that you and Mama stayed married and inside of a year of moving out here, you broke up. Then my marriage was suddenly ripped to shreds when I came here to visit with Mom after you left. Me and Pete had a good marriage before my visit to Shelton Heights. I tried to shake the possibility of everything being related to the myth, but a few days ago, when everything really got crazy, Rachel brought it up and it's starting to make sense to me."

Ted released a light grunt and then puckered his lips in a thoughtful pose. After a short time of silence, he turned and looked at Jan. "Everything can't be explained, I don't reckon; but one thing's for sure, this neighborhood ain't had a thing to do with me and Leona splitting up. We moved to this neighborhood to try to save the marriage. It just didn't work out."

Jan's eyebrows rose. "Save the marriage?"

"Uh-huh. We were having problems long before we moved to Shelton Heights. We been having problems for years, baby. We kept them hid while you and your sisters were at home, but when y'all moved out and we were there by ourselves with nobody to talk to but each other, it just got worse and worse. We had that retirement nest egg, and I thought that moving to our own home after years of renting would be something that would make everything better. But it didn't."

"So, you're telling me that this fling you had with the Mary Kay saleswoman wasn't something that just happened after you moved here? There were other women?"

Jan stiffened when her father leaned his head back and burst into a hearty laugh. He held his protruding abdomen as though her words had come from the mouth of a stand-up comedienne. Not knowing how to respond to Ted's reaction, Jan sat quietly, waiting for him to finish and give an explanation.

"I'm going to tell you the same thing that I told your sisters. There is no Mary Kay lady," he said, causing Jan's jaw to drop. "Let me take that back," he quickly added. "There *was* a Mary Kay lady, but I didn't run off with her. And by the way, she wasn't Guatemalan either. That whole affair was all up in your mama's head because that pretty Asian girl would smile and flirt with me every time she came to bring your mama her orders. I ain't saying I didn't give your mama a reason to worry. I was flattered and I might've flirted back, but that was as far as it got.

"The girl's daddy was a real estate agent and he helped me get my house in Montgomery when I decided to move out. From the time Leona found out about that, she's been accusing me of running off with that child. I'm a deacon in the church. I would have been removed from my post if that was what was going on."

"So, there was no other woman?"

"I couldn't stomach the woman I had, Jan. Why would I run off to go and get another one?"

"Daddy!"

"I'm sorry, baby, but you asked and I'm just trying to be as frank as I can be. And the truth of the matter is, I left for one reason and one reason only. I couldn't live another day under the same roof with your mama."

"But Daddy, you were both in the church, serving the Lord. How does it get to that point when you're living for God?"

"It shouldn't happen like that, but sometimes it does, Jan. The world ain't a perfect place, and sometimes even Christian marriages fall apart. Now, I don't want to be pointing no fingers, but I declare; if there is ever such a thing as being *too* saved, your mother is it. After thirty-some-odd years of being beat across the head with Bible scriptures and never being able to do anything that was good enough or Godly enough, I just got tired. All the arguing wasn't doing me or my soul no good; and after years of bridling my tongue and holding back my fist, I was on the verge of cussing her out and beating her down. And I know God wouldn't have been pleased with that, so I did all I knew to do. I left."

Jan crossed her arms and sat back on the bench, trying to digest all that her father was saying, afraid to ask the question that was dangling at the end of her tongue. "So, Mama's been lying all this time?"

Ted shook his head in quick motions. "No, no, no, baby. In Leona's mind, she's telling the truth. She probably really does believe that I ran off with that woman. The girl refused to sell her anything else after Leona accused us of sleeping together a few months before I left. And I would leave the house for hours at a time just to get away when Leona got on my nerves, so when I'd come back home, she'd always say that I'd been with that girl."

"You never corrected her?"

"I tried, but what was the use?" Ted said with a wave of his hand. "Every time I did, she'd come up with some blame scripture that was supposed to prove me wrong and her right. After a while, I stopped trying. I stopped trying to defend myself, I stopped trying to save the marriage, I . . . I . . . I just stopped trying. I know I disappointed you and your sisters, Jan, and I'm sorry about that. I never meant to let you girls down in any way, and I sure didn't 'tend to let God down."

Jan watched as the lines on her father's face deepened. His countenance was sad and she heard what sounded like signs of regret in his voice as he continued speaking.

"According to the Bible, I didn't have no grounds for divorcing Leona, so I ain't saying I was spiritually right to leave, I'm just saying I had to. A man needs to feel like a man, baby, and when a woman insists on doing and saying stuff to make him feel like less of a man, then that's when he needs to move on."

With her mind wandering from her parents' situation to her own, Jan's eyes dropped to her lap. "So, is that what happened with Pete? Did I do or say something to make him feel like less than a man?"

Ted wrapped his arm around her shoulder and pulled Jan closer to him. "I don't know your situation, so I can't say what went wrong with you and Pete. From what you told me when you first moved in with your mama, I can't see where you stripped him of his manhood. But I don't know, Jan. Only you and Pete can figure that one out. Just 'cause me and your mama couldn't work ours out, don't mean you and Pete can't. I admit that I didn't care for him much at first; especially after he got you pregnant. But over the years, I've seen the way that boy looks at you, baby. I've seen the two of you together. I just can't believe y'all can't work it out."

"That's because you don't know about the letter," Jan said, a lone tear escaping her left eye.

"What letter?"

Just as Jan opened her mouth to answer, the front door of the house opened and Leona stuck her head out, shaking her head in slow motion and looking at her daughter with compassionate eyes. "They done killed another one."

Chapter 21

No militia currently stood guard in the building where five American soldiers had dwindled to three, but even with the freedom to speak, no words were exchanged. Peter didn't know if Louis and Fletcher felt the same as he, but for Peter, he kept his mouth closed for fear that everything he'd ever eaten in his lifetime would come hurling out if he dared to part his lips.

In the early hours of his fire team's capture, Peter had thoughts of being physically tortured—punched in the face, kicked and beaten, burned with hot irons, dunked in water until he gagged for breath. Whether there was any truth to it or not, he'd heard that seventy-five to eighty percent of the men in Iraq were bisexual, so he'd even considered the possibility that he'd be sexually abused. But as much as he dreaded all of those things, he couldn't see the torment of any of them being worse than what they had just endured. The ordeal lasted only a few minutes, but nothing had prepared Peter for being forced to look at the lifeless, bloody head of his murdered nineteen-year-old comrade.

The sight of the red-headed, boyish-faced soldier's dismemberment was more gruesome than anything Peter had ever seen; and war had exposed him to many sights of injury and death. At every other moment of his military life, he had been able to see death and label it as something that came with the territory. Soldiers and death, death and soldiers; the two went hand in hand, especially during times of conflict. But for Peter, this was different. He could not categorize this experience as simply a casualty of war. He couldn't rid his mind of thoughts of the final moments of fear and suffering that Chuck had undoubtedly endured before taking his last breath. The cut at his neck wasn't even a smooth one. It appeared as though the Iraqis had taken a butcher's knife, or at best an electric saw, and cut through the boy's flesh, making the death a slow, agonizing one.

When the enemy soldiers came early this morning and took the boy away, Peter's heart ached as though it were his own son being led to slaughter. He had stayed up with Private First Class Charles Klauser all night, just as had been requested. They'd talked and prayed for hours, and inwardly, Peter hoped for a last-minute miracle. As dawn broke, Fletcher woke up and joined them. When Louis stirred to the sounds of prayer and praise, he sat quietly with his head bowed, seeming not to know how to respond. He cried with them, though, as Chuck gave his final request.

"If any of you guys make it out of here, please tell my family that I love them, okay? And tell them that I'll be all right. I'm gonna miss them, but I'll see them again in heaven if they get to know Jesus. You'll tell them about Jesus, won't you, Sarge?"

Peter's eyesight became a flooded blur as he whispered a feeble, "Yeah."

"And Jericho?"

"Yeah, Klauser?"

"Tell my girlfriend that the last words on my lips before I died were, 'I love you, Katherine.' Tell her I died just like I lived; loving her."

Peter nearly lost his breath as he tried, without success, to swallow back his emotions.

They were still praying when the Iraqis burst into the room in their signature noisy, overstated manner, cut away Chuck's restraints and hauled him away while they served dinner to those remaining. There was fright in the young man's eyes, but he offered no resistance. Just as they exited the door, he turned around and looked at Peter.

"Thank you, Sarge," Chuck called as the door closed behind them.

That was the last time they saw him alive. Two hours later, they were looking at his mutilated head. Now, hours after that, as Peter looked at Louis lying on the floor in one corner of the room and Fletcher sitting not ten feet away with his face pressed against his bound hands, doom was the order of the day.

Have mercy on us, God. It was a futile prayer and Peter knew it. When it came to passing out mercy, God had stopped listening a long time ago. At least that's what it felt like, and with every day and every death, it was starting to be what Peter believed.

With emotions so chaotic that he could barely keep them under control, a part of Peter wanted to weep like a woman in labor, ten centimeters dilated and with no medicine to lessen the pain. Another part wanted to snap the neck of every enemy soldier that stood outside their door. Then there was that frightened part of Peter that wanted to find a magic escape route and run for his life. But where would he run? It wasn't like he was being held hostage in an abandoned home in the United States of

America. There, if such an escape route existed, he would have a chance. He could run out of enemy doors and right into a safety zone. But in this place, there was no friendly territory. If he fled, he'd be running from one adversary to another.

Peter's thoughts were interrupted by the sight of Fletcher moving closer, closing the gap between them. He came to a stop when he was within inches of Peter, sitting in a position mirroring his, with his back rested against the concrete wall behind them. The sun was setting outside, and it was only a matter of hours before their captors would come in with cameras and choose their next victim.

"How are you holding up?" Peter whispered when Fletcher released a strenuous sigh followed by silence. The window in this place was void of the dark curtains that covered that of the other cell Peter and Fletcher shared, so although the sun was going down, there was still enough light to allow him to see the strain on his friend's face.

Slowly, Fletcher shook his head. "I'm trying to keep the faith. Trying to be like the guy in the Bible who held on to his faith even when he was about to be beheaded. What was his name?"

"John the Baptist."

"Yeah, him," Fletcher said. "That J.B. is a tough act to follow." After a moment of silence, he added, "I wonder where they go at night."

"Who?"

"The guards."

"I'm sure they're right outside the door," Peter said.

"I don't think so. They always bolt it shut when they leave, and it's just too quiet for anyone to be out there."

Peter listened to the quietness and then said, "Well, maybe not *right* outside the door, but you best believe they're not too far away. Deadbolt or not, I don't think they'd leave us without some insurance that we don't escape."

"These painful ropes are insurance enough, if you ask me."

Peter looked at his wrists. They were raw from days of being tied up, but the pain from the area where his skin was broken was overshadowed by the throb in his head that refused to completely cease.

"They're probably roosting somewhere," Fletcher said.

"Roosting?"

"Yeah, like a pack of buzzards. You know vultures can't see in the dark, so they roost until daylight."

Peter couldn't help but smile at Fletcher's choice of words. He turned to his friend and took note of the look of deep thought on his face as he stared straight ahead. "What, Flex? What's on your mind?"

Fletcher looked at him and snickered. "You think you know me, now, don't you?"

"Am I wrong?"

"Nah," Fletcher admitted, using his hands to push his glasses up on his nose. "I *am* thinking about something."

"Okay, well, I think I know you pretty good, then. Wanna talk about it?"

As though he wasn't sure whether he wanted to share, a short pause ensued before Fletcher voiced his thoughts. "I think they're saving us for last."

"Us, who?" Peter looked at Fletcher with raised eyebrows.

"Us . . . me and you. I think we're going to be the last two." Fletcher's eyes darted across the room and then his voice lowered even further when he returned his attention to Peter. "Louis . . . I believe he's next."

"Is that wishful thinking?"

"No. I'm serious."

"What are you talking about, Flex? What makes you think that?"

"You met the Bling-Bling brothers, right?"

Peter nodded without delay. The men, known simply as the Bling-Bling brothers, were the proprietors of a family-owned business that sold genuine gold and precious stone jewelry at a fraction of what it would cost to buy in the States. Peter had bought Kyla's earrings from them, and he'd also purchased a matching diamond bracelet and necklace for Jan, but didn't include them in the package when he mailed his daughter's gift. The box containing Jan's jewelry was still tucked away in his belongings at Camp Taji.

The brothers, whose given names Peter never learned to pronounce correctly, lived in Baghdad and were Muslim, but didn't dress in the distinct gear that many others of their faith did. Instead, the two men, who appeared to be in their late twenties or early thirties, dressed in street fashions that were popular in America in the early eighties. They wore Members Only jackets and balloon-style pants, like the ones that celebrities such as Michael Jackson made famous. They would have been laughed at in the United States, but in Iraq, even in the twenty-first century, the brothers were considered stylish and hip.

Unlike most of the younger Iraqis, the Bling-Bling brothers were friendly men and they'd answered many of Peter's probing questions concerning the goings on in their country. Peter was certain that they extended such hospitality to him because of the frequent purchases he'd made from their street corner business. He was careful not to ask anything that would make them feel that by answering, they were betraying their people.

They'd told him that the headdress that most of the Muslim men wore was called *hijab* and the body garment was called *kasari*. The tribal leaders were referred to as *sheiks* and never, ever were Peter or his American friends to refer to an Iraqi as a *hagee.*

"That," one of the brothers told Peter in a heavy accent, "is like a white American man calling you the N word."

Snapping from his brief trip down Memory Lane, Peter realized that Fletcher was sitting deep in deliberation, not offering any further explanation for his earlier thought. "What about them?" Peter urged. "What do the Bling-Bling brothers have to do with this?"

"I bought a watch for my son from them one day, and I overheard them talking to another dude, telling him that Iraqis like black people better than white people."

"What? Why?"

"I don't know. I didn't hear him give an explanation. Maybe because their skin is darker like ours. I don't know."

Peter shook his head. "Was the guy black that he was talking to?"

"Yeah. He was an American soldier. In the Army, I think."

"Then he was probably just saying that to make a sale."

"Maybe."

Unexpectedly, Peter had a quick flashback of Chuck's decapitated head and squeezed his eyes shut to try to erase the image.

"Is your head still hurting?"

Peter opened his eyes and realized that Fletcher had seen and misread his sudden reaction. "Yeah, it is. It's better, though." He wasn't lying. His head was still throbbing and Peter didn't think any good would come of him revealing the real reason behind his actions.

"Pete?"

"Yeah?"

"What's gonna be your biggest regret about life? I don't mean to sound faithless, but I think it's pretty clear that we're all gonna die here. So, what's gonna be your biggest regret? Will it be that you and Jan didn't have the chance to get back together?"

Just the thought of dying without the opportunity to see his wife and daughter again was more persecution than anything the Iraqis could inflict upon Peter. He sighed and relaxed against the cold concrete behind him. "I don't know that it's the not getting back together that will be my greatest regret. I mean, when it comes right down to it, even if I made it out of here alive, there's a good chance that our reconciling might not happen. I said some harsh words and so did she. I can forgive her—I already have. But I don't know how she feels about me right now. So, my biggest regret will be the fact that I never had the chance to tell her how sorry I am; and Kyla too. Just to know what both their last memories of me will be is depressing. I took life for granted, Flex. I thought I'd be around to make it right."

"We all think like that, Jericho. You think I thought I would die here? It's crazy, man, because we see or hear of our brothers dying every single day, but how many of us really think that we're gonna be one of the dead when the final count is tallied? I told you, I promised Chantel that I'd be coming home. I *promised*."

"Shortly before leaving Cali to head here, I talked to Kyla on the telephone and promised her that I'd make things right between her mama and me," Peter said. "God even gave me two chances to at least apologize to Jan, but I didn't."

"What do you mean?"

"Well, you know how they gave us that break to go home for two weeks? Well, I didn't even contact my girls during that leave. I went to Seattle and spent the time with my mom. I figured I'd just wait until my tenure was up to focus on Jan and Kyla. Now look at me."

Fletcher shook his head from side to side like he couldn't even think of words to say that would make Peter feel less guilt. "What was the second time?"

"I called Jan one day and left a message on her voicemail. I could have apologized then, but my stupid pride just wouldn't let me. I called because I was feeling particularly lonely that day and needed to hear her voice. I was hoping that she'd answer the phone. When she didn't, my mind started telling me that she wasn't available to me because she was spending her time with someone else—another man."

"Was she?"

Peter shrugged. "I can't say for sure, because I never talked to her. But I feel like I know Jan well enough to comfortably say that I doubt it. We're separated, but we're still married. I don't think she'd start a relationship with someone else while she's married to me. Lying about her visit to her mom was one thing, but I don't think she would be unfaithful. But whether she was out with someone or not isn't the point. I still should have apologized. At least I could die knowing that she knew how I felt about all this mess. Dying without your family knowing you love them almost makes your life seem worthless."

Stillness took temporary custody of the room, with only the sounds of Louis' light snoring keeping the room from being completely quiet.

"What will be your greatest regret?" Peter asked.

"That I didn't have the chance to share salvation with my family."

Peter looked at Fletcher and smiled.

Fletcher continued. "Man, your life has not been pointless. I mean, yeah, I can imagine that you would regret not being able to make things right with your family, but I have to believe that God will somehow let Jan and Kyla know where your heart is. Your life has in no way been a waste. Look at what you've accomplished in just these few days that we've been on lockdown. You've led two lost souls to Christ, man. Shoot, I don't think I know enough yet to be telling too many other folks about being saved, but I can't imagine that many more things in life are more fulfilling than knowing that somebody has eternal life because of you. Can you imagine how different Chuck's after-life is now than it would have been if you hadn't been here?"

Peter's smile broadened and he said, "Thanks, Flex. I needed to hear that." But as true as he knew Fletcher's words were, Peter couldn't quite erase the disappointment of knowing that he was only hours away from never again knowing the joy of hugging Kyla or the ecstasy of making love to the only woman to whom he'd ever truly given his whole heart.

Chapter 22

"Mr. Greene, is my daddy going to go to heaven?" Kyla looked up at Hunter with expectant eyes, hoping that she'd get the answer she so desperately needed to hear.

They had just pulled into Hunter's parking space at the office where the *Atlanta Weekly Chronicles*, the newspaper that Hunter founded as a college student, was produced each week. Generally, he took Malik home when he picked him up from school in the afternoons, but because he had work to do in order to meet their print deadline, he'd brought the children to the office with him, hoping they'd keep themselves busy while he did the same.

"What makes you question whether or not your dad will go to heaven, Kyla?"

Grabbing her book bag from the backseat of Hunter's Range Rover, Kyla closed the door behind her. She had convinced her mother and grandparents to allow her to go to school today, even though she had hardly slept at all last night. Everybody at Redan Middle School had heard of her father's capture, and she hated that teachers and friends treated her differently. The same thing was happening at home, and it was one of the reasons that she wanted to go to school—to regain some sense of normalcy. But it escaped her there too. The closest thing to normal that she received these days was when she was around Malik and his family, so when Jan gave her permission to ride home with Hunter and Malik after school, she grabbed the opportunity.

"I heard Grandma say that he wasn't going to heaven because he got mad at Mama." Kyla followed closely behind Hunter, and Malik was only a few steps behind her.

"Hey, Lorna." Hunter paused to speak to his secretary, who handed him a folder as soon as he walked in the door. "Any messages?"

"Yes, they're all inside of there," she answered.

Kyla looked at Lorna's fingernails as she tapped the folder. The secretary's appearance always fascinated Kyla. She'd only seen Lorna on three other occasions, but every time she'd visited the place where the *Atlanta Weekly Chronicles* was produced, three things about the secretary were consistent. Her hair would either be very short or extremely long; she'd always have long, colorful nail tips; and the heels of her shoes would be at least five inches high.

Lorna must have seen her staring because she smiled and dangled her diamond-studded fingernails in front of Kyla's face. "Ask your mom if you can get some. I'll take you. They won't be this long, but they'll be pretty."

"Okay," Kyla beamed, knowing all along that asking would be a waste of her breath.

"Yeah, right," Hunter mumbled.

The walk to the break room was a noisy and interactive one, interrupted constantly by Hunter exchanging small talk with other staff members and workers who stopped to hug or pinch the cheeks of Malik and Kyla as though they were toddlers wanting to be coddled by the adults around them. Kyla sighed with relief when they finally made it to the end of the maze, and once inside the calm of the dining area, Hunter placed the Chick-Fil-A bag on the table and pointed toward the sink for the children to wash their hands. After doing so, Kyla and Malik sat while Hunter distributed their food.

"You want to say grace?" Hunter asked, looking at Kyla.

Without answering, she bowed her head. "Thank you, Lord, for this food and thank you for letting Mr. Greene buy it for us. Bless those that are less fortunate and don't have food to eat. And please fix it so that those people are feeding my daddy and not letting him starve. In Jesus' name. Amen."

"Amen," Malik echoed.

Kyla looked up at Hunter and saw him looking back at her with sympathetic eyes. She knew that he wanted to somehow convince her that the hostage-takers in Iraq weren't withholding food from her father, but Kyla had seen the live footage on television. Her dad was never a large man, but she could tell from his picture that he wasn't being fed on a regular basis. He'd lost weight since she'd seen him last. When Hunter handed her a cup of lemonade, he avoided the subject of food and reverted back to the question she'd asked when they first arrived.

"Kyla, parents are allowed to get angry; you know that, right?"

"But Grandma said . . ."

"Listen to me, sweetheart. Husbands and wives get mad at each other all the time. That's a human emotion, not a sin. Getting angry isn't something that will keep a person out of heaven. If that were the case, married folks would bust hell wide open all day long."

Kyla got up from the table and fished through her book bag, pulling out a wirebound notebook. Flipping through the sheets of lined paper, she stopped when she found what she was looking for. “See? Grandma said that in Colossians 3:19, the Lord said that it was a sin for husbands to get mad at their wives. And she said that since Daddy got mad at Mama and won’t have a chance to come back to her and ask for her forgiveness before he dies, she said that he’s going to spend eternity with the devil and his angels.”

Hunter walked to the break room’s counter and opened a drawer near the refrigerator. When he returned to the table, he had a Bible in his hand. Kyla watched as he pulled out a chair and sat between her and Malik. “I don’t know what that scripture says word-for-word, Kyla, but I can promise you that your grandmother has the meaning of it twisted.”

“So, he *will* go to heaven?” Malik asked.

Hunter looked from Malik to Kyla. “Have you two been discussing this all day or something?”

“Not *all* day,” Kyla said. “I don’t take any classes with Malik. But we talked about it after school while we were waiting for you to pick us up.”

“I told her that Mr. Jericho wouldn’t have to go to hell just for being mad at her mama, but she kept talking about what her grandma said.”

“She did,” Kyla insisted. “She said it’s in the Bible.”

“Colossians 3:19,” Hunter said, bringing the attention of the children back to him. “Husbands, love your wives, and be not bitter against them.”

“That’s all it says?” Malik stood and leaned over the table for a better view.

Hunter nodded and turned the open Bible so that Kyla had a clear view. “Sweetheart, sometimes you have to read all of the scripture to get the full understanding. Here, God was talking to more than just husbands. See? In the verse before it, He told wives to be submissive to husbands, and here, He gives guidelines to fathers, servants and children. We all fall short of God's commandments every now and then, Kyla. But when we make mistakes, it's not a one-way ticket to hell."

"Even if we don't have the chance to get it right?" Kyla felt tears dancing around the edges of her eyes, and when she blinked, Hunter picked up a napkin and dabbed them away.

"Time and circumstances may not always allow us a chance to get it right with each other; but if we just ask for God's forgiveness for our wrongdoings, then that's all we need. And I'm sure that your father has done that. He's a man of God, despite whatever mistakes he might have made. The Bible tells us that all have sinned and come short of God's glory. None of us are perfect, and if your dad's allowing his family to fall apart is a sin, it's no bigger sin than anything any of us have done. We'd be in a mess if God dismissed us all to hell for every mistake we made."

"I know that's right."

Kyla's eyes turned to the open doorway where Jerome Tides stood, listening.

"Hey, Uncle Jerome," Malik said.

"Hey, lil' man," he responded, pressing his fist against Malik's and then reaching across the table and lightly pinching Kyla's cheek.

Jerome's tweak was different than those of the other employees. Kyla smiled and ignored Malik's disapproving look. Her mother, and other women she'd overheard talking, raved about Hunter and how handsome he was with his mocha complexion, bald head, and perfectly trimmed mustache and goatee. But to Kyla, Jerome, who wore his naturally curly hair in a short fade and had eyes that seemed to twinkle when he smiled, was the more striking one. By most accounts, he probably wasn't better looking than Hunter, but if she were older and had a choice, Jerome would be it.

"Who needs a testimony of forgiveness?" Jerome asked, pulling up a chair uninvited. "I'm the poster child for redemption."

"You are?" Kyla asked. She just wanted to keep him talking. She liked Jerome's dialogue. He didn't speak in near-perfect English like his sister, Jade, and his older brother, Jackson, but he didn't talk in Ebonics either. To Kyla, Jerome's dialect just sounded cooler than most men. Occasionally, he referred to her as "shawty" and she liked that the most.

"He sure is," Hunter said.

"Uncle Jerome used to live in jail," Malik said, as though he were unveiling some undercover secret.

"So," Kyla said, smacking her lips. If Malik thought that made a difference to her, he was wrong.

Jerome nodded. "No doubt. Ten years."

"And he thought his father had gotten killed while he was locked up," Hunter said. "He had done some things wrong and hadn't had a chance to tell his father how sorry he was. But he still gave his heart to God while he was there."

"Yep, sure did," Jerome agreed. "I mean, I'd talked to my dad while I was on lockdown and all, and we had started getting kind of cool in our relationship, but I still didn't get to really beg his pardon 'til I finally bounced from that joint. And even after I got out, I couldn't apologize to him right away because it was days after that when we found out that he was still alive."

"But even if his father really was dead," Hunter explained, "God would not have condemned him to hell just because he hadn't verbally told Reverend Tides how sorry he was. So, if your dad never gets the opportunity to express himself to you or your mom, he can still be completely forgiven."

Kyla tried to smile. "I hope so."

Jerome placed his hand on top of Kyla's and she stared at it, feeling momentarily paralyzed until his voice broke her trance.

"You see, sometimes we, as humans, are the ones that have trouble forgiving each other. Your grandma is probably having a bit of a problem forgiving your dad for what went down between him and your mom. But what we have to remember is that God ain't like us. I tell the fellas at the prison that same thing when I go there with Dad to minister to them. Sometimes the folks we hurt can't find it in their hearts to let it go, but in the end, God is the final judge. Does that make sense to ya, shawty?"

"I think so. I wish Grandma could have heard it, though. I don't think she'll ever see it that way; even if I try to tell her."

Hunter sat back in his chair. "I wish she could have been here, too."

"Why don't you just put something in the paper about it?" Malik suggested as he sucked the last of his lemonade through his straw.

Kyla looked across the table at her friend and smiled. Then she turned to look at Hunter, whose eyes were locked onto Jerome's.

"What do you think?" Jerome asked.

Hunter reached over and rubbed his hand across the top of Malik's head. "That's a pretty good idea, sport. I think we should do that. You two want to help us put together a story about forgiveness?"

"For real?" Malik asked.

"For sho'," Jerome said. "It was your idea, nephew. You oughta help with it."

"Mr. Greene, can we mention my daddy in the story?"

"I wouldn't have it any other way, Kyla. Finish up your lunch and come to my office so we can get started, okay?

We have a lot of work to do if we're going to meet deadline." Hunter stood to leave and headed toward the door.

"I wish he could be around to read it." Gone was the girl who had just smiled at the idea of writing the story. Kyla's eyes dropped to the table and she tightened her lips, trying to imprison the onset of a sob.

Jerome stood and then bent down to embrace Kyla, allowing the tears she could no longer withhold to flow into the fabric of his shirt. The thought of her father being killed in the same cruel fashion as the men before him made Kyla's heart hemorrhage; so much so that even with the strong arms of the object of her infatuation comforting her, the sorrow mounted.

Chapter 23

"Well, so much for the black thing, huh?" Fletcher laughed at his own wisecrack, but Peter couldn't even pretend to be amused.

Enemy forces had just left the three prisoners of war to themselves after once again interrupting their quiet confinement with lights, cameras, and more action than the Americans cared to be a part of. The room was relatively calm now, but the atmosphere was thick with the stench of Baghdad's air and the musk of the weapon-brandishing men who'd dispersed just minutes earlier.

"Come on, man," Fletcher urged, nudging Peter with his elbow. "Don't shut down on me now. My sense of humor has never been put to the test like this. I don't need you to start throwing tomatoes at the stage at this point in the stand-up routine."

Peter closed his eyes and exhaled. He wanted to cry, but he couldn't. His heart felt cold, and the animosity that was building against their foes was beginning to overshadow his distress. The knots in his stomach hadn't untied themselves since the enemy soldiers pulled Fletcher out of the lineup and made him read the notorious letter that marked the start of his final twenty-four hours.

Fletcher tried again. "Doesn't the Bible say something about laughter being the best medicine? If there has ever been a time when I needed medicine—"

"Stop it, Flex," Peter retorted. "Just stop it. There's nothing funny about this."

"He's doing the right thing, Jericho," Louis cut in. "Owens knows he's next to go and he's dealing with it. As a United States Marine, that's what is required of us."

Peter glared at Louis. He didn't wish death on any one of his comrades, but, *If one of you had to be next to go . . .* Peter shook the thought from his head. It wasn't fair of him to wish that Fletcher had been right about the Iraqis preferring black soldiers over white ones, but he did. He wasn't ready to lose his friend.

"Truth be told, I'm about to think Owens is the lucky one," Louis added. "There ain't no better way to die than to die for your country. And living here is way worse than dying. I was hoping that they chose me."

So was I. Peter closed his eyes and tried to banish that thought as well. *Lord, forgive me.*

"Look, man," Fletcher said. "I know what you're feeling. I'd feel the same way if it were you. I don't want to die, but I can't deny that I prayed to God that He wouldn't let me be last. If I had to go, I wanted to go before you."

Peter looked at him. "Why?"

"Truth?"

"Yeah, truth."

"Two reasons—I'm selfish and I'm scared. The selfish side of me doesn't want to see you hauled out of here, nor do I want to be made to look at your bloody head. The scared side of me doesn't think I can go through a day of this without you. I've been drawing strength from you since the first day, and I don't know if I can make it without having you here with me."

"Drawing strength from me?" Peter's eyebrows and voice pitch rose simultaneously. "Man, I've been feeding off of you since day one. It's been your perfectly timed wit that has kept me from losing it on some days."

"Well, ain't that sweet," Louis quipped. "If my wrists and ankles weren't tied together, I'd give you a standing ovation and ask for an encore."

"What's wrong with you, Malloy?" Peter snapped.

"What's wrong with *me*? What's wrong with you? This is serious business and you two are over there acting like a couple of boy scouts—no, *girl* scouts. All of us have to man up and be Marines. Who cares who drew strength from who? The truth of the matter is that this ain't no Jehovah's Witness assignment. We can't travel in twos and we don't have any control over who goes next. You think Bigalow wanted to be first? And the kid, you think he wanted to die at nineteen?"

Peter got the feeling that Louis was quickly losing the control he'd managed to maintain up until now. He was rambling. Nothing he said seemed to have anything to do with the thing he'd said before it, and none of it was a viable reason to interrupt his and Fletcher's conversation. Fletcher must have felt the same way.

"Malloy, what are you talking about? We know that nobody got to choose the order, and we know neither Klauser nor Bigalow wanted to die. But what does that have to do with what we were talking about?"

Louis' hard patriotic exterior seemed to crack before their eyes. He swore and used both his legs to kick his dinner plate across the room. Instinctively, Peter looked toward the door. It was a very similar outburst that caused the injury to his head. Fortunately, this time, there was no guard present. His mind went back to Fletcher's theory that when the men left for the night, they didn't stand post outside the door. If they did, the open window on the wall would have alerted them of Louis' disgruntlement.

"Look at us, man," Louis said, his voice still at a heightened level. "We're getting our throats cut one day at a time; and for what? We put our lives on the line for our country and it turns around and pulls down its drawers in our faces and shows us where we can pucker up. You know why? Because the United States government couldn't care less about us, that's why. If these murderers kill us, so what? The United States has a thousand more men that they'll just send over to replace us. We accuse these half-baked savages of not valuing the lives of their own, but if this doesn't prove that the United States doesn't value the lives of its own, then I don't know what does!"

The words seemed unfamiliar coming from Louis' mouth. Peter had never known him to say anything negative about his country or the war. He was a fourth generation Marine and had proudly made that known more than a few times. Just two minutes ago, he was the voice of reason; now his tirade was bordering the scene that Silas made when he found out that he was to die first.

"Look, Malloy, I've got less than twenty-four hours," Fletcher said. "I think if anybody has the right to go off on the United States, it's me. But what good will it do? If you don't mind, I'd rather not spend these last few hours arguing with each other or dogging out our country. Because in spite of everything, it's still the best country in the world and I wouldn't trade my citizenship for any other."

Peter nodded in quiet agreement, but inside, he began to feel what faith he had left evaporate in the heat of the Arab world. All of his Christian life, he'd been taught and had read the biblical reference that promised that God would put no more on His people than they could bear. But this clearly challenged that scripture. Although he grieved the losses of both his other military brothers, realistically speaking, in time, he'd get beyond it and be able to move forward. But Peter knew without doubt that he would never be able to rise above the sight of Fletcher being carted away at gunpoint and then having to see his head paraded as though it were a trophy presented for some prized accomplishment.

"Go get your plate." The voice broke Peter's thoughts and he looked up to see Fletcher looking at Louis and pointing his restrained arms in the direction of the plate that had slid clear to the other side of the room.

Louis looked at the plate and then back at Fletcher. His eyes were filled with defiance, but he said nothing.

"Please, go get your plate," Fletcher repeated, this time with less authority. "I'd like to have dinner with my brothers. *Both* of my brothers."

Taking a moment to look at Peter and then again at Fletcher, Louis shook his head slowly and then began the short but tedious journey that would bring him to his banished meal.

"Don't lose your faith, Pete." Fletcher never took his eyes off of Louis, and his lips barely moved, but Peter was certain that he'd heard the words.

"What?"

"You heard me," Fletcher whispered, turning to face him. "I can see it drying up, Jericho, and you can't let it happen, no matter what."

Peter felt his chin quiver, and he rigidly held his emotions in check.

"Remember when you first told me about your last name? I know I said it sounded Indian, and it does, for good reason. But that wasn't the first thing that came to mind. My first thought was the Bible story that I read years ago as a kid in Sunday School. The lesson's title was 'Joshua and the Battle of Jericho.' You know how the story goes. You know how God used this one man to lead His people and to ultimately bring down the walls of an entire city after seven days of marching around it. I can't help but think that in some way, God orchestrated it so that you could be sent to this city to lead us into victory."

A hot, exultant tear rolled down Peter's cheek. "Then I have failed Him miserably."

"Not so, my brother. How many times do I have to keep reminding you? I need you to get this through your thick skull because this time tomorrow, I'm not going to be around to remind you of this anymore. Private First Class Charles Klauser is in heaven right now because of you. The pearly gates, as my granddaddy used to call them, are now being prepared for my entrance because of you." Fletcher turned and glanced toward Louis, who had retrieved his plate of food and now sat nearby, watching and listening. "Malloy will have the opportunity to make a life-changing decision because of you."

Peter used his arms to wipe away wet emotions that had pooled at his chin.

"I'm sure to Joshua, Jericho looked like too big of a war to win. And now, to Jericho, Iraq looks like too big of a war to win. But sometimes what we see as winning isn't necessarily God's definition. You've won souls, Jericho, so you've already won this battle, whether you live or die."

Peter stared straight ahead as the room darkened more, marking the sand that piled at the bottom of the hourglass. "O death, where is thy sting? O grave, where is thy victory?" He looked at Fletcher and saw the confusion on his face. "That's what one of the apostles in the Bible wrote in one of his letters to the Corinthian church." Peter swabbed away the remains of the evidence of his tears. "Paul talks about how death has no power over the children of God. The pain of death is in sin, but because we are no longer sinners, but saved by the blood of Jesus, He gives us victory over the sting of death; so when we are faced with it, we simply step away from a mortal body into immortality."

"Heaven," Fletcher said.

"Yeah."

Fletcher shrugged. "See? So, unlike in the Bible story, in this particular battle, it's Jericho that gets the victory."

Peter forced a smile. "Not just me; all of us. If we know Christ in the pardon of our sins, that is," he added with his sight fixed on Louis.

When Louis broke eye contact and turned his face away, Fletcher bowed his head. "Father, thank you for this food that we are about to receive . . ."

Chapter 24

"So, they moved the meeting to Thursday just because they wanted to pray for the soldiers in Iraq?" Rachel asked the question as she and Jan climbed from the car after finding an empty space in the lot of New Hope Church.

Jan grabbed her umbrella from the backseat just in case the dark clouds that loomed overhead decided to open up during the Women of Hope gathering. Then she pressed the button on her key ring that automatically locked the car doors and set the alarm. When Jan told Rachel of the change in schedule, she had no idea that Rachel would want to come along. Rachel had just finished her shift at the hospital and was complaining of being tired. But when Jan told her about the meeting, Rachel collected a second wind from somewhere and immediately began making preparations to come. Jan knew that her cousin didn't think she was strong enough on her own to handle all of the drama that life had handed her lately, and although she didn't want to hear all of the complaining on the ride to New Hope, Jan was glad to have the support.

Rachel ran her fingers through her short, layered haircut. She smoothed down strands of hair that the continuous light breeze had misplaced, only to have them stray again. "They couldn't just pray on Friday at the regular meeting time?"

"It's not that they *couldn't* pray on Friday night, Rachel. On the message that Jade left for me, she said that Reverend Tides felt an urgency about getting together tonight for a special time of prayer with the women's support group."

"What urgency?"

"I don't know, but to be honest with you, I don't care. I'm glad he called for the service. I just hope I can be a part of it without being singled out because of Pete's situation. I don't want to feel like I'm in the spotlight. I just want to pray and gain strength just like everyone else."

"Well, you can forget that, honey. You and I both have done enough church for us to be sure about one thing. Just like at that women's meeting, somebody is going to talk all sappy to you until you finally break down and cry."

"Nobody spoke sappy to me at the meeting, Rachel."

"Whatever. What I'm saying is that they will probably have a depressing atmosphere to fit the occasion. Half of them are just going to be crying to get attention anyway—just a bunch of Aunt Leonas."

"Rachel!"

"Don't get caught up in their emotion, Jan. You just need to be strong. It's mind over matter. Don't think about what those folks over there are doing to Pete; think about what Pete did to you. If you put it all in perspective, you'll see that you really have no need to cry."

Jan kept her eyes fixed on the double doors that were

still at least one hundred feet in front of them. She was already feeling the water rising in her eyes, and she blinked quickly to try to shoo it away.

"You're not going to cry, are you?" Rachel said when Jan remained silent.

"No, Rachel; but this whole thing is very sad, and I don't think any of the members who might break down will be doing it just for show. I'm not the only one here who has family ties in Iraq, Kuwait and Afghanistan. Their people might not be prisoners of war, but what has happened with Pete and those other men could happen to any of the soldiers at any given time. This is serious business. Night after night of hearing that American soldiers are being brutally killed can get to be too much for those of us who are human." Jan looked at Rachel and pursed her lips. "Even if Pete wasn't there, it would be sad for me, but having my husband there—"

"Stop calling him your husband, Jan." Rachel's voice was saturated with exasperation. "He's the man who abandoned you, the man who took your heart and spit on it, and the man who has quite possibly left you for another woman."

"He's also the man who is still my daughter's father," Jan quickly put in, finding herself irritated by Rachel's body language that silently but visibly told Jan that she was stupid to care. "Rachel, this isn't about me," she added, knowing it was only partially true. "It's very hard having to deal with knowing what's going on in Iraq and trying to keep Kyla preoccupied so that she's not thinking about it all day and dreaming about it all night. And now, on top of all of that, Daddy is in town and Mama's been anointing her whole living room with blessed oil ever since he stopped by yesterday; acting as though he brought in demons or something. Sometimes I feel like I'm about to lose my mind in all of this madness. I can use as much prayer as I can get; for me and my family. That's why I'm here. You didn't have to come if you had a problem with it."

"Don't you even go there. You know how in demand this diva is. I could have been any number of places tonight, but I'm here because I love you. I wouldn't dare let you do this alone."

Jan sighed, suddenly feeling like an ungrateful brat. "I know and I appreciate it, Rachel; I really do. But I need you to understand all of the evil that is coming against me. It's hard."

"That's a big part of the problem right there, Jan. You're trying to make your situation something spiritual. The devil didn't do this to you. You did this to yourself when you moved in with your mama. Your problem isn't science; it's geography. You need to pack up your stuff and get the you-know-what out of that neighborhood you're living in. If you'd get out of Shelton Heights like I told you, that alone would take care of most of your issues."

"For the sake of argument, let's just say that's true."

"It *is* true."

"Fine, Rachel; but moving now is not going to change what's already happened. It's not going to change the fact that my parents hate each other or that my hus—my daughter's father is about to be murdered." Jan's voice quivered.

"See?" Rachel said, stopping in her tracks to turn and face Jan.

"I'm fine," Jan said as she walked around her.

"No, you were doing fine when you weren't watching those stupid war updates. Maybe you should go back to that."

Jan shot a glare toward Rachel, but opted out of replying. They were too close to the front door now, and she had come to the conclusion days ago that her cousin would never truly be able to understand why she still cared about Peter and his well-being. Trying to convince Rachel that one wrong didn't deserve another would be a waste of time. It would only further frustrate matters. Neither of them would ever be able to see through the eyes of the other.

A blast of cold from the air-conditioned sanctuary hit both women in their faces as they walked through the front doors of New Hope Church. The last time they had come for the group counseling meeting, the foyer was empty, except for the dutiful receptionist. This time, many women—at least a hundred of them—crowded into the area, and it was clear that more than just the regular crew were gathering for the unique prayer service.

"Hi, Jan."

Turning around, Jan looked at the perfectly manicured hand on her shoulder and then up at a woman whose face was just as flawless. She could recall very few of the names of the ladies who were at her first meeting, but this one, she did.

"Hi . . . Kenyatta, right?" Jan wanted to be certain.

"Right. Kenyatta King." She seemed pleased that Jan had remembered, but her smile faded as soon as it had appeared. "I'm so sorry to hear about your husband, girl. I know that had to be hard to believe."

Jan's hopes of not being singled out had already been dashed, but she was thankful that Kenyatta had been mindful to lower her voice level enough to keep their conversation private. Jan ignored Rachel's I-told-you-so expression and replied, "It was. It still is, actually."

"I dropped by to check in on you Tuesday, but you had a house full."

Raising her eyebrows, Jan questioned, "You did? You know where I live?"

Kenyatta nodded. "You're just one street over from where I live with my brother and nephew."

"You live in Shelton Heights?"

"Yes, on Waller Drive."

Rachel grunted, using her hands to try to put more space between the women. "Okay, break it up. One person with bad karma is more than enough. You know what? It might be a good idea for y'all to do a quick role call to see if all the girls in your support group live out there in Boogieman Ville. That could be the diagnosis right there and y'all could save yourselves from fighting traffic on Friday nights just to come talk to a sanctified shrink. See how simple that was? For the bargain basement price of five dollars, I just solved everybody's problem." When she was done with her rant, Rachel stood with her hands held out, pretending to wait patiently for the women to pay her fee.

"If you don't back up off me, you gon' get shot for the bargain basement price of free," Kenyatta said, patting her purse as she spoke.

Jan looked at the brown Coach bag and wondered if a concealed weapon was the cause of the bulging sides. True or false, the threat was believable. Rachel must have thought the same and drawn the conclusion that she didn't want to find out. She took two steps back and looked at Kenyatta through narrowed eyes. Had the circumstances surrounding their meeting been less poignant, Jan probably would have laughed. For the first time ever, she believed she'd just seen her smart-mouthed cousin meet a worthy opponent, and the sight of it was amusing.

"As I was saying," Kenyatta continued, equally disregarding both Rachel's stare and her presence. "I came by your house but never got on the inside to see you. Some crazy lady was out in the front yard telling me that I couldn't come in the house because I was showing too much cleavage."

Jan tried to look as if she were totally unaware of who

the "crazy lady" might have been, but she could feel the color drain from her face as Kenyatta continued.

"She started yelling some scripture, Job 31:33, I think; telling me that I needed to cover my transgressions and hide the iniquity of my bosom if I wanted to come in the house. Well, I had on a top almost just like the one I have on now, and I don't think the neckline is plunging too deep. Do you?"

Jan shook her head, half to answer the question and the other half in shame. "No, it's fine. But you know how the older saints can be. They have far stricter views on how they think Christians should do everything, including how we should dress."

"Yeah, well, she was 'bout to meet Jesus and be able to ask Him for herself, talking all loud and having everybody looking at me. If it wasn't for Reverend Tides' son, it was about to be on and popping in your front yard."

Just the thought of a showdown between her mother's overzealous personality and Kenyatta's trigger-happy one was enough to make Jan cringe. "Jackson?" she asked, hoping to change the line of conversation just a bit.

"No," Kenyatta said, sporting a wide grin. "It was Jerome. He came up and started talking to me and that took my mind away from that lady. I see him at church every Sunday, but that was my first time speaking to him. He has a really calming way of talking to you, unlike that crazy woman. Jerome told me that you had plenty of friends and family inside and that Dr. Greene—Jade was talking with you at the time, so I didn't bother to go in."

"Well, thank you for dropping by. I appreciate the thought."

"You're welcome. And like I said, I'm close by, so if you ever want to get together . . ."

"Good evening, everyone." Jade spoke in loud tones as she rounded the corner of the foyer, and in an additional effort to gain everyone's attention, she clapped as she spoke. When she was satisfied that she had the floor, Jade continued. "Sisters, thank you so much for shifting your schedules at the last minute and coming out tonight for this special prayer meeting. I'm sorry for the delay, but far more people turned out than expected, and I'm grateful for the support. The more prayer, the more power. Amen?"

"Amen!" the crowd echoed. A couple of shouts of "Praise God" and "Hallelujah" were mixed in the responses too.

"Amen," Jade reiterated. "The classroom that generally houses our Women of Hope meetings only seats about forty people comfortably; so, in obedience to the instructions given by our pastor, we are going to take tonight's meeting into the sanctuary. And please, don't crowd into the back of the edifice. I'd like you all to try to sit in the front rows of the center section. Thank you."

Jade barely had time to finish her sentence before the crowd began pressing toward the entrance doors as if a concert were about to take place and the tickets were general admission. Jan looked over both her shoulders as she moved forward to avoid being run over. She saw Kenyatta disappear in the thickness in front of her, but there was no sign of Rachel. Once Jan made it inside the sanctuary and into the aisle, the congestion eased, but the women still rushed for available seating that would give them the best view. Jan was forced to sit somewhere near the middle of row six, which was fine with her. She still had an unobstructed view, and the comfortable distance made her feel safe and unexposed. Jan took a quick look over her shoulder and scanned the faces of those nearest behind. *Where did Rachel go?*

Everyone around her suddenly stood and began clapping, drawing Jan's attention to the pulpit where she saw Reverend Tides, his wife, and their daughter enter from the side door. The atmosphere of praise nearly made Jan forget that they were only there to pray corporately for the troops in Iraq.

"Praise the Lord. Oh, how good and pleasant it is for brethren to dwell together in unity. Please take your seats for a moment," Reverend Tides said. Jan watched him lean forward so that the speaker's stand in front of him supported his weight. His face was filled with disquiet. "I want to thank all of you, the members of the mother board, the members of Women of Hope, the intercessory prayer group, and all of you other sisters and friends of New Hope who came out to stand in faith with us on this evening. I hope that you didn't come tonight for any other purpose than to lay before the Lord and beseech His mercy. Our country needs His mercy, saints. Our government officials need His mercy. The troops need His mercy. We all need God's mercy."

"Oh yes, Lord, we need your mercy!" Several people voiced replies to the pastor's words, but the woman sitting next to Jan seemed to be the loudest.

Reverend Tides continued. "Many of the members of New Hope have loved ones that are at war right now. Maybe some of you are in that number."

"Yes," a chorus of voices responded. Some of the women lifted their hands as though the pastor had asked for a headcount.

"Well, we're going to pray for each and every one of them and for you as well. This week, my family and I have spent many hours at the home of Mrs. Leona Grimes, a neighbor of ours in Shelton Heights. Sister Grimes is not a member of New Hope, but she and her daughter are supporters and frequent worshipers here. You all have said that you have family who are fighting in the war. Well, Sister Grimes' son-in-law is being held prisoner in Baghdad. I'm sure you've seen the news footage of the beheadings that have been going on there for the past few days. Sister Grimes' daughter's husband is one of the prisoners set to die at the hands of the Iraqis."

Jan swallowed deeply and stared down at the wood frame of the back of the pew in front of her. Her heart began to race and she felt flush. By the gasps that ran around the audience, it was apparent that many of the women hadn't made the connection between Jan and Peter. She wasn't surprised. She could count on one hand the number of women at New Hope that she'd had a one-on-one conversation with.

"Yes, we will pray for all of you and your loved ones, but I need for each person under the sound of my voice to become selfless for just a few minutes. I dare you to put someone else's needs before your own. Do that and see won't God bless you mightily for your graciousness. In a moment, I'm going to ask each of you who know that you have a relationship with the Lord to gather around this altar. And we are going to pray like we've never prayed before. If you have any doubt in your heart or mind of what God can and will do, then I need you to remain in your seat. We don't have room for doubt or doubters. Somebody's life depends upon this prayer, and we need God to do the impossible. But how many of you know that what is impossible with man is possible with the Lord?"

"Yes it is!"

"Amen!"

"Thank you, Lord!"

"Glory to God!"

The women were standing and clapping now, rallying behind the words of their pastor. Jan's eyes overflowed and the tears streamed down her cheeks. As much as she'd wanted to share a spot on the pew with Rachel, she was glad that it didn't work out that way. Rachel would be outdone at her inability to place mind over matter.

"Is anything too hard for the Lord?" Reverend Tides challenged.

"No!" The shouts came from every direction and resonated in the acoustics of the near-empty sanctuary.

"Sister Jan, if you're out there, I need you to come up front right now."

Jan sat frozen in her seat and used her hands to wipe the tears from her face. She hoped she'd heard wrong. *No . . . please don't call me up. Please don't call me up.*

"Come on, Sister Jan," the pastor said, his eyes scanning the audience for her. "I need you to move in a hurry. God wants to do something, but you got to get in the pool while the water is troubled. Are you here?"

Jan didn't want to get up, but she didn't seem to have a choice. Her body moved on its own, bringing her to a standing position and delivering her all the way to the altar. Kenyatta's manicured hands patted her on the shoulder as Jan passed her second row seat. Reverend and Mrs. Tides walked from the pulpit to the floor to meet Jan. Jade followed, and when she reached the place where Jan stood, she embraced her. Jan could no longer keep her tears in check, and she held on to Jade and wept heavily.

"That's right, daughter; pray for her while you hold her," Reverend Tides instructed Jade. "And to my other praying and believing sisters, gather around and join in. God is in the building."

The front of the church became inundated with women who were praying aloud as they gathered. Jan felt several hands on her shoulders and back and the touches from them sent electrical chills down her spine. Reverend Tides prayed for a while, asking for God's mercy and pleading with Him to give Jan comfort and confirmation in the form of daytime visions and nighttime dreams. Sometimes his prayer transformed into moans and other times in unknown tongues; then he would pray some more. All during the pastor's intercession, the women surrounding Jan prayed too, all of them making their separate requests known to the Lord, all for Jan's sake. After a while, Reverend Tides stopped praying and began exalting the crowd.

"God is able to do exceedingly, abundantly above all that we ask or think." Reverend Tides' voice bellowed through the speaker system. "And even if He don't answer our prayers, we rejoice because we know that He's still able!"

More cries and shouts could be heard around her. Jan tightened her grip on Jade, trying to draw strength for her weakening knees.

"But I said it before and I'll keep on saying it," the preacher pronounced with confidence. "The battle ain't over 'til God says it's over. And in the almighty name of Jesus Christ, we claim victory!"

"Victory!" Jan heard Jade declare in her ear.

Chapter 25

The ride home was quiet. Jan used her cell phone once to call home to check on Kyla; but other than Jan's brief chat with her daughter, no communication was offered for many minutes. The rain was falling on the outside, forcing Rachel to drive at a slower pace than normal. The reduced travel speed, coupled with the lack of interaction, made the ride seem that much longer.

Periodically, Jan glanced toward Rachel. She'd never known her to be silent for such a long period of time, but she was too tired to ask any questions. The prayer service had gone on for just shy of two hours, and Jan felt as though she'd given blood to every woman who prayed around her. Her body felt depleted of energy and she longed for her bed. More than ever, she also longed for her husband.

Rainy nights made her think of Peter because that was the setting that guaranteed to deliver to her a romantic evening. Rarely did it rain in the desert of Twentynine Palms, but on those occasions when it poured on the outside, the inside housed a flood of passion. Closing her eyes, Jan relished in the memories of it all. She made the attempt to convince most people that she was getting accustomed to not having Peter around, but in truth, every month that she'd been away from her husband felt like an eternity.

I will always care about you, but I don't love you. And no, it didn't take me all this time to figure that out. It just took this long for me to get the courage to tell you.

The recollection of Peter's letter snapped Jan from her more tender thoughts. She sat up in her seat and turned up the music that was playing softly in the car. The quietness was too much, but Jan figured that it was for the best. They'd just had an awesome time at church, and somehow, the words of the pastor and the prayers of the sisters had given her some sense that there was still hope. Not for her marriage and maybe not even for Peter being spared from certain death; but she felt hope for her life and hope for her survival. Whatever happened—however God decided to move, for the first time, Jan felt as though she would be able to live on.

"Did you even come around the altar and pray for me?" Jan heard the thought in her head blurt from her mouth involuntarily.

"What?" Rachel reached forward and turned down the volume of the music.

She'd already asked it once, so she might as well ask again. "Did you come to the altar during the prayer?"

"Why?"

Jan looked at her, already knowing the answer. "Because I just want to know if you were praying for me."

"I could pray for you without going to the altar. God's hearing wasn't limited to those who went to the front, you know."

Her evasive answer was all the confirmation Jan needed. She turned her face to the window and watched evidence of the downpour roll down her window. The streams were unending. As soon as one reached the base of the window, another was right behind it. The scene reminded her of tears—her own tears, most of which nobody saw. If the fibers of her pillowcase could talk, they could tell stories that, right now, were only known by Jan.

"You don't seem any happier," Rachel said. "Did the prayer help at all?"

Jan smiled, but never turned her face from the scene outside. "It helped tremendously. I was just thinking, that's all."

"About what?"

Turning from the window, Jan asked, "Are you sure you want to know?"

She could tell from Rachel's heavy sigh that she had already figured it out and wasn't thrilled, but Rachel replied with a dry, "Sure. Why not?"

Leaning her head against the headrest, Jan directed her eyes in front of her. The rain was falling in sheets, making the roadway barely visible. Some of the drivers had pulled over to the side of the road, waiting for the downpour to ease. Some were even getting off at the first exit they could find, perhaps turning around to go back to what seemed safer. Jan admitted that the weather was bad, but in her opinion, it wasn't so bad that they shouldn't keep pressing. Didn't they know that it would clear up after a while? Wasn't what they had at home worth battling the inclement weather?

"I should have reached out to him, Rachel."

"Uuuugh!" Rachel groaned through clenched teeth.

"Just listen." Jan didn't break her stare. "See how it's raining outside now? That's not the norm, Rachel. It rains like this, what, once or twice a year, at the most? And people are giving up on getting where they need to go. See?" she said, pointing at another car that had come to a stop on the shoulder of the road. "They can't even take a twice-a-year downpour."

"Since we just left church, I'm gonna try not to cuss. But what in the fiery pits of darkness are you talking about, Jan? What does that have to do with anything?"

"The letter I got from Pete was so unlike him, Rachel; that's what I'm talking about. Who knows what he could have been going through when he wrote it? War does crazy things to folks, and I should have tried to get some answers before just giving up."

"Answers about what? I didn't see no question marks on that letter, did you? Jan, the man said he didn't want you no more. How could anything to do with war cause him to say something like that? Honey, didn't no war cause that; a woman caused that. Pete chose some other skank over you, and that's all there is to it."

Jan shook her head. "I don't believe that, Rachel. I can't. I know Pete better than that. Something happened to him. He had to have a moment of—"

"Insanity?" Rachel broke out into a loud fit of laughter, causing Jan to close her eyes and struggle to remain composed as she waited for the guaranteed snort. "You are actually going to plead temporary insanity on his behalf? I take everything I said back about you not needing to see that shrink, Jan. You need her and you need her bad."

"I'm not crazy, Rachel. I know what it looks like and what it sounds like, but I really feel in my heart that it wasn't as cut and dry as it all seems. Now . . . well, I'm just regretful that I didn't dig deeper and find out what was under the surface. I keep thinking that maybe those people who captured him made him write the letter."

"What?" The traffic was at a standstill now, affording Rachel the opportunity to turn and look directly at Jan. Her expression indicated that she thought Jan had all but lost her mind.

"Hear me out. What if that's a part of their plot? What if they make the soldiers write letters to their families that will turn the family members against them so they won't even try to seek out ways to save them?"

"Jan, you sound like a fool."

"We don't know what they are capable of, Rachel. That could very well be the answer to the mystery."

"Girl, this ain't no mystery to nobody but you. Pete wrote that letter to you and he meant every word of it."

"We don't know that," Jan said, getting more irritated by the second.

"No, *you* don't know that. I love you, Jan, and I'll do just about anything for you. But I'm not going to let you walk around in a fog. Come on, now; stop lying to yourself. Both you and Kyla got a letter on the same day. Why didn't the folks make him write a nasty letter to Kyla? Why would they allow him to write the usual 'Daddy loves you' letter to her and then write you one that tells you to kiss his behind?"

"It didn't say that."

"Whatever, Jan. You know I'm right."

Jan swallowed to hold back an erupting emotion that she couldn't quite identify. Rachel had brought up a point that she hadn't considered in her pondering, but Jan wasn't sure if having it thrown in her face made her want to cry, or to slap fire from the girl who'd tossed it there. She did neither one. Instead, Jan quietly watched the road ahead as the traffic began moving once more.

"I know you don't want to hear this, Jan, and I'm sorry; but aside from being your cousin, I'm your friend. And I wouldn't be a true friend if I didn't keep it on the real with you. I think that all you should be focusing on now is making a new life for you and Kyla. What's done is done. You are a very attractive woman, old enough to know what you want and young enough to still get it. You are educated, employed and independent. You have a child, but she's not a baby, so guys won't be so intimidated. Plus they won't have to worry about having to battle egos with her father because by then, Pete will be—"

"Rachel!" Jan's face was hot with fury. "I can't believe you were going to say that. You were going to sit right here in my face and say Pete would be dead, weren't you?"

"Would you rather I said it behind your back?"

"I'd rather you didn't say it at all! Were you in the same anointed service I was just in? Did it give you any hope at all? Why do you always have to play devil's advocate? Why do you always have to be a pessimist?"

"I'm not being a pessimist, Jan; I'm being a realist. Yes, I was in the service and yes, I saw all of the tears and heard all of the praying and wailing. But all of that Japanese don't mean nothing in Iraq."

"Japanese? What Japanese?"

"You know; all that honda-honda-kawasaki-yamaha-suzuki tongue speaking that every church person has mastered."

"Rachel!" Jan gasped.

"Okay, okay," Rachel said, tossing a look and one hand toward the sky. "Forgive me, Lord. But I'm being real, Jan. Do you know how many other people have prayed for their sons' and daughters' safety? You've been watching the news lately, so I know you've seen the special prayer services that have taken place all across the country. They had an all-night vigil for that first boy that got murdered. Folks were crying, praying, singing. Honey, they had one up on y'all tonight, 'cause they were burning candles and everything. But guess what? He still got killed. God could have come down to earth and gone to Iraq dressed like and looking just like He be looking in all those Jesus Christ movies, stood in them folks' faces and commanded them not to kill that boy, and they still would have done it. And you know why? Because those people over there ain't scared of God or nobody else."

Jan reposition herself so that she leaned against the headrest and said, "You did the right thing by not coming around the altar. Reverend Tides told all the doubters to stay at their seats, so you were right where you needed to be."

"Say whatever you want about me. I believe in God as much as the next person, but I also know what I know. Don't get me wrong. I think it was nice and very thoughtful of Reverend Tides to pray for Pete and the rest of the men who are left. But he ain't no closer to God than anybody else. Don't the Bible say that God doesn't play favorites? If God didn't answer the prayer requests of all those thousands of other people, He's not about to answer the request of one man. Jan, you have enough people filling you with false hope. When it comes right down to it, I may not be saying what you *want* to hear, but I feel like I'm the vessel God is using to say what you *need* to hear."

Chapter 26

"You still woke, Pete?"

"Flex, man, I couldn't have gone to sleep if I had ingested a whole bottle of NyQuil. Not last night, and probably not for the duration of my stay."

"Malloy?"

"Yeah, Owens. I'm here too."

All three had stayed awake throughout the night; sometimes talking, sometimes praying, other times saying nothing at all. Any tears that were shed were done so in private, with the darkness of the nighttime hiding each man's terror and grief from the others. The room was still dark now, but the men could see shadows of one another. Clear signs of daybreak were peeking through the single window situated high on the wall across from where Peter sat. Some nights, as he struggled to find sleep, he could watch the moon glowing from above through that window. But not last night. Last night, all Peter could see was sinister darkness; a darkness that was now slowly being interrupted by a sun he had prayed would never rise. He didn't know what time it was, but if history was any indication, it wouldn't be long before the enemy barged in.

"Owens?"

"Yeah, Malloy?"

"Are you scared?"

"Scared doesn't even come close to describing it. If I was a kid, I'd be peeing my pants right now."

Fletcher chuckled, trying to make light of the situation, but Peter felt his tear ducts swell at the sound of his friend's words. He wished he could stop the hands of time, create a diversion, anything to change the normal routine. But he was powerless against those that held them.

"What is it now; about six o'clock?" Louis' words slurred with heavy fatigue.

"Probably," Fletcher answered.

God, help us, Peter thought. Even with the backing of the most powerful country in the world, all of them were rendered powerless. Thoughts of Jan and Kyla almost choked back his next words, but he said them anyway. "I wish they'd just kill us all at the same time and get it over with."

"I was thinking the same thing, Jericho," Louis said. "You think if we asked the English-speaking one—"

"Ask?" Fletcher said with a dry laugh. "Man, you think if they knew that you guys would rather die with me, they'd grant your request? These maniacs ain't gonna do nothing that they think we want them to do. Especially the English-speaking one. He's the most hateful one of all."

"Yeah, you're probably right. Well, maybe we should tell them that we want to die separately. Maybe they'd kill us all together."

"Good old reverse psychology," Fletcher mumbled. "Yeah, Malloy, that'll work on people who are barely human."

Peter continued to watch the window. Through it, he saw what looked like a twinkling star. Until that moment, he hadn't even noticed the stars. They were very few, almost non-existent, except the one, and it disappeared as quickly as it came into view. Perhaps it was a falling star. He almost closed his eyes to make a wish, but then realized how ridiculously childish it would be.

Looking at Fletcher through the shadows, Peter noticed him massaging his neck and imagined that Fletcher was pondering the process that he was about to endure. *I have to do something. I can't just sit by and let the closest thing to a brother I've ever had go out like this. If he goes, I go.* "What if we don't give them a choice?" Peter suddenly suggested.

"Huh?" said Fletcher.

"What do you mean?" Louis asked simultaneously.

Peter couldn't even believe he was suggesting the radical plan, but desperation was setting in. He'd come to the conclusion that he didn't want to spend one more day as a prisoner in Iraq, letting others decide when and how he would die. If he had to die, he wanted to choose. Peter silently prayed that God wouldn't define his plot as suicide.

"What if, when they come in to get Flex, we fight back?"

"How?" both men said, still speaking in chorus.

"Pete, our legs and hands are tied together. What kind of fighting can we do?" Fletcher asked.

"Like Malloy said yesterday, we're Marines. We're trained to defend ourselves and our country under the most deplorable conditions. We'll do whatever we can do with whatever mobility we have. Look out the window. There are barely any stars in the sky and the darkness is fading. That means daylight is on the way. The sun is never fully up when they come, which means they could walk in at any minute now. I say we start working our way into a standing position. We're always half-asleep or at least lying down when they come in. If we're standing and fully alert when they burst through those doors, that alone will startle them, maybe even confuse them a little. We'll stand close together with you in the middle, Flex. And when they approach to grab you, we'll just start swinging, yelling, fighting as much as we can with the mobility we have."

"You think that will make them shoot us?" Fletcher asked.

"Or beat us to death," Peter said. "We already know we can't win, but we'll fight to the death. They'll have to kill us. We won't settle for anything else."

"Give me liberty or give me death," Louis said. It was the first patriotic thing they'd heard from him since yesterday's meltdown.

"Are we together on this?" Peter asked.

"Yes," Fletcher and Louis replied.

"Then let's do it."

Standing had never been so difficult. The men grunted and moaned as they tried to use the wall as a means of stability. The more Peter moved, the more he felt the vein in his head pulsate. If he were going to fight, he'd have to forget about the discomfort of his head, and that wouldn't be easy.

"Oh, please kill us all," Louis panted, cursing under his breath as he struggled.

Peter wondered if his comrade should be so ready for death. He still hadn't made a choice to accept Christ. But Peter felt blameless, knowing that both he and Fletcher had offered Louis the opportunity on more than one occasion. Salvation was free, but if Louis was going to receive it, he had to have a heart of acceptance.

"I'm up, guys," Peter said, trying to catch his breath and regain control of the increased aching in his head all at the same time.

"Me too," Fletcher said. "Man, I'm sweating more now than I did in those five-mile runs we did back at the base."

"Okay," Louis said. "I think I'm a year or two older than you guys, so we'll chalk my last place finish up to age."

Fletcher laughed. "Think again. I got you by a year, man. I'm forty."

"Oh," Louis said.

"We won't tell nobody, man," Peter said.

"Cross your heart and hope to die?" Fletcher spoke the words and immediately broke into a giggle that became contagious.

Before long, all of the men were laughing heartily. Peter laughed so hard that he could barely catch his breath. He didn't know if the metaphorical one-liner was that hilarious or if the three of them had finally reached a state of delirium.

"Shhhhh!" Louis said, his voice suddenly at a ghostly whisper. "Shhhhh! Listen, guys, listen!"

There were sounds of a motor of some kind, and it was coming closer. Peter's heart pounded so hard that he could feel it in his feet. His bladder vibrated at the same pace as his head, but he couldn't be concerned with bodily discomforts.

"Is that . . . is that an aircraft?" Fletcher stammered.

It certainly sounded like one, but Peter couldn't be sure. The only thing he was positive about was that it was time. Time to stand like a man. Time to fight like a soldier. Time to meet his Maker. The noises outside were getting louder. The Iraqis must have known that the American soldiers were planning a rebellion attack because if the approaching sounds were any indication, they had brought reinforcements.

Louis shared Peter's thoughts. He swore before frantically saying, "I think this place is bugged, guys. They heard our conversations. They know what we're doing. They've beat us at our own game."

The yelling and gunfire began even before the enemy soldiers reached the door.

Louis collapsed onto the floor. "I can't do this! I can't do this! Ahhhhhhh!"

Peter's breaths came in quick huffs and it was impossible to steady his erratic pulse. Amidst Louis' cries, a wave of apprehension coursed through Peter's veins, but he remained erect as he looked down at Louis' crumpled body and then up at Fletcher. "This is it, bruh. It's now or never. What's it gonna be? You ready?"

Icy fear had Fletcher's eyes frozen in a position as wide as silver dollars. "The Lord is my shepherd, I shall not want," he said, his breath shallow and his body trembling. "Yeah. I'm ready," he interjected, and then continued with quick words as though trying to fit it all in before it was too late. "He makes me to lie down in green pastures, He leads me beside the still waters, He restores my soul. He leads me in the paths of righteousness for His name sake. Yea, though I walk through the valley of the shadow of death, I will fear no evil . . ."

Memories of some of Chuck's final words swirled through Peter's head. *Tell my girlfriend that the last words on my lips before I died were, 'I love you, Katherine.' Tell her I died just like I lived; loving her.*

"I love you, Jan," Peter whispered just as the door burst open, letting in screaming soldiers with guns aimed and ready to fire directly at all three of them.

Chapter 27

"Pete!"

As Jan came to an upright position in her bed, she didn't know whether she'd said the word aloud or just in her dream. The illuminated numbers on the clock beside her bed showed that it was only minutes past eleven, meaning she'd only been asleep for about an hour. She wiped beads of perspiration from her forehead and soon found that the same moisture was seeping from every pore in her body, wetting the sheet below her and the one on top. Covering her mouth with her hands, Jan tried to recall the details of her nightmare. Bits and pieces of images floated through her head, not allowing her to put the full puzzle together. But she remembered enough to know that it wasn't a good sign. The dream had left her feeling like an empty pitcher, a broken wineglass, a wilted flower; a widow.

Tears from Jan's eyes began to mix with the sweat on her cheeks. The sheet that had been covering her body was already clammy and Jan buried her face in it, saturating the fibers with her sorrow. Vivid flashes from her dream, like scenes through the lens of a digital camera, began to zoom in and out of her memory bank. Images of Peter being dragged to an open field, sights of his trepidation, sounds of him petitioning for his life, while enemy soldiers carrying jungle machetes stood around laughing at his calamity as they overpowered him and forced his head against a chopping block.

"Why, God? Why?" she moaned into the covers, her body rocking back and forth.

And even if He don't answer our prayers, we rejoice because we know that He's still able!

Jan recalled Reverend Tides' words at tonight's prayer service. But knowing that God had possibly chosen not to do something that He was able to do only increased her bereavement. She'd known all along that the odds were stacked against Peter's survival, but as long as he was alive, she still held to hope. Had she listened to Rachel she wouldn't be so torn right now, but Jan found comfort living in that fog that her cousin reprimanded her about. And as "real" as Rachel had been with her, Jan still regretted not going after Peter for answers. Now, if her dream was as true as it felt, she would never know what had driven him to write the mean-spirited letter to her or what had caused him to determine that their marriage couldn't be salvaged. Jan desperately needed to know the answers to those unsolved mysteries, but if the only person with the answers was now gone, everything would forever be left to speculation.

Jan snatched the covers from her face and said, "Why am I acting like it's a done deal? Maybe it was just a dream. Maybe he's not really dead."

The ache in her heart told her otherwise. She recalled Reverend Tides asking God to show her Peter's salvation in dreams. Instead, she'd witnessed his slaughter. The dream was too authentic—more realistic than any dream she had ever had in her life.

But it was still just a dream, Jan thought, using her hands to massage her temples, trying to find relief.

Or was it?

The wet bedding was beginning to give her a chill, and in spite of her lethargy, Jan found the strength to get out of bed and wrap herself in the consolation of the silk robe Peter had bought her on their last Valentine's Day together. Tonight, for the first time since their separation, she wore the matching gown. She was missing him more than usual, and wearing it served as a surrogate for the real thing.

Blinking back more tears and walking to her window, Jan opened the blinds and took in the beautiful scene of the neighborhood under a full moon. She crossed her arms in front of her and continued to stand before the clear-paned glass. Few signs still lingered of the earlier heavy, blinding rainfall that had locked traffic on Interstate 85.

The ceased rainfall didn't stop the flood of questions that flowed through Jan's mind. How could a solid marriage take such a steep wrong turn, never to find its way back on the right track? In what way had she failed her husband so much that he needed to find consolation in the arms of another? Were her parents' divorce, her botched marriage, her husband's capture and possible murder, all due to the legend of Shelton Heights? *What's going to happen next?*

"I'm not about to sit around and find out," Jan whispered aloud as she turned to her left and reached for the telephone on her nightstand. "I gotta get out of here."

On their ride home from church, Rachel had been paged and given the opportunity to work a late-night eleven to seven shift to cover for an absent coworker. Even after being frustrated in traffic for an hour, Rachel jumped at the chance to make the extra dollars and be on duty at the same time as the man she was currently seeing.

Jan's quick fingers dialed the familiar number at record speed, and for a moment, she thought that she would have to leave a message. But on the fifth ring, Rachel answered, speaking in very soft tones.

"Hello?"

"Rachel?"

"Yeah, girl, it's me. I just got to work a few minutes ago and I'm in a staff meeting now. I just walked to the back of the room to answer the phone when it started vibrating and I saw your name on the caller ID. What's the matter? I thought you said you were going right to bed when you got home from church. You got home at nine something."

"I did go right to bed. I was in bed by ten."

"Then what are you doing up? Are you all right?"

"Yeah . . . no . . . yeah," Jan said. "I will be, anyway. I'll be quick. I know you're busy. I hope you were serious about allowing me and Kyla to move in with you, because I need to take you up on it."

"Well, yeah. You know you can."

"I don't want to intrude."

"Girl, hush. You know I got you. You're not intruding."

"It'll only be for a couple of months. After that, I'll find a place of my own."

"Jan, why are you explaining stuff to me? I told you I got you. However long you need to stay, the place is available. When do you want to move in?"

"Is now too soon?"

"Uh-oh. What happened? What's wrong?"

Jan took a deep breath. She didn't want to get into this right now. Telling Rachel about her dream would only lead to a long, complicated conversation that neither one of them had time to delve into. Besides, as long as she didn't dwell on the possibility or speak the words, she could make herself believe that Peter was still alive and the dream was just that.

"Nothing's wrong, Rachel," she lied. "I just woke up a few minutes ago, realizing how right you've been. I have to get out of Shelton Heights."

"Well, it's about time you listened to me. I won't get off until seven in the morning, but you can start packing, and by the time I get home, you can be moving in. And don't let Aunt Leona talk you out of it either," Rachel added. "No scriptures, no nothing, Jan. You need to do what you need to do for yourself and for my little cousin."

"I know," Jan replied. "I'm getting ready to start packing now."

"Good."

"Thanks, Rachel. I owe you one."

"Girl, please. You don't owe me nothing. You would do the same for me."

"I really would."

"I know. Now, do what you gotta do. I'll call you when I get home."

After thanking Rachel again, Jan hung up the phone, dreading the thought of having to stay in her mother's house even one more night. She had to leave now. Picking the telephone up and hitting redial, Jan was disappointed when she got Rachel's voicemail so soon after speaking with her. She assumed that her cousin didn't want to chance getting into trouble by walking out of the meeting again. At the sound of the beep, Jan left her message.

"Hey, Rachel. Sorry to be calling you back, but I just wanted to let you know that I wanted to go ahead and move into your place tonight. I still have the spare key that you gave me and I can let myself in. I just want to pack a few things, and Kyla and I can take as much as we can tonight. The big stuff, I'll come back for tomorrow. Thank you so much, girl. You really are a lifesaver."

Jan hung up for the second time, feeling anxious about talking to her mother. She knew that Leona wasn't awake. She was always in bed by ten and was up before the crack of dawn for her personal time of devotion. There was no doubt in Jan's mind that her mother was going to fight her on the sudden decision to move, but Rachel was right; she had to stand her ground. And the best reinforcement she knew was her father. Ted was staying at a hotel that was only five miles away, and he could handle Leona much better than Jan; especially since the divorce. He had tolerated a lot when they were together, but in witnessing her parents' interaction since her father had arrived in town for a visit, Jan noted how much more authoritative he was.

It was late, but the phone rang only twice before Ted answered. "Hello." He sounded alert, almost singing his greeting.

"Daddy, hi."

"Hey, sweetheart. Now, which one of my girls is this?"

Jan giggled softly. "It's Jan, Daddy."

"Hey, Jan. I can't tell none of you apart over the phone. Kyla told me that you went to a prayer service at your church. You just getting home?"

"No, Daddy. I just . . . I need your help with something."

"Okay. What is it?"

"Can you come over right now and help me move?"

There was a short pause and then Ted said, "Move? Where are you moving to?"

"Kyla and I are going to stay with Rachel for a couple of months. I need to move out."

"I understand that, Jan, but why in the world do you want to move at this hour? What's the rush? Can't you wait until it's light outside?"

"No, Daddy. I need to go now." Her attempt to sound blithe didn't work with her father.

"Jan, this isn't about you thinking that Shelton Heights is cursed, is it? I told you that what happened between me and Leona ain't had nothing to do with—"

"This isn't about you and Mom, Daddy. This is about me and Pete." It frustrated Jan that nobody seemed to understand her situation.

"What happened with you and Pete ain't got nothing to do with Shelton Heights either, baby. Half of all marriages end in divorce and—"

"Please, Daddy!" Jan burst into tears. Her emotions were so unstable these days.

"Jan, why are you crying? There's more to this than what you're telling me. Is your mama upsetting you?"

"I'm sorry, Daddy. It's not about Mama. I just had a nightmare and neither Kyla nor I have had a good night's rest since Pete got captured. Maybe you're right. Maybe all this strange stuff has nothing to do with living here, but my baby is all I have left now, and I can't take any chances that something bad will happen to her because I insisted on ignoring all the warnings and living in a community that I knew could be jinxed."

Ted sighed heavily, but Jan could tell that he was up and moving around, preparing to come to her aid. "Have you told your mama about this?"

"Not yet, but I will," Jan replied amid a sniffle.

"And you're sure you want to do this tonight?"

"I'm very sure."

After another quiet pause, Ted said, "I'll be there in ten minutes. That means you have ten minutes to tell your mother. She ain't hardly gonna let me in the house this late if she ain't been told that I'm coming. Knowing her, she won't let me in no way, but I still want you to talk to her."

"I will. Thanks, Daddy."

"Ten minutes," he reiterated.

As soon as Jan hung up the phone, more anxiety began to build. She didn't look forward to talking to her mother, but it had to be done. First, though, she would pack her things. That way, her mom would know that she meant business and there was no talking her out of it. She flung the closet door open and pulled out the empty leather suitcases she had used when she moved from California.

"You have to get out of here, Jan." The pep talk seemed to give her more determination. One at a time, she laid the bags on her bed and unzipped them. Then she went to the wooden drawers and pulled out her clothing by the handfuls, stuffing them in the bags in hurried fashion, not even bothering to place them in any order. She hadn't purchased much since moving to Atlanta, so fitting her garments back in the same cases they'd come in would be no large task.

"Jan." Her mother called her name and opened the door at the same time. All the commotion that Jan was creating had stirred her from her sleep. For a short while, Leona stood in the doorway looking at her, saying nothing more. Jan knew her mother was wondering what all the hustle and bustle was about, but she continued her chore without even acknowledging Leona's presence in the room. "You hear me calling you, girl? What are you doing? Why you pulling all them clothes out, Jan?"

"I'm leaving, Mama."

"Leaving to go where? What in the world?"

"I . . . we . . . Kyla and I are going to stay with Rachel for a while."

"For what?"

"I just need to, Mama," Jan said, not once stopping to look Leona in the face. "I know you're going to think I'm crazy, but I'm just going to tell it like it is. I have to get out of Shelton Heights before something else bad happens."

"What you say, girl? I know I ain't raised you to believe in no witchcraft."

"Mama . . ."

"Jan, the Bible says—"

"I don't care, Mama! I don't care!" Jan screamed the words, taking Leona aback. "Please don't tell me what the Bible says about witchcraft, Mama, because I don't care to hear it."

"Janet Lenore Grimes Jericho!"

Ted had gotten there fast, but the timing of the ringing of their doorbell couldn't be any more perfect. Jan needed her father's backing right now. He would support her even if it was just to oppose her mother.

"Daddy's coming to help me move," Jan blurted as she rushed past Leona, ignoring her scolding calls, and made a beeline for the front door. Hurling it open, Jan froze at the unexpected sight of the two priestly uniformed gentlemen who stood looking down at her with solemn eyes. She'd been a Marine wife long enough to know what it meant when chaplains made personal visits to wives of those in active duty. Looking beyond the men, she saw her father's Chrysler whip into the driveway beside the chaplains' car. He immediately jumped from the driver's seat and began running toward the door. Ted knew what their presence meant too.

"Mrs. Jericho?" one of the men said.

Jan looked at him and opened her mouth to respond, but couldn't. She knew what was about to happen, but she couldn't stop it. Jan had only felt this way one other time in her life and it was five days ago, as she stood in her patient's room, preparing to administer her medication.

"Jan?" Ted said as he stepped between and then in front of the men.

She opened her mouth again, but still too overcome to speak, Jan's knees began collapsing beneath her body weight. The last thing she remembered seeing was her father lunging toward her, and the last thing she remembered hearing was her mother's voice, screaming her name.

Chapter 28

"Are you sure you're all right, Jericho?"

"Yes, sir," Peter whispered, almost cringing as he shifted his body to prevent Colonel Alfred Goodman from touching his shoulder.

This dream was almost like every dream before it. *Almost.* Peter watched closely as Colonel Goodman sat on the floor of the helicopter beside him. But this time, when the man raised his hand to pat Peter on the knee, he couldn't move his leg fast enough. Colonel Goodman made contact, not once, but with three pats in succession. Peter recoiled with regret, fully expecting to wake up and find himself still sitting on the floor of the concrete chamber. But he didn't.

"It's okay, soldier," the colonel said in a comforting tone that suggested that he understood Peter's reaction. "I know you've been through a lot. We're gonna take care of you and get you whatever help you need to work through this. I'm proud of you, Jericho. I'm proud of all of you."

It was then that Peter realized that this time, it was real.

The helicopter ride, his superior sitting beside him, the whole dramatic rescue—all of it was real. He felt dazed, like he was in a state of shock as he lifted his head and looked at the man who sat across from him. Fletcher's eyes were closed, tears streamed down his cheeks, and his lips moved rapidly with no sound coming out of them. Beside Fletcher, Louis lay crumpled on the floor, much like he was when the door to their holding place burst open. At the rear of the helicopter sat three of the men who had risked their own lives to save Peter and his companions. They all looked weary, and for good reason.

What happened? Peter closed his eyes and tried to remember every detail. It wasn't long ago, but he struggled with remembering what had taken place in the last hour. He recalled the noises on the outside of the building where they had been held prisoner. Then there was gunfire that rang out over the sounds of rotating propellers. There had been two helicopters. The other one was carrying the remaining rescuers and was somewhere ahead of the one that carried Peter and his friends.

When the door of the prison house caved in, Peter recalled voices yelling words that echoed around the closed-in space.

"Get down! Get down!" the darkened faces yelled at them. Several of the men carried high-power flashlights, and the beams from them were blinding.

Peter and Fletcher stood their ground, just like they said they would. Even when the men kept ordering them to get on the floor, they stood, trembling, waiting for them to shoot or get close enough to try to grab Fletcher so that they could react according to plan.

"State your names! State your names!"

The orders changed, and that was the moment Peter realized that all of the men were speaking in English—clear, understandable English, with no foreign accents attached. These weren't the Iraqis; these were made up of an army of his own.

Peter's heart leapt. "Peter Kyle Jericho. United States Marines, sir!"

"Jericho!"

When Colonel Goodman stepped from the shadows, Peter tried to stand at attention and salute, but his restraints caused him to topple. Several of the men rushed to his aid.

"Come on, guys; cut them loose," Colonel Goodman ordered. "We've gotta get out of here. Move, move, move!"

Everything before that seemed to happen in slow motion and everything after it in fast forward. The three survivors were rushed to the waiting chopper, and they'd been flying ever since.

"Bigalow and Klauser are dead, sir," Peter heard himself say as his mind floated back to what was happening now.

Colonel Goodman nodded his head slowly. "I'm aware." His eyes were glossy and he looked as if he might cry. "Ramsey, too."

Peter's head hung low. In the drama-filled days since their vehicle was attacked, he'd almost forgotten about Corporal Mike Ramsey, who had died in the crash. "I'm sorry, sir. There was nothing we could do."

"I know, Jericho. There was nothing any of us could do. There's no need for you to feel any responsibility in their deaths. If anyone is responsible, it's me. I take the blame. I should have been able to get to you sooner. We hoped to somehow locate your whereabouts and get to you all before anyone got killed. It was a long shot and it didn't work out that way, but we have to look at the positive side. We have to be grateful that we didn't lose everybody. Corporal Ramsey, Sergeant Bigalow and

PFC Klauser will always be remembered as heroes. And the only difference between them and the three of you is that you all lived to tell the story. You're all heroes."

Their private chat was interrupted by one of the rescuing soldiers. He reached for Peter's arms, and when Peter looked down at his own wrists, he noticed that he was holding them together as if he were still bound.

"Good to have you back with us, Jericho."

Looking up at the man, Peter gave him an appreciative nod. His face was familiar, and Peter knew him as one of the men who'd come over with the same regiment of soldiers as he, but he didn't know his name. The medic poured antiseptic over the areas of Peter's wrists where the flesh had torn from days of being wrapped tightly with stiff, jagged ropes. The resulting pain caused him to flex his muscles and stiffen his whole body in order to endure the sting.

"Sorry, Jericho," he said. "This will be over in a minute."

Peter watched as the man quickly wrapped both his wrists in clean, soft bandages. It was feeling better already. When the man reached for Peter's head, Peter quickly obtained a firm grasp on the medic's wrists to stop him.

"It's gotta be done, Jericho," Alfred said. "Let him do his job."

Peter tried his best to relax as the man gently unwound the soiled cloth that the Iraqis had used. The drying blood that had seeped into the material made the cloth stick to Peter's skin at the site of the wound. He screamed in pain as the medic poured a liquid substance on the area to loosen the attachment. Tears slipped from Peter's eyes, but he hid them behind the new bandages on his wrists.

"You got yourself a beaut, Jericho. I think he's gonna

need a couple of stitches and will most likely need to have a little infection drained," the attendant said as he examined the unhealed injury closely.

"Just clean it real good and patch him up for now. They'll take care of him at the hospital," Alfred replied.

The whole process only took a few minutes, but when it was all done, Peter's head pounded as hard as it had when he first woke from unconsciousness. He tried, without much success, to breathe through the discomfort.

"You okay?"

Opening eyes that he had just closed, Peter looked at Fletcher. He had finished praying, and while the medic now nursed his wrists, Fletcher looked at Peter with concern.

Peter nodded. "You?"

"Yeah," Fletcher said, flinching as one of his wrists was being wrapped. He looked to his left at Louis, who remained in a fetal position, and used his free hand to deliver a supportive pat to his shoulder. "We're all going to be just fine."

"Where are we headed, sir?" Peter asked Colonel Goodman.

"Kuwait City."

Peter remembered that being the same place where the rescued prisoners of war had been taken back in 2003. "Then what?"

Alfred's right eyebrow rose a fraction, as if he were perplexed by the question presented. "Well . . . then you'll be given complete and thorough medical examinations to be sure you're healthy, both physically and mentally. You'll be able to get plenty of rest and some good nourishment for the next forty-eight hours or so. After that, you should be able to go home."

Home. There it was, and the sound of it, just like in his dream, served as a bitter dose of reality for Peter. In his dream, he'd been able to get to Atlanta and eventually, get to his wife and gain forgiveness; but this was real life. All the while that he'd been imprisoned, he'd regretted the fact that he would never get the opportunity to apologize—or so he thought. It was a missed opportunity that haunted him then; now, it was the fear of rejection.

"Switch places with me, Owens," Colonel Goodman said.

Peter watched as Alfred relocated to Fletcher's vacated spot and began helping the medic care for Louis, who hadn't spoken to anyone since they were whisked away to safety.

"I think the guilt is eating at him," Fletcher whispered.

Peter nodded. The soldier who had put on a front of such patriotism and bravery for most of their time together had to be experiencing a great sense of embarrassment at the way he caved in when immediate death seemed like a guarantee.

"I'm still finding it hard to believe that we were saved," Fletcher said. "I had accepted death and had prepared myself for it as much as I could. I never thought—"

"Me either," Peter admitted.

"You know what this means, right?"

Peter looked at Fletcher, but never got an opportunity to speculate.

"It means that God has given me another chance. He's given you another chance, too, bruh."

Peter remained silent, already knowing the road down which the conversation was headed and not at all certain that he wanted to go that route. Fletcher's continuance indicated that Peter didn't have a say-so in the matter.

"I get the chance to lead my family to Christ. *Me*, man," he added with a wide, grateful grin. "I can be the one to get my family in the habit of worshiping on Sunday. I'm looking forward to finding a church home and seeing my wife and son get back to the Christian practices that we all once had, but allowed to die."

The beginning of a smile tipped the corners of Peter's mouth. "You sound excited."

Fletcher cocked his eyebrow questioningly and said, "Aren't you? Man, do you know how close we came to death? I had become what is known on *The Sopranos* as *next*. I was literally minutes away from being butchered, Pete. God gave me this chance. He gave all of us this chance, man."

Peter reached up and touched the fresh bandage that had been wrapped around his wounded head. He knew that everything Fletcher said was right, but their situations were different. Nobody was happier to be alive than Peter, but the "happily ever after" could very well escape him.

"You are going to talk to your wife and daughter, aren't you?" Fletcher asked in the middle of the extended silence.

"I don't know."

"Pete . . ."

"It's not that I don't want to, Flex. You gotta believe that. I do want to, but I don't know if I can. I can't pretend that a lot hasn't happened."

"But you said you'd forgiven for her lying to you, right?"

"I have, but I'd still like an explanation and I'd still like for her to tell me the truth. Plus, there are two of us involved here. I'm not an innocent bystander. She's got to forgive me too, and I don't know where her heart and mind are right now. We've lived in two different worlds, functioning like two separate entities for a long time."

Peter could feel the heat of Fletcher's eyes searing into his skin and he knew that his friend wanted to say more, but Fletcher eventually turned around and relaxed against the wall. Peter knew that Fletcher couldn't understand his hesitation, but that was because he didn't know the whole story. Even if Jan could overlook the mean things he said to her as she and Kyla were leaving for Atlanta, she may not be able to forgive him for everything else. The "everything else" was the part that frightened him the most, but if he was going to regain her full trust and love, he would have to face all of his sins; even the secret ones.

"I need you guys to eat something," Colonel Goodman said as one of the other rescuers began pulling a cooler from the back. He had offered them nourishment shortly after they took flight, but at the time, none of the men were interested in food. "You all look feeble, and while Iraq isn't the most developed country in the world, technically it's not a third world country either; so there's no good reason for me to bring three starving guys back home. We're about ready to land. Eat up."

While he spoke, Alfred handed out turkey sandwiches and cartons of fruit juice. After much coaxing, Louis sat up and now sipped his juice through a straw while keeping his eyes fixed on the floor of the aircraft. Peter and Fletcher ate heartily, the first identifiable meal they'd had in days.

"How long were we there, Colonel?" Peter asked, swallowing the last of his sandwich and reaching out his hand for another.

"Held captive, you mean?"

"Yes, sir."

Fletcher nodded, wanting to know the answer to the same question. "We lost track early on because we were drugged in the beginning."

"Drugged?"

"Yes, sir," Peter explained. "They gave us something in water that put us to sleep, and we don't know how long we were out before finally waking up."

"You were gone for seven days."

"Seven days," Fletcher said.

"It felt longer," Peter remarked.

"*Seven*, Pete," Fletcher repeated. "Seven."

Peter locked into Fletcher's stare, finally grasping the reason for his fixation with the word.

Alfred, on the other hand, was still confused and looked from one man to the next, trying to figure out what it was he had missed. "So?"

"Seven," Fletcher said. "That's the number of times Joshua marched around the walls of Jericho before God gave him the victory. This time around, it was Jericho that won the battle."

Alfred's mouth twitched with a hint of amusement. "Over Joshwa, no less," he said, looking directly at no one and almost seeming to speak to himself.

"What's that, sir?" Peter approached the question with caution.

Looking at both men with illumination in his eyes, Alfred said, "We took a prisoner among the men that camped near the place where you were held. They have him in the other chopper."

Peter's eyes widened. There were several men who had come in and out of the cell during the time they'd been held there. But there was one they saw every single day.

"Tall? Thin? Speaks English?" Fletcher sat forward, voicing Peter's thoughts.

Alfred nodded and retrieved a folded slip of paper from his pocket. "And get this. His name is Joshwa Hassan al-Numan."

Peter's heart pounded at the realization.

Fletcher clapped his hands with elation and then said, "So, God flipped the script? Oh, man! Instead of giving Joshua and his boys the victory over Jericho, like He did in the Bible, He gave Jericho and his boys the victory over Joshwa—and in seven days." Leaning back against the wall and laughing out loud, he added, "Man, I can't even believe I took this long to hook up with a God that is *this* cool! I gotta check my sense of humor, 'cause I think the Lord is trying to upstage a brotha big time."

Chapter 29

Wave after wave of shock slapped at Jan, stinging more than the gentle but effective ones her mother had given her as she and the others struggled to snap her from her daze of near unconsciousness.

"He's . . . he's . . . he's alive?" The astonishment had almost caused the words to wedge in her throat. "Pete is alive?"

Jan sat between her parents, holding both their hands in hers as she looked across the room at the chaplains whose visit she'd misinterpreted. When they pulled her from the floor and ushered her to the sofa where she now sat, the men, who introduced themselves as Nigel Eden and Elliott Slater, shared with her the news of her husband's rescue from enemy territory. Although they'd already told her twice before, Jan needed them to verify again what her ears had heard.

When Chaplain Eden spoke, there was a faint tremor in his voice, as though saying the words caused a sudden emotion to touch him. "In total, we lost three men who were in that particular fire team, but Sergeant Jericho wasn't one of them. Yes, ma'am; he's alive."

Jan could barely hear her father's voice over the pounding in her chest.

"Well, where is he? Is he being taken back to California?"

"No, sir," Chaplain Eden answered. "Their current whereabouts are unknown. Their commanding officer, Colonel Alfred Goodman, reported their rescue at around daybreak."

Elliott Slater interjected. "There is a big time difference between here and Baghdad." He looked at his watch. "Here, it's midnight, Thursday. Right now in Baghdad, it's about eight o'clock on Saturday morning. The ambush to rescue the soldiers happened just a couple of hours ago, between five-thirty and six on Saturday morning."

"Ambush?" Leona scowled as she repeated the word. "Don't that mean that somebody got killed?"

"It doesn't necessarily mean that," Chaplain Slater explained, "but in this particular case, there were several casualties. Not our men, thank God; but several of the Iraqis that were holding them hostage had to be gunned down in order to complete the rescue mission."

"Lord have mercy," she retorted, shaking her head from side to side. "All this killing is against the Word of God. In Deuteronomy 5:17, the Lord told us not to kill. It had to be important because He made it one of His special commandments. How can y'all be a part of this sinfulness? Y'all two men s'posed to be preachers, ain't you?"

Both men looked at her but said nothing.

"Well, is you or ain't you?" Leona urged.

"Mama . . ."

"The Lord say if you be 'shamed of Him before men, He'll be 'shamed of you before His Father in heaven. Y'all 'shamed of being preachers?"

Before the men could answer, Ted jumped in. "You said you didn't know of Peter's whereabouts. Do you really not know or are you just not allowed to tell us?"

"We know they left Baghdad safely," Nigel Eden answered. "At the time, they were headed to Kuwait City, Kuwait, which is about a ninety-minute to two-hour flight. We know where they were scheduled to land, but we haven't had an update, so we don't want to misinform you."

"So, what happens from here?" Leona asked.

"Well, I'm certain there will be a delay in Kuwait before they continue to the U.S. The flight to the States will take quite a number of hours. The plane will probably make at least two stops to refuel and to change pilots, if needed. The journey will take a little more than a full day, I'm certain, but they're in good hands."

Jan heard the conversation as it continued between her parents and the clergymen, but her thoughts were elsewhere. She wasn't quite sure how to react to this sudden, unexpected turn of events. Her emotions were scattered and she tried to pull them and her thoughts together. Jan was both thrilled and terrified to hear of Peter's freedom. Knowing he hadn't met the same misfortune as others in his group was liberating. The news had lifted a burden from Jan's heart, but it left her torn.

Peter had made it clear that he didn't want to be with her. His death, as tragic as it would have been, would have made things less complicated. Jan had found a level of relief in knowing that she wouldn't have to tell her daughter of the permanent dissolution of her parents' marriage. It was something that Kyla never would have had to know. Now, as Jan stared toward the hallway that led to her daughter's bedroom, she knew that she was back at square one. She had to find a way to break the news without breaking Kyla's heart.

"Jan, you hear the man talking to you?" Leona's voice cut into Jan's thoughts.

"I'm sorry?"

"I said is there anything else that you need to know before we leave?"

Looking at Chaplain Eden, Jan shook her head. She had a million questions in her mind, but she knew that he couldn't answer any of them. "No. You've been very helpful. Thank you for coming by to let us know what was going on."

"You're welcome," the chaplain said as he and his colleague stood. "Again, we sincerely apologize for scaring you earlier. I can image how shocking it was to see two chaplains standing at your door at this late hour. But being a long-time military wife, I'm sure you have some idea of how these things work. The military alerts the Casualties Affairs Office and they send over whoever is available to perform whatever duty is pressing at the moment. Tonight, it was the two of us. I'm glad that the news we were delivering was good."

"It's good news, but you might be telling it to the wrong woman."

Jan's head made a swift turn that allowed her to face her mother. She couldn't believe Leona had made the remark. "Mama!"

"No, Jan. Now, these men need to know the truth." Leona turned back to the gentlemen. "Pete wrote a letter to his wife just before he got caught by them soldiers over there, and he told her he didn't love her no more. So, while we're glad that God was merciful enough to spare his life, we're sure that Jan ain't the one he'll be celebrating it with. There's probably some other woman who needs to be hearing this and not Jan."

Clenching her teeth, Jan was furious. She swallowed hard, trying not to reveal her brewing anger, but she glared at her mother with reproachful eyes. Her personal business was not a concern of the two strangers standing in their living room. Though she whispered, her words were singed with displeasure. "You're crossing the line, Mama!"

"What line? The line of the truth? The Bible says in John 17:17 that when we tell the truth, we sanctify the people we talking to. These men need to know the truth about that boy—not just because it's the truth, but because telling it to them will save their souls. Military life will send them to hell, but us telling them the truth will sanctify them and make them holy."

"Woman, shut up!" Ted stood and looked down on Leona, who still sat. A stunned look overshadowed her face, but her ex-husband wasn't finished. "Don't you ever get a nosebleed from being so high and mighty all the time? Now, I don't claim to know all the scriptures like you do, but what you just said sounds so stupid that I'd bet my last dime that you ain't read that verse right."

Jan's blood pounded and her face grew hot with humiliation. She closed her eyes to block out the sight of the astonished expressions on the chaplains' faces as they watched the family drama unfold. It was one thing to have those in her inner circle see the dysfunction of her family, but Jan was utterly disgraced at having it displayed here.

"Bet your last dime? On top of every thing else, you done started gambling too?" Leona said, flinging her arms theatrically. "You gon' bust hell wide open, Ted. A gambler ain't nothing but a thief."

"You got a Bible verse for that too? Tell me where I can find it, Leona. Tell me where I can find it so you can win some more brownie points with Jesus."

"Stop it!" Jan screamed. She had taken all that she could. The tears that ran from her eyes felt warm against her skin. Wiping them away with her hands, she looked at the clergymen. "I'm so sorry." Her voice was just above a whisper.

Both men looked at her with sympathetic eyes, and Jan could only imagine what was going through their minds. She felt their compassion. They pitied her hopeless plight.

"It's all right, ma'am," Chaplain Eden said. "I'm sure you and your family have been under a lot of pressure over the past week."

He'd given her an escape, but Jan felt the need to explain. "My husband . . . Sergeant Jericho and I have been separated for several months—over a year now. But I still appreciate you all keeping me informed. I would have much rather heard this from you than to wait for the news broadcasters to get wind of it. It's been very stressful—the not knowing, especially."

Chaplain Slater nodded. "I imagine so. And I imagine that this information will be plastered all over the morning news. It was important to us that you hear it before the rest of the world does. You deserve that much for supporting your husband, regardless of your current status, as he serves the country with honor."

Jan swallowed, held her chin up and managed to smile convincingly. "Thank you." She stood and shook both gentlemen's hands just before walking them to the door and bidding them a pleasant evening.

"Well, what do you know," Ted said from behind her. "That prayer service that you and your church had tonight must have worked."

Turning to face him, Jan leaned her back against the door and suppressed a sigh. She remained absolutely motionless for a moment and then pressed both hands over her eyes as if they burned with weariness. She didn't know whether to cry, laugh or leap for joy. All of them, and yet none of them seemed like the absolute appropriate reaction.

"Come sit down, baby," Ted said. "This is a lot on you, I know. You need to sit and relax."

"You can go now, Ted," Leona said. "I'll take care of Jan for the rest of the evening. She just needs to go to bed and get some sleep. She can deal with all of this tomorrow."

Jan dropped her hands by her side. "No, Mama. Daddy came by to help me move some of my stuff. I still need his help."

"Girl, you ain't going nowhere. Stop this foolishness. See them men that just left? That right there proved that there ain't no curse on this neighborhood. You were afraid that something bad was going to happen and what happened was something good. Don't that tell you something?"

"Yes, Pete's rescue is something good, Mama. It's something wonderful. Something miraculous, really. But it didn't happen until I made up my mind to move. Good didn't happen until the plan was set in motion, and I can't stop now."

Leona put her hands on her hips. "I can't believe a child that I birthed and raised is talking so foolish. Are you listening to yourself, Jan?"

"Yes, Mama, that's just it. For the first time, I'm listening to myself and doing what I think is best. Pete is alive and I'm glad; but he's still not mine anymore. Since the time that our family got connected to this neighborhood, I've lost my father and my husband, both all of a sudden."

"Jan . . ." Ted reached for her, but Jan stepped away.

"No, Daddy, it's true. I know you still love me and I know you'll always be there for me, Christina and Wanza. I'm sure Pete will always love and be there for Kyla too; but it won't be the same for her and it's not the same for me. Maybe I am foolish, Mama, but I can't chance letting Shelton Heights take anything else from me. I feel alone enough as it is. Don't you?"

Fighting more tears and leaving her parents to their own thoughts, Jan tightened the belt of her robe and walked in the direction of the hallway. Prior to her and Peter's separation, she loved moving. It was one of her favorite parts of being a military wife—transferring from one location to another and getting to travel the world. Now, as she headed toward Kyla's room to wake her for their second move since leaving California, Jan suddenly realized that the thing she used to hold so dear had now become a despicable chore.

Chapter 30

In spite of the fact that Peter recalled the happenings on the helicopter that delivered him and his surviving team members to Kuwait, and the poking and prodding that his body endured early in the morning at the hands of the medical staff who gave him a complete physical examination, it wasn't until he woke up seven hours later, in the military hospital in Kuwait City, that he was fully convinced that his freedom was real. It was the first time in more than a year that his eyes had opened voluntarily, not being forced to do so by the call of duty. Peter had nearly forgotten what it felt like to get a full night of rest. He looked above his head and saw a bag of fluid that was feeding some type of liquid into his arm, by way of a needle.

"How ya feelin', soldier?"

Peter turned his head to the left and saw the brunette beauty who asked the question in an unmistakable Southern accent. He smiled. "I'm alive, ma'am. I can't complain."

"And the whole country—the United States, that is—is celebrating the fact that you're alive. They been talkin' 'bout y'all's rescue on the news all morning and afternoon long."

All morning and afternoon long? Intuitively, Peter scanned the room in search of a clock. "What time is it?"

" 'Round about two in the afternoon." She suddenly reached over and turned up the volume on a radio that sat on a shelf beside where she stood. "They're talking 'bout it again. Hear that?"

Being careful not to disturb the catheter in his arm, Peter brought himself to a seated position and faced the radio as though it were a television. His bare feet dangled off the side of the bed as he listened to his name and the names of the other rescued soldiers called repeatedly throughout the report. Peter hunched over, his arms resting on his thighs as he listened intently, taking in every word. His mouth curved with tenderness and a smile was on the horizon, but it retreated when the reporter began speaking of the Iraqi who had been captured during the ambush.

"The President of the United States and the United States government is celebrating the arrest of Joshwa Hassan al-Numan, one of the men on the top ten most wanted list of Al-Qaeda war criminals. He was taken into custody by the soldiers who rescued Owens, Malloy and Jericho."

As far as Peter was concerned, it was a bittersweet victory. Joshwa needed a dose of his own medicine. He didn't deserve a trial. A trial was a waste of American taxpayers' money. The murderer deserved much worse. Even death was too good for him. Peter's thoughts were reeled in by the correspondent's next words.

"The United States and the United States Marines are

mourning the deaths of those prisoners of war that were murdered this week—killed by the Iraqis. The first to die, twenty-six-year-old Corporal Michael William Ramsey of Virginia Beach, Virginia, leaves to mourn his death a wife and a four-year-old son," the newscaster said, leaving a dramatic pause and then continuing. "Twenty-three-year-old Lance Corporal Silas Royce Bigalow of Iowa City, Iowa, leaves behind a wife and two young children. Bigalow would have turned twenty-four today."

"I didn't know," Peter whispered to himself. But when he heard the last name, it stung in a way that the others hadn't.

"And our youngest American victim of Iraq's most recent violence is Private First Class Charles Martin Klauser, of St. Louis, Missouri. At only nineteen years old, he was not yet a husband, but he has surviving parents, a high school sweetheart whom he wrote letters to often, vowing to marry her when he returned home, and an infant daughter whom he never had the opportunity to meet."

"Sergeant Jericho, are you all right? I didn't mean to upset you."

Not until the attending nurse said those words did Peter realize that water was streaming from his closed eyes. He wiped them away with a twinge of embarrassment, then looked at the woman and managed a small, tentative smile. "I'm fine, ma'am. I just feel like I lost a brother; *three* brothers," Peter quickly amended.

"I can only imagine what y'all went through," the nurse said, placing her hand on her chest. "Every soldier I tend to that's been hurt over there has a different story to tell about the violence and the devastation that he or she was forced to witness."

Colonel Alfred Goodman entered the quarters alongside a doctor, just in time to cut short the image of

Chuck's severed head that had begun forming in Peter's mind. As the colonel neared, Peter straightened his back and saluted.

"At ease, Jericho," Alfred said, and then patted him on the back.

"Well, you look much better this morning." The doctor had a wide-shouldered, rangy body. He smiled and offered Peter his hand. "Dr. Ben Carson. How are you, Sergeant Jericho?"

Peter raised his eyebrows at the sound of the name. "I'm fine; thank you, Doctor."

Dr. Carson grinned. His smile was wide and his uneven teeth were strikingly white in his lightly tanned face. "I'm far too pale to be *that* Dr. Ben Carson, but I get that reaction all the time. I was fortune enough to meet Dr. Benjamin Carson a few years ago when he spoke at a medical convention I attended. He said that I was free to claim him as my brother from another mother, so I do."

"It could happen," Peter said, chuckling.

"You look good, Sergeant," the doctor repeated. "You had a little dehydration, but I think the meds are taking care of that." He pointed at the bag of fluid that hung at the head of Peter's bed. "How's your head feeling?"

Instinctively, Peter reached up and touched the place where the bandage had been. It was no longer there. At that moment, a stored memory flashed before his eyes and Peter reached for the back of his head. "You gave me stitches."

"Yes. You don't remember?"

"I do now; vaguely."

"You were pretty out of it at the time. You only needed eight of them. It wasn't a large wound, just a deep one. For precautionary measures, we're giving you some antibiotics to kill any residual infection. You'll be fine."

"That's good to hear," Colonel Goodman injected.

"How are Owens and Malloy?" Peter asked. He wasn't used to being in a room where they weren't; especially Fletcher.

Dr. Carson and Colonel Goodman exchanged glances.

"They're fine, Jericho," Alfred said.

Their hesitation concerned Peter, but he knew that they wouldn't disclose any personal medical information, so he refrained from pressing the issue. "When can we head back to the States?" Peter looked at the doctor as he asked. Whatever date the man gave wouldn't be soon enough, but he hoped for a date that was sooner rather than later.

"Well, I want to keep you on the fluids for another twenty-four hours. By then, all of your tests results will be back and if everything checks out, so will you."

Peter smiled without words.

"Is there anything else you have concerns about?" Dr. Carson asked.

"No. Not right now."

"Good." The doctor shook Peter's hand again and then turned to face Alfred. "Colonel, I'm going to go and check on the others. Will you be joining me?"

"In a moment, yes. Let me have just a few minutes with Sergeant Jericho."

"Certainly."

When the doctor walked away, the nurse, to whom Peter had never been formally introduced, followed.

"Sleep well, Sergeant Jericho?" Colonel Goodman asked as he took several steps to his right to mute the sound of the radio that the nurse had left on.

"Very well, sir," Peter responded, knowing full well that his sleeping pattern wasn't the real reason for the private chat.

"You heard the news reports, I see."

"Yes, sir. I wish all of us would have made it back alive."

"So do I, Jericho; but this is war. All of us never make it back alive."

"I know, sir."

Colonel Goodman sat beside Peter on the bed. "Each of your families have been notified of your rescue."

Peter stiffened.

"I wasn't aware of your separation."

Rank wouldn't allow Peter to tell Alfred to mind his own business, but he really didn't want to discuss his marriage right now. He remained silent, even through the pause that lapsed. Peter hoped the lingering quietness would somehow transmit the unspoken message to his commanding officer, but it didn't.

"Military life can be very stressful on a marriage, Jericho. I'm a married man and I'm talking from experience. I'm over six-two and my body mass is comprised of 250 pounds of mostly muscle. That woman of mine isn't even five feet tall and she weighs nearly half of what I weigh. But don't let the size fool you. She's a trash-talking, no-nonsense kind of girl who is not intimidated one bit by my stature or my military ranking. But when it comes right down to it, I know she's got my back. You know what I mean? I know she loves me, and if the situation called for it, she'd come to physical blows with anybody who dared to cause me harm."

Peter shook his head. "Well, as much of a turn-on as something like that would be, I can assure you that Jan's not about to scrap it out with nobody because of me. She definitely wouldn't do it now. And I'm not sure that she ever would have. It's just not her personality."

"You'd be surprised," Colonel Goodman said. "Someone once said that a woman was like tea; you never know how strong she is until you dip her in hot water. When the heat is on, our women will do things for us that we might not expect. The point of the matter is that I'd give my life for my wife and I think she'd do the same for me. We have problems just like everybody else, but whatever obstacles we come against, we talk it out, take it to the good Lord and go on.

"I don't know what happened to split your marriage, Jericho, but if you love her and she loves you, fight for it. Don't ever give up on a good thing. I'm speaking, not Colonel to Sergeant, but brother to brother. And when I say brother to brother, I'm not talking about child of a black man to child of a black man. I'm talking about child of God to child of God."

Peter looked at Colonel Goodman and he watched the burly man as he pointed his index finger from himself to Peter. Peter sat quietly with his eyes locked onto Colonel Goodman's as the man continued to speak.

"If your deliverance in Iraq taught you only two things, it should have taught you that everything is not always as it seems, and that nothing is too hard for God. By man's calculations, you should be a dead man right now, Jericho, but when it comes right down to it, God is in control. I *know* you have a strong faith in Jesus Christ. You didn't tell me that, but I've watched you from the time our regiment got together until now. I *know* you're a praying man."

Peter never took his eyes off of Colonel Goodman, even as his commanding officer walked back to the radio and turned up the volume. The newscaster was still talking about the miraculous rescue of the three remaining soldiers.

Pointing at the radio while taking slow steps toward Peter, Alfred said, "You won this one, Sergeant, and that's great; but the fact of the matter is, family comes first. So, regardless of what Owens said,"—he paused and then gently placed his index finger on the left side of Peter's chest, tapping the area behind which his heart rested—"the battle of Jericho really ain't over 'til you win *this* one."

Chapter 31

It would be another four hours before Peter had the opportunity to be reunited with the man who, in seven days, became the best friend he never knew he needed. At 1800 hours, 6:00 P.M. civilian time, the men came together for the first time since being unloaded from the helicopter upon arrival in Kuwait City. Peter and Fletcher shared a long, warm embrace, both of them struggling to remain composed in front of the medical workers who surrounded them.

It was dinnertime and the two men shared a genuine hearty laugh when they looked at their prepared meals.

"Fried pork chops!" Fletcher exclaimed. "I owe the cook a kiss. Where is she?"

When a short, stubby, bearded gentleman raised his hand, a roar of laughter filled the small quarters.

"Ahh, will a simple 'thank you' do?" Fletcher asked.

"Absolutely, sir," the man said, grinning.

"Yes, thank you. This is great," Peter said as he looked at the healthy portion of Cajun chicken gumbo on the plate in front of him. "This is great," he repeated after taking his first bite.

"Where's Sergeant Malloy?" Fletcher asked, looking around as he chewed.

Peter looked too, wondering the same. "I don't know. He's probably on the way."

It was a few minutes later when the men noticed Colonel Goodman entering the area with Louis by his side. He held up his hand to stop Peter and Louis from standing at attention at his entrance. A meal consisting of meatloaf, rice and corn on the cob was placed on the table and Louis sat quietly, not looking at either of the men sitting across from him. Colonel Goodman sat too, and a plate filled with a mix of steamed vegetables and one baked chicken breast was placed in front of him.

Peter's eyes darted to Louis and then back to Alfred. He opened his mouth to speak, but Colonel Goodman shook his head slowly from side to side, silently hushing the remark before Peter could voice it.

"How's the food?" Alfred asked.

"Good," Peter said.

"Almost as good as home," Fletcher agreed.

Colonel Goodman began eating, but Louis remained quiet, with his eyes staring into his plate and his hands resting in his lap. Peter's heart went out to Louis. If his behavior was due to the embarrassment of retreating when he thought death was imminent, Peter wanted to tell him that he was being too hard on himself. The truth of the matter was that if Fletcher had caved when Peter asked if he was ready, Peter would have too. Neither he nor Fletcher held the reaction, no matter how cowardly it was, against Louis and maybe if he knew that, he wouldn't be so withdrawn.

Peter looked at Colonel Goodman for a second time

and his commanding officer must have read his thoughts because once again, the colonel shook his head, denying permission for a request that still went unspoken. Returning his attention to the plate in front of him, Peter resumed eating.

"It looks like you guys are going to be able to head back to the U.S. tomorrow."

Fletcher's eyes lit up like a child's on Christmas Day. "Have we been cleared already, sir? The doctor told me that he wouldn't know for another twenty-four hours."

"We won't have the final word until then, but early signs indicate that you will be on a plane by this time tomorrow. I don't want you to get too excited, though, because you won't exactly be headed home just yet."

Peter and Fletcher exchanged glances. Colonel Goodman continued.

"We're going to send all of you to VA Greater Los Angeles Healthcare System for further testing before fully releasing you."

"Why is that, sir?" Peter asked. "It feels like we've already been given every medical workup known to man—both physical and spiritual."

Alfred smiled, aware that Peter was referring to the talk they had just hours earlier. "I know, Jericho. But when soldiers have been through all that the three of you have been through, we can't be too careful. You all endured a great deal of physical and psychological trauma. You not only saw comrades dragged away to their deaths, but you were forced to look at portions of their dead carcasses." He shot a glance at Louis and continued. "Under the circumstances, some of you have slept remarkably well since being rescued, but others have not slept at all. How you've coped with everything in the past hours since your freedom plays a heavy part in all of this. Even if Dr. Carson releases you all tomorrow, he's already told me that he is doing so under strict recommendations that each of you have an extensive psychological evaluation to check for PTSD."

"Post-traumatic Stress Disorder." Immediately, Peter knew that it was more for Louis than Fletcher and him.

"That's right, Jericho. I know you may feel fine right now and your greatest desire is probably to go home and be with your families, but the Marines are responsible for you beyond today. We have to be concerned with your tomorrow and your next week; your next month, even. This complete analysis may seem pointless to you, but it is very necessary for your total well-being."

"How long will we have to stay there, sir?" Fletcher asked, breaking a short silence.

"There's no absolute answer to that question, Sergeant. It may be a longer process for some of you than for others." Colonel Goodman was careful to keep his eyes on Fletcher and Peter. "Ultimately, that decision will be left to the professional discretion of your assigned physician."

Fletcher seemed disappointed as he placed his fork on his plate. "What about our families, sir? Will they be able to visit us at the hospital?"

"I'm sure that would be contingent upon the predicted length of your stay there. If everything checks out well, you may be in and out inside of twenty-four hours. In such a case, I doubt your families will be encouraged to visit you, because in a short while, you'll be back with them anyway. If your doctor there feels that you need to stay longer for treatment, then yes, your families will be allowed to visit.

"Each of your families will be contacted as soon as we know for sure the date you will be landing on American soil, and of course, the armed forces will provide the means for them to be onsite when you arrive in California." He looked at Peter and then continued. "You will be able to be greeted by family members and to spend a few minutes with them and with the media before being taken to the hospital, but we won't allow media at the hospital at all; and we'll discourage family from visiting you at the facility until the length of your stay is determined."

Knowing that his family would be able to greet him seemed to be enough for Fletcher. He smiled to himself as he leaned back in his seat and began eating the rest of his food. When Peter saw his friend's happiness, his mouth curved into an unconscious smile. He was genuinely happy for Fletcher, but couldn't help feeling a prelude to the loneliness that would await him at the gate.

Chapter 32

"Mama, wake up! Look!" Kyla watched as Jan's eyes flew open and she sat straight up in the bed.

"What? What's the matter?" Her eyes took a quick scan of the room, trying to find the emergency that had called for her daughter to wake her.

"Nothing's wrong, Mama." Kyla laughed at her mother's wild-eyed appearance. "I just wanted you to see this."

Jan turned toward the television in the direction of Kyla's pointing finger. While her mother rubbed her eyes for clarity, Kyla bounced on the bed, almost unable to contain her joy. Together, they listened to the reporter tell the story of the pending return of the U.S. soldiers that had been rescued in Iraq. The last day and a half had been sheer jubilation for Kyla. Ever since her mother woke her up, merely minutes after the clergymen left her grandmother's house, and told her that her father had been rescued, Kyla had hardly been able to eat or sleep.

"Daddy's coming home," she sang. "Now we can all get back together again, right?"

Kyla looked at her mother, and even though a smile trembled over Jan's lips, she didn't appear to be happy. Kyla knew that Jan was tired from the lack of sleep since they moved into Rachel's house, and seeing her weariness made Kyla regret her selfish decision to wake her.

"I'm sorry, Mama. Go back to sleep. They'll be talking about this all day long. You can watch it later."

"Well, I'm woke now, Kyla," Jan said, looking at the clock on the wall. "I should have been up three hours ago. I never sleep this late on Saturday. It's already almost noon." Jan stretched her body as she spoke.

Not an ignorant child, Kyla knew that her mother had doubts about whether she and Peter would reconcile. They had been apart for a long time, and while Kyla loved living in Atlanta and didn't like the notion of leaving behind the friends she had made, she would readily give it all up to have her family back together. Her father had promised her, in a letter he sent just prior to leaving for Iraq, that he would mend the family when his time at war was done, and she believed him. Whatever it took to make it happen, she knew Peter would do.

"I'm so tired," Jan said through a weary yawn as she removed the covers from her legs.

"That's 'cause you still haven't caught up on your sleep from when Rachel came home early from work yesterday." Kyla laughed at the thought of it all. "Whichever side of the family she gets her craziness from, I hope I don't catch it."

"Go wash your face," Jan said, laughing with her. "I promised your grandmother that we would come by her house for lunch today. We're supposed to be there in less than an hour, so hurry."

Kyla jumped from the bed, leaving her mother watching the latest news updates on television. Stepping into the hallway, Kyla heard sounds from the television in the living room. The channel was set on the Comedy Central station, and they weren't playing any of the updates on her father's release. Kyla knew that her mother's best friend wasn't Peter's biggest fan and probably had heard enough of the continuous broadcasting. She could hear Rachel doing something in the kitchen area, and with only one bathroom in the apartment, Kyla jumped at the opportunity to get in before anyone else needed to.

Rachel's apartment was cozy and nicely decorated. Kyla had always enjoyed the few times that she'd come over with her mother for a visit. But living here was a different story. The apartment was much smaller than her grandmother's house, and although she loved her mother, she didn't exactly like having to share a bedroom with her. At Leona's she could decorate her room the way she wanted. Posters of her favorite movie stars and entertainers decorated her walls, and there was enough space on her dresser to display her honor trophies and the recognitions she'd received from her participation in track and field and cheerleading. In her mother's room, she couldn't showcase any of those; not to mention the fact that she couldn't display her favorite photo of her and her dad. Jan hadn't forbade it, but knowing the circumstances, Kyla just didn't feel comfortable placing the picture on the corner of the dresser that housed her other things.

After rinsing the soap from her face, Kyla turned off the faucet and blindly felt around the counter for the towel she'd placed there just moments earlier. Even Rachel's towels weren't as comfortable and soft as the ones at her grandmother's house. The bathroom door was closed, but

Kyla could hear Rachel in the living room, laughing at something on television.

"She sounds like Julia Roberts on crack," she remembered her father saying about Rachel's laughter. While his description was a bit over dramatized, it wasn't by much. In the smaller quarters of Rachel's apartment, her laugh sounded louder and more annoying than ever. Everything about Rachel, in Kyla's opinion, was overdramatic. When she talked, her body gestures were exaggerated and she seemed to always make every situation more theatrical than it had to be.

Last night was a good example of that. Just as Jan had asked, Ted helped them move a few items into Rachel's apartment. It was nearing two in the morning by the time they'd packed and transported the belongings from Shelton Heights to their new quiet neighborhood, and the move had been quite uneventful until Rachel arrived.

"Girl, I got your message," she said as soon as she burst through the front door of the apartment, winded as if she'd run the distance, instead of driven from her job to her house.

"Rachel, what are you doing here? I thought you didn't get off until seven," Jan said.

"I do," Rachel said as she began tidying the living room, hurriedly gathering items in a floral decorated box that she'd left on her coffee table and then straightening a stack of magazines that was in disarray. "Well, I guess I don't anymore," she said. "I heard your message on my cell and I thought I'd come and help you."

"You didn't have to do that, Rachel. I told you Daddy was going to help me."

"I know I didn't have to, Jan. I did it because I wanted to. Men aren't the best creatures to have around to help set up a house. Where is Uncle Ted? Is he gone already? See what I mean?"

"I told him he could leave, Rachel. He helped Kyla and me bring our things over and once we were situated, he left. It's not like I was moving into my own place and needed help in setting up a whole house. I can't believe you got off from work for this."

"You might have needed me," Rachel called from her room, where she had gone to put her things away.

"Rachel, if I needed you, I would have called. You're making me feel like I made you miss out on that extra money you wanted to make."

Rachel rejoined them in the living room. "Girl, don't even worry about it. I was really ready to leave after that long meeting. I need to rest up anyhow; I got another date with the rich white cardiologist. He has a friend who's a neurosurgeon. You wanna double date?"

Kyla saw her mother's eyes bulge with disbelief as she looked in her direction and then back at her cousin. "Rachel!"

"Oops," Rachel said, accompanying the word with a loud laugh and then a halfhearted, "Sorry."

"You should be."

Rachel shrugged. "Well, at some point you're gonna have to face the facts, Jan. Kyla's not a baby and opportunities like this won't come around every day. You'd better get in while—"

"Pete got rescued."

When Jan said those words, Rachel's jaw dropped like a foul ball in Turner Field. Kyla had wanted to be the one to break the news. But while she was looking for just the right moment to do so, all the while hearing Leona's voice in the back of her head telling her to stay out of grown folks' business, Jan beat her to the punch. Either way, the moment was golden, and Kyla would have loved to have a still frame image of Rachel's stunned expression. It was clearly not what she expected to hear.

"What?" The word could barely be heard over Rachel's gasp.

"Military chaplains came by Mama's house and told us just before we left to come over here."

"But how? When? What happened?"

"Apparently, the U.S. sent out a search party to find out where the men were being held, and when they found out the information that they needed, they carried out an ambush of their own. Kind of like a hostile take-over, I guess. They aggressively went in before daylight and took them back. They killed several Iraqi soldiers in the process."

"Granddaddy said that the prayer at New Hope worked," Kyla threw in just for good measure.

After that, she didn't know what happened. The happy child left her mother and Rachel to themselves while she went to bed to finish up on the sleep she started before leaving Leona's house. Kyla knew that the second half of her night's rest would be far more peaceful than the first. Her father was alive and well, and New Hope wasn't the only body of people who had been praying for that. God had answered her prayers too. She dozed off shortly after crawling into the bed, but she remembered waking up briefly when her mother finally joined her around six in the morning. What she and Rachel had to talk about for all that while, Kyla wasn't sure.

On most days, Kyla liked Rachel because of her colorfulness and because of the fact that she sometimes purposefully ruffled Leona's feathers. It was always entertaining to see the two of them butt heads. But the thirteen-year-old didn't like the way Rachel spoke negatively of her father. Jan tried to keep all of her conversations with Rachel concerning Peter private, but Kyla sometimes overheard them.

By the time Kyla walked out of the restroom, her mother was emerging from their bedroom, looking refreshed, despite her abbreviated sleep.

"Hey. Where are you all headed?" Rachel asked when both Kyla and Jan entered the living room.

"When we left last night, Mama asked if I was so scared of the legend of Shelton Heights that I wouldn't come by for lunch." Jan smiled. "I told her I'd come by, but that I would take her out to lunch instead of us eating in. You know, Picadilly used to be her favorite restaurant to stop by after church when we were kids. There's one on Memorial Drive and she hasn't been in a while, so I think I'll take her. You wanna join us?"

No, no, no, no, no! Kyla screamed in her head. She wanted to be able to celebrate Peter's release without any negative feedback from Rachel. It would be quite enough to deal with her grandmother.

"No thanks," Rachel replied to Kyla's relief. "I would, but I need to find myself an outfit for tonight."

"Okay," Jan said as she leaned over to hug Rachel. "I know I've said it a million times, but I really do appreciate everything you've done for me and Kyla. I promise we won't be here much longer. I don't want to become a problem for you and your dates."

"What problem? He's got two houses, girl. Believe me when I say you're not going to impede anything we have planned. You and Kyla are welcome to stay here forever if you want."

Forever. The word had never rung so loudly in Kyla's ear. Rachel didn't expect her parents to ever make amends, and it didn't look like Jan held out much optimism either. But Kyla refused to allow the doubts of the grown-ups to take away the only hope that kept her going.

The ride to her grandmother's house was less than twenty minutes. Kyla would have to get used to the longer car ride because now, with their new living arrangement, Jan would have to drive her to school on a daily basis. She'd miss standing at the bus stop with K.P., Tyler and the Lowman boys, but . . .

Why are all of your friends boys? Kyla's thoughts were interrupted by the line she remembered from one of her father's last letters, and she almost laughed out loud as her mother maneuvered their car into her grandmother's driveway.

"Come on in," Leona said when they reached the front door. "How y'all doing?" She walked with a slight limp that she didn't have yesterday or any of the days prior to it.

"Fine, Mama," Jan replied. "How are you?"

"Well, my bones are aching a little bit, but I s'pose I'll make it. Since I'm living by myself now, I gotta pray a little harder that the Lord keeps me with my health and strength."

Kyla looked up at Jan and set her lips so that she wouldn't laugh. She could tell from the look in her mother's eyes that she was trying to do the same. The dramatics definitely came from the Ellis side of the family.

"You got some mail there on the table," Leona said to Jan while she hobbled down the hall to get her purse.

"I got something UPS?"

"Yeah," Leona called back. "It's a military shipment and I had to sign for it, so I hope it ain't divorce papers. That boy free now, so ain't nothing holding him back."

Her words struck a nerve with Kyla, and she wanted to snatch the envelope from her mother's hand and throw it out with the garbage. It must have had a similar effect on

Jan because Kyla watched her hold the envelope in her hand for several moments as though she was contemplating whether to even view the contents.

"You want me to open it, Mama?" Kyla couldn't even believe she'd asked the question. She didn't want to open it any more than Jan did.

Jan looked at her and smiled. "No, sweetie."

Kyla wiggled onto the space beside Jan as she sat on the sofa, staring at the brown-and-white cardboard envelope. Unless divorce papers only consisted of two or three sheets of paper, the packet looked far too thin to be the forms that her grandmother predicted. When Jan began tearing away the strip that kept the envelope sealed, Kyla held her breath. *Daddy wouldn't do this. He promised that he would work on settling things on his return, and now that he is back, he wouldn't go back on his word. Daddy wouldn't lie. He just wouldn't.*

"What is it, Jan?" Leona asked as she walked into the room just in time to see her daughter slip her hand inside the opening.

"It's another envelope," Jan said when she viewed the contents.

"What's in it, Mama?" Kyla leaned in to see what would be revealed next.

Leona inched closer too. "Yeah, Jan; what they got in there?"

"Plane tickets. Two tickets to California." Jan said the words as if talking to herself. Handing the tickets to Kyla, she unfolded the paper that had shared the envelope with them. Her eyes scanned the wording quickly. "Pete is catching a flight to Los Angeles tomorrow. He'll be landing on Monday, and the tickets are for us to be there to greet him."

"Lord have mercy, girl. What you gon' do?"

Jan stared at the tickets, slowly shaking her head from side to side. “I don’t know. Under the circumstances, I don’t think it would be proper for us to be there.”

Kyla looked at her mother with earnest eyes. “Oh, please, Mama; can we go? I wanna see Daddy. Please?”

Chapter 33

Most times, when Peter flew from one assignment to another, the time passed rather quickly. But as they now made the twenty-five hour flight to Los Angeles, every hour felt like two. Just like in his dreams, Colonel Goodman accompanied them along with a medic, who at first seemed like an unnecessary addition to the crew. Just three hours into the flight, Peter realized that the medic's presence was one they could not have done without.

"I don't understand what happened," Fletcher said after Louis woke up from his second nightmare, screaming and violently swinging at images that were apparently locked in his psyche. "He was fine right up until the time that we were rescued."

Peter watched Colonel Goodman effortlessly wrestle Louis to the floor and hold him there. This time, instead of just waking him up and helping him back to his seat as they'd done before, the medic injected a needle in Louis' arm. Shortly thereafter, the traumatized soldier was guided to his seat and strapped in. His eyes were open, but clearly, the medicine had served as a sedative.

"Like Colonel Goodman said earlier, the effects of war can creep up on a man. I hope he's going to be okay. I hope *we're* going to be okay." As Peter spoke the words, his eyes followed his commanding officer. Colonel Goodman dropped into a nearby seat and leaned his head against the window. It was paining him to see one of his men suffering.

"You think your family is going to meet you when we land?"

Fletcher's question pulled Peter's attention away from the happenings in front of him. Turning to face Fletcher, he shrugged his shoulders while simultaneously shaking his head. "I doubt it."

"Do you *want* them to be there?"

Peter took a moment to mull over a question that should have been simple to answer. There was no doubt that he wanted to see his wife and daughter. The apprehension lay in what he would say to them. There weren't any right words except to apologize and somehow, saying "I'm sorry" just didn't seem like enough. For more than a year, he'd allowed his own stubbornness to keep him apart from them. He'd missed both Kyla's and Jan's birthdays, his and Jan's thirteenth anniversary, all of his daughter's PTA meetings, honors programs and every holiday that had come and gone since his disagreement with Jan. Even when he factored in the lie that Jan had told him, there was no good reason for his absenteeism.

"Well, do you?"

"Of course I do. I don't expect them to be there, but if they are, I'd be happy. I don't know what I'd say to them or even what they'd say to me, but seeing them . . ." Peter allowed his voice to drift and then released a burdened sigh. "It would be nice. You know?"

Fletcher smiled. "Yeah, man. Nothing like a near death experience to make you want to celebrate life with the people you love most."

"Yeah."

"I always did love Chantel and Flex, Jr.," Fletcher continued, "but I have to admit that there have been times when I've taken both of them for granted. When we were over there, I kept trying to imagine what their lives would be like without me. My wife is a nice looking woman, Pete. Men would have been chasing her before my body could turn cold, and I didn't even want to think about her being with another man. And Flex, Jr. . . . well, you know that boys that have to grow up without their fathers have a higher chance of turning to drugs and violent crimes. I didn't want them to have to live without me, and I wouldn't want to live without them either."

"Yeah," Peter said for the second time.

"What about Jan?"

"What about her?"

"Is she pretty?"

"Man, yeah," Peter said, his mouth curling into a reflective smile. "Plus she's fine, so I know the fellas would be all over her if she ever became available. And then there's Kyla. In a few years she'll start to date, and I need to be around for that just in case I need to shoot somebody. There's some snot-nosed boy in Atlanta that she spends a lot of time around."

"Puppy love?"

Peter grunted. "Not according to Kyla, but I'm not convinced."

"Well, you definitely need to be checking that out."

"Right."

"So, you're gonna work on putting the Jericho family back together, then?" Fletcher's voice asked a question, but his eyes made a statement.

Peter looked at his friend and then at his commanding officer, who had now dozed off as he sat with his head rested against the side of the cabin. It had been a long couple of days for Alfred. He'd been so busy taking care of his soldiers that he'd had little time to rest his own body.

"Colonel Goodman broke it down for me real good yesterday," Peter said.

"Yeah?"

"Yeah. I have to fight for her, Flex. Whatever it takes, I have to fight for Jan with just as much determination as I fought for my country. Family comes first, right?"

"Right. That's good to hear, man. That's what I've been wanting to hear you say. Fight for them, Pete; *both* of them."

Peter shook his head no. "I don't have to fight for Kyla. That's my baby girl and she loves me no matter what. If her mother and I called it quits, she'd be real disappointed, but I think Kyla would forgive me once she was convinced that I'd be there for her regardless. But Jan . . . Jan is a different story. She's the one that I'm going to have to fight for. I hurt her on more than one level in all of this, Flex. I said things, I've done things—I'm going to have to fight for her love and her trust. It took seven times of marching around the city for Joshua to get the victory over Jericho. It took seven days of captivity in Iraq for Jericho to get the victory over Joshwa. I don't know how long this next battle is going to take, but if it takes me seven days, seven weeks or seven years, I have to fight for Jan."

Chapter 34

According to their normal worship schedule, she should have been sitting in the pews of Glory Temple with Leona, but on Sunday morning, Jan made the decision to fellowship with the body of saints who had set aside a special night just to pray for a miracle on her behalf. She and Kyla arrived early, even before the start of the service, and when Jade saw them enter the foyer of the church, she embraced both of them and insisted that they sit with her family.

"Hey, Jan. Good to see you this morning."

Jan smiled at Hunter's words as he met them halfway down the aisle and escorted them to their seats. He was so tall, broad-shouldered and handsome. Jan hoped that she wasn't visibly blushing. It sure felt like it. "Thanks. I was hoping for a chance to speak to you today. I wanted to thank you for the touching article on forgiveness that appeared in this weekend's edition of your paper. It was really powerful and I appreciate your allowing Kyla to work on it with you. She got a real kick out of seeing her name in print, not to mention the photo of her and her father."

"It was my pleasure. It was way more her work than mine. I'm real big on fatherhood, so when a girl has such high regard for her dad like Kyla does, it's worth printing." Hunter winked at Kyla as he spoke. "I'm thinking of starting a youth corner in the newspaper. Think about letting her submit something on a regular basis."

Jan nodded in approval, and Kyla's grin reflected the sentiment that she would enjoy the opportunity to do something like that. The ability to write was a gift that the child had inherited from her father. Peter had always been good with words, and Jan believed he had the potential to be a bestselling author if he ever desired to follow that path.

The view provided from the section reserved for the pastor's family and special guests was so unlike the one afforded from the rear that it almost looked like they were in a different church. Malik beamed when he spotted Kyla approaching, as though he hadn't just seen her yesterday when Jan took her to Greene Pastures to spend the afternoon with her friends. For her own reasons, Kyla wasn't very happy today, but she managed a smile in Malik's direction. Jan noticed that her daughter's grin widened just a bit when Jerome Tides walked by with his brother, Minister Jackson Tides, and stopped to kiss Kyla on the forehead.

"God is still in the miracle-working business," First Lady Mildred Tides said as she walked over to hug Jan. Before Jan could respond, she continued. "The same God that delivered my husband has delivered yours. Satan tried to take him once, baby. Don't sit by and give that old devil the chance to take him again."

Jan swallowed and then looked in the direction of Jade, who was now standing off to the side, chatting with

Hunter, Kenyatta and Stuart, the handsome, midnight-skinned security guard who had come to speak at the Women of Hope meeting. Hearing Mildred's words, Jan couldn't help but wonder if Jade had been discussing her situation with her mother-in-law.

"Hey, Tyler; come sit with us!" Malik called to the boy standing next to Stuart.

Jan's eyes were fixed on the child who looked to be about the same age as Malik and Kyla. She'd never seen him before, but assumed he was Stuart's son since he looked so much like him; only not nearly as dark. The scene prompted her to recall Kenyatta's reference to her brother and nephew who lived in Shelton Heights. Putting two and two together, Jan concluded that Kenyatta King and Stuart Lyons were siblings. *That's why she was so friendly with him at the meeting.*

"I prayed for you last night." Mother Tides brought Jan's eyes and attention back to her as she spoke. "The Lord showed me where the enemy was out to destroy your marriage in a way that defies even your own understanding. I don't know the details of your situation, baby, and the God-in-heaven truth is, it don't matter none anyhow. All I know is that the Lord sent you to this church today for a reason, and a part of that reason was so that you could hear what I had to say. The Lord put you and that soldier together, Sister Jan; you hear me?"

Jan nodded, her eyes bordered with tears. She desperately wanted to believe what her ears were hearing, but she had too much evidence that proved otherwise to be able to fully accept it. Even if God had put them together, if Peter didn't want to be with her, did God's plan even matter?

"And you know what happens when God has His hands on something?" Mildred looked her straight in the eyes as she posed the rhetorical question. "The devil will use whoever he can, however he can, and whenever he can, to try and demolish it. He will do anything to shake your faith. Satan is a conniving little devil and the Bible says that he comes for one purpose and one purpose only: to kill, steal and to destroy. The scripture says that he walks to and fro in the earth, seeking whomever he may devour. And you best believe the people he seeks to destroy most are the children of God. He already got them other folks. It's *us* that he's after. If he can kill your faith, he can steal your marriage and destroy your victory. Don't let him take away your victory."

As the final words left Mildred's mouth, the organist began playing soft music, signifying the start of the service. Jan was pulled in for one final hug, and she bit her lip to control the sob that felt as though it wanted to choke her. When Mildred left her and the congregation rose for the opening prayer, Jan took that moment to wipe away tears that managed to escape. She was more torn than ever before. Yesterday, Jan had polled all of the people that she knew loved her the most, and until now, she thought her decision was final.

Ted told her that he had mixed emotions. He'd always respected his son-in-law for the way he'd stepped up to the plate and taken responsibility for his unborn child after Jan's premarital pregnancy was discovered. Ted valued the fact that Peter had been a good husband and father, and he was proud of the honorable service that he had given to his country. But the letter that had been written to Jan overshadowed all of that. Speaking honestly, Ted told his daughter that he didn't understand why she'd even want to see Peter after all he'd done.

"I want to see him too," Ted concluded. "But I want to see him so that I can punch him in his face. He did you and Kyla dirty, Jan, and it's gonna take a long time for me to forgive him for that. I'm glad those folks didn't kill him, but to be honest, if they had-a broke both his legs, I'd say he had it coming."

It was the first thing Ted and Leona had agreed on since her father had come for a visit. Jan's mother had made it known clearly that she didn't think it was a good idea for her to go to California. As a matter of fact, according to Leona, to do so would be a sin.

"That's the devil trying to get you to go against both God and nature," Leona emphasized. "Common sense ought to tell you that you ain't gonna do nothing but make a fool of yourself if you go flouncing your narrow end all the way to California to meet that boy and you run into some other woman who's there to meet him too. What you gon' do when you see that, Jan? And how is something like that gonna affect my granddaughter? Plus—and I told y'all this a long time ago when y'all were children—the Lord ain't never meant for us to fly. And if the devil can make you look like a fool and then make you go against God's will on top of that, then he got you just where he wants you."

"Mama, none of us know for certain that Pete has another woman. You let Rachel plant that in your head and both of you have been running with it ever since. And I've never understood why you insist on thinking that getting on an airplane is a sin."

"It's in the Word, Jan. I ain't insisting on nothing. I'm telling you what the Lord said. When the people of God stop trying to get around His Word, this world will be in a better place."

"For years, I've heard you say that it's in the Bible, Mama, but to be honest with you, I've never read it or heard it preached from the pulpit."

"That's 'cause all these modern day preachers are half scared to preach anything that they know people won't agree with. Everybody trying to fill up the church and while they're shouting, what they're really doing is dancing around the Word, trying to avoid reading certain scriptures because they know it will hit home and they'll lose members. God ain't never meant for man to fly, and I believe with my whole heart that anybody who dies in an airplane crash goes straight to the pits of hell."

"You don't really believe that, Mama."

"Jan, if you die in sin, then in sin you shall remain. And a sinner can't make it into heaven."

"Where is it said in the Bible that flying is a sin, Mama?"

"You challenging me? Girl, you know I read the Bible every day. I know my Word like I know my Jesus, so if I say it's in there, you can stake your life on it. In Matthew 28:20, the Lord says, '*lo*, I am with you always, even 'til the end of the world.' "

Jan took a moment to reorient herself, then said, "And that means it's a sin to fly?"

"Anything you do that God ain't with you when you do it is a sin, Jan."

A tumble of confused thoughts and feelings assaulted Jan. She sat back, momentarily so confused and badgered that she couldn't speak. Her quietness didn't adequately conceal her inner turmoil because Leona looked at her and shook her head in obvious shame.

"As much as I brought my children up to know the Lord, I don't know how in the world you got to be so ig'nant about the Word of God." Clearly running short on patience, Leona placed her hands on her hips. "He said, '*lo*, I am with you always,' Jan. He ain't said nothing 'bout high. That means we need to stay on the ground if we want God's protection. He ain't promised us no protection in the air. And if God ain't getting on no plane, He don't intend for us to get on one either."

Even now, as Jan stood and clapped to the music that accompanied the praise team, she was barely able to keep from laughing at the thought of it all. Ultimately, she made the decision not to go to California, but not because of her mother's misguided scriptural reference, but because of what Rachel said last evening when they sat up talking after Kyla had been sent to bed.

"Jan, it's really not about whether Pete wants to be with another woman. What this is about is the fact that he *doesn't* want to be with you. You might be torn between believing or not believing that there is some other woman involved, because you're right when you say that we don't know that for sure. But the one thing you *do* know for sure is that Pete no longer wants to be with you. And while Aunt Leona—bless her heart—is way off base with her conviction that flying is a sin, she ain't nevah lied when she said you'd look like a fool flying all the way to California, chasing after a man who has made it very clear that he doesn't love you."

Rachel was right, and remembering her words dried up Jan's earlier desire to laugh. Her decision to rip into shreds the complimentary airline tickets came to Kyla's dismay, but Jan stood her ground, knowing that she was doing the right thing for both of them. Or so it seemed. But now, just when she thought she had it all figured out, Mother Tides' words rang in her ear, bringing back the uncertainty that Jan thought she'd finally put to rest.

Lord, please show me your will for my life. What is it that you *want me to do?* The thought froze in Jan's brain and a terrifying realization washed over her. This was the first time she'd gone directly to God and asked for guidance. Before now, she'd sought answers through other people: Leona, Rachel, Ted, even Jade. Astonished at the sense of fulfillment she felt in knowing she'd finally released her problem, Jan sat, as directed by the pastor and exhaled, feeling lighter than she had in months.

"Let's give God a handclap of praise," Reverend Tides

said as he laid his open Bible on the book board in front of him. "He answered our prayers, saints. He didn't have to do it, but He did. Give Him praise!"

The applause sounded like thunder to Jan's ears. She returned to a standing position along with the rest of the congregation and clapped until her palms burned. No matter what the outcome of her marriage, God had indeed answered the cries that had been sent up to heaven just three days ago. Jan could only trust that He'd do the same with the request she'd made less than three minutes ago because more than ever, she needed His guidance.

"You may be seated," Reverend Tides said. "Now, turn to your neighbor and say, 'If God did that, then He can do this.'"

When Jan turned to look into Jade's eyes, she knew in advance that the Lord had tailor-made today's sermon just for her.

Chapter 35

"Okay, guys, the pilot says that we have begun the landing process and should be on the ground and at the terminal in the next twenty minutes or so."

Colonel Goodman was directing his words at Peter and Fletcher only. Louis had been sedated for most of the flight and remained quiet and detached as he sat in the same seat, in the same position where he'd been placed after Colonel Goodman and the medic wrestled him to the floor for the third time.

"Security officials are going to be on the grounds and throughout the terminal so that we can have as much of an uneventful disembarkation as possible," the colonel said, taking Peter's attention away from his mentally imbalanced comrade. "I can tell you now that the media is at the airport in full force, but that's not anything that we didn't expect. Security will make sure they don't get too close.

"Ground transportation will be out front, waiting to take the two of you to your respective undisclosed hotels, where you'll be allowed to spend the night. Sergeant

Malloy will be taken directly to the hospital. His family has been notified and they will meet us there. If you have family at the terminal, they can go with you to the hotel. You'll also be assigned security, and hopefully, that will ensure an enjoyable and quiet evening with your family. Tomorrow, you'll be checked into the hospital and will spend at least twenty-four hours there before being released."

Peter's heart pounded within the confines of his chest. He was very much looking forward to stepping out onto American soil, but he could appreciate returning even more if he didn't have to celebrate his homecoming alone. Curiosity forced him to ask, "Do you know whether we have family waiting on us?"

When Colonel Goodman looked at him, his eyes answered the question before his lips even began moving. "At the last report that I received from the ground, there is family waiting for Owens on the grounds and Malloy at the hospital, but no one had checked in for you yet."

Hearing the words would have been far more devastating had Peter not expected them. Still, the pain they brought mercilessly carved lines on his face. Nodding slowly, Peter silently accepted the harsh truth.

"I'm sorry, man," Fletcher said. His expression said he meant it.

"Yeah; me too," Peter said with a faint smile that struggled to form.

"You're welcome to come and hang out with me and my family, Pete. As a matter of fact, I'd love to have you meet and get to know them."

"Thanks, Flex. But I think you might have better things to do tonight that my presence might hinder."

Fletcher shook his head. "No, man. You being there won't be a problem."

"Hey, man," Peter said, holding up his hands. "I want

to try a lot of things before I die, but that ain't one of them."

"You stupid," Fletcher said through a burst of laughter. "What I meant was Flex, Jr. will be there, so me and Chantel won't be taking our celebration that far; not tonight, anyway. I mean it, Pete. You can come and hang out with us. I won't feel right knowing that you're by yourself. We've stuck together this long. Might as well keep on hanging tough, man."

This time Peter's smile came easily and it was genuine. He couldn't remember the last time he wanted to tell a man that he loved him, but the words to Fletcher were hanging off the edge of Peter's tongue. If it weren't for the close ears of their commanding officer and the medical personnel who were riding along with them, Peter would have made his thoughts audible.

"What do you say?" Fletcher urged. "It'll be fun."

"Thanks, man, but no thanks. I really do appreciate the offer, though."

"I mean it, Pete."

"I know you do, Flex, and that's why it means so much to me that you would offer to lend me your family. I mean, I still want to meet your people and all, but I think that time alone may be just what I need. I've got to find out the next step in this ongoing battle that I'm in." Peter glanced at Colonel Goodman as he spoke. "As hard as Iraq was, the next phase of this fight might be even harder. I need some time with God. Not just to talk to Him, but so that I can hear what He has to say to me."

"Right," Fletcher said, recalling the talk that he and Peter had in the early days of their confinement.

"Listen, guys," Alfred interrupted. "I know you're going to be ready to get to your rooms and get some rest, some alone time, some family time, whatever. But remember this: You're high profile war heroes now, and there have been a lot of people praying and pulling for your safe return. I know you're tired and you really don't want to be bothered by the media, but I think it would be a good idea just to give them a little of your time."

Peter dropped his head and sighed. He didn't mind the press being there, but he wasn't looking forward to talking to them.

"It doesn't have to be long, Jericho," the colonel assured him, noting Peter's demeanor. "Just a few words will be satisfactory, I'm sure. Look, you guys are some of the most respected men in the country right now. America knows you've been to hell and back. The media will be sympathetic to the fact that you're not running over with words on your first day back at home. But I think we owe them a little talk time."

"Yes, sir." Peter sat back in his seat and watched out of the window as trees, cars and houses drew closer. His body was tired now. Staying awake for much of the flight was starting to take its toll.

When the wheels of the plane hit the runway of Los Angeles International Airport, Peter suddenly wished they had twenty-five more hours to go. As the aircraft was directed to its stopping point by those on the ground, Colonel Goodman walked toward Peter and Fletcher, hauling two large and familiar-looking duffle bags.

"Our stuff!" Fletcher exclaimed. They hadn't seen the luggage since they left camp on the day that they were captured.

Alfred grinned. "Thought you guys might want these. I had them flown from camp into Kuwait. You won't be going back to Iraq, so anything that couldn't fit in the bags is being shipped."

Peter grabbed his case and immediately opened it. Carefully running his hand along the inside of the bag, he blindly searched until he found what he was looking for.

Peter pulled out the black velvet box and lifted the top, taking care to lightly finger the jewelry he'd purchased for his wife months ago.

"Nice!" Fletcher stood behind him and admired the set. "Real nice."

Peter smiled and then placed the box back into his bag for safe-keeping. He hoped the jewelry would win points for him when he made the trip to Atlanta to try to mend his family.

"Look," Fletcher said, pointing in the direction of the window and then waving.

Peter followed the path of Fletcher's eyes and saw scattered airport personnel standing outside the plane, applauding. It was just the beginning of a hero's welcome.

Stepping out from the plane and onto the grounds of the same California airport that began his pilgrimage to Iraq a year ago proved to be too much for Peter to digest all at once. Spiritually, he had grown by leaps and bounds in the time that had lapsed between the start and finish of this full circle moment, and he hadn't prepared himself for the sensation of being swept away by currents of gratefulness.

Peter's legs buckled and he dropped to his knees, overcome. "Thank you, Jesus." Accompanied by a heavy flow of tears, the words weren't easy to distinguish, but Peter repeated the phrase over and over.

Many moments passed before he realized that his sentiment was being echoed by Fletcher and Alfred. They were kneeling too, one on either side of him, praising God with no embarrassment for the media cameras surrounding them or those that hovered in the aircrafts overhead.

"Sergeant Jericho, what happened over there?"

The questions began as soon as the men gathered themselves and were in listening range of microphone-bearing reporters.

"Sergeant Owens, were you with the soldiers who were killed?"

"Colonel Goodman, how did you find out where the soldiers were being held?"

"Were the bodies of the murdered soldiers recovered?"

"Are things in Iraq getting any better?"

"Were you tortured in any way by the Iraqis?"

"What can you tell us about the Iraqi prisoner who was taken into custody?"

"What are your feelings about the President of the United States not being here to greet you all today?"

Along with the questions, applause and cheers rang out and camera flashes were coming from every direction as they walked into the airport terminal. Security guards directed the three men to separate areas, and microphones and tape recorders dangled in the air, aimed toward Peter's mouth. Turning to his right, he saw Fletcher being mobbed by his family while reporters took photos. He caught a glimpse of Chantel. She was pretty, just like Fletcher said. And Flex, Jr. looked like a regeneration of his father. Turning to his left, Peter saw Colonel Goodman answering questions that were being directed toward him. Looking out of the window just behind him, he saw the medics place Louis in the ambulance. A small number of media representatives were there too, catching it all on film.

"Were you afraid for your life at any time during the detainment?"

Peter turned his attention back to the men and women that stood in front of him, but couldn't determine which one of the men asked it.

"Step back, please," Peter's assigned security guard said to the reporters who were getting uncomfortably close.

"Is there anything at all that you can tell us, Sergeant Jericho?" a female reporter asked in a voice that pleaded for an answer.

Peter looked into the faces of the anxious journalists who desperately sought information to take back to the rest of the world. Looking at his provided security, Peter nodded the silent message that all was well. Then clearing his throat, he finally spoke.

"I just want to thank all of America and beyond for their support and especially for their prayers for us. I'd be lying if I said that I was not afraid for my life. At times, I was terrified. I think we all were, and for good reason. All I can say is that God will ultimately judge the hateful men who killed my brothers. I want to send my thoughts and prayers to the families of Corporal Michael Ramsey, Lance Corporal Silas Bigalow and Private First Class Charles Klauser." Peter took a moment to gather his trembling lips. "They are the true heroes in all of this. They embody what it means to give one's life for his country.

"And please allow me to say to the fiancée of PFC Klauser, if you are listening, Chuck asked me to tell you that he loves you. He was going to make it a point to say those words just before he was killed so that you would know that he died just as he lived—loving you and the daughter you gave him. To his father, I'd just like to say, you should always remember your son with pride. It was important to him that you were proud of him. *Very* important." Peter took a step backward and then said, "That's all for now. Thank you."

The reporters were still asking questions as he was escorted away by the protective military guardsman. Two stretch limousines awaited, and just as Peter's door was being opened for him, he heard Fletcher calling his name. Turning, Peter spotted his friend running toward him, holding Chantel's hand and with his son following.

"Hey, man. You can't run off before you meet my family."

"Of course not," Peter said with a wide grin, glad that security was not allowing the television cameras any farther than the exit doors near baggage claims. "You must be the lovely Chantel. Flex talked about you very frequently and very favorably."

Chantel hugged Peter, wrapping her arms tightly around his neck, leaving a pleasant smell of some kind of perfume in his nostrils. "He's talked nonstop about you since you all arrived. For whatever you did to keep him so positive and to save his life, I thank you." Tears were streaming down her cheeks as she pulled away.

"He did," Fletcher said, patting Peter on the shoulder. "He saved my life big time. I'll have to fill you both in on it tonight."

Smiling knowingly, Peter extended his arm to Flex, Jr. and gave him a firm handshake. "You should be proud of your father."

"Yes, sir," the teenager responded with glistening eyes. "I really am."

"See you at the hospital tomorrow?" Peter embraced Fletcher.

"You sure you don't want to hang out with us tonight?"

"Yes, please," Chantel added.

"Thank you," Peter said, all the while shaking his head. "But there will be other times."

"I'm gonna hold you to that," Fletcher said. "See you tomorrow."

Through the tinted windows of the luxury car, Peter watched Fletcher and his family share a collective embrace. It seemed that the limousine circled the entire city twice before finally driving into the parking lot of the luxurious Four Seasons Hotel at Beverly Hills. The security guard who rode with him explained to Peter that the purpose of the long ride was to ensure that they weren't being followed.

"Those news hounds can be a real pain sometimes, you know," he said.

As both men checked in, the eyes of the employees revealed their knowledge of who it was that was staying under their roof for the night, but they all remained professional, not once revealing to others the star status of their special guest.

"I'm right across the hall from you in case you need anything," the security guard said after he'd done a thorough check of Peter's room to be sure that everything was in order.

Peter chuckled to himself as he locked the door behind the guard's exit. If he were getting this type of attention and protection, he could only imagine what movie stars and music artists went through as they traveled from city to city.

The Four Seasons had definitely earned its five-star status. Peter's accommodations looked like an immaculate home away from home. Everything was plush and posh: the chairs, the carpet, the curtains, the bed. It was a room fit for a king—or a hero.

Before doing anything else and before his body became any more fatigued than it already was, Peter fell to his knees at the foot of the bed, in much the same manner as he did at the airport, and prayed. This time, though, he was able to verbalize words that emotions wouldn't allow him to the first time. For every blessing the Lord had provided since the days of his childhood, Peter gave thanks. For all of the small miracles he'd taken for granted over the years, he gave thanks. For the battle that he and a portion of his fire team had won, he gave thanks. For the souls he was allowed to lead to Christ, he gave thanks. There were moments during his prayer time that Peter could think of no words to say. He went from kneeling to lying prostrate before the only One who he knew to have saved him; not just from the captivity of Iraq, but from the bondage of sin.

It was an hour later when Peter finally peeled off his clothes and stepped under the shower, feeling refreshed and renewed. This one was the first real shower he'd had since leaving Twentynine Palms for his near-fatal tour of duty. He stayed in the hot waterfall for so long that every surface in the bathroom was covered by a thick layer of mist by the time he stepped out. Peter hummed a tune of whose origin he wasn't even sure. It was a new song, of sorts; and although he was not the best singer, it sounded good with the help of the bathroom's acoustics.

Peter suddenly came to a standstill. A moment later, he received confirmation on what he thought he'd heard the first time. There was someone knocking at his door. Wrapping the hotel towel around his waist, Peter emerged from the bathroom and peered through the peephole. Through the small glass, his commanding officer's face looked distorted.

"Colonel Goodman, sir," he said with a salute as he opened the door.

"Sergeant," the colonel acknowledged and then turned when the door across the hall opened and the security guard stood in the doorway. "It's okay. It's just me."

"Yes, sir," the man said, his eyes wandering a bit to the side of the colonel just before closing his door again.

"Come in, sir," Peter said as he stepped aside.

"I'm not going to stay, Sergeant. You had a package that arrived and I just wanted to be sure it got delivered to you safely."

"A package, sir?" Peter hadn't had the time to go

through his bag to see what may have been missing, but if there were any remaining belongings, he wasn't expecting them to arrive so soon.

When Colonel Goodman took two steps to the right, Peter heard himself gasp.

Chapter 36

The words being spoken weren't loud enough for her to decipher, but Jan could hear Peter and his commanding officer exchanging low-volume dialogue as she walked around the suite where Peter had been placed for the night.

After getting over the initial shock of seeing her, Peter had invited her inside. At first glimpse of him, his body glistening and only a towel around his waist to avoid nudity, Jan's mind raced. Her first thought was that Peter's infamous "other woman" was inside the room with him and that the colonel's knock had interrupted their evening. Peter's invitation for her to come inside didn't lessen Jan's skepticism. Even now, as she walked around the one-bedroom suite, she found herself looking behind doors and inside closets to see if *she* were temporarily hiding until Peter could get rid of the unexpected company.

Whoever's footing the bill for this room is paying a pretty penny, Jan thought as she walked through the living room area and out onto the balcony of the tenth-floor accommodations. It would be dark now in Atlanta, but the three-hour time difference left a bit of sunlight still lingering in California. The early evening view of the city was beautiful, so she could only imagine what it looked like under a full moonlit, star-filled sky.

"Jan?"

At the sound of her name, Jan flinched, but didn't turn to face the man who had said it in such an unsure manner. What was she going to say? What was *he* going to say? Peter had been brave enough to put his life on the line for a country full of people he didn't even know. But he'd chosen the cowardly way to tell her that he no longer loved her. *Now that I'm here, will he be man enough to say it to my face?* That was the real reason she'd come—to hear it for herself. The country may have been proud of Peter, but Jan had never been so disappointed in anyone in her entire life.

"Bay?"

It was a nickname that she used to love. There was no deep history behind it; it was simply what her mother called "a lazy man's way of saying *baby.*" But how dare he call her by the same term of endearment that he used when he loved her? Jan spun around and glared at Peter, still standing on the inside and still wearing nothing but a towel. *Am I supposed to be turned on by this?* she thought, trying to be unmoved by his sculpture, but struggling not to be distracted by the attractive view that Peter so openly displayed.

"You want to come in and talk?" he asked.

Talk? She didn't want to talk to him. What was there to talk about? He'd made his stance crystal clear. All at once, Jan regretted her last minute decision to purchase that expensive ticket to replace the complementary ones she destroyed. Once again, she'd gone against Rachel's advice, and once again, she'd lived to regret it. Peter's Marine-prompted chiseled frame was no longer appetizing. Reality made the sight of him repulse her.

"I'm leaving." Jan tried to push past Peter, but he grabbed her by the arm.

"Leaving, why?" His face was filled with bewilderment. "Where are you going? You just got here. Where's Kyla? Did you bring her with you?"

Jan snatched her arm away. "Why would I bring Kyla to see this fiasco? She's already been hurt enough."

Peter dropped his head. "I know. I'm sorry."

"You're *sorry*? Is that the best you can do? You're sorry?" The tears that surfaced in her eyes made Jan even angrier. She'd promised herself that she wouldn't allow Peter to make her cry; yet, here she was.

"Listen, Bay."

"Stop calling me that!"

Her hysteria apparently caught Peter unprepared. He held his hands up and took a step back. "Calm down, Jan; okay? I know you're angry and you have every right to be. But we're two adults. We can talk to each other without screaming."

"Didn't you mean to say that we are two *reasonably smart, reasonably attractive* adults?" Jan scoffed, recalling the words that had been used in the letter. Words she'd read so often that she could recite them verbatim from memory.

"Huh?"

"You know what, Pete? I don't even know why I came here. I suppose you really think I'm an idiot for doing so, and guess what? I think I'm an idiot too. But I was stupid enough to believe that if I came here, I could somehow find closure on all of this."

"Closure? So, what are you saying—we're over?"

Jan wiped tears from her cheeks and laughed at the

same time. "Oh, that's just brilliant, Pete. That's right; try and get me to be the one to say it so that you can use that to try and turn our daughter against me when she finds out. I don't know why I didn't tell her already. I should have showed her the letter on the day that it came, but I was so busy trying to protect her and protect you that I didn't even think about protecting myself."

"So, you're admitting that you know about the letter?"

Jan looked at Peter and scowled. "Stop playing stupid, Pete. Of course I know about the letter."

"And your reason for not showing it to Kyla was to protect *me*? Okay, Bay . . . Jan. If we're going to talk about this, let's at least be honest with one another. First, let me say that I've forgiven you. Iraq taught me that life was too short not to forgive."

"Forgiven *me*? For what?" Jan was so annoyed by Peter's behavior that she wanted to reach up and slap him across the face. "Whatever or whoever knocked you in your head must have knocked out your brains in the process."

"That's not funny, Jan. This is a war injury. I could have died over there."

"Do you see me laughing, Pete? It's not funny to me, either. It's pathetic."

"What's pathetic is that you're still lying after all this time."

Jan flung her arms up in the air and then allowed them to fall to her sides. "Here we go with that again. I am so sick of you calling me a liar."

"You need to see the letter to jar your selective memory?"

"Oh, don't you worry yourself, Sergeant Peter Kyle Jericho. I *have* the letter. But it wouldn't prove your point; it would prove mine." Jan watched through tearful eyes at the look of confusion that covered Peter's face as she retrieved the envelope out of her purse. His reaction was almost authentic enough to believe, but she knew better.

His eyes remained locked onto envelope, even as she began speaking. Jan imagined that he was trying to think of another lie to tell, but she was at her wit's end and had no intention of giving him the opportunity to dig a deeper hole for himself. Jan's blood was near boiling and her teeth were clenched when she began speaking again.

"You know what, Pete? I prayed for you while you were in Iraq. Even after I got this letter, I prayed for your sorry behind. I spent time in therapy—that's right, *therapy*, trying to cope with everything, and after all of that, you still haven't changed. I don't know what happened to us, Pete. Maybe Shelton Heights really is cursed and haunted by some dead warlock's spirit, and maybe my going there is what sent our marriage to the pits of hell. But whatever the case, I deserved better than this. After thirteen years of marriage, I deserved way better than a stupid Dear Jane letter."

Simultaneously with her final word, Jan used her closed fist, and as much force as she could, to shove the envelope into Peter's chest, causing him to nearly lose his balance. Ignoring his calls, she stormed out of the room and ran the full length of the hall to the nearest elevator. Once the elevator doors closed behind her, Jan wept heavily into her hands. What had happened to the level-headed woman who just this morning declared her strength and made unfulfilled promises to her mother and cousin?

"Girl, don't you go there crying and carrying on," Leona had said. "Psalm 30:5 tells us that weeping endures for a night, but joy comes in the morning. That means that God don't intend for none of His children to cry when the sun is up. The sun will still be up when you get there, and crying in the daytime is a sin. You already flying when you ain't s'pose to. Don't add to it by crying while it's light outside."

Jan knew her mother had once again misinterpreted a scripture, but she wasn't about to try to correct her.

"I wish you wouldn't go, Jan," was Rachel's hardnosed stance. "This is crazy. The boy has already told you how he feels. Why are you making a fool of yourself?"

"I have to hear him say it, Rachel. Sometimes things aren't what they seem," Jan had replied, remembering Mother Tides' words. "Sometimes you can read something and the tone that it comes across in isn't the same tone that's meant."

"Stop being stupid, Jan!" Rachel retorted, interjecting a side of profanity despite the presence of her aunt. They were in Rachel's house, and in her house, Leona couldn't tell her what and what not to say. "No matter what tone he says 'I don't love you' in, he's still saying he doesn't love you. Don't let him make a fool of you, girl. The best thing you can do for yourself is to never speak to him again. The only thing you need to be talking to him about is how many zeros you want to see on his monthly child support check. I can't believe you can't see the idiocy in you going to California."

"I do see it, Rachel, but I still have to go. I know it doesn't make sense, but I have to do this for me. I'm not taking Kyla because I don't want her to be exposed to whatever transpires. But after I get back, I'll sit her down and tell her the whole truth. The inevitable can't be put off forever."

"I still don't think you should go," Rachel voiced, "but since you're insisting on it, then at least refuse to let him break you. Pete's not going to tell the truth, so you can forget that. Don't even get your hopes up. In fact, don't even mention the letter to him. Play crazy like you didn't even get it and see if he brings it up. If he's a real man, he'll bring it up. If he's not, he won't. And believe me when I say Pete won't."

The elevator traveled down ten floors faster than Jan wanted it to. When the door opened, she took a moment to dry her tears with her hands and put on her best face before walking out into the lobby of the lavish hotel. She didn't want the employees to see her anguish. Jan walked as quickly as her legs would carry her.

As she stepped through the doors that placed her outside, Jan noticed the setting of the sun. It didn't seem like she'd been in Peter's room that long, but darkness was now moving in and taking its proper place. Looking at her watch, Jan made a decision to head back to Atlanta. She was sure that she could move the next day's flight up to this evening. It was Monday and those traveling on business had probably already taken afternoon flights back to wherever they needed to go. Changing her ticket wouldn't be too much of a task.

"Jan!"

She had just reached her rental car when she heard Peter's calls. Looking in the direction of his voice, she saw her husband running toward her, wearing only boxer shorts. He was shirtless and his feet were bare. Jan was finished talking. She needed to leave with whatever dignity she had left. Peter wouldn't be allowed to strip her bare. Using the keyless entry feature, she unlocked the doors of the car and got inside as fast as she could.

"Bay . . . wait!"

Peter reached the front passenger door and opened it before Jan could find the correct button to push to lock the doors in the unfamiliar car.

"Get out, Pete!" she barked, hoping her uncharacteristically forceful mannerism would discourage him from pressing the issue any further.

"We need to talk, Jan." The sprint to catch up with her had rendered him breathless.

"Get out of my car. I mean it, Pete. Get out!"

"No. Not until you answer one question. Answer one simple question and I'll leave."

Jan was so angry that her body trembled. "Fine! Ask your stupid question so I can go." She cranked up the car for emphasis.

"Where did you get this letter from?"

Jan looked at him and rolled her eyes. "Get out, Pete. I don't have time for your sick and twisted games. Get out!"

"I'm not playing games!" Peter shouted back for the first time. "Where did you get this letter?" When Jan glared at him without an answer, his aggravation heightened. "Where did you get it, Jan? Tell me!"

"Stop acting dumb, Pete. You know where I got it. I got it through the mail from you. Where else would I have gotten it?"

Peter looked at her, then at the letter in his hand, then back at her again. "But I didn't write this."

Jan closed her eyes and released an infuriated sigh. "I really do look stupid to you, don't I? Pete, I know your handwriting. You did write that."

"Yes, I wrote it. What I'm saying is I didn't write it to *you*. How could you have gotten this in the mail?"

Searching his face in the dim light, Jan saw frightening authenticity. Either Peter had lied so much that he'd become a professional at it, or he was telling the truth. "What do you mean you didn't write it to me? What other woman did you lead to believe you loved her? What other woman gave you a baby that served as the only reason for you not viewing your relationship with her as a total waste of time?"

Again, Peter looked at the letter and then back at Jan. "I wrote this to Rachel—thirteen, probably fourteen years ago."

Chapter 37

After Peter answered Jan's question, he found himself in an even bigger war, trying to convince her not to leave and to give him ample time to explain. "Thirty minutes, Jan. Just give me thirty minutes and I promise I can clear this all up."

They had walked back to the hotel room together, under the watchful eyes of the front desk clerk who had seen Peter run out of the facility half-clothed. Despite his erratic behavior, he was a rescued prisoner of war, a man who had almost paid the ultimate price for his country, and they were not about to cause trouble for him. They even provided him with a new key to his room since, in his haste to catch Jan, he'd left his on the nightstand beside the bed.

The elevator ride back to the tenth floor was quick and quiet. Peter took note of the dispassionate expression on his wife's face and knew that she was already aware that what she was about to hear wasn't what she wanted to hear. After letting Jan step into the room ahead of him and assuring his security guard that everything was fine, Peter walked in and closed the door behind him.

"You want something to drink?" he offered.

"The clock is ticking, Pete."

She was not in the mood for stalling tactics. Peter walked closer to where she sat on the edge of his bed and handed her the letter. "Read it again, Jan."

"I don't want to."

"Please. Read it again."

Jan snatched the paper from his hand and Peter sat on the bed beside her as she read it aloud. When she finished, she looked at him, seeming to open the floor for his defense testimony to begin.

"Don't you see, Bay? I wrote that letter to Rachel when I was breaking up with her to fully pursue you. She was the one I knew I didn't love but didn't tell right away. We'd had a nasty fight a few days before I wrote the letter because she wanted me to work on building a relationship with her, but I knew it wouldn't work because I knew where my heart was."

"That doesn't make sense, Pete," Jan said. "You say here that if you never had your relationship with me, then you never would have been able to hold Kyla in your arms."

"No, that's not what it says," Peter replied, pointing at the words on the paper. "I was telling Rachel that had I not had a relationship with *her*, then I never would have been able to hold *you* in my arms. You were the precious gift I was talking about. This was written before Kyla was even a thought."

A single tear dropped from both of Jan's eyes. "If what you say is true, Pete, how did this letter get mailed to me?"

"I don't know, Bay; but on the date of the postmark, I was already in Baghdad. See? This letter was mailed from within the States. Rachel must have mailed this to you is all I can think."

"Rachel wouldn't do that," Jan snapped.

Not wanting to run her away, Peter immediately conceded in spite of the mounting evidence. "Okay, then I don't know how it got mailed to you. I just know I didn't do it. I would never have said this kind of stuff to you. We had a fight, yes. But I have never stopped loving you, Bay. You have to believe that."

He watched as Jan stood from the bed with a fresh stream of tears staining her cheeks. "Oh, I'm supposed to believe that, but you won't believe that I never lied to you about my visit to Atlanta? How lopsided is that, Pete?"

"Jan, it's okay; really, it is. I've come to accept that you just needed some time away from me and Kyla for whatever reason."

"But that's not true. Why won't you believe me when I tell you that I only intended to stay with Mama for a week? Things just happened to make it longer."

Why does she keep insisting on lying to me? I can forgive her for the original lie, but I need her not to continue lying to try and cover the first lie. Peter just wanted to put his life back together. If that meant throwing in the towel, then he was willing to do so. "Okay, Bay."

"Pete, you're patronizing me."

"No, Jan. I just want to stop fighting. For the love of God, can we stop fighting? If you'll accept that I didn't write that letter to you, I'll gladly forget everything else. I just want my wife and daughter back. I don't care about nothing else right now."

"But in your heart of hearts, you'll always believe that I'm lying about this. What kind of life can we have if you believe I'm a liar? I don't understand why you would think I'd do such a thing. If I wanted to spend more time with Mama, I would have just told you that."

"I found the letter, Jan," Peter blurted. He'd never intended to take it that far, but Jan left him no choice but to call her to the carpet. She was beginning to sound pathological and that frightened him. "I found the letter tucked in your Bible in the backseat of my car."

"What letter?"

Peter stood and walked to his duffle bag. He had pulled the letter from her Bible and placed it in his before leaving for Iraq, but he didn't know if it had been packed with all of his other belongings or if his Bible was one of the things that would be mailed to him later. Peter began pulling items from the bag and stopped when he saw the leatherbound book. He retrieved it and immediately pulled the envelope out from between two pages.

"What's that?" Jan said as he handed it to her.

"The letter that you wrote to Rachel, but apparently never mailed. The letter where you were telling her that you needed to get away from me; that I was making your life so miserable that you needed to make up a lie to tell me so that you could go and stay with your mother for a while. Is any of this ringing a bell for you?" Peter was beginning to get angry. If she denied it still, he was prepared to walk her back to her car and call it a night.

"Oh my God," Jan whispered.

"Remembering it all now, are you?" Peter's voice was filled with sarcasm.

"I wrote this fourteen years ago, Pete." There was terror in Jan's eyes when she looked at him. "I wrote this letter to Rachel during that time when she wasn't talking to me; after you and I got together. She was making my life a living hell at the time. Rachel and I were sharing an apartment, remember? That was the place I was telling her I needed to get out of because of the resentment in the air. Remember how I left Florida and went to stay with Mama and Daddy for a few weeks? That's what this letter is talking about—my agonizing relationship with Rachel; not you."

Peter returned to his place on the side of the bed. "So, you gave it to Rachel?"

"Yes."

"So, how did it get in my vehicle?"

Jan remained quiet, but Peter knew that her mind was racing.

"You don't see the connection here, Jan? Rachel's behind all of this. She doesn't want us together. She's still angry."

"About what? This is just too crazy, Pete," Jan said, standing from the bed once more. "It's been thirteen years and Rachel moved on a long time ago. It's not like the two of you were married or anything. If Rachel is capable of this—if she's doing something this crazy, then she's acting like a woman scorned. I mean, I could understand if you all were engaged, but you weren't. You weren't even sleeping together. Why would she . . . ?"

Peter immediately knew that his demeanor had given away the long-withheld secret. There was no sense in trying to deny the truth. Enough accusations of lying had been tossed between them to last a lifetime. It wasn't just time to face this demon head-on; it was *past* time.

"You slept with Rachel?" When Peter didn't reply, Jan said it again, but this time, much louder. "You slept with Rachel?!"

"I'm sorry I didn't tell you before, Bay. I just—"

Before Peter knew it, Jan had slapped him across the face and continued swinging at him with all of her might. As each slap and punch hit its target, Peter thought of his commanding officer and what he'd said of his wife. Peter had never seen this side of Jan, but knew he had it coming. Easily, he could have stopped her raging, but instead, Peter guarded his face and his fresh stitches and allowed her to swing on him until she felt he'd been punished enough.

"I can't believe you, Peter! How could you do this to me? My husband and the woman who was supposed to be my best friend? I hate you and I never, ever want to see you again!"

"Wait a minute, Jan."

This time, when she swung at him, Peter caught her arm in mid-air. She was much stronger than he'd ever given her credit for. Or maybe it was the angry adrenalin that propelled her strength. Either way, Peter had to restrain her arms and then wrestle Jan to the bed, where he straddled her body and pinned her arms over her head, using both his hands.

"Get off me!"

"Stop yelling before security throws us out of here." Peter had no sooner said the words than Jan opened her mouth and inhaled deeply in preparation for a scream. He quickly released one of her arms and covered her mouth with his hand just in time to muffle what would have surely been enough to get him arrested. "Bay, please. Please just give me a minute to explain," he managed to say despite the stinging of his arm from the slaps that Jan was delivering with the hand he'd freed in order to cover her mouth. Tears from her eyes wet the side of his hands as he kept it clamped over her lips.

It didn't take Peter long to realize that no matter how much he pleaded with Jan, she was not going to *give* him anything. She was just too angry to be reasonable. If he wanted a minute to explain himself, he'd have to take it. "I didn't cheat on you, Bay; you have to believe that. Yes, I slept with her, and yes, I should have told you before now, but what happened with me and Rachel happened *before* you and me got married. It happened before we even started dating. I promise, Bay. I didn't cheat on you. I promise to God, I didn't cheat on you."

Peter breathed a sigh of relief when Jan stopped hitting him and he felt her muscles relax a bit. Still, he kept his position, not yet certain that he trusted her not to scream or to yell at him. He was being truthful with her, but that still didn't change the fact that he'd kept this from her for the duration of their relationship.

"I'm sorry I didn't tell you. At first it just didn't seem like anything worth telling, seeing that you and Rachel were no longer close and everything that had happened between her and me had happened before you and me. Then when you all got close again, everything got complicated. Rachel knew I didn't want her around, but she kept popping up over our house. And any time I acted like I didn't want her there, she'd hang our past over my head, saying that she'd tell you if I ever tried to prevent her from coming over. After a while, it started feeling like it wasn't really you that she was coming to see, but me."

Peter paused and watched the rise and fall of Jan's chest. Her breaths were slowing down now. They weren't coming as fast or as hard as they were just a few moments earlier. Taking a chance that he wasn't at all sure about, Peter turned his body so that he rolled off of his wife and into a seated position beside where she lay. Jan didn't move and her stare was frigid. Even so, Peter was encouraged that the hatred that blazed in her eyes at the start of their exchange had disappeared. He continued.

"When I got the assignment to move to the base in Twentynine Palms, it was the best news my ears could hear. Remember how much we struggled in the beginning of our marriage and how much better things got once we were in Cali? Going there put some real distance between us and Rachel; distance that she couldn't erase with a few hours' drive. I'm not trying to pretend to be innocent in all of this, Bay. I'm just trying to be totally honest with you, and I apologize in advance if anything I say hurts you.

"I knew when I slept with Rachel that I didn't love her, and I knew that one of the reasons she did it was because she thought it would keep us together. I . . . I took advantage of that at the time. But I did apologize right afterwards," Peter added quickly, sounding like a child who was trying to explain away the pain of a pending leather strap. "When she first read that letter from me, she said that I might as well have called her a . . . well, you know . . . because I didn't bother to address her by name."

Recalling that Rachel had planted the same seed in her head, telling her that Peter had just basically referred to her as the same derogatory identification, Jan closed her eyes and swallowed while Peter continued.

"She kept calling me a dog and she promised that I'd live to regret the day I ever met her. Boy, was she right. I always knew that she didn't want us together, but I would have never guessed that she'd go to these lengths to make it happen. I don't know why I kept it from you all these years. I guess the truth is that I was afraid of losing you." Peter released a vinegary laugh. "Looks like I screwed up either way."

"She made me believe Shelton Heights was the reason that everything fell apart."

"What?" Peter watched Jan sit up and wipe water from her cheeks. It accomplished little since new streams were already replacing the old ones.

"The whole legend that Shelton Heights is haunted—she made me believe it. She told me that the reason my world was falling apart was because I made the choice to stay in the house with Mama. She pretended to love me and to want to protect me from being hurt."

Jan's tears flowed heavier and Peter said a quick prayer

before taking the risk of sliding nearer to her. Placing his arms around her shoulders, he pulled her head into his chest.

"We grew up like sisters, Pete. How could she do this to me?"

Hell has no fury like a woman scorned, Peter thought. "Shhh. It's my fault, Bay. I should have been honest with you. In her defense, I don't think she did it to hurt you. I think it was just meant to hurt me."

"How could it not hurt me?" As Jan wept, her body trembled and she clung firmly to Peter.

During the brief silence that followed, he felt his heart drumming heavily in his chest. He hadn't felt his wife in his arms in nearly sixteen months. Closing his eyes, Peter savored the moment. "I know you're hurting, Bay, but I prayed for this. When I was in Iraq, sitting on death row, I prayed for the chance to hold you and tell you how sorry I am for everything. I'm sorry for hurting you, Jan, I really, *really* am. But, God . . . this feels so good." Peter squeezed tighter. "I miss this."

Quietness rested among them for several moments and Peter didn't care if they ever started talking again. He'd said what he wanted to say. Now all he wanted to do was hold her. But Jan broke the silence.

"You know what I really missed?"

Her voice was muffled, but Peter heard her. He loosened his grip, hoping that whatever she said had nothing to do with Rachel. He didn't want to talk about her anymore. "What?"

"Your massages." She smiled at him for the first time. It wasn't a full smile, but it was a smile, still.

Peter brushed her moist cheek with his fingers. He felt tension mounting in every muscle of his body. "You want one?"

He could see the apprehension on Jan's face as he fully

released her. She touched his bare chest with the tips of her fingers, almost in a manner that questioned whether she had the right to touch him at all. Peter reached up and wrapped his hand around hers, pressing it down so that her palm was flat to his skin. Taking control, he maneuvered her hand in slow motion, allowing it to travel the full width of his chest and then down to his stomach.

Apparently finding pleasure in the involuntary exploration, Jan moaned.

"Let me give you one," he whispered.

When Jan's eyes met his, Peter couldn't tell whether he was seeing the flames of his eyes reflecting in hers or whether hers were just as smoldering. No longer unsure of himself, Peter lifted her chin and slowly brought his lips to hers. Gently, he eased her down on the bed. It had been so long since they'd touched like this that he wanted to devour her with the passion he'd been forced to keep at bay. Instead, Peter made his kisses delicate and brief, pausing between each one to whisper his love for every part of her body that his lips came in contact with.

It was Jan who was losing control, clawing at him and begging for more. But Peter refused to be rushed. He'd fought too hard and waited too long. This would be a victory of which every aching moment, he would relish.

Chapter 38

When Jan's eyelids lifted at six o'clock the next morning, she jolted to a seated position, feeling as though she'd awakened from an erotic dream. The strange setting that surrounded her brought her comfort. It meant that she really wasn't in Atlanta, and when she looked at the long, sleeping form beside her, she knew it wasn't Kyla who she had shared a bed with last night.

Jan smiled as images of last night's passionate marathon replayed themselves through her head. Maybe it was the extended length of time that she'd gone without the touch of the man she loved that made their evening seem so extraordinary—whatever the case, it had been a phenomenal experience. The last thing she remembered before falling asleep was feeling Peter's hands caressing the lower part of her back as he finally got around to making good on his offer. By that time, Jan had been depleted of all strength and the fact that Peter still had enough vitality to deliver such an effective massage was impressive.

Now, he lay on his back. He wasn't snoring, but she could hear his breathing. As was normal for him, at some point during the night, he'd kicked off the comforter that covered him, and today that habit allowed his wife to appreciate the whole of him. Noticeably, he'd lost a few pounds, and Jan wondered if it was weight that had been shed over the full time that they'd been apart, or if he'd dropped the pounds in the week he'd been held captive. Either way, it really didn't matter now. He was home.

Jan brought her face slowly to Peter's and gently placed her lips against his. Subconsciously, he returned her kiss, not once breaking his breathing pattern or opening his eyes. Seeing him lying there in such a natural state stimulated new desires in Jan, but in spite of the temptation, she refrained from waking him. Peter had worked hard to satisfy her every need last night. He'd earned the right to rest.

Easing from the bed, Jan pulled one of Peter's shirts out of his duffle bag and slipped it over her head. *Thank you, Jesus.* She wouldn't dare start another day without giving credit where credit was due. God had had to perform several miracles in order for them to get to this point. He'd spared Peter's life, directed Jan to take Mother Tides' advice to hold on to hope, and allowed her to get angry enough to shove the letter in Peter's chest. Had she not walked away, leaving the letter in his hand, Peter would have never uncovered Rachel's plot.

Rachel. Jan closed her eyes and shuddered as if a draft of cold air had suddenly swept through the room. The fine bumps that surfaced on her arms were driven by quite a different emotion than the ones of last night. Jan couldn't remember the last time the treachery of a loved one had hurt so deeply. Probably never. She walked out of the bedroom, through the living room, and out the doors that led to the balcony. Jan had been right in her estimation of what the view would look like under the stars. The sun was beginning to rise, but the dimly lit view was perfect. It was simply beautiful.

The striking landscape gave the false impression that all was right with the world. From this view, no one would ever know that a country that housed this kind of beauty had also lost thousands of soldiers in an evil war that had gone on far too long. No one would guess that a country that housed this level of splendor would also house hunger, poverty and other destitution. And for Jan, it was hard to fathom that a country that housed this display of majesty also accommodated people who were capable of the level of betrayal that Rachel had exemplified.

How could you do this? Tears welled in Jan's eyes. She didn't want to be sad, but she was. Rachel had been her best friend for the better part of her life. Growing up, Jan was closer to her cousin than she'd been to either of her sisters. They'd shared so much over the years: homes, laughs, tears, meals, vacations, secrets. Jan cringed when she thought of all of the confidential information she had entrusted to Rachel. Knowing what lengths the now seemingly unknown woman had gone through to tear her marriage apart, Jan was left to question every single thing Rachel had ever said to or done for her.

As a woman, she could understand Rachel's pain. It was reasonable to expect her to dislike Peter after he rejected her in spite of her advances and intimate offerings. Jan recalled how frightened she was at the notion of having to tell Peter that she was pregnant with his child. She imagined that she would have been devastated too, if, after trusting him on that level, he had turned his back on her. But Jan knew that she would never have devised such a hateful plan to find revenge.

A stream of moisture trickled down Jan's cheeks. She knew that she had to find some way to forgive Rachel, but at the same time, she would never again be able to allow her back into her life. Not as a friend. Not after she'd committed such a dastardly act. The first thing on Jan's agenda, when she returned to Atlanta, was to remove her belongings from Rachel's apartment. She couldn't believe she'd let Rachel talk her into moving in with her, insisting that all of the folly in her life was due to the legend of Shelton Heights.

That's why she told me not to read the letter to him; because she knew if Pete heard the words written in the letter, the truth would be revealed. "Ugh!" The realization of it all almost made Jan sick to her stomach.

If her relationship with Rachel hadn't been what she thought was a tried and proven one, the reveal wouldn't be so shocking. But theirs wasn't a trust that had been established overnight or even in recent years. Hers and Rachel's was a twenty-five-year bond that had been established when they were in middle school. *There's no telling what else she's lied about or been hiding from me. Always acting like everything she did was to my benefit. Going to counseling with me, going to prayer with me—she probably just wanted to know what was being said so that she could twist it around to fit her agenda.*

Jan felt raped. Not physically violated, but mentally and spiritually desecrated because of her relationship with a woman she trusted wholeheartedly. If it had been any other friend or acquaintance who had duped her, Jan could have handled it with much more poise. *But Rachel . . .*

"Good morning."

Jan turned to see Peter approaching her from the shadows of the living room, wearing a bathrobe provided by the hotel. Walking closer to erase the spacious gap between them, Peter wrapped his arms around Jan's waist and pulled her close to him. He moaned as if just the feel of her body against his had excited him. Jan slipped her hand inside his robe and felt his muscles quiver. The silence seemed to last forever before Peter ended it.

"It's beautiful out here, isn't it?"

"Yes," Jan replied, placing her cheek against his partially exposed chest and looking out over the balcony.

As though he could feel the heaviness of her heart, Peter said, "It's going to be fine, Bay. I know it hurts right now, but give it some time. You'll get through this. *We'll* get through this."

"I know." Jan took a moment to savor the kiss he placed on her forehead. She wanted the moment to last much longer, but the romantic setting came to an abrupt end at Peter's next words.

"Colonel Goodman is going to be here in an hour to pick me up. I have to get showered and ready to leave."

"Leave?" Jan blurted, pulling away. "You have to go back? So soon? Why?"

Peter chuckled. "Calm down, Bay. I'm not leaving for Iraq. I'm sorry, I guess I just assumed you knew since Colonel Goodman escorted you over here. I figured he'd told you that I have to check in to the VA hospital for a complete physical and mental checkup."

"What for? You're fine. Lord knows after last night I can definitely vouch for that."

Peter laughed and then fished for more compliments. "Yeah? Was I that good?"

"Oh my goodness, yeah."

"There's more where that came from, you know. I can't wait to . . . show you."

Jan looked up at him and saw that the earlier laughter in his eyes had been replaced by something far deeper. "Me either."

Peter released a lustful groan before pulling away and putting some space between them on the balcony. He seemed to struggle to change the heated subject. "This, uh . . . this visit to the hospital . . . it's just a necessary precaution. It'll just be overnight. We'll be released in the morning."

"Oh." Jan suddenly felt lost and a little disappointed. She was looking forward to spending the day with her husband and hoped he'd be catching the early afternoon flight back to Atlanta with her.

"You look real good wearing my shirt," he remarked, scanning her from head to toe with approving eyes.

"Thanks." Jan reached forward and untied the belt of his robe and watched as it fell open. "And you look real good in . . . nothing."

Laughing, Peter appeared to blush as he crossed his hands in front of himself in mock embarrassment.

"I was hoping we could spend all morning together," Jan said through a sigh.

Peter felt her disenchantment and wrapped her in his arms once more as he led the way back inside and closed the balcony doors. "It's only one day, Jan. Why don't you spend the day here, and tomorrow when I'm released, we'll head to Atlanta together and surprise Kyla. I can't wait to see her."

"Believe me when I say she feels the same. But my ticket back is for today."

"So what? We'll change it. That's not a problem."

Jan pulled away from Peter and her eyes dropped to the carpet. "I think I'll go ahead and turn in my rental car and catch my scheduled flight today."

Peter protested. "No, Bay. We've spent way too much time apart. I want us to leave here together."

"I do too," Jan said, stepping close to him again, "but like you said about your visit to the hospital, it's only one day. I need to take care of some things in Atlanta *now.* It can't wait." Jan searched Peter's eyes for approval, or at least a sign that he understood the urgency.

"Okay," he said, nodding slowly. "But don't let those *things* get you into any trouble. She's not worth it."

Jan smiled and then stood on her toes while she pulled Peter's face toward hers. What began as a planned simple kiss turned into an impromptu early morning session from which her husband barely had time to recover before his commanding officer arrived.

Chapter 39

"Sit still," Leona scolded as she pressed a makeshift icepack against the side of Jan's eye. "If you wasn't grown and married, girl, I'd take a leather belt to your behind. I ain't never been so embarrassed in all my days."

Jan closed her eyes and endured the initial pain of the cold compress before settling back in her chair. Not thirty minutes ago, it had taken two policemen to pry her off of her one-time best friend, and now Jan was left to recall it all in her head and wonder if she'd do anything differently if she had it to do all over again.

The first stop that she, Leona and Kyla had made on the ride from the airport was by Rachel's apartment to remove all of Jan's and Kyla's belongings. With Rachel still at work, the timing was perfect. As she and her daughter were collecting the last of their things, Jan wandered into Rachel's bedroom for no reason in particular, and stumbled across the same floral box that Rachel had hurriedly removed from the coffee table on the night that she and Kyla moved in.

Curiosity got the best of her, and inside of the box, Jan

found several journals in which Rachel had been keeping a frequent record of her devious plot to destroy Peter at all costs.

"This is why she rushed home that night," Jan told her mother as she revealed her findings. "She wasn't interested in trying to help me and Kyla get moved in. She needed to get here so that she could hide this box of journals before we noticed them."

Rachel's chronological entries dated as far back as ten years and read like the diary of an obsessed woman. For a fleeting moment, Jan felt sorry for her. Rachel had clearly been profoundly hurt and insulted by Peter's decision to end their brief relationship and she wanted to attack him where it would hurt the most—the family that he held dear. Essentially, they were the people she defined as those that he'd valued higher than her worth. Ever since it began its early blossom when they were middle school students, Rachel's body had always been her best bait to lure the opposite sex. And when Peter took the bait and, in essence, tasted it and tossed it back into the ocean, unwanted, it had apparently been too much for her to accept. From the entries, it wasn't difficult to conclude that Rachel had an undeclared love for Peter. Her cousin had been in many relationships that didn't turn out to be lifetime ones. The only thing that could possibly make this one different was that she loved Peter.

Rachel loves my husband. It was a thought that hit Jan fast and hard, but one that made everything that had happened make sense. Rachel's was a love that, over the years, had twisted and turned into something dark and dangerous. All of Jan's pity was expunged, replaced by renewed anger when she thought of how close Rachel had come to finding the warped victory she sought.

Once they were back at Leona's house, Jan and her mom were sitting on the front porch talking when Rachel arrived to welcome her cousin back home as if all were right with the world. When Jan saw the familiar car pull into the driveway, her body took on a mind of its own. After listening to a forty-minute sermon from her mother on the ride from the airport, and another thirty as they sat on the porch, Jan thought that she was spiritually strong enough to handle the situation in a Christ-like manner; but she wasn't.

"Jan, remember what I told you. Leave it in the hands of the Lord. The Bible says . . ."

As Jan stood from her seat, she heard Leona talking, but her words faded as though several yards of space had suddenly been placed between them. At a slow pace, Jan descended the steps and then held her hands up to stop the embrace that Rachel had set in motion. To Jan, it would have been the equivalent of Judas kissing Jesus as a mask for his betrayal.

"What's wrong with you?" Rachel asked, looking wide-eyed and guilty of a sin for which she'd not yet been verbally charged.

"You," Jan said as brewing anger caused her breaths to come in quick, short puffs. "That's what's wrong with me. That's what's been wrong with me for years, Rachel."

Cursing, Rachel put her hands on her hips and said, "I knew that fool was gonna say something to flip the truth and turn you against the wrong people. What cockinbull story did he tell you, Jan? He probably denied everything, didn't he? I knew it . . . old dirty dog. I'm disappointed that you'd still be gullible enough to believe anything that liar said after what he wrote to you that—"

"Shut up!" Jan screamed with tears burning her eyes. "*You're* the liar, Rachel. All this time, you've been making Pete and some old dead warlock out to be the enemy when it's been you doing things to destroy my family. I thought we were friends, Rachel. I thought you had my back, when what you really had was a knife stuck in it. How could you be so sick and evil? How can you even look at your own smug, lying face in the mirror, Rachel?"

Jan's elevated voice had brought the neighbors on both sides of them and the ones across the street out onto their porches. But the growing audience didn't faze either of the angry women.

"Who you calling a liar? I know you ain't calling me no liar. I *have* had your back. But if you want to believe your crazy church friends, your stupid shrink and your lying husband, who done did me and probably every other woman he can sweet-talk into bed, then you go right ahead, sister-girl. I don't need you and nobody else. But don't you *ever* call me a liar. Not after all I've done for you!" Rachel took on a threatening stance, one that Jan had seen many times in their more youthful days. But never had she seen it directed toward her.

Jan's vision became clouded with tears and her lower lip trembled. "You've never done anything for me, Rachel. All you've ever been is a devious, hateful, jealous manipulator."

More profane words spilled from Rachel's lips. She ended her vicious rant by saying, "Ain't nobody jealous of you. You ain't got nothing that I want, you lil' no-house, no-money, no-man, trifling—"

"That's enough, Rachel. We know the truth," Leona said from the porch before her niece could reference her daughter by the highly offensive term that she knew was coming. To put a permanent end to her niece's award-winning theatrical performance, Leona held up the box of journals so that Rachel could see it. "Now, shut your mouth and g'on home, girl. This ain't nothing but the devil trying to stir up trouble."

"What were you going to do next, Rachel?" Jan shrilled. "What were you going to do if none of your other plans worked? Were you going to try and hurt me so that I'd think I'd gotten hurt because I lived in Shelton Heights? Were you going to hurt Kyla? Is that why you kept telling me to leave before she ended up suffering because of my address?"

"You betta step up out of my face!" Rachel said, holding her open palm eye-level to Jan and not answering the string of questions that were tossed at her.

All of a sudden, Jan's eyes bulged. "Oh my God, it was you, wasn't it? You were the one in the car that almost hit her that day when she was walking to the bus stop in the rain."

"You even stupider than you look," Rachel spouted. "How could that have been me? I drive a Honda, not an Audi."

Jan stared straight into Rachel's eyes, daring her to give the wrong answer to her next question. "How did you know it was an Audi?"

"You told me."

"No, I didn't. I couldn't have. I never even knew what kind of car it was." Jan knew her suspicions were right and she could feel herself starting to lose control.

Leona apparently could sense it too, even from as far away as the porch where she continued to stand. "That child done did some stupid stuff, Jan, but she ain't tried to run over my granddaughter. Stop letting the devil plant his evil thoughts in your mind. That's enough, now . . . both of you. Jan, you get in this house and Rachel, you go on home so these nosey devils standing 'round my house will go home too. When all is said and done, we still family, and just like Jesus forgave those that nailed Him to the cross, Jan, you gotta find a way to forgive Rachel so y'all can move on from here. After everybody cool off, we'll talk about this some more. Ain't no sense in talking 'bout it no more tonight."

"I don't need her forgiveness!" Rachel yelled.

"Good," Jan said, " 'cause I don't have any to give you. Now get off my mama's property. I can't even stand to look at you anymore."

When Jan turned to walk away, Rachel grabbed her by the arm and pulled her close to her face.

"You think you better than me, don't you?" Rachel hissed. "Ever since you got with Pete, you've thought you were better than me."

Jan wondered how Rachel had come to that conclusion, but she didn't have the opportunity to reply before her cousin spoke again.

"Well, remember *this*: Every time you lay with Pete, you ain't doing nothing but feasting on my leftovers. Make no mistake; I can get any man I want, including yours. So don't fool yourself. I could have had him if I wanted him."

Snatching her arm away, Jan replied, "Oh, you wanted him, Rachel. As a matter of fact, you still do. Otherwise, none of this would have happened; so I think we can dismiss that claim right now."

"Oh, pah-leeze! If I wanted Pete, I could have him in a heartbeat. Look at my body and look at yours." Scowling, Rachel pointed from her ample cleavage to Jan's petite frame as she spoke. "Think about it, *Janet*. If Pete really had the option of living on *this* land versus *that*, why wouldn't he?"

Jan shrugged. "I don't know. Maybe you've had so many squatters and loiterers that the value of the property has depreciated."

That insult earned Jan an angry fist to the side of her face. The unexpected blow left her stunned, but only for a moment. Throwing her arms around Rachel's neck, Jan wrestled her to the ground, where the two of them tussled relentlessly. The crowd that had been standing in the distance closed in to get a better view of the escalated action. And while Rachel was by far the more experienced fighter, it was Jan who, by majority consensus, won the split decision.

The commotion had stirred the normally quiet and relatively mundane neighborhood, and though Leona tried, she was ill-equipped to bring an end to the live showdown. At some point in the mayhem, someone called the police, and fortunately for all parties involved, Officer Lyons was one of the men who responded to the call.

"Get in the car. Get in the car!" Stuart commanded as he lifted Jan from the ground and forced her in the backseat of his cruiser. He climbed in after her, closing the door behind him. "What are you trying to do, get yourself thrown in jail?" He fought to catch his breath from the efforts it took for him and his partner to peel the battling women apart.

With her face turned from him, Jan watched as another police car pulled up and two more officers joined the one who stood outside talking to Rachel. Facing Stuart, but struggling to define his features in the darkness that surrounded them, Jan's only response was, "She hit me first."

The officer's despondent sigh was unconstrained. "What do you mean she hit you first? Do you know how elementary and utterly ridiculous that sounds? How old are you . . . ten?" His voice was reprimanding. "Okay, listen to me and listen to me good. We can make a big issue out of this or we can stomp out the fires right now. You with me? According to you and the other witnesses, she was the aggressor. So, the good news is that how far this goes will be up to you. You can press charges, which would mean that we'd take both of you downtown for statements, or you can let her off the hook and let it go. I can't tell you what to do, but for the sake of everyone involved, I suggest the latter. Is it worth pressing charges to you?"

"As a matter of fact, it is," Jan said emphatically and

without pause. "She lied on my husband. She wants him and she lied on him to try and ruin our marriage, not to mention what she tried to do to my daughter. I want her treacherous, lowdown, scheming butt to go to jail. By the time Big BonQuesha 'nem get through working her over, I'll bet she won't throw her body up in nobody else's face."

"You can't be serious."

"Do I look like I'm kidding?"

Stuart took a breather, rubbed his hands over his face, and then tried again. This time, his voice was calmer. "Look, let's start over, okay? I know who you are, but I can't recall your name right now. So, why don't we start with you telling me your name."

"Jan."

"Okay, Jan, I'm Officer Stu—"

"I know who you are."

"Good. So, since you know who I am, I hope that you know that what I want is what is best for you. So, listen to me carefully. I have two sisters and I know women are far more emotional creatures than men. But I need you to stop thinking with your heart and start thinking with your brain. Sending that woman to jail isn't going to rectify any of this. It'll just be a selfish move on your part that you most likely will regret as soon as you calm down. There are more people to be considered than you. You with me? If you end this now, I can pull some strings at the department and make it go away. But if you press this juvenile issue, you're going to pull your daughter, your mother, even your husband into all of this senseless pandemonium. Think of your husband, Jan. Hasn't he gone through enough? He just left a war zone. Can his welcome home be a peaceful one?"

Jan wiped a tear from her face and released a sigh. She didn't know who she was angrier at; herself, for not having enough discernment to identify the treachery, or

Rachel, for being such a ruthless chameleon. Her life had undergone so much turbulence over the past year that it didn't seem right for Rachel not to suffer too. She had been the antagonist all along, and for her to just walk away with only a few scratches from a five-minute fight somehow didn't balance the scales. Jail might not solve the problem, but at least she would feel some sense of compensation for what Rachel had put her through. It just wasn't fair.

"Can we squash this?" Stuart asked, breaking the silence.

"I guess." Jan's voice lacked enthusiasm as she ran her fingers through her hair to try to smooth down what the fight had mussed. She could only hope that she was doing the right thing.

Stuart pulled her close to him and briefly held her to his chest, speaking as though he had read her mind. "You made the right decision, Jan. Some things just have to be left in God's hands. I'll talk to the other officers and we'll be sure to escort the subject off of your mother's property." He released her. "In the meantime, I suggest you make your daughter your first priority. She witnessed much of this, so you need to go inside the house and let her know you're okay. Sometimes, for the sake of our children, we have to at least *pretend* to be mature adults. Whatever that woman did or said couldn't be worth traumatizing your daughter by allowing her to see the two of you clawing at each other out on the front lawn like a couple of rabid stray cats. It's not sensible and even more . . . it's not Christian."

The newest tear that streamed down Jan's face was more from the sting of Stuart's words than from the lingering pain that Rachel's right hook had delivered.

"But for the record, I have to say this," Stuart added just before opening the door to let both of them out. "Call it egotism, call it shallow arrogance, call it whatever you want. But whether it's Christian or not, every man loves a ride or die chick who will fight for him if it comes down to it. And if a championship belt were on the line tonight, you'd be wearing it right now."

The ordeal was over almost as suddenly as it began, and coming to physical blows with Rachel didn't bring Jan nearly the satisfaction that she'd hoped. But in retrospect, she was already glad of her decision not to press charges. Stuart was right. Sending her cousin to jail wouldn't have brought satisfaction either. Not long-term, anyway. In the end, Jan wasn't proud of any of it. While she felt that Rachel deserved any punishment she got and more, Jan didn't like feeling that she'd stooped to the level of a liar to try to even the score.

"Does it hurt, Mama?" Kyla asked, gently touching the red, slightly swollen spot by her mother's left eye.

"A little. But I'm okay. Mama's real sorry that you had to see that, Kyla. I never meant to scare you, and I don't want you to think that fighting solves anything. It really doesn't."

"It sho' don't," Leona butted in. "Just a shame and a disgrace 'fo God; that's what it is. If you had-a came in the house like I told you to, none of this would have happened. Put that ice back on it, Jan, else your eye gon' be shut in the morning."

In obedience, Jan placed the washcloth filled with crushed ice back against her skin.

"I know fighting don't solve nothing, Mama, but you beat Rachel good. I can't wait to tell Daddy. What happened, Mama? What did she do to make you so mad?"

"Hush your mouth, Kyla," Leona scolded. "This is grown folks' business and you need to stay out of it. It don't make no never mind what happened, and you ought to be 'shamed for your daddy to know anything about this mess. It ain't like it's nothing to brag about. It don't matter what Rachel did; fighting wasn't the answer. She just need saving, that's all. And no matter how much you beat on somebody, you can't beat the devil out of them. Besides, I didn't see no swelling on her face, so who's to say who beat who? Ain't no winners in none of this foolishness, Kyla, you hear me?"

"Yes, ma'am," Kyla called over her shoulder while watching Leona leave the bedroom. Then, taking a second glance to be certain that her grandmother was out of listening range, she leaned toward Jan's ear. "You might nota beat the devil out of her, Mama, but you still beat her good."

Jan couldn't help but giggle as she wrapped her arms around Kyla's shoulders, pulling her even closer. "I did, didn't I?"

Chapter 40

The circumstances surrounding the temporary reunion weren't the best, but Peter was glad to see Fletcher and Louis again. It was to no one's surprise when only two clean bills of health were handed out. Louis would have to remain in the hospital for an indefinite amount of time for further treatment and observation. Fully clad in the most distinct of Marine garb known as Dress Blues, Fletcher and Peter spent some time by their military brother's bedside as they waited to be officially released. Louis' family surrounded him, showing a strong system of support and level of pride, and while they all sat in fellowship, the staff doctor stood nearby, enjoying the exchange.

They joked about things that went as far back as their days of basic training. It was no secret that the Marines had the toughest basic training of any branch of the United States military, and the men's humorous stories of the days of wanting to throw in the towel were amusing. Peter purposefully avoided any talk about their most recent assignment, and Fletcher didn't mention it either.

During most of their gathering, Louis seemed to be his

normal self, laughing and recounting highlights of a military career that was winding down for all three men who had barely survived the Iraq war.

"For me, it was Germany," Louis said while they chatted on the topic of their favorite assignments. "I liked Korea, too, but I think we all liked Germany better. Don't you think, Laura?" He turned to his wife.

"Yeah," the bleached blonde, full-figured woman agreed. "I saw Tina Turner on stage two times over there."

"Well, that alone would have been worth it for me." Fletcher laughed. "Man, if I was fifteen years older and she was fifteen years younger . . ."

Peter butted in with an additional reminder. "And if you weren't already married?"

"Minor details, my man," Fletcher said over the roar of laughter in the room. "This is Tina Turner we're talking about; the *original* Beyoncé. A brotha could shift some things around if need be."

"You stupid," Louis said through a beet red face.

"Then you'd be on the news for nearly getting killed by her boyfriend instead of nearly getting killed by those people in Iraq." Louis' father's hand flew over his mouth as soon as the words were complete, but it was too late.

That was the remark that sent Louis back into his shell, sealing it shut. His laughter came to an abrupt halt and the soldier shut down like a robot whose battery had suddenly died.

"I'm sorry." His father lowered his head as he apologized and was granted immediate forgiveness. He'd made the comment, but in reality, it wasn't his fault.

"That's all right, Mr. Malloy," the doctor assured as he walked closer to the bed to service his patient. "This kind of sudden detachment will happen occasionally. It's his way of blocking it all out. We're going to work on all of that while you're here, aren't we, Sergeant Malloy?" The doctor patted Louis's arm in a reassuring manner as he spoke.

The door opened and Colonel Goodman stepped in, standing tall and looking like the qualified commanding officer that he was. Even the uniform couldn't hide his bulging muscles. Peter and Fletcher stood in a synchronized salute.

"Are you ready to go, men?"

"Yes, sir," they replied.

Colonel Goodman looked past them at Louis, who still lay quietly, staring at nothing in particular. "There is security outside the door who will escort you to the car that will deliver you to the airport. I'll join you shortly."

After saying their goodbyes to Louis and his family, Peter and Fletcher marched toward the door, where there were two military police waiting. One of them shook both soldiers' hands and then motioned for them to follow him. The other stayed behind, no doubt to wait for Colonel Goodman. The walk to their awaiting limousine was a quiet one, with no words spoken until the doors were closed, shutting them inside the car.

"We're really going home now." The warmth of Fletcher's smile echoed in his voice.

Peter nodded and one corner of his mouth pulled upward. "Yeah, we are."

"Now you can set everything straight with Jan. Don't let the fact that she didn't show up yesterday make you not want to try, Pete. Sometimes circumstances—"

"She did show up yesterday." Peter's whole face spread into a grin when he saw Fletcher's reaction. "She showed up a couple of hours after I'd already checked into my hotel and was settling in."

"And?"

Peter sobered. "And we got into a very heated argument."

"And?"

"And then she left."

"She left?" Fletcher's face fell.

"And I went after her and coaxed her into coming back."

A grin overtook Fletcher's features. "You did?"

"Yeah, but then we got into another argument that ended up in a physical altercation. That was a first."

"You fought?" Fletcher's eyes bulged.

"She was swinging like Laila Ali, man. I'd never seen her that angry and I never knew she was that strong. I thought the hotel security, or at least the security guard who was in the room across from me, would bust up in there at any moment."

Fletcher was clearly disappointed when he relaxed in his seat. "So, what now? You're not giving up, are you?"

"After the way she loved me last night? Are you crazy?"

Fletcher's eyebrows shot up in surprise. "What? Y'all made up?"

"Man, I'm getting ready to go to Atlanta and start another fight, just so we can make up again."

The men shared a hearty laugh, one just as happy as the other for the way things had transpired.

"You never met her," Peter said. "When we get settled, we have to plan for our families to get together, either wherever you settle or wherever the Jericho family decides to call home. I was thinking of moving to Houston, but Jan and Kyla have established roots in Atlanta, so we'll just have to see how it all works out."

"Can you live that close to your mother-in-law?"

Peter sighed. "Man, after all God has brought me through, Leona won't be nothing for me to handle."

"I know that's right."

"So, it's a deal?" Peter asked, leaning forward in his seat. "We'll get our families together soon?"

"I would like that," Fletcher said as he grabbed Peter's extended hand and then pulled him into an embrace. "Love you, man."

Peter beamed, happy that one of them finally had the courage to voice the sentiment. "Love you too, Flex."

"Glad to see you guys are all . . . *chummy* and everything," Colonel Goodman said as he climbed into the car and watched the door close behind him. "But can you at least wait until you are officially honorably discharged before you come all the way out?"

Peter and Fletcher threw each other sideways glances and then launched at their commanding officer, embracing him and sharing a prolonged, jovial laugh.

Epilogue

Dear Daddy,

Even though you have been home for almost two months, I still like writing you letters and it makes me happy when you write me back. One day, when I'm grown and you and Mama are old (ha-ha!), I'm going to publish a book with all of your letters in it. I don't know what I'll call it yet, but I'm thinking about calling it Letters From a Hero *or something like that. What do you think?*

Daddy, I'm so proud of you and I love you to pieces. You promised that you'd put our family back together and you did it. I knew you would, so I wasn't surprised like Grandma and Granddaddy were. But I admit that I was *surprised when you decided to stay in Atlanta. I'm sooooooo glad you got us a house here. Now I get to keep all my new friends, and since everybody in the city already liked you before they even met you, you have friends here too. And since Rachel all of a sudden moved back to Florida, I'm glad Mama had already made friends with Malik's family and with other people at the church.*

Speaking of Malik, tell me what you think about him. You haven't said much, but I see you watching him all the time when we go to church or to Greene Pastures to ride the horses. You think he's nice, don't you? He's not my boyfriend or anything, but I still want you to like him. If he's still my friend when I'm a senior, I might let him take me to the prom—unless Mr. Jerome wants to take me. Then Malik will be out of luck. Okay, I'll stop before you never let me out of the house again. LOL!

I love you, Daddy. And although the war in Iraq is still going on, I know that the battle has been made easier for those left behind just because Sergeant Peter Kyle Jericho was once there. I believe that with my whole heart, Daddy. I really do. Write back soon. I love you.

Kyla

After kissing the signature line, Kyla folded the letter carefully and placed it in a plain white envelope. She tucked it under her pillow, in the same place where she'd put all of the letters she'd written to her father since his return. She knew that at some point during the night while she was sleeping, Peter would come in to check on her. When he did, just as always, he would kiss her on the forehead, pick up his letter and take it back to his room, where he would read it with fondness. In a day or two, Kyla could look forward to another letter from him for her collection. It was a ritual that she and her father practiced at least once weekly.

Just before Kyla turned off the lamp on the nightstand of her new bedroom, she looked at the awards on her dresser. Not her own awards. She'd replaced hers with the ones presented to her father at a nationally televised banquet in honor of him, his surviving colleagues, and the men of his fire team who had been killed while serving. The President of the United States presented each man (or for those who had died, a proxy surviving family member) with the Bronze Star, Purple Heart, and the Prisoner of War Medal. Peter had had his honors professionally framed, and when Kyla asked to keep them in her room, Peter agreed.

She still remembered Malik's wide eyes of disbelief when she told him that her father had allowed her to keep the priceless mementos. With fatigue setting in, Kyla sighed, nestled her head in her pillow, and smiled. *A Daddy's girl and proud of it!*

Reader's Group Guide

1. What is your overall viewpoint on legends and superstitions such as the one involving Shelton Heights? Do you believe truth could lie in such folklore?

2. Discuss your early thoughts on Peter's and Jan's sudden separation. Before the full story was unveiled, what was your assessment?

3. How do you feel about the Women of Hope ministry and groups like it?

4. Prior to being informed in this story, were you aware of the alarming statistics surrounding women in abusive relationships?

5. Share your opinion on the church and psychotherapy. Do you believe Christians should seek the professional help of psychologists/psychiatrists, or should they just rely on their faith in God in difficult times?

6. When Rachel was first introduced to the story, what were your thoughts about her?

7. Did she surprise you in the end? Why or why not?

8. Leona was an uncompromising woman who took her beliefs to a whole new level. Do you know of similar people? What are your thoughts on others like her?

9. Throughout the story, Kyla remained relatively strong, considering her age. Why do you think she

was able to handle herself better than most of the grown-ups?

10. For the readers of *In Greene Pastures*: Were you pleased or disappointed with the reveal of how Hunter's and Jade's relationship turned out?

11. During the scenes that highlighted the goings-on in Iraq, were you drawn into the described settings and the emotions of the soldiers?

12. After all that he experienced, how realistic do you believe Louis' mental outcome was?

13. Peter and Fletcher formed a solid bond of brotherhood in the time of their distress. Do you think these types of friendships are lasting; or do they wane once life returns to normal?

14. What were your feelings on Peter's secret? In your eyes, was it a "forgivable sin"?

15. How did you perceive some of the secondary characters such as Corporal Alfred Goodman, Kenyatta King and Officer Stuart Lyons?

16. Discipleship played a pivotal role in this book; specifically with Peter's role in the lives of his imprisoned military comrades. How important do you think it is for Christians to be effective disciples for Christ?

17. Who was your favorite character in this story? Why?

18. Who was your least favorite character in this story? Why?

19. If you could rewrite any portion of *Battle of Jericho*, which scene would it be and why?

20. Discuss the current war in Iraq. What are your personal thoughts on why it happened and your prognosis on when or if it will ever end?